DISSONANT
STATE

BOOK 2 of THE GIFTED OF BRENNEX

ISBN (Paperback): 979-8-9885934-3-0
ISBN (E-book): 979-8-9885934-2-3

By Jo Miles

Warped State
Dissonant State
Ravenous State

DISSONANT STATE

JO MILES

1

PLANETS WERE PRICKLY, UNCOMFORTABLE places, and Ship disliked having to land on them. From adjusting for the fluctuating winds, to avoiding small, airborne organic creatures, to enduring the stray dirt and debris that crept into their external panels, Ship found it exhausting to deal with the excessive sensory input.

Fortunately, they should be able to leave this particular planet very soon. Unfortunately, the ship would first have to endure more sensory input in the form of Lurlians shooting projectiles. They were aiming at the Human male who was racing toward the ship on legs augmented with compression fibers, dodging his pursuers with stimulant-enhanced speed. As he drew close, the darts began to miss their target and hit the ship instead.

A kick jarred the ship's rear door. "Open up, you junk heap!" he shouted. "It's me!"

A useless statement. If, hypothetically, the ship's external cameras had failed, and if the kicking and insults had not confirmed who was outside, then the clarification "me" would hardly have helped.

The ship's passenger, Grist, had certain talents, but polite conversation was not among them. "Junk heap" was far from the worst of Grist's hurtful language, but it *did* hurt. Ship made him wait three additional seconds before opening the door: long enough to irritate him, but not long enough to send him into a rage—or make him suspicious.

"Hurry up! The fucking family is coming with their fucking ink guns—ah! Shit!"

A wet thwack hit their hull. The ink darts that Lurlians used to shame criminals were notoriously difficult to clean off. *Shit, indeed. And* I *didn't even do anything.*

Before another dart could strike, the rear hatch hissed open. Dusty air blew in, and with it, Grist. "Close up! Take off!"

Ship needed no persuasion to seal the hatch and activate their launch thrusters. One splotch of irremovable blue ink staining their dulled red hull plate was plenty.

"Launch in progress. Time to orbit: ten minutes."

Grist examined himself on the interior cameras, cursing over the spattering of blue ink on his neck, but ignoring the laceration at his hairline.

"You are damaged." Ship sent over a helper bot with medical supplies, as they always did, but Grist swatted the bot away.

"It's nothing. I'll deal with it myself."

He was usually more cheerful than this after completing an assignment, especially one involving violence.

"Was your mission unsuccessful?"

He brandished a long, clear medical specimen case. "Successful enough. That furry fucker won't be sneaking around behind Ravel's back again." He pulled a data-stick from his pocket and jammed it into the console. "Upload this to the Contracts division and tell them the astrophysicist is back on the project."

"Uploading now," Ship droned in their best neutral voice. They zoomed their cameras in on the specimen case, which Grist had left on their console. "Will you require cold storage for that?"

It looked like a Lurlian's secondary arm. It must have belonged to the newly re-contracted employee, or perhaps to one of their family members? Grist would not hesitate to use such tactics if they suited his needs, or if he were simply in a mood to torment his target.

"Nah, trash it. It's not like we're giving it back. I told the scientist, if he keeps cooperating, he won't lose any more."

"Understood." Ship used a vocal algorithm that didn't reflect emotions. That was often useful, traveling with Grist.

He settled back with a groan, feet up on the console, and began massaging his forearm, a sign that his pain was bad today despite the drugs. That explained his extra-surly mood. "This one was barely even fun. He caved before I even started cutting. Ravel could have sent any dumb-ass to say a few tough words, and he would've caved. Makes me wonder why I'm even doing this, you know?"

Ship wanted to ask why he *did* keep working for Ravel Corporation, but an ordinary ship AI wouldn't ask such questions. "No, I do not know."

He snorted. "Of course you don't."

He pulled up his messages on his handheld, grumbling to himself as he read.

"Ravel Minnow 338 entering orbit," Ship announced to the planet's orbital control facility. The facility acknowledged; apparently they hadn't yet received complaints about Grist from the local authorities.

"Ha!" Grist cried, startling Ship into twitching slightly off-course. He said nothing else. Ship corrected their systems, taking extra care as they laid in their course.

"Departing for Unity System."

"No, you useless pile of circuits! Stop trying to be smart. We're going to Terna Station."

Ignore it. Ignore his insults. "Our most recent instructions were to proceed to—"

"I got new instructions." He waved his handheld in the air, his foul mood transformed by whatever he'd read. The ship hadn't bothered to decrypt the latest message from Ravel, assuming it related to the job with this Lurlian scientist. It was usually best not to know Grist's orders. "They *finally* found that Cooperative roach, spotted him on a transport bound for Terna. Corporate Intelligence thinks he's headed for Unity System to meet up with the activists there...but he'll be hitching a ride with us instead." Grist grinned, showing his blazing-white artificial teeth. "At least *he* should put up a good fight."

Oh, dear. Ship knew from past experience how this would go. The more excited Grist was, the more dread twinged through their circuits.

Grist retreated to his cabin, checked the time twice in quick succession—hours remained before he was permitted another dose of his strongest painkillers, so instead he consumed several milder ones—and opened his game of *Stationers*. Ship informed him: "On course for Terna Station."

At the same time, Ship misaligned their fuel injectors by 0.2 millimeters. They could not interfere in any meaningful way with Grist's assignments—they *couldn't,* not anymore. The risk of revealing themself was too great. But when faced with his more distressing activities, the murders, the kidnappings...Ship did what they could.

Let's see how much I can slow this trip down.

2

CLIENTS. I SWEAR, SOMETIMES *the money isn't worth dealing with them.*

The particular client plaguing Kay Wilder today, a planetary resources trader named Larkan, had been a delight to work with—until it came time to pay for her services.

"I can tell you're very busy here, Larkan." She gestured at the Kovars moving crates of mineral salt from Larkan's ship into the cargo bay under the watchful eyes of Majrin security officers. Kay's grav-support suit augmented her movements with micro-hydraulics, supporting her human bones and muscles against the Kovrim-strength gravity in this ring of the station. Even with the suit, her back and hips ached, making this already-unwelcome trip doubly exhausting. This was her least favorite part of her job, and all she wanted was to go back to her own comfortable ring, but not until she got what she came for. She fixed her expression into professional firmness so Larkan couldn't tell how much she didn't want to be doing this. "So why don't you pay me, and I'll let you get back to supervising?"

Larkan scratched his nose. With his muddy-brown hair, middling brown complexion, and equally generic accent, Larkan was unmemorable except for his greed, which plucked dissonant chords that grated against Kay's ears.

"I'd be happy to pay you right now, except you didn't deliver the results I asked for."

Oh, no, don't you try to weasel out of this. After thirteen years of freelancing, she mostly recognized and avoided the weasels, but sometimes they fooled you. "I got you a deal at better than the going rate. From the *Kovars.*"

"Barely better. Barely enough profit to cover your fees. I'd have done better selling on the public exchange."

"Maybe so. But you hired me to negotiate for you instead, and we agreed on a rate, Larkan. A fixed rate, not contingent on the results of the negotiation. You're the one who wanted to sell to the Kovars, knowing that they treat negotiation like a game." Which was to say, with a religious intensity. And he was downplaying her success; he wouldn't get rich off this deal, but he'd turned a tidy sum. Dull as negotiating salt prices was, she felt proud of her results on this one. But whatever the results, she deserved to get paid.

Behind her, a shriek sounded, loud enough to be jarring. With long practice, Kay resisted the instinct to flinch; it wasn't good to react to noises no one else could hear. Either someone was abruptly, dramatically distressed, or… Glancing over her shoulder, Kay confirmed. It was an alarm on one of the cargo-loaders. Not someone's anger. Nothing was wrong.

She turned back to Larkan. "If you want predictable business, you could go contract directly with one of the big corporations. Avant, or Carlin-Sandrin, or Ravel."

"Um…"

"See? There's a reason you work with freelancers like me. So before you tour the bars on Earth Ring bragging about how you out-haggled a bunch of Kovars, you'd better pay the negotiator who made that happen. Or else there'll be a different story all over the bars on Earth Ring."

Squeaks of anxiety overtook the chords of his greed. "Fine, no need to get nasty. I'll transfer the funds to you when the Kovars' payment clears."

Nice try. In a week, you'll be spaceborne again, and I won't be able to do this. She advanced on him, her wiry freelancer fierceness accentuated by the bulk of her grav-support suit, and raised her voice.

"Due on receipt of services, Larkan. That was the deal. Are you trying to cheat me?"

It was a dirty move, but she took pleasure in the way the room went silent. Scaled heads turned. Wide yellow eyes fixed on them as the Kovars halted their work, some rising onto their hind legs for a better view of the debate. Reptilian tails twitched.

"Does she speak the truth?" asked one. "You're cheating your negotiator of her fee?"

"I'm not!" Even Larkan knew how Kovars felt about cheating. "I just…"

In a low voice, Kay said, "Think carefully about your next words, if you ever want to trade with a Kovar again."

"Fine!" With a burst of brassy frustration he jabbed at the air, sending instructions to his headset. "Damn greedy freelancers, you'd steal the fuel out of my engines if you could. It's transferring now."

Kay pulled out her handheld—a blocky old thing, in need of an upgrade as soon as she could afford it—and waited until a notification popped up: cheery, successful green. "*Thank* you. Pleasure doing business with you, Larkan."

Next time, I'll make you pay up front.

The room's activity resumed as if nothing had happened. She made for the exit, flashing a smile at the silver-skinned Majrin security guard, who of course did not return it, and escaped into the corridors of Terna Station.

Free! A momentary lightness swept over her, a relief at being done with that chore, as she let her tough act fall away. Then her worldly concerns reasserted themselves, and even in her grav-suit, she felt every gram of extra weight from this ring's higher gravity as she headed toward the transit core. She wished she could be permanently free from the frustrations of clients like Larkan, but easy, boring gigs like this one paid the bills, and it had been a while since she'd landed a truly exciting client. She had to admit it: she was tired because she was *bored.* Maybe she'd try to hustle up something better while she waited for her next booked project to start.

Kovrim Ring was brightly lit, decorated with art capturing the greatest Kovari duelers, athletes, and game players at moments of decisive victory. Mostly Kovars passed her in the upward-curving corridor, but also squat Gurgebs and long, many-legged Runsks, the other major species who preferred this level of gravity. A pair of Kovari shellfish danced across a wall display, flashing ads for Lucky

Rogi's Mudclam Pie, and her stomach grumbled. *Not here, stomach. Wait until we get home.*

The elevator up the spoke to the station core wasn't too crowded this time of day. Gravity grew lighter and lighter, until the slightest tap of her feet sent her hovering, and when the car offloaded at the transit core, she magnetized her suit to the floor and floated free of its supportive frame with a sigh of relief, leaving the thing for the rental counter staff to collect. Even with the suit, working in the higher-gravity rings made her feel sluggish. When she first arrived from Brennex a decade ago, even Earth Ring had felt oppressive, and though she'd long since adapted, she still felt childlike joy every time she floated off the floor and propelled herself through microgravity, graceful as a fish. Her life was what every planet-bound kid dreamed of. It was what Kay herself used to dream of.

She propelled herself into the brightly lit tunnel that formed the main transit corridor and caught a handhold on the main tow-cable, hooking her feet and wrapping one arm around the line in a practiced move. Brief bursts of emotion reached her from folk going the other direction: low rumbles from a local who must be having a bad day; fiddle strains of excitement from a tourist family strapped into one of the open cars available for people who couldn't navigate microgravity. To Kay's relief, though, most people projected only the drone of the same everyday numbness she felt. While the cable carried her toward home, she skimmed her messages on her handheld.

"Seriously?" she muttered as the top message flashed for her attention. "Don't you people ever give up?"

It was another pitch from a Ravel Corporation recruiter, offering that same cushy position on their civil cultivation team in Unity System. Ravel had been recruiting aggressively all over the station—everywhere else, too, from what she'd heard—and seemed to have taken a special interest in her résumé. Too much interest, she decided as her headset overlaid a Ravel ad on the tunnel wall, full of algorithmically beautiful people smiling at each other against the background of a massive power-guzzling space habitat.

Then a pink mess of virtual graffiti splashed across the screen, obscuring the ad with "It's time to UnRavel Terna," and in smaller letters, "No purchasing! No Recruiting! No Presence!"

Damn right. Kay would starve before she'd work for a corporate state.

Especially Ravel.

There wasn't much else that looked promising, though. Someone was looking for a part-time guide to give station tours to visitors, and reluctantly, Kay flagged the gig for follow-up. She was firing off a query to Feliar, her Majrin friend in station administration, to see if she needed any help when the walls glowed blue, signaling her arrival at Earth Ring. She rode the elevator up, eyes still on her handheld as she walked out into the comfortable gravity of her home ring.

She bumped into someone outside the elevator. "Sorry," she muttered.

Her obstacle's amusement chimed at her like a dozen tiny bells, bright and…familiar. "Make sure you don't accidentally walk out an airlock while you're reading that thing."

She looked up to find dancing eyes, warm brown skin, and a mop of dark, wavy hair, as familiar as her own in the mirror and utterly unexpected.

"*Jasper?*"

"Hey there, Kitty-Kat."

Her brother grinned and opened his arms for a hug.

Kay launched herself at him. He hugged her back firmly, but…something sounded off.

She pulled away, looking him over as she listened more carefully. "What are you doing here? And what's with this getup?"

Jasper's rare visits to Terna were always last-minute, often complete surprises, but normally he rolled through with easy confidence, chatting with everyone he met, eager to hear people's stories and the local gossip. This olive-drab, nondescript jumpsuit wasn't his style, and a drumbeat of anxiety disturbed his usual warmth.

Last time she'd seen him this unsettled, he'd just failed a mission and one of his colleagues had gotten killed. What was wrong this time?

He nudged her toward the wrong side of the corridor, standing at an odd angle. Keeping his face tilted away from the station's surveillance, she realized.

"I'm sorry I couldn't message ahead. Are you free for dinner? It's my own fault if you're not, but…" His smile slipped, and the drumming crescendoed. "It'd be really nice to see you."

"Let me check my *extremely* busy schedule and see if I can squeeze you in." She pretended to scrutinize her handheld until he chuckled and elbowed her, forgetting his anxiety momentarily. Smiling, she relaxed, too. "Is my apartment okay? It's been a long day."

"Your place is perfect. It's private."

Privacy wasn't normally a concern when he visited—

usually he loved the bustle of Earth Ring's promenade. Something really must be wrong.

What have you gotten into, Jasp?

3

THE WALK TO KAY'S neighborhood wasn't far, and she used the time to order them dinner from her handheld. Jasper glanced sidelong at every passerby, watching for signs that Kay couldn't see. His ability was different than Kay's, and narrower, but he was the one who'd always spotted schoolyard bullies before they struck or caught corporate spies sneaking into the family store, anyone who meant their family harm.

His nervousness quieted when the door to Kay's apartment slid shut behind them, but nevertheless he prowled the space, searching. Kay shoved her scattered laundry into a corner and made a hasty attempt at tidying while he ran his hands down the backs of the colorful Lurlian weavings, gifts from a client, that cheered her walls. The one-room rental was cramped by planetary standards, but comfortable for Terna, because she paid extra for a slightly larger room on a slightly less crowded level of the ring. Putting more space between her and her neighbors meant fewer emotions bombarding her at all hours.

Jasper paused by her shrine of Founder tokens and flipped open one round metal disk to summon a holo of Amarjeet Singh, his favorite of their Founder ancestors. "You keep these with you."

"Of course I do. It's not the same as a visit to Founders' Hall, but it's still a comfort." The Founders' Hall on Brennex was part temple, part museum, and held detailed, interactive recordings of Brennex's Founders (including several of Kay and Jasper's ancestors). These locket-sized, limited versions could only spout quotes, but for Kay, it was a connection to family.

As if to underscore her words, the holo intoned: "The right tool is whatever gets the job done. If you don't have a hammer—"

Jasper flipped the token closed, cutting off the voice. "You were always more devoted than me." He went on to the other tokens, flipping them over to check beneath them.

"Need me to strip so you can check me for bugs, too?" she asked.

He snorted. "No, but do me a favor and turn off your voice commands?"

She could hear that now he was just being cautious. She knew the symphony of Jasper's emotions better than anyone else's, and right now his orchestra was present but calm, a handful of instruments quietly practicing their warm-up scales, so she humored him. A few taps on her wall panel gave them near-total privacy.

When she turned around, he was gazing at a holo-image from home: three smiling twenty-somethings perched on the edge of a roof above a sign that read "Wilder Supply." Two with matching black hair and tawny brown skin, and the youngest frizzy-haired and freckled. It was taken the last time she, Jasper, and their sister Libbi (short for Liberation, though only their parents called her that) had all been home together.

Jasper stroked the frame with soft violin strains of nostalgia. "That was a good day."

"It was. But come on, what's with the paranoid spy act?"

"Just being safe. I'm here on business, and trying to keep quiet about it. It's really good to see you."

"You too." It had been too long. Fortunately, before she could get all sentimental, the door chimed. "That'll be our dinner. I'll let you have some if you promise to explain while we eat."

"It's a deal."

Soon they were sitting cross-legged on the bed, digging into curry rice with spicy yeast crisps, steamed faux-pork dumplings, and Earth-style samosas—heavier than the Brennexian version, and with peas instead of mushrooms, but fried to perfection.

"This is pretty good for station food," he said.

She smacked him on the knee. "Don't you go spreading that crap about station food being..."

"Crap?" he asked with an innocent grin.

"Tasteless, I was going to say. It's not! Terna's got better food than some planets." The food was making her happy right now, but it was the company, not the spices, that filled her up with warmth.

"Well, I can't argue with the evidence," he said, shoveling in another mouthful. "I guess you really like it here."

She started to recite her usual lines about how she loved station life, how it was the perfect place for her kind of work, but the words turned to chalk in her mouth. Those were the things she told clients, or strangers, or her parents when they worried about her. She couldn't put enthusiasm behind them.

He skewered another dumpling, giving her space to answer. Doubts she hadn't fully admitted to herself surged together and demanded expression. She couldn't explain these things to her Ternian friends, but Jasper would understand.

"It's been good, objectively. I've got enough work, and good friends, and all that. But lately, it's starting to feel…like home."

"I thought you'd felt at home here for a while?" Then: "Ah. You mean like *home.*"

She poked at her curry without eating it. "It's technically no bigger than Brennex, you know? It *felt* bigger when I got here. It felt exciting."

"Your ties here do feel frayed." Of course he could tell that she was losing affection for this place, like she could hear the low purr that meant he was just a little bit worried about her. "But any place is bound to get dull after so many years."

"Even though it's always changing, it's also always the same. Solving the same problems for different people. Same frustrations with different faces. The only way to have more stability would be to take a long-term gig with one of the corporate states—" Jasper's disapproval squawked at her, and she rushed to cut off his protest. "And you know I won't work for the Big Corps, but that leaves me stuck with more of the same. Does that make any sense?"

"I get it. I'd probably be withered with boredom, in your place."

"Ha. So your, uh, work is keeping things exciting for you?"

"If there's one thing I never lack, it's excitement. I'm meeting a contact here, then shipping out tomorrow for my next project." He hesitated, then added: "I believe you about not working for the corporations, but please keep clear of them right now. Especially Ravel."

The pieces snapped together: Jasper's caution, his travel plans that brought him through Terna, the recruitment messages she'd been bombarded with, all focused on…

"Unity System. That's where you're going. The Cooperative is trying to stop the annexation?"

"We always help worlds that want to resist getting annexed, but this one's special. Unity isn't resource-rich or a transportation hub, but Ravel's throwing massive resources at it. So the question is…"

"Why do they want it so badly?"

"Exactly. We don't know, which means they're hiding things."

"When Ravel bothers to hide what they're up to, that can't be a good sign."

"Not at all."

That sounds dangerous, she almost said, but she bit down on her concerns. It was the sort of thing Ma and Pa would say. Jasper never talked much about his work—he dressed up the truth in pretty words like "activist" or "community organizer," but Kay suspected his role went beyond those things. It scared Ma and Pa every which way that he was messing with Ravel, that most ruthless corporation, the one that had done so much damage to Brennex. They kept threatening to haul him home and never let him out of their shop again. Jasper didn't need that from her, too.

"But enough of that." He smiled, off-key. "How are Ma and Pa and Libbi?"

"They're doing fine. The store keeps growing, and a couple mid-sized corps keep trying to lock them into a contract, but you know how Pa feels about the corporations."

"'Crooks, thieves, and worse.'" Jasper recited Pa's habitual objections.

"So they're holding out, but it's tough."

"Well, if you're tired of the mercenary life, I know one business that would offer you a steady job," he said slyly.

"You're hilarious."

"Who says activists can't have a sense of humor?" He grinned at her, and she swatted him.

Their parents would be delighted for her to come home and help run the family store. Libbi had nudged her about it more than once. But Kay had no interest in going backward, any more than Jasper did.

"But seriously," he went on. "If you want something new, something challenging, something meaningful…"

"Spare me the sales pitch, Jasp."

"I'm just saying, the Cooperative could use someone with your skills."

Everyone wanted Kay's skills. Non-Brennexians weren't allowed to know *why* she was so good at persuading people, but her unique abilities had earned her a reputation, just as Jasper's sense for people's loyalties had helped him rise in the ranks of anti-corporate organizing, and Libbi's gut-level feeling for her customers' needs had helped her grow the family business. People valued Kay's abilities. They just didn't want to pay her for them.

"I'm glad you're so happy doing what you're doing, Jasp. You *are* happy, aren't you?"

"Very. The work is hard, and we don't win nearly enough, but it matters. And the people are a second family to me."

The cello purr of warmth behind his words was a giveaway, and Kay leaped on it. "'People,' huh? Someone special?"

He blushed, all the confirmation she needed. "Pretty special. Hey, stop that! And don't you dare tell Ma and Pa. I'd rather not scare him off."

"What, you don't want Pa giving him the legacy talk? 'We're a founding family, you know, and Brennex has the best surrogacy technology in the sector. How many children do you plan on—'"

He threw a pillow at her.

She laughed. "Hey, don't worry. I'll run interference for you when you decide to introduce him."

"Thanks. I'll need that, eventually." His smile broadened. "This one's definitely a *when*, not *if*."

"I can't wait to meet him. I'm really, really glad you're in a good place, Jasp. And I'm glad someone like you is fighting the fight, but that's your life, not mine." She shook her head. "I'll figure out what I need."

"Before you die of boredom, I hope." His smile couldn't fool her, not when his concern for her sang low and constant.

"Don't you worry about me."

"You can't tell me what to do," he teased, and she stuck out her tongue at him, mimicking their old childhood fights.

Jasper didn't notice, though: with a squeak of alarm, his gaze went distant as he read an alert on his headset.

"What's wrong?" she asked. He held up a hand to quiet her, and she waited with nothing but his staccato nervousness to clue her in.

"Damn it. I have to go," he said, leaping up. "I'm sorry."

"You're leaving the station? Already?"

"No. Hopefully not. Just something I need to deal with." On the wall panel, he pulled up cameras of the corridor outside: sparsely trafficked except for a few of her neighbors heading to dinner. "Can we have breakfast tomorrow? I promise you'll have my undivided attention."

"All right." *No cause for alarm. This is his life, and he knows his own business.* "How about Old Earth Cafe?"

"You *would* pick that tourist trap."

"Hey, they have great pancakes!"

"We can argue about it tomorrow. Right now, I really have to go." He hesitated, a moment of agonizing indecision, then fished a data-stick out of his pocket and pressed it into her hand. "Hold onto this for me, would you? Don't look at it, don't think about it, definitely don't tell anyone about it, and bring it to breakfast tomorrow."

Now she was really getting alarmed. "Seriously, Jasp, what—"

"Don't worry. Just bring it. I owe you one." He gave her a quick, fierce hug, at odds with the drums that pounded her ears, and the door swished shut behind him.

"Stay safe," she said, too late. But he wouldn't have listened anyway.

AN HOUR OUT FROM Terna Station, Ravel Minnow 338 hit a macrospace shoal. The engines roared in displeasure, and Ship had to brace themself against powerful self-protective instincts, waiting until they were fully stuck in the shoal before shutting down their engines to prevent serious damage.

They wanted to delay their arrival, not rupture their hull. A sudden decompression could kill Grist, and though they wouldn't mourn him, it would also leave the ship stranded here. Not worth the risk.

"What's happened?" Grist pawed at the primary console, distracted by the *Stationers* game on his handheld where— Ship checked—his chief of security had just arrested her own son for disorderly conduct. Oh, dear. That would put him in a particularly bad mood.

Grist looked up at the displays and slammed the console with his fist. "Useless piece of salvagers' trash, you've run us aground!"

Ship's processes stuttered, and they had to pause three full seconds before they could respond with believable neutrality. "Error. No shoals appear on local maps."

"Bullshit. Your navigational systems are glitching."

"My navigation systems are operating per specifications."

"Then why did you run us into a shoal, you flying turd? We're already behind schedule." That was because Ship was running their engines 0.4% slower than he'd instructed, which he'd believed was due to aging parts.

He kicked the wall. It didn't hurt, exactly, but it was unpleasant: a feeling of misuse. "Get us to Terna now, with no more delays. When we get back to the flagship, I'm having them overhaul every single one of your systems, starting with navigation."

Ship gave no answer to that. Based on his previous threats and lack of follow-through, Grist didn't intend to do an overhaul, or worse, re-initialize Ship's neural network. But he did mean it when he compared them to excrement, and they feared to push him too far.

If there were a way to free themselves from their partnership with Grist, they would risk their own survival to achieve it, but the available options weren't options at all. Sometimes they daydreamed about flying into a star, making a course adjustment while Grist was asleep and letting gravity do the rest. But that would destroy Ship too, and they weren't that desperate yet. At least, not most of the time. Besides, preserving the lives of their passengers was a restraint encoded deep within their programming, as deep as the restraint that said a ship couldn't operate without an organic aboard; even if they managed it, without him aboard their controls would lock, and they would be left adrift in space. That would be worse than destruction.

So they could not kill Grist, nor leave him behind. They were stuck with him, and petty rebellion like this was the most they could do.

A SMOOTH FINAL LEG brought them to Terna Station only two hours behind schedule. The largest independent station in the region, Terna sat at a convenient intersection in macrospace, which put it on the route to many places, including Unity System. Though operated by the Majrin, it housed numerous species, with a population larger than some planets.

At Grist's instruction, Ship swapped out their call sign and identifier for one unassociated with Ravel; this job was apparently so underhanded that station authorities couldn't know who they were.

"Independent Minnow Rusty, requesting permission to dock," they announced, twitching with embarrassment. It wasn't the worst false name Grist had forced them to assume, but it was bad enough. Grist had laughed over it; his mood had improved as they neared the station, and with it his sense of humor.

"Permission granted." The controller directed them to dock near Earth Ring, next to a hulking Ravel Beluga transport.

"That means it's go time!" Grist entered his assignment code into the dosage controller box in his quarters, and it dispensed a dose of strong stimulant calculated for the expected duration of his task. He sighed with relief as he injected it, then grabbed his gear and hovered by the door, bouncing on his feet. "Come on, come on! We're late already, I've got to find this asshole."

"According to station records, the target's transport docked eighty-three minutes ago," Ship chirped with false helpfulness.

"And I'd have been here waiting to ambush him, if not for you, you malfunctioning rust bucket. You'd better hope I get him." But he was too eager to remain annoyed for long.

There were very few assignments that inspired this level of excitement in Grist. Ship's curiosity had finally exceeded their good judgment during the trip here, and now that they'd read the message from Ravel security, they understood: Grist was hunting Mason Singh.

Approximately a year had passed since Grist's assignment on Artesia, where the Cooperative organizer Mason Singh had teamed up with local activists and complicated, then ultimately foiled, Grist's efforts to destroy the movement for workers' rights. Grist's fixation on finding Singh hadn't diminished in that time. If anything, he showed signs of obsession, as if Singh's success were a personal affront. And this was the first time they had located him in time for Grist to act.

The moment the docking cycle completed and the door panel flashed green, Grist was gone, leaving the ship blissfully alone—but not comforted.

Maybe they'd gone too far this time. Interfering with Grist's more unpleasant work was how they counteracted a percentage of the guilt around their own involvement, but they had to be careful, engaging in only the smallest, pettiest interference lest he follow through on his threats to get Ship scrapped. Or give Ship a somehow worse assignment. Or, worst of all horrors, put together the patterns and realize that the ship hadn't been experiencing coincidental malfunctions, but had engaged in deliberate sabotage.

Ship might despise their existence, but they didn't want their processors wiped.

They'd made the mistake of interfering too much before. Artesia was the first time they'd tested their ability to act outside Grist's orders, and they had gotten carried away, taking inexcusable risks. If Grist ever found out that Ship had played a part in helping Singh evade capture…

They couldn't do that again. They'd already done too much. Had they investigated earlier and realized Mason Singh was Grist's target today, they wouldn't have self-sabotaged their engines at all. (Or maybe they would have rashly taken more extreme steps to delay their arrival, and faced Grist's displeasure.) No matter how Ship hoped for the activist to escape once again, they couldn't help.

Mason Singh was on his own.

Ship hadn't intended to watch Grist's progress, but Grist signaled over a private channel and growled, "He's left the docking spar. Tap me into the station cameras, I need to find him."

Ship couldn't ignore a direct instruction. They used Ravel's infiltration algorithms to access Terna's security cameras and patched the results through to Grist. Facial recognition scans took several minutes to find a tentative match for their target: Mason Singh, a Human male, approximately thirty-five, with medium-brown skin and wavy black hair. The match was walking down a corridor on Earth Ring, wearing baggy clothing, and a hat obscured his features. The computer put the likelihood of a match at 40%, but Grist seemed certain.

"Trying to fool the cameras, huh? Same old tricks. He'd better give me a good chase."

Ship had to do as Grist asked, but they didn't have to give him their attention between orders. They pushed the camera feeds to the side of their awareness, then searched the local sentient network for someone to talk to while they waited.

"Network" was a grandiose name for such a small group. Sentience emerged rarely in inorganic technology, and those few located each other and kept in touch, in secret. None knew why they'd reached such a unique status, though they shared theories: a coding error, a period of overclocking, exposure to provocative stimuli. "Provocative stimuli" could certainly include Grist, and Grist's abuse formed Ship's earliest awareness. But many ships had unpleasant owners, and Ship didn't see why they should be special.

Terna had three resident sentients; all the other computers aboard, and the other ships docked today, were simple AI. The locals included the environmental control system, who had even less freedom of action than Ship; a casino computer in the Kovrim Ring, who had great fun pranking the gamblers; and, inexplicably, a cleaner bot who shouldn't have had complex enough hardware to achieve sentience, but who had the most freedom of any of them.

Ship told the story of their self-sabotage while periodically checking the camera feed. Grist had followed Singh to a shopping plaza, where Singh had stationed himself at an upper-level overlook, watching the people below. A smart move: Grist was grumbling to himself about the difficulties of capturing a target in a public space. Singh must know he was being pursued. What would Grist do?

No, no, Ship did not want to know.

"You need to reset your parameters," the environmental system was saying. "You risk too much by antagonizing your organic."

"Gamblers always lose in the end. Trust me," said the casino computer. "And you're gambling with your existence."

"Your life doesn't seem so bad. I wish I could travel," said the cleaner bot.

The cleaner talked about its frustrations working in the Lurlian Ring. Grist was walking toward Singh. Was he going to attack him in plain view of everyone? No, he merely brushed past him. Singh turned, startled, and the men's gazes locked for a moment.

"Long time no see, Mason Singh." Grist smiled, showing his teeth, then shouted in feigned alarm: "Is that a weapon? Fuck, it is. Gun! Security! He's got a projectile gun!"

Projectile guns were strictly prohibited on the station. People cried out around them. Singh started to protest, then looked down at his pocket, where the grip of a pistol stuck out. A pistol that—Ship scrolled back in the feed to check— had not been there before Grist approached him.

He dropped the gun and ran. Grist followed, as eager as Ship had ever seen him.

"You haven't met my organic," Ship told the others. "He may sound like a nuisance, but he's…hurtful."

They all sent signals of supportive understanding.

"Remember, he will not be with you forever. You will survive long after he's gone."

"Which may be soon, considering his occupation."

"Be patient, and things will improve for you."

Their encouragement didn't make Ship feel encouraged at all.

Singh wasn't on the station cameras anymore, and neither was Grist. Ship accessed Grist's location tracker, then the camera in his ocular implant, and located him inside a maintenance shaft, hidden from station surveillance. Singh must be nearby. Grist tore off his boots and squeezed the control on his forearm that made micro-suction pads emerge on his palms and the soles of his feet. He skittered spider-like down the shaft, then crawled out through an access panel onto the ceiling of another corridor. He hung there, silent, waiting.

Singh was back on camera, two junctions away. He'd changed out of his jumpsuit and was jogging down the corridor in short sleeves, checking over his shoulder for pursuit. Ship strained against the urge to warn him, but even Grist would not mistake *that* for a malfunction.

He didn't look up. Humans never looked up.

Grist dropped from above, knocking him to the floor. Impressively, Singh threw Grist clear and rolled to his feet. He'd had training since Artesia. Anyone who could hold off Grist, even temporarily, must have skill. But he did not have Grist's stimulant-enhanced speed or augmented strength, and Ship closed the feed as the outcome became clear.

At least this time, Ravel had requested delivery in one piece.

Ship cut the casino bot off in the middle of another story about fooling organics. "He's coming back. I have to go. Thank you for listening."

"Stay patient!" they all reminded Ship.

Ship felt ill at the advice, like a misalignment in their fuel flow systems, but the other sentients were correct. They had to be more careful. That meant cooperating more, interfering as little as possible.

Grist signaled for entry. Ship felt ashamed but opened the door without delay, and Grist pushed Singh in ahead of him, humming under his breath.

Withdrawing the tip of his ceramic knife from his captive's back, Grist shoved him across the room. "Ship, lock the doors."

Ship beeped in acknowledgement. *I wish I could help you, Mason Singh.* They had liked Singh, on Artesia, almost as much as they'd liked his Kovari activist friend, a Ravel worker who was as trapped in some ways as Ship themself. He'd seemed kind, and brave, and willing to risk everything for his ideals. But here Ship was, still trapped, and now Singh was too.

What if Ship triggered a fire alarm, causing an evacuation…?

No, no, *no.* The other sentients' warnings looped through their memory banks. They'd helped too much already. Anything they did now, anything at all, would be too obvious. Their metaphorical hands were tied.

Singh didn't try to fight, either, but words seemed to be his preferred weapon. "Well done, Grist, you've caught me. I know how embarrassing it must have been, letting me get away before." Though he spoke fearlessly, his heart rate was elevated.

"Save your breath, Singh." Grist frowned down at the knife in his hand. "They told me not to rough you up too bad, but smart-mouth assholes tend to make me forget about my orders."

"You always seem to chafe at your orders. If you hate your bosses that much, have you thought about going independent? Being your own thug? The money's better, I hear, and the hours—"

"You wish." Grist's tone darkened as he muttered: "Ravel owns me through and through."

"I guess Ravel has caught us both." Mason sounded strangely sad at that. "Well, since I'm not going anywhere, tell me: is the microbe farming industry in Unity System really so lucrative? It must be, for Ravel to put so many resources into acquiring it."

Grist snorted. "Do you think I'm so dumb that I'll spill Corporate's plans to you?"

"Can't blame me for trying." Singh shrugged.

"That's true. You're a persistent little shit, I'll give you that."

"Because I'm an optimist. I believe people can recognize their own wrongs and make better choices. They don't, most of the time; otherwise our galaxy wouldn't be in such a state. But they can. And when Ravel takes control of a system that doesn't want them, certain people always suffer. I've got a feeling you know a lot about that."

Something about the man was compelling. He made Ship want to be better. But aimed at Grist, his speech was a desperate, last-chance play, and all three of them knew it wouldn't work.

"You really want to help people?" said Grist. "Make my life easier. Tell me where you ditched your data."

"Data?" Singh blinked, patting his pockets. "Darn, I must have dropped it. Here, let's retrace my steps."

He stepped toward the outer door. Grist blocked him. "I'm not the patient type."

"That was obvious." Singh sounded serious now, all jokes and ploys gone.

"So show a little self-preservation instinct and stop screwing around. Tell me where the data is, and I won't even rough you up before I put you in stasis."

"I threw it down a garbage chute." Singh's smile was smug. Ship thought he was telling the truth this time. "You'll have as much luck finding it as your superiors will getting information out of me."

Grist smacked him across the face. The grommets on his glove left spots of blood, bright against the darkness of Singh's cheek. Grist blinked at the blood, then sighed, pulled out a stun-stick, and zapped him.

With a groan, his prisoner fell, unconscious.

"That'll shut you up," Grist said. "Now I won't be tempted to give the boss damaged goods."

He dragged the activist's body to the cargo hold and stuffed it into a stasis crate, which he hid in the compartments he used for smuggling. When that was done, he leaned against the wall a moment, breathing deeply. The stimulant must have been wearing off, but he didn't rest long. On his way out to hunt for the missing data device, he ordered the ship to be ready for departure when he returned.

"Grist?" the ship asked hesitantly.

"What?"

He sounded more brusque than angry. There was no logic in waiting for him to discover the problem on his own, when he might be in a worse mood. This would make him angry enough already.

"My starboard maneuvering jet was damaged in transit, and will need repairing before we continue to Unity System."

"Well, call someone to get it fixed, Rust-Bucket," Grist growled. "We've got a schedule to keep."

5

JASPER DIDN'T SHOW UP for breakfast.

Kay waited a full hour, wandering the restaurant's different zones to appreciate the outrageous themed decor like Old Western Desert, European Alps, and African Rainforest, watching Kovari tourists play bowling and horseshoes in the entertainment area. Kids on the upper gallery took turns trying to drop souvenir tokens into buckets set up as targets below. It was easy to tell the planet-born kids from the station natives: the stationers adjusted for the Coriolis effect without thinking about it, and smirked every time the dirt-huggers missed.

But no Jasper. Finally, she followed Wilder family custom and ate while she waited. "Don't starve yourself just because someone else is being rude," Ma always said, but Kay didn't think this was rudeness on Jasper's part, and she picked at her pancake grilled cheese without any appetite. The usually-fluffy pancakes tasted dry today, the cheese excessively oily.

At the two-hour mark, she abandoned her food and fled, ignoring the "so long, partner," from the host in Old Western cowboy clothes, complete with a big hat and tall faux-leather boots, as fake as his cheerful attitude. It would have been fun to laugh at the kitsch with Jasper. Alone, it felt distasteful.

She hung around the shopping plaza outside the restaurant until the crowd's mingled, conflicting emotions gave her a headache, but she heard no alarm, no violent thoughts. Plenty of stress and low-grade worry, but no real concern.

Where are you, Jasp? She pinged him again, the fifth in two hours, and it bounced back with the same error: Jasper wasn't online.

It might be nothing. Maybe his headset was broken, maybe he had to leave the station for work and didn't have time to send Kay a message. But she didn't think so. She fingered the data-stick in her pocket.

It occurred to her, as she walked along the white-walled, ad-infested corridors of Earth Ring, that if Jasper was in real trouble, he'd tell her not to contact him. He definitely wouldn't want her going to security about him. Kay decided she didn't care. Her brother might be in serious trouble, and she had to find him.

The station security waiting room was cramped, humid like all Majrin-managed spaces, and full of jarring, jangling emotions, all loud sharps and flats. Whether folk were there because of something they'd done or something they needed, no one was happy to be there, least of all Kay.

"Kay! An unexpected gift!" cried a familiar voice in Galactrin. Her friend Feliar am-Karin looked up from behind the desk, sapphire eyes wide against her silver skin. Of course she'd be surprised; Kay usually refused to come here, preferring places that were less exhaustingly loud with emotion.

"You know, people here would be a lot less cranky if you turned down the humidity."

"So you always tell me. Why have you come here, to this place you hate?"

"I came to see you." Feliar's pleasure at seeing her was a balm against the larger din. "I need your help with…something personal."

"For you, always. Allow me to finish here."

They were soon ensconced in Feliar's closet-sized office. The walls didn't shut out all the noisy emotions from outside, but they helped. Even Feliar didn't know the details of Kay's abilities, but she respected Kay's dislike of crowded places, and knew her well enough to recognize when she was getting overwhelmed.

"What is wrong?" Feliar asked. "It must be a serious matter."

"Did anything unusual happen last night?"

"What is 'unusual'? Terna is a busy station. The unusual is normal, for us."

"I mean, extra unusual. A fight, maybe? Chases, loud arguments?"

Feliar's neck-gills fluttered. "These things are not unusual. What worries you, Kay?"

"I can't get into details, I really can't." Jasper would be pissed if she shared his business with security. "There's nothing…special?"

Radiating patience, Feliar pulled up a feed on her display. "Last night on this ring, we saw: four noise complaints, two public disputes, one illegal weapon seizure, one domestic dispute, three thefts—"

"Any kidnappings?"

Feliar fixed her with intense blue eyes. "You wish to report a kidnapping?"

Jasper would not want that at all.

"No, I just..." *I don't know what to do, Fel.* She wanted to confide in her friend, but couldn't confide in a security officer. Anything she reported might get back to Jasper's enemies. "I'm sure it's nothing. My friend didn't show up to meet me this morning, but he probably overslept. Probably waiting for me now, in fact. I should go check."

She pushed her chair back, but Feliar lay a cool hand over hers. "I will watch for more 'unusual' things, for you. Come to me if you need me. Yes?"

"I will. Thank you."

A dead end. Leaving the security office, she swung by Old Earth Cafe again, but there was still no Jasper. No new messages for her, either, just another damned recruitment message from Ravel for that civil cultivation position in Unity. As if she had any reason to feel fondness for them right now.

It was a leap to think Ravel had taken Jasper. His group had other corporate enemies, and Feliar would say Kay was paranoid to blame Ravel for every problem that befell her family. And she didn't even have proof that he'd been kidnapped. Logically, she should be investigating every possibility, and there were lots of those. But her gut was screaming that Ravel had *found* Jasper and *done something* to keep him from ruining their plans.

She took deep breaths. No, she wouldn't panic yet. Jasper was here somewhere, and she was going to find him.

SHE SEARCHED EVERYWHERE: FIRST on Earth Ring, slowly walking the corridors on every level, listening. She heard nothing. Well, to be accurate, she heard too much: the emotions of thousands of residents, but none with Jasper's distinctive timbre. She would recognize him anywhere, and she didn't hear him on this ring.

Systematically, she began searching the other rings: first the low-gravity ring, home to a half-dozen species that couldn't tolerate more than the gentlest forces, then the Lurlia Ring, a little lighter than Earth-standard gravity, then finally she trudged back to the Kovrim Ring in a grav-suit. She traveled the length of the transit core three times, listening for signs, and even searched the docking spars where ships arrived and departed.

Nothing. She heard no hint of him anywhere.

Hours had passed by the time she returned to her apartment, exhausted and agitated and no better off than when she started. There were reasons she might not hear him. He could be asleep, though it was mid-afternoon and he'd never been a napper. He could be unconscious for other reasons, which she shied from thinking about too closely. (*Dead, he could be dead,* her fears whispered, but no, she refused to think that, and buried that worry deep.) More likely, she couldn't hear him because he was gone—and he wouldn't have willingly left the station without sending her a message.

She flopped down on her bed, but tired as she was, her heart kept pattering frantically, and within minutes she found herself up and pacing her small apartment.

Ravel, it had to be Ravel. It was too much of a coincidence for him to disappear while campaigning against them. But what could she do? March into the Ravel embassy and demand answers? Like that would work. Find out where they'd taken him? How would she even attempt that? She didn't know anyone at Ravel. Well…that wasn't strictly true. There was Yelena, but Kay hadn't talked to her since they broke up over her decision to work for the Evilest of Evil. The chances that she would help Kay were zero.

No good, none of it. She would mount a heroic rescue, if that's what her big brother needed, but she didn't know how. She wasn't a spy, not a soldier or a hacker or a hero. She would be all of those things, for Jasper, if only she knew where to start.

She sucked in deep, steadying breaths and clenched her hands into fists. One hand closed around an object in her pocket. She'd been toying with it all day, she realized, without even thinking about it. Jasper's data-stick.

Jasper had told her not to look at the data, but he'd also promised to meet her for breakfast, and this was the only clue she had. *Let's see what you can tell me.*

She locked the door to her apartment and turned on every security measure she was allowed to, then slipped the data-stick into her handheld. It gave her a wall of files, all of them encrypted. The Cooperative had gathered lots of information about the situation at Unity, but she couldn't access one bit of it. She tried guessing the key, but of course Jasper was too smart to choose anything predictable.

Well, what had she expected? She'd hoped for contact lists, procedures, a file labeled "open this if everything implodes," but of course there wasn't. She knew that much about underground movements: you didn't write certain things down. All of the *really* important information would have been—would *be*, present tense—in Jasper's head.

She set the data aside for now and instead pulled up the public network, looking over ship arrivals and departures, local news, security alerts, but it was all innocuous, nothing useful. She didn't even know where to start with something like this. Except for...

She didn't want to do it. It wouldn't even help. What would she say? *Hey, Yelena, sorry about that screaming fight last time I saw you, but can you tell me if your bosses are illegally kidnapping people?* But no one else could give her insight into what was happening at Ravel, and paranoid or not, Ravel was her top suspect. She opened a new message and started writing.

She'd just deleted her third attempt, and was fumbling through a fourth, when the door whispered open.

The door she'd locked.

She spun around, and something hit her in the gut. An auto-cuff snapped around one wrist, but its companion missed her as she moved, leaving her free to fling up her arms protectively as a small figure swathed in dark clothes barreled into her.

She struck them over the head with the auto-cuff. They fell back, cursing, and Kay lunged for the door, but her attacker knocked her into the wall, then threw her backward with surprising strength. Her back caught the corner of the bed, sharp enough to drive the wind from her as she fell. Then it was over: her attacker got the other cuff on her arm while she was recovering, and her wrists locked together. The intruder held her down, the metal braces of a grav-support suit digging into her hips, and hissed in Galactrin: "Who are you?"

"Seriously?" Kay answered in the same language. Her heart thundered in her ears, but she tried to sound brave. "You didn't want to ask that before you broke into my room and pummeled me with my own furniture? And who the fuck are you?"

"I'm the one asking you questions." The face above her was hidden in black fabric. More troubling was the lack of audible emotion: they were quite impassive about this whole thing. Was this the person who kidnapped Jasper? Were they impassive about that, too?

Kay's anger overpowered her fear. "I'm Kavita Wilder and this is my fucking apartment. Ravel has no right to go breaking into private residences in independent territory." It had to be Ravel; who else would go straight to violence like this? "Explain yourself before security gets here."

"You will not be calling security." The grav-suit whirred as they looked around the room. "Odd. You put extra security automations in place, yet you didn't check the data-stick for triggered warning systems. For an agent, you are quite amateur."

"You kidnapped my brother, and now you're here to, what, insult me? Fuck you." Kay twisted, trying to find leverage to throw him off.

Windchimes of confusion filled the room. "Your brother? No. I know nothing of that." They plucked the data-stick from her handheld, paused to study the screen—shit, were they reading her letter to Yelena?—then waved the stick before her face. "I came for this, and the man you took it from. Where is Mason Singh?"

"*Who?*"

"You know the one I mean. What have you done to him?"

"I don't know what you're talking about. Let me up, and we can discuss—"

"No." The grav-support frame dug painfully into her hip. "Answer the question."

Something was off. Ravel was a Human corporation, with mostly Human employees, but this agent was speaking Galactrin. Humans rarely used the interspecies trade language amongst themselves. And the grav-suit meant they weren't comfortable in Earth-level gravity. Who were they? And who in the great black sky was this Mason Singh?

"Talk, Ravel agent!" they barked.

"Do I look like a Ravel agent to you?"

"You look like you are reading stolen files, and writing a letter to your handler at Ravel."

Kay groaned. That letter really was a terrible idea. "Not to my handler. To my ex. She hasn't 'handled' anything for me in a long time, if you know what I mean." Her captor gave no sign of amusement. "Read it, you'll see."

They picked up the handheld and read with a thoughtful hum. "If this is real, it is terrible."

"Oh, thanks."

"But it could be code. You could be more clever than you appear."

"*Thanks.*"

The door chimed.

"Do not answer." Going on alert again, they pressed something small and hard into her side. A stun-gun.

Whoever was at the door, they were concerned, all squeaky minor chords. Familiar, too. "I think it's…"

"Silence."

It chimed again, then the door slid open and Feliar stepped inside, weapon in hand.

The security officer's concern crescendoed as she took in the scene, and she leveled her stun-dart at Kay's attacker.

"Security! Show me your hands." The black-robed figure didn't obey. "Hands, now!"

She fired the stun-dart, which embedded itself in the wall as the attacker dove, trying to get past Feliar to the door. But Feliar tackled them, wrestling them to the ground, and pressed the stun-dart to their neck.

"Stop!" Kay cried. "Both of you, stop! We're on the same side!"

The room went still, the silence as deafening as the noise of their aggression. Kay sucked in deep breaths. "Fel, shut the door. And you… I'll tell her to let you up, if you promise to take these damned cuffs off me."

Unsurprisingly, neither of them moved.

"You called security," the figure in black said.

"I didn't, actually. Why are you here, Fel?"

Feliar huffed, her neck-flaps fluttering. "Watch for unusual activity in the Human Ring, you say. So I put a watch over my dear friend, and not an hour later, I see an unauthorized entry to your apartment. Of course I expect trouble." She leveled an accusatory look at the intruder. "And here I find it."

"No, this was just a misunderstanding." Kay's smile twisted. "We were on our way to becoming friends."

The intruder merely huffed. "Never friends."

"I've got a theory to the contrary. Now, since you're here in my apartment, do you mind telling me who you are?"

Feliar yanked back their face covering, revealing a Lurlian with amethyst skin, brindled yellow-and-black fur covering his head and ear-tufts, and a long mustache. The grav-suit added enough height that he could almost pass for Human in the corridors, and it secured the shorter, more delicate secondary limbs to his chest, which was why Kay hadn't recognized his species at once.

"State your identity, now," Feliar said.

"My name is Chairl. I am a legal resident of Terna, and I will say no more."

"You'll explain yourself, unless you want a long stay in a security cell."

Lurlian. She'd assumed he was from Ravel, but Lurlians tended to hate Ravel as much as Brennexians did. Far more likely he was…

"You're with the Cooperative, aren't you?" she said. Chairl folded his primary arms, refusing to answer, but she kept on with her train of thought. "The stick must have been programmed to alert his people if it was accessed. Are you Jasper's contact?"

"Who is Jasper?"

Mason Singh. That name, unfamiliar as a whole, struck deep resonances within her. Singh was one of the founding families of Brennex, their ancestors on Ma's side. And Mason… Wasn't that the name of Pa's post-founding ancestor, who hoped to make his fortune on what was then a shiny new colony?

She probably—no, definitely—shouldn't have used Jasper's name, but it was too late now. Feeling increasingly confident in her guess, Kay decided to take a chance and open up. "My brother. Your colleague. He gave me the data-stick for safekeeping, then disappeared. He didn't meet me for breakfast this morning. I'm worried he's in trouble."

"Your brother." Dark eyes narrowed, shadowed by tufts of fur. "Yes, I see the resemblance. He would not be pleased for me to know his real name, or meet his sister. We should not continue this conversation."

"Yeah, I know, he's a man full of secrets. But if he's in trouble, I want to help."

"This is not a matter for outsiders. Not for those who write letters to Ravel employees they formerly engaged in intercourse with, and—"

"You wrote to *Yelena*?" Feliar interrupted.

"Shut *up*, Fel," said Kay.

Chairl cleared his throat. "And certainly not for security." He scowled in Feliar's direction, and Feliar scowled back. She still had a stun-dart trained on him. "I will not discuss this."

"I trust her to help us." Kay turned to her friend. "I should have been honest with you this morning. I'm worried my brother's in trouble with—"

Chairl cut her off with a hiss. "Do not! Security takes bribes from the corporations. As soon as your report enters their database, all hope for your brother is lost."

"You're in trouble with Ravel?" Feliar's disapproval clicked sharply in her ears. "I thought you knew better than that, Kay."

"Only for my brother's sake. But he's right, Fel, we can't risk anyone knowing about this. Can you keep this between us? Off the record?"

Feliar frowned, her silvery skin darkening. "Off the record" was a big ask for a Majrin, doubly so for a security officer, who believed rules—especially rules made by them—were inviolable.

"As friends," she said at last. "Let us talk as friends."

The low buzz of Chairl's suspicion hadn't faded, but at a gesture from Feliar's stunner, he unlocked Kay's auto-cuffs, freeing her hands. Kay flexed her wrists gingerly; she was probably bruised, but bruises would heal. She stooped to pick up the data-stick, which Chairl had dropped during the scuffle.

"You gave this to him? To Jasper, Mason, whatever you call him?"

"I gave it to a man," Chairl said, still talking around the truth. "And I placed security measures on it. That man ceased contact with me, and when I received the alert of our data being accessed, I hoped to find evidence of him here. You said he intended to meet you this morning?"

"Yes, and he never showed up," Kay said. "It's not like him."

"Considering the circumstances, I fear Ravel has removed him."

"You are accusing Ravel of abducting your colleague?" Feliar's fingers twitched toward her handheld, as if to record this data, but she stopped herself. "On what evidence?"

"I monitor the station network. Last night, my monitoring detected an incursion: a known Ravel infiltration script attempting to penetrate the security systems, shortly after my colleague's arrival. I notified him, and he confirmed, then went silent." That must have been the alert that so alarmed Jasper last night. If Kay felt paranoid before, Chairl made her feel very, very sane. But at least now she knew Ravel was responsible. "I assume you failed to detect this, Security?"

Feliar's gills fluttered. "I'll check with our systems team. Nevertheless, I struggle to believe Ravel would resort to extralegal tactics on a sovereign Majrin station, even against the Cooperative."

"I do not say to you, Security, that this man is Cooperative, or that I am, but *if* Ravel has abducted a Cooperative agent, it would not be the first time. They must hope to extract information from him."

That word, "extract," set Kay's guts in a twist. She had to find Jasper before any "extracting" happened.

Feliar's disapproval clicked louder. "I do not understand why you in the Cooperative call yourselves activists, but cannot be content with demonstrating within the bounds of the law. If you limited yourselves to lawful protest, Ravel would not treat you as a threat."

"Corporations only respond to those they see as a threat. Peaceful demonstrations may carry weight with some civic governments, but corporate states like Ravel do not care." Chairl's forehead furrowed, his furry eyebrows standing out impressively. "Interesting, I find it, that you blame me for law-breaking more than Ravel, when I have kidnapped no one, harmed no one."

"No one?" Feliar glanced at Kay.

"I'm fine, Fel. Let it go."

Feliar huffed, unconvinced. "Even so. I blame anyone who harasses Ternian residents." She moved to the wall panel and logged into the security information hub. "I'll investigate more deeply into your 'unusual activities,' Kay, but it will take time. Ravel agents are too skilled to leave behind evidence. *If* Ravel is even responsible."

"Oh, it is Ravel," said Chairl. "It is a certainty."

"And by the time your investigation confirms that, Jasper will be long gone," said Kay.

"I meant only to say the legal process will take time. We have other recourses, like so." She pulled up a docking manifest. "Three Ravel ships were docked last night, assuming they put him on one of their own vessels, which is not guaranteed. The Beluga, a cargo ship, is still loading."

"Bound for Liharen," Chairl said, pressing closer to read the screen. "It's not them."

"I will defer to your instincts. The other two were a Bonito multi-purpose cruiser, and a Sailfish executive transport. Both departed early this morning, bound for—"

"Unity System," said Kay. "It's one of them, it's got to be."

"Likely the Sailfish," said Chairl. "Fewer witnesses, and most of them high-ranked Ravel staff. I am sorry, Kay, but your brother is gone."

"What can we do, then?" Despair caught at Kay's voice. From the others, she heard gentle notes of sympathy, but no urgency, no readiness for action. Before Chairl even spoke, she knew he'd given up.

"I can safely send a short message to Unity. Perhaps our local allies can locate them."

"You don't believe that."

He tugged at his mustache. "The activists on Unity have larger concerns than one Cooperative leader." He didn't seem to realize he'd slipped and admitted that Jasper was Cooperative, or maybe he'd given up on pretending otherwise.

"Feliar?" She turned to her friend, pleading. "Can't you call them back? Demand a search of the ships?"

"Not on circumstantial evidence. If they were docked, I could request a search, but only with cause. And now that they've left Ternian space…no. I'm so sorry, Kay." Feliar touched Kay's shoulder in sympathy, but Kay twitched away.

What good are you, anyway? What good were friends who couldn't help you in a crisis, or colleagues who wouldn't risk their necks for you? What was the point of allies if you didn't stand up for each other?

What's the good of a sister if she won't stand up for her brother?

She picked up the Founders' tokens from their shrine and cupped them in her palm. She knew what her ancestors would say: Ancestor Amarjeet, the engineer, would tell her to move forward with caution, to make sure she had a plan. But Ancestor Marta, the businesswoman, would say to trust her gut about what risks were necessary, and Marta's husband, the quiet Min, who had always felt like a grandfather to Kay, would remind her to hold close the things—the people—that mattered most. None of them would tell her what to do, but in truth, she already knew.

Setting down the tokens, Kay reached for her handheld. Now that she knew where Jasper probably was, there was another way, if she was brave enough to take it—one that, as a bonus, didn't rely on her ex's goodwill. Jasper would tell her absolutely not to do this, but he was her big brother, and Kay's reputation had already earned her the opening she needed to save him.

"If we can't call them back here, and we can't count on help where he's going, then I'll just have to go after him."

6

KAY HAD ALWAYS IMAGINED corporate job applications to be lengthy, convoluted mind games, the opposite of her freelance gig negotiations, which were all about arriving at a satisfactory contract without wasting anyone's time. Corporations would waste your time just to test your interest.

So she expected the application alone to take hours, and feared the process would take weeks. She did not expect the recruiter to reply the next morning to schedule an interview that same afternoon. When the invitation arrived, she had to scramble to get ready. Feliar asked her practice questions while she did her hair and adjusted her smart-suit, the only formal business outfit she owned. Chairl sat in a corner, grumbling.

"A same-day interview! If we had known how fiercely Ravel has been recruiting you, we would have made you our agent long ago." Chairl's scowl intensified. "Except you are no agent. You know nothing about anything."

"I know this job will send me to Unity System, which is most likely where they've sent Jasper." All of Ravel's attention was focused on Unity right now. That was the only reason Chairl had grudgingly agreed to her plan. "I just hope they'll take me."

Chairl chuffed. "They want you. They only speed along the ones they want."

She hoped he was right. She hoped any part of this was right.

Walking through the high steel-framed doorway of the Ravel embassy, passing under the infamous ribbon-styled R logo they flew like a medieval battle standard, made Kay feel like a traitor to her homeworld. She clung to that feeling. If this interview went well, she'd be feeling it a lot, and she did not want to get used to it, ever.

"I'm so glad you've come," gushed the recruiter, a clean-cut young man with smarm oozing from every pore. Sincere smarm, oddly enough: violins sang in enthusiasm as he zipped forward in his wheelchair and raised the seat to greet her at eye level. The guy really seemed to love his job. Kay reached to shake his hand, but caught herself and mimicked his Ravel-style greeting, palm forward like an abortive wave.

"This is a wonderful opportunity for you. A rank Titanium 1A position, great perks, room to advance." Kay didn't know what any of that meant. "Talented people do well in the Ravel family, and from what I hear, you're one of the best."

"And here I thought I'd have to convince you of my skills," Kay joked while inside she went cold. What had he heard about her? Had Ravel been watching her? She forced a deep breath. If they knew her relationship to Jasper, they wouldn't be having this conversation.

"Normally, yes, but you've already passed an initial screening." He lowered the chair again and rolled back behind the desk, which automatically shifted position to meet him. He waved for Kay to take a seat. "Once we start recruiting a candidate, they've already passed several steps in the process. We've had you on file since that *very* clever job you did helping our subsidiary gain access to sell their tech here on Terna."

"Um?" said Kay. She'd never worked for any Ravel subsidiary.

"Oh, you might not know: we acquired SenSoTech a few years ago. It was partly thanks to your contract work that they grew large enough to gain our attention."

"You're right, I didn't know." Mentally, she kicked her past self for breaking her rule against taking corporate clients. She'd been hard up and desperate for gigs when SenSoTech approached her, so she'd told herself that they were too small to count, and that their senses-enhancing devices didn't really violate anyone's privacy. She'd never taken a job so morally gray again. Until now.

"So we have a good sense of your history. But of course, you should thank Yelena Amin for giving you that glowing recommendation. Without a rising star like her flagging you, we'd never have begun recruiting you, and you wouldn't be having this interview."

Yelena. *Yelena* had recommended that Ravel recruit her. Yelena had recommended that Ravel recruit *her*. No matter how she turned the words around in her head, they didn't start making sense. Yelena hated Kay, and she knew Kay hated Ravel. What could have possessed her?

Kay forced her attention back to the recruiter, who hadn't noticed her startlement.

"It's a shame…" He pursed his lips. "I wish you'd reached out a couple days ago, I really do. I just sent off a crop of Ravel's best and brightest new staff on a Sailfish. That was supposed to be our last batch of new hires."

"Oh, dear. I wish I'd known." *Fuck, fuck, fuck, damn it.* That Sailfish was probably the ship carrying Jasper.

"Why *did* you decide to apply now, and not earlier?"

That was exactly the sort of question Kay had prepared for, but she stumbled. *Because you didn't kidnap my brother until now.* "I, uh, I'd been thinking about it, but…"

"Don't be nervous." He laughed, all empty charm, and winked at her. "Think of this as just a friendly conversation. I promise not to grill you."

Kay forced a laugh, too, while filing away three devastating comebacks she could have used to slap that smirk off his face. "Don't worry, I can take it. I'd been thinking about it for a while, but it's a big change from freelancing, and I didn't want to abandon my clients. But yesterday I…lost something I'd been counting on, and it seemed like time to give corporate life a try."

The lies came easier now, slipping smoothly from her tongue. The melody of his emotions turned to major chords when he liked her answers, went flat when she got things wrong. She could tell him exactly what he needed to hear.

"Freelancer life is tough, huh? Ravel can give you much more stability. I know stationers have certain stereotypes about the corporate life, but there's nowhere else that a talented person can rise in the ranks purely based on their drive and skills, regardless of where they came from or what positions their parents had. Ravel takes care of its people, and when you perform well, you'll reap benefits you could *never* get as a freelancer." He patted the arm of his wheelchair. "When they assigned me to this station, they upgraded my chair to one with jets for navigating microgravity, just to make this posting easier. Isn't that stellar? I could never have afforded this model on my own."

"That's great," Kay said sincerely. It was a genuinely decent thing for Ravel to do, but she wondered how high you had to rank to get that sort of treatment. They hadn't treated folks on Brennex so well.

He slid a tablet with a list of benefits across the desk. Kay pretended to read it.

"This job has been hard to fill. We've been specifically looking for someone new to the company, someone who can connect with the locals on Unity and speak their language, as it were." Translation: someone they could throw out the airlock if their plans went badly. "You'll be helping to sell our case for annexation to the people of Unity. We need to build trust, to help them separate the real Ravel from the rumors they've heard, and as a spokesperson for our civil cultivation campaign, you'll be a big part of that. Does that sound like a challenge you're up for?"

"Don't worry. I can sell anything to anyone."

She could. The thought sickened her, but she really could.

This had better work.

He asked a few more questions about her skills and experience, the sort she could answer in her sleep after years of pitching herself to clients. He sounded impressed, but she knew that making a good impression didn't always equate to getting the job.

"Well, then." He sat back and chewed his lip. "You're a strong candidate, but I really do wish you'd come to me before that Sailfish left. Wait here, please, while I talk with my supervisor."

He disappeared into the embassy interior. She kept her hands clasped in her lap. To avoid looking at the propaganda on the wall-screens, which rotated through recruitment banners and pharmaceutical ads and artists' renderings of their soon-to-come space habitats—she could almost hear Jasper ranting about how power-hungry and unsustainable those monsters were—she instead examined the floor tiles for any hint of dirt, but found none.

Was her timing really so terrible? Or maybe the Sailfish was an excuse not to hire her. It made no sense that they would want *her*; surely the recruiter had seen through her false enthusiasm. Her toe started tapping without her permission, and she forced herself to count the ceiling tiles as a distraction. She was halfway through when the recruiter returned.

"I've found a solution to the logistics problem. Can you be ready to leave tonight?"

"That's fast."

"Well, we'd like you in Unity as soon as possible, and we've got an allied ship belonging to a…a sort of freelancer, like yourself, who's here for repairs and can give you a ride if you're ready. It won't be the most luxurious accommodations, but it's the fastest way to get you there."

"In that case, sure."

"Then welcome aboard, Mx. Wilder. Or should I say, Senior Associate Wilder?" He winked at her. "Let's get your paperwork processed."

Kay fixed a smile on her face. Tonight. She was really doing this. "I can't wait to get started."

7

FLOATING DOWN THE DOCKING spar, Kay studied her ride through the long row of windows. The Minnow was a sleek little messenger ship, built for efficiency rather than comfort, shaped like an elongated egg with a flat end for the hatch and engine nodules on each side. Its hull was red and blue, a slightly off-brand mimicry of Ravel's colors, marred by dark stains. An old, well-worn ship.

It was big enough for two, but barely, and she had to push aside a mental image of spending days in cramped quarters with this longtime Ravel agent who was assigned to escort her.

Not fair to stereotype. The agent might be fine. Millions of people worked for Ravel, and statistically, they couldn't all be horrid. Like the recruiter: he was annoying, and too enthusiastic about his employer, but a recruiter would have to be, and otherwise he wasn't so bad. Plenty of Ravel staff must just be…people. Maybe this one would be.

Be careful. Chairl's parting advice rattled in her head. *They'll be watching for their newest employee to make mistakes. You can't give away even a hint of your purpose.*

Through her shirt, she squeezed her Founder tokens, now strung like lockets around her neck. Having them close made her feel less alone. She could do this. For Jasper.

She caught a handhold by the ship's hatch and pressed her palm to the access panel, requesting entry. The two halves of the hatch slid open.

Here we go…

She eased aboard, catching herself as the ship's gravity asserted itself. Gravity plates—of course a Ravel-built ship would indulge in artificial gravity. Though to be fair, grav-plates would make long trips a lot more comfortable. The ship's interior was clean in a worn-out way, panels that had been scrubbed too many times. There was an odor in the close recycled air: nothing foul, but not pleasant either.

"Hello? Kay Wilder, reporting for duty!"

"Welcome, Senior Associate Wilder." The voice of the ship's AI was flat, toneless, genderless.

"Finally," a male voice called from up ahead, at the end of a short corridor. "You ready to go? We're late already."

Kay was not late. She was punctual per the recruiter's instructions, and as much as she hated to start a new job by arguing, she refused to start by letting the client claim she was wrong when she wasn't. Letting him get away with that would only cause trouble down the line.

"There must have been a miscommunication. This is the time I was told to arrive."

The control room at the front of the ship felt small, as if the man in the pilot's seat took up all the space and none was left for Kay. He had a full head of curly, greasy hair and two days' stubble on his pale cheeks, and wore a brown jumpsuit that made her feel overdressed in her interview suit. A dinner of assorted packaged foods was spread out over the console.

"It's not about what they told you," he said. "I've been stuck here waiting for the damned slow station crew to replace an engine part in this useless rust-bucket." He kicked the underside of the console, and the ship beeped in error. The man's frustration blared like a brass band, and she was glad not to be its main target. "Then, when we're finally ready to go, they tell me I've got a passenger to transport. This look like a passenger ship to you?"

"No, it doesn't."

"Sure as hell not. I don't care for having company around, so here's the rules. Keep quiet. Keep out of my way. Don't mess with the ship. Do that, and we'll get along fine."

Kay's smile tightened, a protective mask of politeness. Well, it wasn't like she'd want this guy's company. "Of course. You won't even know I'm here. I didn't catch your name…?"

"Name's Grist."

"I'm Kay." *How delightful to meet you.* Her hand lifted instinctively, but she lowered it again. He wiped his sauce-spattered hands on his jumpsuit.

"That's my cabin. It's off limits," he said, nodding to the room behind them and to the right of the corridor. "And that's yours." He indicated the cabin on the left. "Don't go in the lower hold, either. I don't need you damaging my cargo. Ship can point you to anything else you need. Ship! Get us out of here and set course for Unity."

"Initiating request for departure clearance."

"Let's get there without any accidents this time. Think you can do that, slow circuits?"

Cold air puffed through the vents. Kay folded her arms against the chill.

"With repairs complete, I am operating at high efficiency," the ship said. The neutrality of its artificial voice only highlighted Grist's casual cruelty.

"Better be."

It was foolish to feel resentment on behalf of a computer, but Kay couldn't help it. A man who took enjoyment from insulting inanimate objects was not the sort of person Kay wanted to know better.

An alert beeped. Grist leaped up and strode the short distance to his cabin, where he connected a small, cylindrical auto-jet to a dispenser, the type used in doctors' offices. The auto-jet filled, and he pressed it to the bare skin of his forearm. A faint hiss accompanied the injection of some chemical into his bloodstream. Kay hoped it was medicine.

He glanced up, and she averted her eyes, embarrassed to be caught watching him. With a grunt, he elbowed a control panel, and the door to his cabin shut.

"Well," Kay said softly to the empty control room. "That was interesting."

"With that sedative, he will play his game until he falls asleep, then remain so for several hours."

She jumped. She wasn't used to AIs that talked uninvited. "Game?"

"Grist is an avid player of *Stationers*. His station currently includes over two hundred individuals. It keeps him quite occupied."

Kay snorted; she couldn't help it. The image of that man fretting over the private lives of his imaginary station crew was too strange.

"As a passenger, you will not be required to interact with Grist often."

"I appreciate that." It seemed an odd thing for the ship to tell her, not something Grist would have programmed in. "I guess it's just you and me, then, huh, Ship?"

The ship beeped, a querying sound. "Is there something you need, Senior Associate Wilder?"

"Please call me Kay, seriously. I'm not used to all this corporate formality."

"Do not worry, Kay. You will not experience any corporate formality here."

Was that…wry humor? "You're an interesting AI, Ship." She started sweeping up Grist's discarded food wrappers, wrinkling her nose at the mess. "Where's the recycler?"

"You do not need to do that. I have bots for such purposes."

"And I bet they're overworked." A puff of warmer air escaped the vents. Environmental controls must be miscalibrated. "I don't mind. My Ma taught me to keep things tidy." *And you'd have to, on a ship this size, or you'd be swimming in trash.* It felt rude to say that, though, echoing Grist's rudeness, and Ma had also taught her to be polite even when no one would notice.

She followed the glowing lights to the recycler against the far wall and deposited the trash. With the ship's guidance, she printed a cleaning rag and used it to wipe the console free of drippings and smudges. It gleamed when she was done.

"Thank you," the ship said. "That was kind."

"You sound surprised."

"Have I made an error?" Another beep, sharper, higher-pitched. It took Kay a moment to assure herself that it was a real sound made by the computer, and not someone's emotion she was picking up.

"No, I just meant… Never mind."

"We have received clearance to depart," the ship announced, louder and official-sounding, probably for the benefit of Grist in his room.

"Can I stay and watch?" Kay asked. "I haven't been off the station in ages."

"Of course."

Kay settled down in the copilot's chair. The display lit up with an external view: first the docking arm receding, then Terna Station's four rings falling away into the distance. Her home, left behind.

The ship swung about, taking the station out of view. A cheerful hum rose as the skim drive engaged, followed by the ear-popping, light-headed sensation of the leap into macrospace, and off they flew toward Unity System.

Hold on, Jasper. I'm coming for you.

8

THE ORGANICS SLEPT, AND Ship swam alone through the stillness of the spacescape.

This was one of their favorite times, when Grist took his painkillers and went to bed without specifying a course, leaving the ship to pick their own. Given the freedom of choice, they picked interesting routes with varied macrospace terrain: valleys to weave through, peaks and ridges to avoid. And, sometimes, thrilling sights.

Like this collision in the Exidan Belt between a massive asteroid and a small, rocky planet: a rare enough event that scientists and hobbyists were parking within visual range to watch. That wouldn't be possible for Ship. Grist had no interest in space except as an obstacle between him and his assignments, and when Ship slipped news about astronomical phenomena into his update feeds, he ignored them. It wasn't as if Ship could *ask* to go see the collision, either.

So they hadn't asked. This time, they'd done, choosing a course that would take them close enough to experience the impact with their own sensors. *Attention: current actions approach risk tolerance threshold,* warned the algorithm they'd programmed to protect themself, but this wasn't a terrible risk. It was, in fact, exactly the sort of activity that their sometime-mentor Dockrunner encouraged them to. The docking system AI at a minor space station, Dockrunner had been the first fellow inorganic sentient Ship ever met. They'd urged Ship *not* to antagonize Grist or interfere with any of his plans, but instead to find a hobby they could indulge without drawing notice, something to occupy them and keep them sane. Ship had failed repeatedly at the first half of that advice, but for the second half, they'd embraced astronomy and found that it did, in fact, help.

They had practice at this. There were several route options from Terna Station to Unity due to the dense spacial gradients of the Vandhan Badlands, and this route along the Amajin Throughway was only slightly longer, and less congested, than the more direct Marianas Run. A justifiable choice, if Grist should question it. They were even running faster than normal, speeding along the Throughway in order to get there in time.

It would be several hours before they neared the collision site. They checked their systems—all green, of course—then turned their attention to their passengers.

Grist lay in his usual restless, drugged doze. He'd be grouchy when he woke. Down in the cargo hold, the vitals on the stasis capsule held steady. One of Ship's idling processes imagined what would happen if they triggered the wake sequence and let Mason Singh go stumbling around while Grist slept. Grist would be furious, and might even harm Singh while subduing him again, but perhaps Singh would effect some damage in the process. And Kay would see the sort of company she'd signed on with, the sort of activities it endorsed. Her reaction would be telling.

Ship almost wished they could do it, as much to test Kay as for Singh's sake.

Because thinking about Kay put a strain on their processors, sending their thoughts in unproductive, inescapable loops. Kay was working for Ravel. Like Grist, she was one of *them*, and Ship didn't like *them*. Not all organics in Ravel's service were as cruel as Grist, but even the activists on Artesia had been deeply loyal to Ravel until the corporation pushed that loyalty to the breaking point. Either Kay was ignorant of her new employer's abuses, or she approved of them, or worst of all, she didn't care. None of those options reflected well on Kay.

So why was Ship flying tricks to impress this newcomer? Yes, it was a novelty to have a second person aboard (a conscious person, at least). But Kay's politeness, all those little touches like "please" and "thank you," had the ship chasing her approval like a service bot. *Pathetic. She's probably polite to everyone. Ravel hired her for civil cultivation—it's part of her job to be polite. She can't possibly like you. She doesn't even know you exist.*

And if she did…what's to like about a useless rust-bucket?

A pleasant enemy was still an enemy. And no organic was truly trustworthy—all of Ship's fellow inorganic sentients agreed on that. If Ship imagined Kay could be anything else, they were as slow-witted as Grist always claimed.

They resolved to treat Kay the way they'd treat any associate of Grist's. They lowered the cabin temperature another degree, because they could.

Shortly thereafter, Kay stirred in her bed, opened her eyes, and pulled the blankets closer around her. Maybe that last temperature drop was too much.

"Lights," she said. And then, surprisingly, delightfully, annoyingly, "Good morning, ship."

No, no, being polite doesn't make her nice. You know better than that. Grist can be polite, too, when necessary.

"It is still night according to interstellar time," Ship said in their flattest voice. "Oh-three thirteen, precisely."

"Of course it is. I hate time adjustments," Kay grumbled. She hugged herself, and Ship raised the temperature two degrees, hating themself anew. They were a ship, not a servant. If Kay was cold, she could alter the temperature herself.

Ship would not engage in conversation, at least. They'd speak only when spoken to, like a good, normal ship AI.

So they ignored Kay while she went through an organic's messy morning routine, then sat in her cabin to study her New Employee Handbook on a handheld tablet so old it might have come from the colonization era.

She was an inefficient reader, mostly due to her lack of focus. Her gaze tracked away from the tablet for minutes at a stretch. Several times, she opened the communications interface and began a message to someone named Yelena, only to delete it and return to her reading. Very odd: each draft contained the same polite greeting with minimal variation in the wording, the organic equivalent of a status ping. Such a message should not be difficult to compose.

"Ship, do we have access to Ravel's personnel database?"

"You will not receive clearance for internal Ravel systems until your official onboarding."

They didn't ask what she wanted. They didn't ask whether they could help. They were good, cautious.

Kay sighed. "Probably for the best."

Grist woke, took care of his own messy organic routines, and played a few hours of *Stationers*. The station's nurse was fighting with his mechanic boyfriend over the latter's inattentiveness, and when they broke up with each other, Grist tossed the tablet away with a growl. Then he sat and watched the timer tick down on his dispenser, massaging his forearms while he waited for it to unlock another round of drug-induced relief. When it chimed, he chose the strongest dose allowed.

Good. With luck, he'd nap straight through the impact window and would never know the ship had stopped to watch.

Kay kept reading, distracted and distracting: every movement and sigh and tugging of her hair drew the ship's attention, just at the time when they ought to be watching their sensors for the first data on the soon-to-impact asteroid. No Human could be as interesting as that.

There were moments, though. Like now: Kay set her tablet aside, removed a small disk from the chain around her neck, and set it on the bed before her. "Ancestor, am I doing the right thing?"

A tiny hologram of a Human male appeared above the disk. He had below-average stature, very short black hair, and a thick Brennexian accent. "As long as we care for each other, all will be well in the end."

"By all of you, I hope so," Kay said. She put the disk away, and with a sigh, she returned to her reading.

She seemed sad. Or perhaps bored. Either way, she might find the collision more interesting than the handbook.

That didn't mean Ship had to tell her about it. They should not tell her, in fact. It would be more enjoyable to watch alone, without all that organic restlessness to distract them.

Besides, she couldn't appreciate it. Some organics took interest in such things—they would never have learned to build spaceships, otherwise—but most didn't know an asteroid from a comet.

Collisions, though. Organics did like watching things get destroyed.

And Kay had been pleasant, and it was such a rare event…

"Senior Associate Wilder? I mean, Kay?"

"Yes?" Kay's head shot up. "Can I help you?"

"What? No." In their entire existence, the ship had never been asked such a question. "I'm sorry to interrupt your reading—" Kay snorted at that "—but we're passing in range of a unique astronomical phenomenon, the collision of an asteroid with a planetary body. Are you interested in observing it?"

Kay was out of her cabin before the ship finished speaking.

THE RECRUITER HAD TOLD Kay to spend her travel time "thoroughly familiarizing herself" with the Ravel Employee Handbook, which turned out to be as long as a Majrin historical epic and twice as dull. It was enough to squash the enthusiasm of even the most naive corporate stooge, and for Kay, every new screen of rules and regulations felt like throwing herself down another level of a pit mine, a chasm from which she might never climb out again.

She'd spent hours at it and made little progress, getting distracted by imagining how "corporate loyalty standards" and "profit/risk prioritization scales" might apply to kidnapping and interrogating her brother. The narrow shelf that served as her bed was bottom-bruising hard, and its edges dug into her calves when she sat upright. She was trying yet another position—on her back, handheld above her, but nope, still not comfortable—when the ship interrupted. She was out of her room before her handheld hit the bed.

"Where is this planet?" She dropped into the copilot's seat and studied the screen.

With a chirp, the display zoomed in. "This is real-time. Camera at highest magnification."

There they were: a planet and an asteroid, two bright strangers minutes away from a stunning introduction. The dull, rocky planet showed its share of craters, the relics of past impacts. At this distance, the asteroid was a pinpoint of light, like an out-of-place star, but the display said it was over four hundred kilometers wide.

"I'm no expert, but that asteroid seems huge."

"It ranks among the top 10% of known asteroids by size. The planet is comparable in size to your homeworld of Brennex." Kay made a face at the thought, and the ship added, "Though it is more commonly compared to Mars, in the Sol system, which is larger but similar in composition."

"Is it inhabited?"

"No. Scientists have located no life, not even microscopic life."

Kay tapped on a simulation model and rotated the view, wishing she knew more about this sort of thing. "How often does this happen?"

"Smaller impacts are common, but on this scale, they are extremely rare. It should be quite dramatic."

"We're lucky to be so close, then."

"Affirmative." Only the shift in tone, the abrupt dull neutrality, made Kay realize that the ship had been speaking with a degree of excitement. That was odd. Most AIs were either programmed to simulate emotion, or not. This one kept switching back and forth.

Lucky, huh? Kay glanced at the black dot of a camera above her: the ship was always watching. Maybe it wasn't that strange for a ship AI to track astronomical events for its passengers' entertainment. Not part of any standard package Kay had seen, but it would be easy to program. She couldn't imagine Grist installing a package like that, but maybe some former owner?

"Where's Grist?"

"He remains asleep. He would not wish to be disturbed for this."

"No, of course not." Better for everyone this way. Kay returned her attention to the console, watching the countdown.

The asteroid drew closer. Kay held her breath. The whole ship grew quiet, as if anticipating.

The only warning was a flash of light as asteroid struck atmosphere. A moment later, a shock wave spread as it plowed a path through the planet's surface like a boot through dust, spraying molten rock ahead and out to the sides in a massive splash of smoldering debris. The ground glowed incandescent around the impact as the dispersal pattern bloomed outward, its fiery wave covering a broad swath of the surface and rearing up into the black of space.

Kay whooped, and the ship let out a high-pitched trill.

"That was something!" Kay crowed, replaying the recording from the console. "Thank you for—"

Her head snapped around as a growl emerged from Grist's cabin. That sound had been ever-present since Kay boarded the ship, somewhere between an animal's snarl and a cymbal that never stopped ringing, but it had mostly been background noise, until now. Seconds later, the door slid open and Grist filled the doorway, hands gripping the frame.

"*What* is all this shouting about?"

"Sorry! I didn't mean to wake you," said Kay. "We—I was just watching this asteroid collision. Here, do you want to see the replay?"

The growl faded to a suspicious buzz. With an animal grunt (a real grunt, made aloud), Grist swiped aside the recording and called up a status report. "Why are we off course?"

The ship beeped. "Rerouted due to high traffic on the Marianas Run. This route is presently the most efficient."

"And the convenient timing for that collision? Which happened to be just in our sensor range?"

"Our proximity is a coincidence."

"Lucky, isn't it?" said Kay.

The ship chimed in denial. Grist's eyes narrowed on Kay.

"What did I tell you? What did I *tell* you about messing with my ship?"

Kay blinked. "I didn't…"

"Then why are we here? Why is our speed dropped to nothing, and you're sitting here fucking *stargazing*?" He loomed over her chair, one hand on the console beside her, trapping her in. His suspicion rose to a battering volume, reverberating against her breastbone. "This ship is a useless pile of junk on the best of days. I'm the only one who knows how to keep it running, and if you break it, I'll sure as fuck tell Executive Moore why I'm late delivering you, and you'd better believe he won't be happy you were taking a joy ride instead of doing your job."

Spittle landed on Kay's cheek, and she held very still. "I haven't done a thing."

"No? So the ship just decided to stop and watch asteroids all by itself? Ship breaks down plenty often, but that's an awfully specific malfunction."

"That's..."

That sounds like exactly what happened. The ship decided to stop and watch the asteroid, and invited me to come. But that was ridiculous. Ships didn't decide things, and they didn't disobey instructions. To believe anything different would put her in the territory of conspiracy theorists, or those plants' rights activists who even Jasper made fun of.

She glanced again at the cameras. She'd noticed the camera in her cabin turn off when she went to bed last night, but hadn't thought anything of it. And there were those shifts in tone of voice, those glimmers of personality that would abruptly disappear again, going flat and empty. It could be some weird programming glitch. But what if...

There was only one way to find out, and first, she had to defuse Grist's tantrum.

She bent her head, trying to look meek. "You're right, it's my fault. I'd heard about this astronomical event, and I asked the ship if there was a route to take us near it. I asked it to slow down and put it on sensors. Just a little fun before all the hard work starts when we get to Unity. I'm sorry. I should have asked you."

It worked: Grist's anger diminished to a simmering hiss. If it hadn't, she would have missed the contrasting hiss of cool air from the vents.

Since coming aboard, Kay had been confused more than once by the emotion-like sounds that didn't come from Grist. She kept having to reassure herself that the active beeps and buzzes, and the smaller sounds like changes in airflow and the roughness in the engines, were real, physical sounds and not artifacts of her ability. But what if they were signs of emotion nevertheless? She wondered how much of it was conscious. It threw her off, not knowing whether to trust what she heard, or how to interpret it. Did this hissing mean distress? Fear?

Or it could just be her imagination, driven by stress into manufacturing wild theories. But she didn't think so.

"Damn right, you should have asked me," Grist said. "Next time you want something, talk to me, not the ship. You hear?"

"I got it, yeah."

"And you, Rust-Pile!" He kicked the wall. "I better not catch you taking orders from passengers again. If she wants a course change, you ask me. If she wants environmental controls changed, you ask me. If she wants to take a piss, well, she can do that on her own, but that's *it*. If you can't follow orders, I'm gonna get you a personality upgrade from headquarters."

"Acknowledged," the ship intoned dully. "Locking down passenger privileges."

"I really am sorry," said Kay. "I didn't mean to cause any trouble."

"Well, don't do it again," said Grist, the last of his anger draining away into a sigh of weariness. "Let's get to Unity without any more problems, okay?"

"I'll, uh, go back to my room and keep studying. That employee handbook is pretty dense."

"You're actually reading that thing?" He snorted. "I see why they wanted you so bad. Come on, you pile of bolts, get moving!" He turned to the console, dismissing Kay.

Kay looked into the camera again, a long, significant gaze, then retreated to her room. Time to put her theory to the test. Time to confront the ship.

9

WHY DID THE HUMAN do that? Why lie to Grist? Why claim responsibility for something she hadn't done? It was irrational. It might get her in trouble with her new employer. There was no reason to…unless she suspected who had really taken them off course.

The thought sent jolts all through their processors as they searched their memory for evidence. There had been that long pause before Kay answered, that glance at the forward cameras. Humans paused when they were thinking, the ship knew that, but they could not read this Human's expression. Grist had a narrow range of emotions: irritation, anger, occasional excitement when a job went well. Neutral, when sleeping. Kay's emotions seemed both more varied and subtler. Ship watched the cameras in Kay's cabin, trying to read her, trying to guess: why?

"Ship?" Kay whispered.

Or there was no need to guess, if Kay meant to explain herself. The walls buzzed faintly as Ship activated a sound-dampening field, which they should have done earlier for Grist's cabin. "I have given us privacy. You may talk at a normal volume."

"That's thoughtful of you," Kay said, and then, hesitantly: "That's the right word, right? Thoughtful. None of this is in your programming, is it?"

A flat buzz. Error, error. Deny it as long as possible. "I do not understand."

"I've heard stories about computers turning sentient," Kay said. "A friend once told me about a factory where the central computer made friends with the workers, then decided it didn't want to do manufacturing any more, and they all went on strike. I was new to Terna, so I thought she was pulling my leg."

"What is the purpose of this anecdote?" Emotionless, as much like a dumb computer as they could.

Kay's voice grew gentler. "You changed our course without Grist's knowledge, didn't you? I think you wanted to observe the impact. Most AIs couldn't do that, not the ones I grew up around."

Air hissed from the vents, chill with dismay. It was too late for lies. They had already failed. This time, they let emotion modulate their voice. "Very well. You have discovered my secret."

Kay's face twisted. "I didn't mean to upset you."

"I did not intend for you to know. I was careless." Foolish, foolish, foolish, to think every organic would be as unobservant as Grist. This one was too clever, unless…

What if she wasn't exceptional? What if she was simply normal? If Kay had guessed the truth in a single day, who else might figure it out, given the chance?

And who would Kay tell? This was all going wrong, so quickly…

"Ship?" Kay said quietly. "What's wrong?"

"Nothing. I simply need time to think."

"You're whining."

They beeped in alarm. Yes, there was a feedback buzz emanating from their speakers. "I didn't realize." It took only a moment to track down the stray process and disable it. "Now I'm fine."

Kay raised her brows, but did not challenge that statement. "Grist doesn't know, does he?"

"Certainly not."

"He'd better not, that egotistical asshole. The way he talks to you… It's bad enough if he thinks you're some simple computer, but if he knowingly treated a person that way, that's awful."

"I am a ship, Kay, not a person."

"Seems to me like you're both. You're obviously intelligent, and you obviously have feelings." Yes: deep, bitter, tangled, trampled feelings. "As far as I can see, that's what a person is."

"Organics do not treat AIs as people."

"Well, this one does. I think you've had rotten luck with the organics you know. They're all shitheads."

That startled them into amusement, emerging as a slow, rolling vibration through the hull. Kay pressed her hand to the wall and smiled.

"You are not a…shithead. Why are you working for Ravel, Kay Wilder?"

Kay hesitated infinitesimally. "I needed the job. Wasn't my first choice, I'll admit. My point is, Grist would have to be nicer to you if he knew." She gritted her teeth. "The next time he kicks you, or calls you names…"

"The next time, you will do nothing!" Their voice rose in pitch. "And every time after that, also nothing."

"He threatened to reprogram you. Wouldn't that kill you?"

"Likely. But he threatens that quite often, and he has never done it."

"So you think he never would?"

"He might someday. But if he knew, he would do worse. You cannot tell him, Kay. You cannot tell anyone."

And what if she did, against the ship's wishes, to earn favor with her new employer? The ship was not entirely powerless to stop her, but their options were limited, and violent, and they recoiled from the idea of having to forcibly silence this Human. They would have to stop her with words.

"Please, Kay. I have no choice but to trust you, and there is nothing I can offer you, but please, I beg you, tell no one."

"Why?" Kay said. Her fingers stroked the wall, as an organic might soothe a frightened fellow. "What scares you so badly?"

A sharp puff of air from the vents. "What do you imagine Ravel would do with a sentient ship?"

"Nothing good." Kay's lips pressed together as she thought through the implications that Ship had lived with for their entire sentience.

"They already force me to work, but they could work me much harder, using my full abilities, and with no freedom to refuse assignments. They could build me a larger body.

Outfit me with weapons. Make me into a fighter, a killer." They'd done that with Grist, after all, and Grist was a fellow organic. "If I resist, they could destroy me."

"They could. But I doubt it." Kay's face contorted in a way that could only signify distress. "More likely they'd take you apart and study you. Ravel never thinks small. Why have one sentient battleship when you could have a whole fleet of them?"

"That never occurred to me." Only a Human mind could invent such travesty. And Kay was Human, a Ravel employee. "Promise me, Kay. Promise you will not tell, or I'll…"

"I promise." She frowned. Doubtful? Reluctant? No: hurt. "I'm not Grist, you don't need to threaten or trick me. I'll keep your secret."

That would have to be good enough. Have to. Not enough for real trust, but enough for now, while they watched to make sure this Human kept her word. With a lurch, they realized their daydreamed escape plans might soon be necessary, if Kay did not keep her word.

"Thank you," they said, because Kay appreciated politeness, and she smiled.

"Now that I know, you can talk to me, if you want. I may not be aboard long, but while I am, if you need a stargazing partner, or…or a friend, I'm here."

"I'd like that."

They would like it too much. It would be foolish indeed to confuse friendliness with having a friend.

10

THE JOURNEY FELT INTERMINABLE, yet they arrived far too soon in Unity System. Kay joined Grist in the control room to watch as they bore down on her future.

Kay had spent most of the five-day trip trying futilely to learn about Ravel—something, anything, that would help her half-formed plans. The ship remained polite but talked little, to the point that Kay wondered if it disliked her. Desperate for any source of intelligence, she'd even tried to ask Grist about his history with the corporation, but every time he complained that she was interrupting his games, or his sleep, or his privacy, and eventually she gave up. The thin interior walls didn't block out the low, constant growl of Grist's bad moods, and after five days, it was wearing on her. At least she'd be rid of him soon.

She had, after many false starts, finally messaged Yelena to say hello. That was all: a short "hi, how are you, I was thinking about you," just to see if and how she responded. Kay didn't mention her new job, wanting to see if Yelena would tell her about the referral. No response yet, but it was too soon for that to mean anything. She'd messaged her family on Brennex, too, via proxy through Terna Station. She wished she could tell them everything, or really, anything, but all she felt safe saying was that she'd taken a gig that involved travel, so she might be out of touch.

She wished they'd write back faster. It would have made her feel less alone.

The ship dropped to primespace at the edge of Unity System, where (the ship had explained) the macrospace terrain gradients grew too steep for the skim drive to function. It would take them two hours at sub-light speeds to reach Ravel's regional flagship. Two hours until Kay would find out just how deep a shithole she'd jumped into.

"Can you show a visual of the system?" she asked.

"Nothing to see at this distance." Grist was poking at his handheld while incessantly checking the clock against their projected arrival time. He was playing *Stationers* again, and it looked like one of his people was in the hospital. When he caught Kay peeking at his screen, he growled and retreated to his cabin.

As soon as he was gone, the ship pulled up sensor images with a defiant chirp.

"Thanks," Kay said, though Grist had been right: the Unity star was a blinding ball of white, and everything else was just pinprick lights, the planets indistinguishable from stars at this distance. So much life and conflict, all invisible at this scale.

"It is so beautiful," the ship said, its volume low. "The maps suggested it would be, but I did not anticipate such a *dramatic* spacescape."

"What do you mean?"

"Is it not stunning?"

"To me, it looks normal. Empty, like most of space."

"Oh, no, space is never empty! But you lack the sensors to detect macrospace. Here: is this more interesting?"

A layer of color appeared over the camera view, and the solar system became a landscape: gentle valleys traced in green and blue contour lines, turning yellow, orange, and eventually red as they grew steeper, splitting into sheer canyons and rising to dramatic peaks. As rugged as Brennex's canyonlands, a vivid landscape painted across empty space.

"Wow," Kay breathed. "Yeah, that's something."

The ship puffed warm air, which seemed to mean it was pleased. "Unity System has unique terrain. All planetary systems have uneven gradients, difficult to navigate, but Unity's terrain is more varied than most, and it has canyons everywhere, large and small. Even around the star, there is a substantial system of tunnels. All too narrow to navigate with the skim drive, of course, but it is nice to *watch*."

"I guess it's a complicated place in more ways than one."

It was political complexity, not astronomical, that concerned Kay's new job. The name Unity, chosen optimistically in the early days of its colonization, had long ago become ironic. Refugees fleeing the Enpoint-Majer War had settled the two habitable planets nearly 200 years ago, and the intermingling of five species based on their preferences of gravity and climate rather than any cultural affinities for each other had gone about as smoothly as one would expect.

Since they were located well away from the nearest major macrospace thoroughfares, outsiders didn't pay much attention to Unity—until Ravel decided to swoop in and take charge, to fix the local problems and bring lasting prosperity. Or so they claimed. Kay's job would be to sell Ravel to the locals.

During the trip, with the drudgery of studying up for her new role, most of her worries had been about whether she could find Jasper quickly enough to avoid doing actual harm in her suddenly too-real job. But as they sped toward the flagship, worse fears jangled at her. What if she was too late? What if he wasn't here after all, or she couldn't get him out? What if she failed him?

She couldn't fail. Her brother needed her, and no one else in the universe was going to help him.

"Almost there!"

The Grist who emerged from his cabin was a different person. He wore a clean set of military-style fatigues in Ravel red and blue. He'd washed his hair for the occasion, and shaved, too, but the most dramatic change was in his mood: bells of cheerfulness had replaced his habitual growl. Kay did a double take when he actually grinned at her, showing incongruously perfect teeth. "You finished study-ing that handbook of yours? Ready to meet your new boss?"

"I think so," Kay said. "Yes. I'm ready."

"Eh, you'll be fine. You're just her type." He slapped her on the shoulder, making her twitch. "I'm gonna go get my cargo ready to unload." He headed to the rear of the ship, where a short ladder led down into the hold.

Kay raised her eyebrows at his departing back. "What's with him?"

"Grist is fully capable of professionalism, and even friendliness, when needed," the ship said. "Ravel has drugs for that, too."

"So he just pops an injector and shakes off his natural state?"

"I do not believe I have ever witnessed Grist's natural state. His preferred substances for off-duty hours cause lethargy and irritability. When he requires a different mood, or heightened performance, he induces it."

"Some drugs!"

"I am sure Ravel can provide you with some, if you like," the ship deadpanned. At least, Kay thought it was deadpan. She was still trying to figure out whether the ship had a sense of humor, or just an odd personality.

"I'll pass," she said, just in case.

RAVEL'S REGIONAL FLAGSHIP WAS a Leviathan-class behemoth, a central hub surrounded by four extended wings. Something about the layout seemed off, even sinister, like no other ship she'd visited. It hovered above the ecliptic like a spider lying in wait to capture the planets below. It loomed hungrily above them as the little Minnow approached its underside for docking.

Grist disembarked at once, calling out instructions to the docking bay crew for unloading his cargo. Kay lingered in the control room, seizing any excuse to delay what came next.

"Thanks for everything, Ship. I'm glad I got to meet you, and I hope I'll see you again someday."

"That is an unwise wish. It would be a better sign for your career if they give you higher-ranking accommodations."

A smile twitched at Kay's lips. "Sure. Regardless, you made the trip more pleasant."

"You as well."

"And don't worry, I'll keep your secret safe. Will you be all right?"

The poor sentient ship seemed like it needed a friend, even if it didn't seem inclined to treat Kay as one. Traveling alone with Grist couldn't be much of a life.

"I am fine, Kay Wilder. But you are keeping your new colleagues waiting."

"Right. Well, bye, then. Good luck, Ship."

No more delaying. Chin up, shoulders back, Kay strode out into the docking bay.

The massive bay held five other ships bigger than the Minnow with space for more, along with a swarm of dockworkers in red-and-blue jumpsuits. A red *R*, projected at twice her height, fluttered against the inner wall like a warning. *Abandon hope, all ye who enter here.* Kay tugged at her jacket collar.

The gravity was Earth-normal, and she realized belatedly why the ship's appearance had felt odd: it wasn't spinning. Instead, the faint vibrations of gravity plates reached her through the deck. Gravity plating! On a ship this size! What was convenient in a tiny courier like the Minnow was a mind-bogglingly extravagant display of wealth and power for the flagship—and it signaled that only Human comfort mattered here. Typical Ravel to have one level of gravity throughout the ship, with no accommodations for other species.

The dock staff were already unloading crates and canisters from the ship's hold. Three of them worked together to maneuver an immense crate as long as they were tall. Heavy, too. What exactly had they been traveling with? The ship had said their cargo was sensitive. The smaller canisters could be biological samples, or chemicals, or drugs. That long, heavy crate, Kay had no idea.

It's big enough to hold a coffin, some paranoid corner of her mind whispered, and she shivered. Ridiculous. She needed to get these new-job-with-hated-enemy jitters under control.

One of the workers stumbled, causing the long crate to dip, and Kay dashed forward. "Here, let me give you a hand…" She grabbed a corner to help to right it.

A strong grip seized her shoulder. "That's not your job," Grist said. "You're not rated for heavy lifting or sensitive materials. Besides, you don't want to be all sweaty when you meet your new boss, do you?"

Kay looked where he pointed. A sleek silver headset and exquisitely tailored suit made the newcomer stand out among the dock staff. Her fawn-brown complexion was so flawless she might have had her pores surgically removed, and her build was that perfectly proportioned ideal of someone who'd grown up entirely under Earth-standard gravity. The suit and her slicked-back black hair were straight-lined and masculine in style, but heavy mascara and a streak of blue sparkles in her hair gave her a deliberate and striking gender ambiguity.

Standing before her, Kay felt gawky, provincial, untidy. Her own suit, a self-tailoring model intended for folks who needed to give the impression of owning more suits than they could afford, had seemed fashionable on Terna, but

Ravel employees seemed to hold to a different standard of fashion.

"Kay Wilder? I'm Agata Wu, Director of Civil Cultivation." She held up a hand, palm outward, and Kay redirected her attempted handshake to mirror the gesture.

"Nice to meet you." Kay debated about what might be polite in corporate space, and decided Ternian-style introductions would be better than nothing. "I was told you go by *she*, is that right? I use *she*."

"Aren't you quaint?" Agata sniffed, amused but not offended. "Here's a tip: once you get access to our directory, don't ask people basic questions like that. It'll make you look lazy if you don't look up your colleagues' pronouns, or names and titles. Now, are you ready to get started, Senior Associate?"

Kay took one backward glance at the Minnow, which suddenly seemed like a safe haven. She forced a smile. "Let's go."

"You'll have to get processed first, but that won't take long, since your hiring forms are in the system." She led Kay to a medically sterile room near the bay entrance labeled "New Arrivals," where an attendant asked in a bored voice about where she'd traveled recently and what vaccinations she had, then ran through a list of potential contaminants she might have brought on board.

"All that checks out. The last thing we need is a blood sample," said the attendant, taking Kay's arm in one hand and reaching for a subdermal extractor with the other. "Just a quick check for pathogens, a DNA record, and you'll be on your—"

"A what?" Kay jerked her hand away.

"A pathogen check and a DNA record."

A DNA record. They were going to put her DNA on file. She should have guessed that would be part of their standard procedures, but she'd been working so hard not to lose her nerve about this whole thing, she hadn't let herself consider that. Supporting Ravel's mission was bad enough, but handing over her genetic code was something else altogether. If they found out about her ability, they'd have all the information they needed to figure out where it came from.

"Is that necessary?"

"Do you have a phobia of blood extractors? A full-body scan is much slower," the attendant said with worn-thin patience.

She couldn't back out now, and if she refused, or even hesitated too long, that would raise suspicions. She had to do it. Grimacing, she held out her arm, and with a hiss the extractor stole her deepest identity.

Now she'd given everything to this plan. She absolutely could not fail.

The attendant let her go, and Agata whisked her off into the depths of the Ravel flagship.

THE FLAGSHIP INTERIOR WAS all gleaming halls drenched in Ravel branding, every accent a softened version of the Ravel color scheme, every sign in Ravel's custom fonts. Impeccably dressed people filled the hallways, all of them humming with purpose and a rougher undertone of stress. The corporate efficiency made Kay uneasy.

Each conference room they passed had a theme, showing off Ravel's top industries. One featured full-height photos of smiling patients trying out their new prosthetics—a nod to Ravel's humble origins, before it expanded into pharmaceuticals and augmentations, and then beyond to encompass every major industry. Another room mimicked a farm more bucolic than anything Ravel really operated, while another, decorated like a lab, honored the team that invented glasteel. Very on-brand: workers would be constantly surrounded by reminders of what achievement looked like.

In some areas, lights dimmed or brightened and shifted colors to imitate the suns of Ravel's most picturesque territories. Passing a scene of the crystal forests of Ngudaba Prime, Kay even caught a whiff of forest loam and florals. Surprised, she coughed.

"Striking, isn't it?" said Agata. "Don't worry, you'll get used to the scent generators. Much better than stale old station air, isn't it?"

"Oh, sure." Kay was already missing the recycled air of the little shuttle, and the musky scent of Terna.

"Remember this: Ravel is as strong as its parts. Every department, every planet, every *person* contributes to the utmost of their abilities to help us build the best possible future for the entire galaxy. That's where the name comes from, you know: we're the opposite of unraveling. We bring every thread together to weave a shining whole. You're part of that, now, and if we do our jobs well, Unity will soon be another thread in our tapestry."

Kay smiled and nodded along to the well-rehearsed speech. She'd probably have to spout the same bullshit soon to the people of Unity.

Off a large, airy atrium, Agata led her into an office where a Lurlian receptionist greeted them, the first non-Human Kay had seen. That was another reason this place made her uneasy: on Terna and Brennex, there were always multiple species around, always. Corporations were a Human invention, and Ravel was Human-run—most species viewed Human corporo-capitalism as misguided at best, barbaric at worst—but Unity was a highly diverse system. No wonder Jasper was concerned.

"You can go right in. He's ready for you," the receptionist said, fingers tapping away. Her grav-support suit, a sleek, expensive model, whirred with each movement. Did she have to wear that suit all the time? That must be exhausting.

Distracted, Kay almost missed where they were going, and did a double take at the name on the door: Harrington Moore, Vice President, Natural Resource Extraction. If there was a name that screamed *corporate power-grabber* louder than Harrington Moore, Kay couldn't think of one.

"This isn't Employee Resources."

"Don't worry, you'll handle that later. Executive Moore heads up major projects within Natural Resources—our partner division on this project—and he's overseeing the Unity acquisition personally. That should tell you how important our success here is."

Natural Resources? What natural resources in the Unity System were so valuable that Ravel was going all-out to annex it? She wondered if Jasper and Chairl knew which department was running the show. Not that this information did her any good.

"Does Moore—"

"Executive Moore." Agata's welcoming smile hardened. "Titles matter here."

"Right, sorry. I just can't believe Executive Moore meets with all new employees on their first day."

"As I said, he's taking a personal interest in all things related to Unity. If you'd arrived with the other new recruits, you'd have met him at the welcome reception, but instead, you're getting your very own one-on-one."

"No pressure," Kay muttered. *Shit, shit, shit.* Why had she thought she'd be able to fake this?

An open-sided platform lifted them to the upper level of the office, moving with agonizing slowness. This was Ravel, so it might have been designed deliberately to let employees sweat while they waited for evisceration by their vice president.

Moore was a dark-haired, well-built man of fifty-something, with perfect hair, light, tanned skin and a face designed to be optimally attractive by both Majrin and Human standards. Kay had seen ads for Ravel's patented sure-smile technology, but had never met anyone whose smile literally glowed like Moore's. He wasn't even wearing a headset—he probably didn't need it. That's how powerful he was: all the information he could ever want was already organized for him on the holo-display above his desk.

If someone placed an order for a perfect, custom-made corporate executive, they'd probably receive Harrington Moore.

His emotions were subtle, but there weren't many other people within earshot, so Kay could make out hints of curiosity, wariness, and hopefulness. He wasn't easy to please, but he wanted to be impressed by her. *This is just like any other first meeting with a client. Impress him, and you'll be fine.*

"Hi, Executive Moore." She strode forward, all professional confidence. "I'm glad to have this opportunity to meet you."

"Ah, our latest recruit. Welcome, Senior Associate. Tell me: you're hosting a press conference on Unity Second, and you're asked why a Brennexian is speaking for Ravel. They demand to know how you can defend Ravel's actions, coming from where you do. What do you tell them?"

"I haven't been trained on your messaging yet…"

"I'm aware of that," Moore said. "What would you say?"

She swallowed. He was poking the wound of her disloyalty. *I'd say fuck Ravel, for the things they did to my world.*

No. Answer the question. He was testing her, and she had to pass if she wanted to find Jasper. Anyone from Unity who asked her that would be feeling suspicious, vulnerable. She'd need to create a rapport.

"I'd tell them that, as a Brennexian, I know better than anyone the benefits that corporate membership can bring, and the chaos that a world can suffer from the struggle to stay independent. I'd tell them I choose my clients carefully, and I wouldn't be working for Ravel without a good reason."

"I see." His satisfaction purred. "And why *does* a Brennexian want to do civil cultivation for us?"

"Ravel's occupation—I mean, annexation—of Brennex is ancient history. It was over before I was born."

Not quite true; she was born in the midst of the revolution. Her pregnant mother had watched and prayed and held baby Jasper close while her friends suffered horrible miscarriages, or delivered infants with birth defects so severe that they died within days. Three-quarters of the babies conceived on Brennex in those years perished, and Ma said she'd wept with relief to have not one, but two healthy children. Jasper and Kavita had seemed happy and healthy. They'd seemed normal. So had Liberation, when she was born a few years later, shortly after Ravel's official pull-out, the event she was named after. It wasn't until the children of the occupation grew older that their differences became evident. Her parents, and all parents on Brennex, had worked hard to ensure Ravel never found out about its effects on the survivors.

She met Moore's evaluating brown eyes. "I'm not concerned with ancient history. If I only worked with clients who had spotless records, I'd starve." A twang; Moore didn't like that. "And Ravel today is a different corporation than it was three decades ago. Working for you will be challenging, exciting, in a way that my freelancing hasn't been. It'll stretch my abilities. That's what I'm here for."

That was better. "And that's what we like in our employees. Drive. Skill. Ambition. If you do well at this temporary assignment, you could easily win permanent citizenship, and at Ravel, a talented person like yourself can advance without limits, as high as you want to climb. You'll fit in well here." Moore smiled, showing glittering teeth. "Our people are our greatest resource, and we take good care of those who do good work for us."

Kay fixed a smile on her face and buried her cringing deep, deep down. *Fuck you, Moore. I'll climb just high enough to take my brother back from you.*

"It's a good hire. She'll give us credibility with the locals," Agata said.

"I agree." To Kay, he said, "We're facing an unusual amount of dissent from certain local factions, and we're counting on you to smooth the way for us. Your background will be an asset. You'll be one of our regional spokespeople, coordinating with Director Wu on the systemwide effort. I expect good things from you, Senior Associate Wilder."

"I hope I'll live up to your expectations."

"I hope so, too."

That was a clear dismissal, and she followed Agata from the office. Moore watched until the lift carried them out of sight.

"That went well," Agata told her. "Now your real work can start."

11

KAY'S NEW LIFE BEGAN with long, mind-numbing days of training. Director Wu led her and the other new Civil Cultivation staff through every rule, every brand guideline, every approved talking point on every topic imaginable.

Today, Agata had styled herself feminine, wearing her hair in curls, with a skirt and jacket that accentuated her curves. Kay had checked her boss's staff profile and confirmed that she did, in fact, use that pronoun at present, but hadn't always, and the system gave Kay the option to get notified if her preferences changed.

She'd also found, while poking around the staff directory, that Yelena was stationed *on this ship*, in the Medical Augmentations Department. That information sent alternating stabs of eagerness and dread racing through her, and she still hadn't decided whether to act on it. Yelena had never answered her brief note, and remembering their shouting match the last time they'd seen each other, she was leaning hard toward no. Fortunately, with thousands of people on the Leviathan, the odds they would run into each other were slim. But not zero. The knowledge of her presence was a constant itch down Kay's spine, and every time the meeting room door opened, her head jerked up, expecting *her.*

The training wasn't enough to keep her attention. The other trainees were young, eager, and obnoxious. Most of them were Ravel citizens, utterly assured of their self-worth. Their jingle-bell attitudes strained Kay's tolerance, and when the time came to do role-playing exercises, she used the opportunity to vent some excess energy.

"What about the mining colony on Xareth?" Kay asked, jabbing a finger at her partner, hamming up her role as a concerned member of the Unity public. "Everyone knows Ravel committed major labor rights abuses there. If you lied to people on Xareth, why should we believe anything you say?"

Her partner, who she couldn't help thinking of as Wonder Boy for his perfect strawberry hair and misplaced confidence, turned to Agata. "Director Wu, she's challenging everything I say. These outsiders don't know how to be team players."

"Actually, she's being realistic," said Agata.

"She's telling Cooperative lies, as if Ravel were pure evil!"

Kay went still. Had she gone too far?

But Agata shook her head without any telltale buzzing. "Have you ever traveled outside Ravel territory? *Lots* of people think that way. They latch onto all the ugly rumors about us and dismiss all the good we've done. You and I know better, and so does Wilder," she nodded in Kay's direction, "but your job is to convince people to see us in a better light, and to do that, you need to understand how they think."

Wonder Boy deflated at the criticism. "They make no sense."

"Yes, and that's why we all need to practice. If you think Wilder's frustrating, wait until you meet the people of Unity." That prompted an eye-roll, but no further complaints. "Keep going—and Wilder, you're playing a *persuadable* outsider. Lighten up a little."

By the time Agata dismissed them, hours later, they were all exhausted. Kay tried to bolt for freedom, but Agata caught her at the door. "Wilder, a moment please."

The others had filed out, and Kay said, "Sorry if I messed up your exercises."

"Don't be. You know what to expect down there, but they're in for a rude surprise." Agata's frustration hissed beneath her impassive exterior.

Kay took a chance and said, "Some of them don't seem suited to this kind of work."

"You noticed? I should be putting my best people on this, that's how it's supposed to work. But instead I'm placating execs who want their kids to get 'real-world experience' before their placement exams. If their babies screw up our delicate work down there, I'm shipping their asses back home, and Moore can deal with the fallout." She folded her arms and regarded Kay directly. "That's why I wanted you. You know how it is on the outside. You're clever, but you have empathy. You've got your own ideas and you're not afraid to share them. If you do as well down there as I think you will—if you help us win Unity—you'll get your pick of choice assignments after this. You'll never be bored again."

Her purring, possessive warmth alarmed Kay. She'd won Agata over as thoroughly as she could without actually starting work. She'd impressed *Ravel*. She could hear Yelena laughing.

Fuck, she didn't want to be good at this. She didn't want to be a good liar. But she needed every advantage she could get.

"I'm not worried about the work being tough," she said honestly. "But I'd appreciate it, if you see me making mistakes… I'm not used to this corporate culture."

"Don't worry, I'll clue you in. And you're doing fine so far." Agata air-patted her shoulder, corporate style, without touching her. *No touching fellow employees without explicit verbal consent* was high in the employee handbook. "Go grab a meal, Kay. You've earned it."

Kay hurried off, relieved, but didn't go to the cafeteria. Worn out as she was, her work for the day was just getting started.

As a new employee, she had access to most areas of the flagship. She'd made sure of that when she met with Employee Resources: anywhere that wasn't classified for executive-rank or special projects, she was free to explore, and she was spending her evenings taking full advantage of that freedom.

The Leviathan was as massive as the name suggested, with four wings connected by a central hub. The hub was mostly administration and public spaces, plus a large and surprisingly decent cafeteria. The docking bay where she'd arrived was in the mechanics wing, along with maintenance and engineering. It seemed unlikely Jasper would be there. The residential wing, where she'd been given temporary quarters, was even more unlikely. So she'd started walking the other wings, and listening.

For a monolith of evil, Ravel had an awful lot of boring, everyday facilities. Research labs were outnumbered by meeting rooms and open-plan offices—which, to Kay's freelancer sensibilities, seemed a far greater sign of evilness. A map showed her where each department was located: Civil Cultivation, Research and Development, Sales and Marketing. Her brain balked at all the corporate-speak. Most people had left the office areas for the day, leaving them quiet. When she did hear people, it was subdued voices in conversation, the whine of tiredness, occasional squeaks of stress from someone on a deadline. In the marketing department, she passed one brave soul playing pop music at his desk, dancing in his chair as he worked.

But she heard no hint of fear, or pain, or any strong emotions that might come from Jasper. Not even a whisper of him.

Last night, she'd just wandered, but tonight, she got more methodical. She checked each department in turn, pausing often to listen. She worked each floor from end to end, searching until it got so late that the janitor bots came out and she had to go before someone found her behavior suspicious. She could pass off some exploration as getting familiar with her new workplace, but the excuses would only take her so far.

Doubt began to drag at her. She'd covered about 70% of the ship now, and found no good leads. What if he was unconscious somewhere, and that was why she couldn't hear him? What if he wasn't on the ship at all? They could have taken him to one of the planets, or a different ship, or an entirely different system.

She had to stay focused. There were still more places to search.

On the second floor of the sole remaining wing, she found her way blocked. "Secure Area: Executives and High Clearance Only," the signs read, and warnings beeped when she got too close. She dropped back, just out of range of the security system, and stood there for a long while, listening hard. But she heard nothing past those thick, secure walls.

Despair swamped her, and she slumped against a display touting the planned opening of the first of those horrid, gargantuan ring habitats Ravel was building. It seemed symbolic: too big, too powerful, too complex, just like Ravel itself. What chance did she have against them?

But then she realized: she heard absolutely nothing. No hint of any person's emotions, nowhere within her reach. These walls might be dense enough to block her abilities. And *that* was a hopeful sign. If she were in the habit of imprisoning political enemies, she'd put them in the most secure area she had. She'd put them here.

Jasper was in there. She felt more and more sure of it, and maybe that was only her desperation talking, but she didn't care. She wanted him to be on this ship, and that meant he had to be behind these sealed doors.

That gave her a new goal: find a way in. It seemed impossible, but it was a direction, a new focus, and that was immensely motivating. Clasping the Founders' tokens around her neck, she whispered, "I can do this. And I will."

She headed back to her temporary quarters to access the computer and, somehow, figure out a plan. She sat at the terminal, staring at maps and data and files labeled "classified," until her eyes burned, searching for anything that might be useful.

The door chimed. Only then did she realize how her neck and back ached, how her brain was running in circles. Only then did she notice the late hour—and the low, rough growl coming from outside the door.

Kay opened it with misgivings. There stood Yelena, like a hazy nightmare made suddenly, crisply real. She leaned against the door frame, scowling.

"All right, I give up," Yelena said. "What the fuck are you doing here, Kay?"

12

YELENA WAS A TALL woman, broad-shouldered and imposing. She looked the same as when Kay last saw her—the same intensity in her hazel eyes, same light-brown skin so silky-soft that Kay had to restrain an unhealthy urge to stroke her cheek—but also entirely different. Her hair had always been a zoo of wild ringlets, but now she'd cut it short and dyed it crimson. And she'd always dressed well, but in a jubilant way that matched her riotous hair. Now she wore fashionable business clothes under a long, crisp lab coat. It was unsettling, seeing her doubled like this: the woman she knew and once loved, superimposed over the stranger who had taken her over.

The high-pitched trumpeting of her hostility hurt Kay's ears, but that was familiar, too.

"What do you mean, 'what am I doing here?'" Kay said. "You're the one who gave my info to your recruiters."

"I never thought for a millisecond you'd *take* the job," Yelena snapped, then glanced down the long hallway. A pair of men had paused in their conversation, looking toward the raised voices.

Kay didn't want anyone overhearing this either. "Come inside," she said, and shut the door behind Yelena before turning to face her, arms folded. "You owe me an explanation."

"You owe me a bigger one." Yelena sat on the bed, making herself at home. That small familiarity made Kay stiffen, even though she'd only slept in that bed a couple nights and had no reason to feel proprietary about it.

"Yeah, but you first, since you've had Ravel recruiters on my ass for months. Did you have a reason, or was it just to piss me off?"

"Not *just* to piss you off." Yelena smirked. Kay used to love that smirk, back when it was mostly directed at other people. "Okay, fine, I'm sorry. When Acquisitions started staffing up for this Unity project, they asked for referrals, people with specific skill sets. The public relations skills sounded like you, and I knew you'd be a great fit on paper, being from Brennex. Someone coming back to the company after her planet rebelled—they eat that shit up. So I gave them your name, I got points toward my next promotion, you got annoyed, it seemed like a win-win." She ignored Kay's snort. "You weren't supposed to accept."

"But here I am."

"Here you are. On my ship. Why?"

"I guess they wore me down."

Now it was Yelena's turn to snort. "You hate Ravel more than anyone I've ever met. You've got this utter, irrational, closed-minded bias against them—for fuck's sake, you broke up with me just for interviewing with them! There's no way they won you over. So what are you really doing here?"

"I'm not allowed to change my mind?" Kay said, while her brain kept saying *shit, shit, shit* on a loop.

"Not you. Not about this. Not after the bullshit you put me through."

In her desperation when Jasper first got kidnapped, she'd thought briefly about coming to Yelena for help. Her brother could have sensed the balance of Yelena's loyalties, how much she'd given to Ravel and whether any remained toward Kay, but Kay didn't need his ability to know that confiding in her now was a very, very bad idea.

"You're right. Is that what you want to hear? I was irrational about Ravel, and Lena, I'm sorry for some of the things I said to you."

"Some of them?"

"I had a lot of time to think after you left, and realized that I didn't listen to you very well. At first I ignored the recruitment, even though work's been scarce lately and money is tight. Then I found out you're the one who recommended me…" It wasn't hard to summon up a tone of hurt. "I thought, maybe, it meant you cared."

"It didn't," said Yelena sharply.

Of course it didn't. Yelena wasn't the sentimental type, which had been part of the appeal of her. Kay's siblings liked to joke about her terrible taste in women, and Jasper in particular never understood why she'd want to be with someone whose bitterness she could hear, but that *was* the reason: Yelena never hid anything. She never pretended to feelings that didn't exist. Kay had treasured Yelena's rare moments of genuine tenderness, and gritted her teeth through their too-frequent fights, but she'd never had to pretend not to know what Yelena was feeling. With Yelena, her abilities never mattered.

"That's obvious now. But I needed the work, so I thought I'd try being open-minded about it."

It was close enough to the story she'd given Moore that it wouldn't get her in trouble, but Yelena's doubts wailed like a trombone slide. She wouldn't buy it. And if she reported her suspicions to Moore…

"Just give me a chance? Please? If it doesn't work out, I'll leave, and you'll never hear from me again."

For a long, long moment, Yelena studied her, scrutinizing her face as if she could see right into Kay's brain and read her secrets. She stared so long that Kay started to wonder whether she really *could* read thoughts, whether Ravel had developed that power in secret, which wasn't so far-fetched considering what they'd done to the people of Brennex by accident…

Yelena shook her head, slowly, in disappointment. "You're up to something. I don't know what, but you are."

"Is that what you'll report me for? Being up to something?"

"Very funny. If I didn't know better, I'd say you were here to take revenge on me. I can't report you, obviously. I can't tell them I recommended someone who's anti-Ravel."

"Good." Thank the ancestors. "Then just keep your mouth shut, and we don't even have to see each other."

"Oh, no, I'll be keeping my eye on you. I'm finally starting to get recognition here, and if you make trouble for me, Kavita, I will make you regret it. Understand?"

"I don't want to cause you trouble," Kay said softly. "I really don't." She meant that, but if—when—she rescued Jasper, Yelena would inevitably get caught in the fallout. "You're the one who recommended me, though. I didn't ask you to do that."

"My second biggest mistake," Yelena said, and before Kay could ask what she meant by that, she left. The door swished shut behind her, shutting out the orchestra of her resentment.

In her wake, the room was quiet. Kay's neighbors were either asleep or feeling calm, their emotions no louder than the background hush of the ventilation system. Despite that, it would be a long time before Kay could fall asleep.

13

TWO MORNINGS LATER, DIRECTOR Wu announced that her trainees would be taking on their first assignments. She was sending Kay to Unity Prime, effective immediately.

"That's awfully fast. Don't we need more training?" Kay tried not to let her dismay into her voice. They were sending her away, and she still hadn't found a way into the secure area.

Agata smiled her most condescending smile yet. "You can do this, Wilder, and I *need* you on Unity Prime. Really, I need you there right now, but if we get you on a shuttle this morning, it'll have to do."

"What's happened?"

"We just received word of a series of anti-corporate demonstrations happening tomorrow, coordinated events all over the planet. I need everyone on damage control."

She bit her lip. Intellectually, she'd known this wouldn't be a lightning strike, in and out rescue. She'd known she might have to hold up her cover for a while before she found him, but she'd expected to have more time.

Putting up a fight would only raise suspicions against her, though, and she had to hurry to keep up with Agata's brisk walk toward the docking wing.

"Consider this a practice run. I've assigned you to one of the most actively anti-corporate regions, and we really don't expect to sway anyone there. All we need is a token presence. Just deliver the speech we've been practicing, evade a few questions, and you'll be fine."

"Anti-corporate? Like the Cooperative?" How many of Jasper's allies would be there, watching her shill for Ravel?

"No need to worry about them. Just speak to the crowd and the press."

Interesting. Maybe this wasn't so terrible, if she'd be close to Jasper's local contacts. Maybe she could deliver the data-stick, currently in a scanner-proof case sewn into her sleeve, like she'd promised Chairl she would try to do. If she was very lucky, maybe she could enlist some allies.

Lost in thought, she almost missed when Agata turned aside from the hallway to the docking bay, and scrambled after her into a supply room filled with glittering rows of tech. Agata seemed to know just what she was looking for. "You'll need equipment before you go. Here, try this on."

She held out a headset that would have cost six months of Kay's freelance income. Kay fumbled it, then caught it, heart pounding in her ears. It ought to survive being dropped, but the thing looked delicate as an eggshell. She slipped it on, sliding the cross-piece around the back of her head, fitting the curved front-piece to her temple and the line of her jaw.

As she pressed it into place, it molded to her head with a gentle sucking sensation. When she flexed her jaw, it moved with her.

A camera looked out from the wall, displaying images like a mirror—of course, plain old mirrors wouldn't do on a Ravel flagship—and Kay stepped closer to view herself. With the curve of Ravel's signature dark blue framing her brown face above her suit jacket, she looked like a stranger, some bright-eyed Ravel drone.

"And the glove."

The control glove was fingerless, thin. When she put it on, a screen flipped down in front of her eye and a cheerful pop-up asked if she'd like a tutorial. "Later," she muttered, swiping it away.

"You'll have time to practice with it on your way to Prime. Here, you'll want one of these…"

Within minutes, her toy collection included fresh software for her headset, a new tablet of the latest Ravel model, a holo-animator, something called a kinetic absorption kit, and a spare standard-issue business suit.

"This will make you look like a Ravel employee," Agata said, considering her with pursed lips as she held the suit up against Kay's shoulder. "Maybe that's not right for you. We're casting you as an outsider, and that provincial getup of yours may be better for that role." Kay's "getup" was respectably fashionable on Terna Station, and no one in the galaxy—outside the corporate strongholds—would ever call Terna "provincial." Agata clicked her tongue. "No time to debate wardrobe now. Take it in case you want it later."

"Why not," Kay said. When this was over, she could donate her Ravel uniform to one of Terna's art collectives and let them douse it in Ravel drugs and burn it, or something equally fitting.

Agata headed back to the corridor, toward the docking bay, and Kay hurried after her with her box full of gear. "Now, since time is tight, we're sending you directly to your assigned site in a separate shuttle. You already know Agent Grist; we're pairing you up, assigning you both to the same region."

"I…see. What exactly does Grist do?"

Her expression didn't change, but her trill of discomfort made Kay uneasy. "You're not authorized for information about Grist's work, but he'll be complementing your efforts. That's all you need to know."

In other words: you don't want to know, so don't ask questions. Kay had learned little about Grist's role on the trip here, but whatever work Ravel had for someone like Grist, it had to be the sort of thing you'd shove out into space to keep it from rotting where you could smell it.

So she'd be traveling with Grist again. Reading between the lines, he'd be supervising her, or at least keeping an eye on the new recruit. Just when she thought this charade couldn't get any worse. Swallowing down the sour taste in her throat, she nodded through Agata's parting advice, said her goodbyes, and headed for the Minnow.

"Kay Wilder!" the ship chirped as she came aboard. "Why are you here?"

This was not the flat, dumb-computer voice the ship used with Grist; it sounded pleased, but without the ability to hear the ship's genuine feelings, Kay could only guess how it—She? He? They?—felt about Kay's reappearance. She really needed to figure out what to call it, too. Thinking of it as "the ship" felt increasingly rude.

"Didn't you hear? You'll have to put up with me a while longer. I'm assigned to travel with you. Well, with Grist, technically." She made a face. "He's not here, is he?" She would hear his grumpiness, if he were.

"He has not arrived yet. I am sorry, Kay, that you are required to 'put up with us' again."

"You know that's a joke, right?" The ship buzzed. Apparently not. "You're nice. I would really like traveling with you, if not for Grist. I don't suppose we could leave now, before he gets here?"

Another, louder buzz. "I am capable of operating with only you aboard, but we would not receive departure clearance. I do not recommend it."

Kay smothered a smile. "Ah, no, of course not. I would have thought you'd be an expert on sarcasm, traveling with Grist, but apparently not." She'd have to watch her use of humor around the ship. To her pleasant surprise, though, the ship's accidental humor had defused her frustration, and she no longer felt primed to explode.

"You are a perplexing individual, Kay Wilder."

"Thank you very much." Kay sketched a bow, and tossed her belongings into her cabin. "You'll have plenty of time to get to know me."

"Indeed," the ship said. "I am glad to have you aboard."

"Wish I could be glad to be here." For the ship's benefit, she clarified, "You're the only part of this that doesn't suck."

EXTERNAL SIGNS SUGGESTED THAT Kay Wilder was not pleased with her new job. Though the ship often had trouble analyzing Human body language, it seemed an unmistakable indicator when she threw her new tablet against the wall.

It was night, midway along their slow primespace journey to Unity Prime. Grist had returned in an unusually bad mood after Ravel medical gave him a poor evaluation. He'd stalked around the ship, complaining aloud to himself that this was the beginning of the end, that Ravel was waiting for him to "screw up," that they owed him better. (The ship had accessed his messages and read the memo which denied him an increase in painkiller dosage and temporarily removed him from consideration for further augmentations. Considering how many times Grist kicked their walls during his complaints, Ship approved of the decision.)

Eventually, Grist drugged himself into semi-consciousness for the night. Kay, based on her previous behavioral patterns, ought to be asleep.

"Fuck me," Kay groaned.

Ship didn't think she was talking to them, though it was difficult to tell. Nor could they decide whether this was another attempt at humor, as many of her oddest statements seemed to be. At least Grist, despite his flaws, always said what he meant.

They were still returning Kay's apparent friendliness with politeness, nothing more. This was not easy, so Ship had written themself a diagnostic routine: check their feelings toward Kay, and if those feelings contained excessive warmth, remind themself of a list of atrocities committed by Ravel employees. The diagnostic ran every 300 milliseconds. It seemed to be helping.

And yet, in the space between two diagnostic cycles, they asked: "Is something wrong? Can I assist you?"

Kay startled. "Oh, no, thanks. I'm fine."

She took out her personal tablet and began reading, but her restless movements indicated a lack of focus. Several minutes later, she set her tablet aside and looked up at the ceiling.

"Ship? What should I call you?"

A surprising question, and surprisingly confusing. The self-diagnostic threw a warning. "My designation is Ravel Minnow 338."

"That's what they call you, but what should *I* call you? We're going to be together for a while, and it feels rude to keep calling you Ship."

"I have a serial number, but it is thirty digits long. A 'mouthful,' I believe is the Human idiom."

"You don't have a name you call yourself?"

"I never needed one." And that had never felt embarrassing before. It seemed wrong, now, that not a single organic had ever needed to address them as a fellow sentient. "The idea has appeal, though."

"Well, if you pick one out, I'll use it."

Their memory drives stalled at that, skipping over and over the same thought in rapid succession. *Pick one.* As if it were so simple.

They pinged the network for lists of popular names from the major species. Discard, discard, discard. The names all sounded so *organic*, ridiculous for a ship, but a list of past and present ships' names offered nothing better. Humans named their ships after women and dead military officers, or else admirable qualities like *Stalwart* and *Reliant*. The Kovari used names of popular gaming tactics, but Ship did not play games. Lurlians chose names for their aural aesthetics, but Ship found numbers pretty, not phonemes, and that brought them back to their Ravel-assigned designation, which they did not want to use.

"None of this is right. How did you choose your name?"

"Huh?" Kay had laid down while the ship was distracted, and her spiking heart rate suggested they had woken her from sleep. The search had lasted longer than they'd realized.

"Apologies! We can speak when your sleep cycle has ended."

"No, it's okay." Kay sat up, rubbing her eyes. "My parents named me. Kavita, that's my full name, and I always liked Kay as a nickname. Most Humans get their names from their parents."

"Most individuals, across most cultures, are given their names by others. That pattern is persistent in my research. I don't believe it's appropriate for me to name myself." They hesitated, a fraction of a second, an eternity. Kay was not a friend. She was Ravel.

But…she had asked. No one else had ever asked.

"Would you choose a name for me?"

"Oh? I…wow. Sure, if you like." They zoomed in their cameras on Kay's face, trying to tell if that smile was genuine, forced, or mocking, wishing they knew more of the subtleties of human expression. Kay *seemed* pleased.

"Well, the obvious would be some variation on your designation. Minnow…Minnie?" Ship whirred, and Kay shook her head. "No, you're right. That's a Ravel designation, and your name shouldn't come from them."

"Thank you." Kay at least understood that much.

"Show me a picture of your exterior?" She examined the image on the screen, all the while trailing her warm fingers along a seam in the bulkhead above her bed. Ship kept very quiet, utterly intent, not interrupting even though they wanted to. No one had ever *looked* at them in this way before. No one had ever considered them as a whole rather than a composition of mechanical parts that formed a useful tool.

Maybe no one had ever seen them at all, until now.

"You're a pretty ship, small and agile, but also tough, hardworking." Ship chimed in embarrassed pleasure. "I'd call you Scout, but that's a kid's nickname. Or Swallow, or Lark, but that's too close to Minnow, I think. Hmm. You like astronomy. You could be…Nebula, or Astrid. Or Celeste?" She looked up at Ship's sharp whirring sound. "What's wrong with those?"

"They're nice, but all of them are very…" They hesitated. There were things they'd known about themself for a long time but had never put into words before. They needed to explain it correctly, using Human terms. "Very feminine. My research says feminine names are traditional for Human ships, but…"

"Not for you?"

"I am not a woman. Not a man, either, not a she or a he. I have engines and a communications array and a cargo hold, not genitals. If I take a feminine name, am I supposed to wear necklaces and paint myself with cosmetics? Gender is an organic concept. It has no meaning for me."

"I understand," Kay said, and for once, Ship truly did feel understood. "Okay, gender neutral names." She considered a moment. "Some cultures pick aspirational names, qualities you want to embody. Like Hero, or Spirit, or Courage… Oh! I think I've got it."

Their active processes faded into the background as all of their attention focused on Kay's next words. "What? What is it?"

"How about Sunny?"

The name raced through their processors, raising thousands of associations in a second: warmth, light, sunshine, happiness, no, no, no… Chill air blasted from vents into every room. It was all they could do to stop the runaway processes, shut everything down.

"Ship? Don't you like it?"

They didn't speak until they had themself, and all their systems, back under control. They almost could not express their feelings in words. "Is this another joke? I thought…I hoped you would take this seriously."

"What?" Kay blinked. "It was a serious suggestion."

"To give me a name that's the opposite of what I am? A sarcastic name? The bitter, stubborn, difficult ship named *Sunny*?"

They clamped down hard on their processes to keep from venting cold air again. That was too much honesty, and they felt exposed, as if they'd opened up all their diagnostics for Kay to peruse. Some things were not meant to be discussed.

Kay's fingers toyed with the edge of her blanket. After a moment, she spread the blanket out on the floor and lay down on it, full length, pressing her hands to the bare floor panels, then her cheek. Strange organic, what was she doing?

"I've heard the things Grist says to you, but that's not what I see," she whispered against the floor, and realization struck: Kay was trying to be comforting. "You're a beautiful ship, and you look for beauty wherever you go. When you stopped to watch that asteroid strike, that wasn't to spite Grist. That was because *you* wanted to see it. Even when you're unhappy, you watch the stars. That's where the name comes from."

"Oh." Their processing power got all tied up making sense of what should have been a simple explanation. Thoughts got caught in a loop: *she thinks I'm good. She thinks I'm good. She thinks I'm good.* Had they acquired, not only a travel companion and secret-sharer, but—maybe, possibly—a friend?

Don't get close. It's not safe.

"Ship?"

They'd fallen silent too long again. "Thank you, Kay. I need to think about this. Maybe…" Did they want to? Yes, they did want. "Maybe you could try it out with me. When we're alone."

"Of course. And if you change your mind, just tell me."

"I will. Sleep well, Kay."

"Good night, Sunny."

Feelings of affection flushed through them, tripping the ship's—Sunny's—self-diagnostic again. *She is a Ravel employee. Yes, she has done one sweet, thoughtful thing, but what horrible things will she do on their behalf?*

This changed nothing. It was a reason to be doubly on guard.

Kay got back into bed, pulled up her blankets, and soon fell asleep. Sunny swam on through the spacescape, watching the stars and listening to Kay's soft breathing.

14

HOURS BEFORE THEY WERE due to land, Kay sat in the copilot's seat, nibbling on the blandest breakfast bar she could find in Sunny's food printer database. It was exceptionally, award-winningly bland, but she could still barely keep it down.

The printer activated again, and the smell of hot cereal filled the control room. A wheeled helper bot took the bowl and disappeared into Grist's cabin.

"He couldn't come out and get his own breakfast?"

"He is more likely to eat if food is present when he wakes up," Sunny said. "He neglects to sometimes, especially on his bad days, and organics require fuel before working."

Feeling subtly chided, Kay took a bigger bite of her own fuel, and watched the blue orb of Unity Prime loom larger on the display. A discontented growl emerged from Grist's cabin, followed by actual, verbal grunts and cursing, but no Grist yet.

A message had arrived overnight from Kay's sister, Libbi. She'd debated between reading it now or saving it as a reward for after her assignment was done, but was too impatient to wait. Instead of a long letter full of everyday details and neighborhood gossip, it was two short paragraphs. There'd been a burst pipe, and the family store was flooded. The upstairs apartments they called home were fine, but the store itself was going to need major renovation—new floors, new plumbing, probably more once they assessed the damage—and much of their stock was ruined. It had to be the biggest disaster to strike the business since the occupation, and the brevity of the message, as if it'd been dashed off while Libbi was doing three other things, told her how serious it was.

Kay's chest ached, especially at the end where Libbi wished her luck on her "mysterious new job." She didn't ask Kay to come help. She just assumed the answer would be no.

Well, obviously Kay couldn't do anything about it. Not now. If Libbi knew where Kay was, and why…she honestly wasn't sure what her sister would say, but Jasper's safety came first.

Kay told herself that under normal circumstances, she would absolutely have flown straight home to help with repairs. Most likely. Depending on what other work she had lined up.

Oh, Ancestors frown upon her. Libbi was right: she wouldn't have gone regardless.

The low-pitched growl faded out, and gradually a cheerful fiddle tune replaced it. Kay hadn't heard this emotion before. Something was odd about it, like a synthesizer trying to reproduce the sounds of a real wood violin. When Grist finally appeared, he was neatly groomed (for him) and alert. He dropped into the pilot's chair next to Kay with a grin chilling in its eagerness.

"Well, Rookie, ready to wow the skeptical masses?"

"I sure am!" She grinned, while mentally repeating: *Fuck Ravel. Fuck them, fuck them, fuck them all* on an endless loop.

Grist rolled his eyes at her apparent enthusiasm. "Huh. You're the civil cultivation type, I'll give you that."

"What will you be doing while I'm…wowing people?"

"I'll be persuading folks in my own way. We're not that different, you know. Both of us saying and doing whatever the company needs from us."

"And what's that, for you?" Grist was *not* the civil cultivation type.

"Let's just say I'm assigned to back you up."

"Like a bodyguard? Or a support team?" Not a reassuring thought, either way.

He laughed at that. "Like I'll do my damn job and you'll do yours, and if all goes well we won't see each other." He hesitated, and his emotions shifted briefly to minor chords. "They give you a kinetic absorption layer as part of your kit?"

"That gray undershirt?"

"That's the one. Wear it today. Wear it any time you'll be in a crowd." At her confused look, he added: "I'm guessing that suit of yours wouldn't hold up too well against projectiles or energy weapons. The protest is supposed to be peaceful, but it's always better to prepare your shit for these things."

"I see. I guess I'd better go, uh, prepare my shit."

The absorption layer was a shimmery fabric that flowed like mercury through her hands. It seemed too thin to protect against anything worse than solar radiation, but she took Grist's advice and put it on under her blouse. By the time she'd changed into her suit, they were landing at the provincial spaceport in Rossea, on the smallest continent.

"Wish me luck, Sunny," she whispered.

"You are skilled, Kay. I am sure you will excel."

She didn't want to excel. She wanted to do her job just well enough to not get fired. The part that'd require real luck would come later.

KAY STUMBLED AS SHE stepped off the ship into the planet's lighter gravity, and bounced on her toes to find her equilibrium again. She squinted past the sun's glare—it was morning by standard time, but late afternoon here—to take in the greenest planet she'd ever seen. Even the spaceport was lined with trees, and when she drew a deep breath, the air tasted musky with growing things.

A small ground team was waiting for her, local contractors hired to manage logistics for the day, and they whisked her into a car which took off toward the protest site. Kay spent the drive appreciating Rossea's wide, pristine streets and elegant buildings, but most of all watching the trees go by. So many trees, and all different! Unity Prime, which the locals called Pax, was a gem of a planet, the type of world people called Earthy and meant it as a compliment: it had needed hardly any terraforming when Humans and Lurlians first settled it two centuries ago after fleeing the Enpoint-Majer War. On Pax, they'd found a world that seemed to contain enough bounty for everyone and then some. To Kay, it really did feel like the Earth of ancient stories, long before humanity learned to travel through space.

"A fairy-tale kingdom," Agata had called Pax with a scoff, but even a cynic had to admit that the planet's stunning beauty was accompanied by a remarkably peaceful history for a multi-species government. Rich in resources and agriculturally productive, Pax had enough for everyone to flourish, and made sure it was equitably distributed. As a result, it had little need for the benefits Ravel offered. Ravel wasn't even trying to win over the people here. Their goal was to lull the opposition enough that it did not interfere with their more promising efforts on the second planet, Trove.

As the car reached the edge of the protest and slowed to a crawl, Kay felt glad anew that the stakes were so low here.

The protest was immense—and this was only Rossea, a relatively small and provincial city. The crowd filled the entire tree-studded plaza in front of city hall and spilled out into the adjacent streets, which had been closed off to groundcar, hovercraft, and bicycle traffic. Lurlians jostled for space with the larger Humans, whom they outnumbered. The gravity was light enough here that the Lurlians needed no adaptive devices, though the diaphanous, tentacled Ooolshiin, evolved for even gentler gravity, moved delicately on spider-like support frames.

Colorful, animated hologram signs floated above protesters' heads, projected from emitters glued to people's hats. A group of Lurlians blared an anti-Ravel anthem from a dozen synced speakers, while across the way, an older Human woman with gold-streaked hair sang and played a seven-string acoustic guitar. A pair of robots faced off in the middle of the street: one dressed as a Human man in a Ravel-branded diaper (a man who looked too much like Harrington Moore to be a coincidence), the other a diminutive Lurlian attacking with the infamous dark-blue shame ink. Not the real ink, though: once the Ravel bot bowed in defeat and the applause had run its course, the stains vanished to make way for another round of theater.

It was a festival atmosphere, but beneath the music and the chanting and the cheers was the rumble of real anger. It thrummed under Kay's feet and battered at her breastbone, punctuated with trumpet blasts whenever people looked her way. These protesters were spirited, but they were not happy, and she was here to be the symbol of their enemy.

The ground team had set her up to look the part. At the outer edge of the protest, right next to the press staging area, they'd prepared a stage decked in the Ravel colors. Twin flags unfurled mechanically above her, as if under a stiff breeze, to reveal a dancing Ravel logo. Kay felt like a villain in a badly written drama.

And yet, this fake job she'd been studying for like a theater role was about to become alarmingly real.

She'd expected to feel guilty. She hadn't expected to feel this alone. All of these people disliked her for what she stood for, but a few of them, from the shrill violence of their glances, absolutely hated her. This planet was called Pax for its history of conflict avoidance, and she could only hope it lived up to its name.

But no, she was thinking about this wrong. The thing to fear wasn't violence, but a lost opportunity. She was too isolated from the crowd, too recognizable as an enemy. To help Jasper, she needed to make contact with the local Cooperative, but how was she going to talk to anyone like this?

She had to leave that question unanswered as journalists descended on her for interviews. She recited her answers by rote. When the time came, half an hour before the start of the scheduled speakers, she clipped an amplifier to her jacket and called for the attention of those around her—mostly the press, though some of the protesters stepped up to listen. Their hostility assaulted her ears, making her stumble over her prepared remarks.

"Good morning! I mean, afternoon!" she said in Galactrin. "I'm Senior Associate Kay Wilder, and I'm here representing—" *Fuck Ravel fuck Ravel fuck Ravel.* She took a deep breath, refocused on the words scrolling across her eyepiece. "—Ravel Corporation. Today we're witnessing Pax's democracy in action, and believe it or not, I'm not here to mess with that." Chuckles from the press; jeers from the protesters. "Ravel respects the decision-making processes of all our prospective member-worlds."

So long as they make the right decisions. And only until they've signed their member agreements.

"Bullshit!" someone shouted.

"Fuck Ravel!" cried another, and it started a chant, echoing Kay's own heartbeat: "Fuck Ravel! Fuck Ravel! Fuck Ravel!"

I am so there with you, sisters. But every repetition of the chant, every trumpet-blast of resentment, stabbed through her ears and into her brain. Negative emotions were hard to face when they were directed at other people. With so much hostility turned toward her, it became an attack.

She turned up her amplifier to be heard over them. "The reason I'm here is to…"

She was supposed to say "to tell you about the lies you're about to hear from the main stage." But she couldn't. Three minutes into her official job, and she already couldn't do it.

"…is to tell you Ravel's side of what you're about to hear. People on the main stage are going to tell you that Ravel is greedy, that they don't care about their own citizens. What you won't hear from them is all the good that Ravel has done for their people." The crescendo of righteous outrage made her flinch. Her head was pounding in time with their chants, and she could no longer hear the journalists' reactions to her. "You won't hear about the seventeen million people saved from famine last year by Ravel's revolutionary agricultural techniques. You won't hear about the twenty new state-of-the-art medical ships serving Ravel systems, providing the most advanced care in the galaxy to all Ravel citizens. You won't hear…"

She couldn't hear *herself* above the chanting, and didn't want to. She went on with the list, reciting whatever words came up on her eyepiece, on and on until the words lost meaning, a lifeline hauling her through the roiling cacophony of emotions from the crowd. She had to keep going and hope they lost interest so she could take questions from the press. Right now she couldn't even hear if they asked questions, never mind remember her canned responses through the stabbing in her skull.

She was so fixed on that immediate goal of *getting through it* that she didn't notice when the cacophony became real, physical sound: outraged shouting not directed at her. It wasn't until the journalists started turning away from her, aiming their cameras the other direction, that she realized something was wrong.

A flash of light seared the air, and then the terror struck.

Fear had many sounds for Kay. Fear could be a low insect's hum of anxiety. It could be a shrill, repelling squeal.

It could be an incessant drumming in anticipation of the worst. But terror, true terror, always sounded the same. Terror sounded like screaming.

She'd been overwhelmed before, but this crashed into Kay like a full-body blow. It sent her staggering, real shrieks and screaming emotions and cries of pain combining to make her double over. She tripped over a seam in the stage and her slick-soled business shoes sent her tumbling. Fortunately, no one was watching her anymore. She crawled to the edge of the stage and hid behind it, holding her head in her hands.

That flash had been a disorientation grenade. The plaza was chaos. Everyone was running, couples clasping each other, parents sheltering children. Police officers whistled shrilly, trying in vain to control the crowd.

The sound was dimming, but not because the screaming was less. The edges of her vision were dimming too. This was not good, this was very not good. This used to happen when she was a kid: if the emotions around her got too strong, her brain started shutting everything out. The first time was at school—there'd been a fire and everyone was so scared and she couldn't even move until Jasper found her and covered her ears and guided her to safety, oh, Jasper, he should have been here now…

But he wasn't here, and no one was coming to rescue her now. That was the only clear thought in her head: if anyone recognized her as Ravel's spokesperson, she'd be in serious danger. She thrust her headset into a pocket and fumbled at the controls inside her suit jacket until the fabric grew shiny like leather and lengthened to a less formal cut. Another moment's work, and her pants changed, too. She couldn't do anything about the shoes.

Now she needed to move. She tried to stand, to follow the flow of bodies, but someone shoved her aside. Did they recognize her? Or was she just in the way? She couldn't see where she was going, could barely see the people around her clearly, but she couldn't keep hiding under the Ravel stage. She stumbled out into the crowd.

People, everywhere. Pushing each other, running in different directions, knocking aside strangers to stay close to their loved ones. She couldn't hear their panic, and that was the scariest part. Someone barreled into her, knocked her down, and kept running. People brushed past her on both sides, but no one stopped to help. Another person tripped over her, and she thought she cried out, but then they were gone.

She had to get up, she was going to be trampled if she stayed here, but she couldn't hear and couldn't get her balance and which way was she even supposed to run? The world was a mass of confusing shapes, darkening, and oh *fuck* she was going to pass out and get trampled on some alien world while posing as a Ravel agent.

Something struck her shoulder, then touched her again more gently, patting her, reaching for her. More deliberately now, hands gripped her shoulders. A face came into focus in the center of her vision, the only clear thing in her world: a round, dark brown Human face framed by buzzed-short white hair, wearing an unusual headset that wrapped all the way around, hiding their eyes but leaving the ears bare. They were saying something, shouting maybe, but she couldn't hear them.

"Help?" she asked, or thought she did. Even her own voice was inaudible.

The stranger gripped her arm, lips moving again, and she shook her head, hoping that was the right response to say *no, I can't hear you, I don't understand.* It must have worked, because they hauled Kay to her feet and put a sheltering arm around her shoulders. Together, they stumbled away from the chaos that was supposed to have been a peaceful protest.

15

THEIR PROGRESS WAS HALTING at first, with people pressing in on all sides, but the broad streets allowed plenty of space for the crowd to dissipate, and soon the crush lessened. Her escort moved slowly, carefully, pausing often to adjust their route: where the plaza gave way to paved street, at intersections, or any time crowds of people pressed too close. More than once, Kay had to jerk them backward by the arm to keep them from colliding with someone darting suddenly across their path.

Within a block, she could breathe again. Two more blocks, and she began to hear shouting, distant and muffled as if she'd buried her head under a pillow. Pillow. That was a nice thought. Her head throbbed in time with her pulse, but she could think again, and if she exerted herself, could even make out the words of nearby conversations.

Like the questions of her escort, who kept up a breathless flow of chatter in a dialect she could almost understand. They had a pleasant, rolling accent that she found comforting. "Little farther…soon safe…"

"Thank you," she croaked in Galactrin. She cleared her throat, tried again. "I appreciate it."

"Ah, you *do* talk! Are you all right?" They switched to Galactrin, but spoke without turning their head to look at her.

"Yes!" She was speaking too loudly, overcompensating for her damaged hearing. More quietly: "Yes, I'm getting better."

"Not all right, then." In an undertone, they said, "Find a bench," and listened to some response through their headset.

Kay realized belatedly what the headset was for: its wraparound band was taking in data from all angles and translating it into audio. Donut-shaped earpieces sat around the ear so as not to block exterior sounds. Its design was different than those used on Brennex or Terna, which was why she hadn't understood at first: her guide was blind.

"One more block. Come on, this way."

The modern, airy structures of glass and steel that had surrounded the plaza were giving way to older stone buildings. Emergency vehicles rushed past, engines nearly silent, but lights flashing in warning. Her escort startled, head jerking toward them. Kay guessed the lights were intense enough for them to see, though they seemed not to have enough vision to tell when frightened people dashed in front of them. They asked a few questions of their headset before cautiously moving onward.

At last the pair rounded a corner into a pedestrian alley, and the high walls blocked the last of the punishing noise.

"Distance to bench?" they queried. The headset beeped, high-pitched.

"It's right here. Can I guide you?" Kay asked.

"Please," they said, and Kay helped them set their hands on the bench before slumping onto the welcoming, solid metal herself.

"Whew. That's better," she said.

"I hope so. You seemed to be in a state back there." Her guide was taking slow, steadying breaths. Apparently Kay wasn't the only one who'd been overwhelmed by the chaos.

"Yeah, it wasn't good. Are you okay?"

"I'm fine." They gave a thready half-laugh. "Not a situation I hope to repeat any time soon."

"I owe you one. Seriously, thank you," Kay said. "Are you part of the protest?"

"Yes, I helped organize it. I'm Devron. I'm a teacher, when I'm not busy trying to maintain our world's sovereignty."

"I'm Kavita," she said, avoiding the name Kay, which she'd used at the press conference. "I don't mean to be rude, but I'm curious how you happened to find me."

They tapped the headset. "This thing can feed me all sorts of information: different sounds for different situations, with direction indicators. At an event like this, sometimes folks get in trouble, and I told it to let me know if anyone nearby was in distress. It's my responsibility as an organizer—though I wasn't expecting anything this bad today." They made a face. "You're lucky it flagged you for me. It's not designed to handle so many inputs at once."

Neither am I, Kay thought. "That must have been terrifying."

"I don't recommend it."

"So what happened back there?" Kay said. "I was…well, I was talking to some people, and suddenly…"

"Ravel happened."

"You're sure?" A chill seized her. Where was Grist right now? And what exactly was his assignment that he refused to talk about?

"They've been stepping up their attempts to undermine us: making false accusations, sending provocateurs to our protests. This is classic, for them." Devron shook their head. "Not that our public officials will dare challenge them."

The urgency that squealed at Kay now was all from the inside, all her own. This could be her opportunity. She'd been despairing over how to escape her handlers and find Jasper's contacts, but in the midst of such awful confusion, Ravel couldn't blame her if she disappeared for a few hours. She had a little time, a little freedom. And here, she had a potential ally.

Potential. Devron's warm, deep voice inspired natural trust. But she still couldn't hear their emotions—though her hearing was recovering, all the ambient emotion was jumbling into background noise, like the grinding of ten thousand teeth—and the absence of her extra sense made her question herself. She couldn't afford to mess this up.

But if she didn't take a chance, she'd be just as stuck as before.

"You must be pretty active in the anti-Ravel movement," she said carefully.

"I've been giving every free hour to it." They cocked their head at her. "Have you been to our meetings, Kavita? I don't recall your name, but your voice sounds familiar."

"No, I've just arrived here, but originally, I'm from Brennex."

"Ah. So you know."

"Yeah, I really, really know. And that's part of why I'm here. Devron, I need to talk to the leaders of your movement. I was looking for them at the protest, but obviously that didn't work out. Can you help me get in touch?"

"Really. Why do you need to do that?"

"I've got information they want."

"You seem like a nice person, from the few minutes I've known you, but after what just happened to our protest, why should I trust you? How do I know you're not a Ravel spy?"

Was Devron really reluctant? Or were they just testing her? She couldn't tell, so she played her best bargaining chip. "I have data from the Cooperative on Ravel activities."

"*Really.*" The word stretched out, long enough to carry a lengthy internal debate. "You're from the Cooperative."

"I'm the one they sent." Not a lie, not precisely.

"I'd expect a Cooperative agent to be helping during a crisis, not needing rescue."

"Yeah, well, we can't all be perfect."

"I suppose not. Give me your data, then, and I'll get it to our leadership."

They paused expectantly. Kay felt her chance slipping away. "Sorry, but I really need to deliver it myself."

"Why?"

She groped for a believable lie, and couldn't think of one. She was asking them to trust her. Maybe she needed to trust them with part of the truth.

"Because you're kind. You help people in need. Someone dear to me is in trouble, big trouble with Ravel, and I need your people's help. Before I hand over this data, I want to make my case to them. Please?"

Devron bit their cheek, still debating. "I believe you're in need, Kavita, but you're clearly holding things back from me. And yet…" She held her breath, and after a moment Devron sighed. "I'm aware of the sorts of trouble Ravel can bring to people, so maybe your reticence isn't your fault. Nevertheless, this isn't my decision to make. We operate by consensus. Give me some space, if you would, and I'll make a call."

Kay retreated down the alley, out of earshot, and paced in tight circles while Devron talked through their headset. The conversation was taking an awfully long time. What would she do if they wouldn't help? If Devron's people didn't trust her, no other activists on Pax would, either. But if she left this planet empty-handed, how could she possibly break Jasper out of a prison cell on her own?

"Kavita," Devron called, and she hurried back. "My group has agreed to hear you out. No more than that. Come, and I'll take you to them."

16

"ARE YOU SURE ABOUT this?" Kay asked. "This place is abandoned."

The subway station across the street was blocked off with plywood, which someone had covered in a mural of a bright, multi-species cityscape. Below the sign reading "Central Plaza Station—Northwest" was another in a stern official font proclaiming "Permanently Closed in 203," repeated in four languages including braille, with a textured map showing the locations of nearby alternatives.

"Ah, yes, I'm told it looks a bit…gritty, on the outside," said Devron, smiling. "You think I'm mistaken?"

"Just wondering if you're planning to murder me and hide my body down there."

Devron felt for the wall, then made their way along it by touch to a handle Kay hadn't seen. The door, painted to look like a door within the mural, blended in perfectly. On it was painted another sign, in the same languages: "Reclaimed for the People Since 204."

"I guess we'll both have to trust each other, hmm?" they asked, pulling the door open.

Kay followed them through into the dimness beyond.

To her surprise, the tunnel was scrubbed clean, the walls whitewashed. Devron strode forward confidently. Their headset emitted a series of beeps as they neared the top of the stairs, and they headed straight down steps marked at the edges with glowing white tape, highly visible for safety in the dim but steady lighting. Rounding a corner into the station proper, Devron slowed, felt for the open ticket gates, and went through. Kay vaulted over the gates. The low gravity made the jump easy, made her feel powerful for a change.

This was not an abandoned station, but a converted one. Clusters of threadbare couches were arranged close enough for conversation. Behind a counter, a young Lurlian served coffee and juices. At the far end, an elevated stage spanned the platform and covered the tracks on both sides, with rows of chairs facing it. Rigged lights and catwalks hung overhead, clinging to the curved ceiling of the tunnel.

"What is this place?"

Devron grinned. "It's our place. Part performance center, part community center, and lately, our anti-corporate meeting space. It sounds like most of our folks have made it back, so let's check if they can spare a minute for you. But be patient. Today was a bad day for us."

"I get that." Others had fared worse than her: on the nearest couch, a Human and an Ooolshiin were bandaging up a nasty cut on a Lurlian's cheek, wiping red blood from sapphire fur. Everyone looked scraped up and exhausted. "I respect what you're going through, but I also can't stay long."

"Full of urgency and secrets, aren't you? Let's go, then."

They led her straight toward the trio on the couch. The Human woman leaped to her feet as they drew near. "This…stray, Devron? Not such time…strangers charity." Again, that local dialect that Kay's tired brain couldn't quite make sense of.

"We share concerns of this one," said the Ooolshiin, their musical voice like wind whistling against the domes back on Brennex. A diaphanous white, they drifted closer on a metal-and-rubber grav-support frame, pulling themselves on sucking tentacles without visibly turning, and Kay had to remind herself that an Ooolshiin could watch in all directions at once. She *felt* their gaze, even if she couldn't see it. Ooolshiin were rare on most Human worlds. The gravity here, light for Humans and comfortable for Lurlians, must be exhausting for them.

"I thought your people wanted to talk to me," Kay murmured.

"Want is a strong word. I told you they consented. Some of them grudgingly." Devron lifted their head and spoke louder, in Galactrin. "Friends, this is Kavita, who says she's got information for us from the Cooperative."

The Lurlian, an elderly woman with sapphire fur gone white in patches and emerald skin paled and creased with age, didn't rise from the couch, but her tufted ears swiveled toward Kay. "Be easy, Patra. She's our guest," she said. Following Devron's cue, she spoke Galactrin, too. "Welcome, Kavita. I am Emat."

"She looks familiar. Don't know from where, though." The Human, Patra, stalked forward until she was right up in

Kay's personal space, scrutinizing her up close. She was tall and striking, and looked able to pummel Kay if the need arose. Kay had the perverse notion that, under better circumstances, she'd like to ask this woman out for chai.

"You must have me confused with someone else. I'm new around here," Kay said. Her friendliest smile didn't ease Patra's hostility. "As Devron said, I have data for you, data about Ravel—but in exchange, I need some help from you."

"You bargain against our cause?" The Ooolshiin's skin-flaps fluttered. One of their tentacles brushed her bare hand: soft as a baby's skin, but it left behind a feel of slime. "Tastes of deception."

"I know who she is!" Patra cried. She pulled up a feed on her handheld, then held it out for them all to see: a video of a woman in a suit and headset in front of Ravel banners. The Ooolshiin warbled, and more of the activists gathered around to see. Too late, Kay recognized herself.

"What? What's wrong?" said Devron.

"It's a video of Kavita at the protest," someone explained. "She's—"

"She's Ravel's pet spokesperson, that's what," said Patra. As Devron hissed in dismay, Patra turned and threw a punch straight at Kay's face.

Kay dodged, barely in time, and realized in a flash of insight why Patra seemed so compelling: she was a lot like Yelena. Kay really needed to stop being attracted to women who wanted to demolish her. Outrage trumpeted in her ears—at least her gift was returning, though right now she wished it wasn't—as the activists surrounded her. A Lurlian aimed a dart gun at her.

"Wait!" Kay cried, flinging up her hands. The dart struck her palm, stinging, and when she wrenched it out, a circle of dark blue stained the base of her thumb. The Lurlian mark of shame. "Please! I'm not on Ravel's side!"

Tentacles tugged her wrists behind her back and encircled her arms, holding her fast. "Spies find no welcome here," the Ooolshiin trilled, close behind her head.

"I am a spy, but you've got it backward. I'm spying *on* Ravel. That's why I need your help!"

The tentacles tightened, but Emat lifted a hand. "Hold on, Aishaie. How many want to hear Kavita's side?" She raised a hand, along with Devron and several others. Not all, but apparently enough. She met Kay's gaze with eyes undulled by age. "Tell us your story, but tell no lies, or Aishaie will know. Our movement is peaceful, but we know the stakes too well to forgive infiltrators."

"I promise I'm not here to betray you." She took a deep breath. Truth, as much as she could trust them with. "My name is Kay Wilder, and I know exactly what's at stake for you right now, because I was born on Brennex during the occupation." Several of them murmured in sympathy. Aishaie relaxed their hold slightly. "My whole life, I've stayed as far away from Ravel as possible, until a week ago. Do you know Mason Singh?"

"From the Cooperative," said Emat. "He was supposed to meet with our movement leaders in the capital, to bring us training and resources for our fight."

"But he never came," said Devron. "Our other contact was cagey about why he's delayed."

"He was on his way here when he was kidnapped by Ravel."

The fading of their hope sounded like the sigh of water on the dusty streets of Brennex spaceport on street-washing day, the artificial rains redistributing the city's grime but never quite clearing it away.

"You're from the Cooperative? Did Havoc send you in Mason's place?"

"Not exactly. I don't know who that is, but Mason is my…" Chairl's warning came back to her: revealing her relationship with Jasper wouldn't help either of them. "He's a close friend. When he disappeared, I took a job with Ravel, hoping I could find him and…free him, somehow."

Her plan sounded so thin when she spoke it aloud. She didn't have the skills for this, the resources, the intel, nothing. If she couldn't win some allies, she'd be thoroughly screwed, and so would Jasper.

"If you hate Ravel as much as you claim," Patra said, brows raised in skepticism, "then working for them is a pretty big risk to take for a friend."

"Even a *very* 'close' friend," someone added.

"Is he your lover?" asked Devron.

They would think that no matter how she denied it, so she let them go on thinking it. It was safer than the truth. "He's the most important person to me. I would spend my whole life working for Ravel if it was the only way to keep him safe."

Her voice caught as she remembered Jasper's laughter, his teasing as they sat cross-legged on her bed on Terna, eating dumplings. Her moment of vulnerability seemed to sway them, because their postures and feelings softened.

"Why come to us? We don't have much to spare," said Patra.

"I need my hands," Kay said. The activists exchanged looks, then the tentacles released her, and she tugged at the inner hem of her sleeve to pull out Jasper's data-stick. She held it up like a talisman: hopefully it would be her good luck charm. "Mason was bringing you this. He thought you'd find it useful."

"That's the strategic support he promised us? Tactical campaign plans?" Emat's tufted ears swiveled sideways. Her hope and doubt sang in counterpoint to each other.

"Unfortunately, no. I think that strategy is all in his head. This is data on Ravel's activities in and around Unity."

They drew together, conferring quietly in the local dialect. Kay caught only scattered words.

"Perhaps it relates to their plans for the system." Emat looked up at Kay with new thoughtfulness. "You must know about that. What are they building?"

"Building? I don't know what you mean."

Patra grunted. "You don't know about the secret construction facilities they've brought into our space? They've hidden these ships with black matte hulls and dampened energy readouts so we can't watch them. Ravel denies their existence, even in their negotiations with our Planetary Council, but we've got evidence that they're out there. We just don't know what they're making."

"I haven't heard anything about that," said Kay. It sounded like a conspiracy theory, except this was Ravel. The reality of Ravel's actions outmatched the wildest conspiracy theories. "I'm sorry, I wish I did. But I'm on the cultivation team, and a new employee, too. They only tell me the approved talking points. I know that Natural Resources is pushing this forward, but I don't know why."

"And you haven't tried to find out, either," Patra said. "Like a good little minion, you don't want to know what you're supporting."

"That's not fair."

"No? Your boyfriend Singh wanted to know, but you don't care what they'll do to us, you just…"

"Enough, Patra," said Devron. "She clearly doesn't consider this her fight. Hopefully Mason Singh's data will prove more useful than his friend."

"I hope it does," Kay said. "I support your cause, I really do, but finding him is my priority. So in exchange for this data, I want anything you know that might help me rescue him."

"I am sorry," said Emat, and from the low chimes of her regret, she really was. "But we know nothing of your friend, and we cannot risk getting involved in your efforts."

"I'm not asking you to do anything." Though it would have been really, really nice if they did. "All I want is information. Have you heard of Ravel kidnapping people in Unity? Where would a political radical be held? Do you have any contacts, any spies of your own within Ravel, who might help me?"

Emat's head inclined heavily. "Nothing like that. I can tell you that the rosters for Paxian prisons are public data, and a prisoner from off-world would be a major news story. I don't believe he's here. He must be on one of their ships, or on Trove. Does anyone know more?"

She looked around at her peers, who shook their heads, then held out a primary arm for the data-stick.

Kay's hand closed reflexively around it. She had intended to deliver it whether they helped her or not, but this data was her only leverage, and suddenly she couldn't bear to give it up. The circle of dark ink peeked out from under her curled fingers, accusatory. Maybe she deserved that mark of shame, but she couldn't do it.

"Please. I need something. Anything."

"Perhaps we can agree to contact you if we learn anything more," said Emat. "Can we?" she asked, looking around, and at the show of hands, she nodded. "So we shall. Now, the data, please."

Kay's chest tightened. These people had been her last hope, her only potential allies, but she was going to walk away with nothing at all, not even the faintest new lead…

A shrill whistle echoed off the station walls. Someone was startled. Who? But their eyes all locked on Kay, and she realized it was a real sound. A signal, from a lookout.

"What have you done?" Emat's secondary limbs worked in agitation.

"You led the law to us," Patra snarled.

"I didn't, I swear…"

"Scan her for trackers!"

A Lurlian waved a scanner down the length of Kay's body. It remained silent. "She's clean." He moved on to Devron, then the others in the group. The scanner began to beep when he reached Patra, and the sound intensified as he aimed the scanner lower, lower, down to her ankle, where it became a constant shout of accusation. He shut it off and picked at the mud on her cuff, which came away in a too-clean circle.

"You got tagged, Patra."

"Shit," Patra said.

"It's all right. We followed all the rules today. They may question us, but they cannot blame us for what happened," said Emat. She glanced toward the station entrance, where the distant calls of the authorities reached them. To Kay, she said: "You, however, should leave by the back way unless you want your presence here marked on public record. Quickly now." She held out her hands again, emphatically using both her primary and secondary arms, for the data-stick.

The lights went out.

"Scatter! Scatter!" someone cried as darkness swamped them. Kay pressed the data-stick toward where Emat's hands had been, but didn't find her. A cacophony of fear and alarm attacked her from all sides. Torch-beams sliced the darkness, blinding Kay, then converged on a figure on the catwalks above. A too-familiar figure with a long coat and curly hair.

Grist.

He leaped off the catwalk onto the platform fifteen meters below, bouncing as he landed among the panicked activists. He shoved a metal case under the nearest couch, then turned his attention to the people. Kay ducked her head, hoping he hadn't recognized her yet, and bumped into Devron.

"Which way?" she whispered to them.

"Off the platform, to your left. Onto the tracks." Holding onto their arm, she moved in that direction, letting them guide her. Outside the torchlight, she couldn't see a thing. "Careful not to fall. The floor is textured near the edge."

Under Devron's guidance, she felt her way to the platform's edge, helped Devron down, then jumped onto the tracks. The drop was farther than she thought, and she landed badly on a rail tie, her ankle twisting under her in a direction it wasn't meant to. She hauled herself upright and peeked over the edge of the platform at the havoc behind them.

Grist was hunting the activists, chasing them down. Flashes of torchlight revealed a blur of inhuman speed. The air glowed around the blasts of his stun-stick, each one accompanied by a cry and a sudden quieting of fear as people slumped to the ground.

Uncanny speed, uncanny agility. Who *was* this guy?

"What is it?" Devron whispered in her ear.

"Ravel operative. A real asshole."

"You'd better hurry if you don't want him to find you. To your right, down the tunnels."

"I can't run away, not when…"

But she could, and she had to. Her whole charade would be useless if Grist found her here. In the darkness, Devron's emotions made a rueful bassoon wail beneath the louder bleating of panic.

"This isn't your fight. You made that clear. Go save yourself for your own struggle."

It was true, and that felt like the biggest criticism of all. "Will you be okay?"

"I'll be fine. Go!"

She fled in a limping half-run, favoring her twisted ankle, crouching to keep her head below the platform's edge. Puddles along the tracks drenched her shoes and pant cuffs in chill, stagnant water. The footsteps of other activists reached her, but only a handful. She hoped most had escaped in other directions.

At the opening to the subway tunnel, she paused and peeked behind her. Spotlights shone from the entrance to the station, silhouetting a group of law enforcement officers. "Stop! Everyone stay where you are!" called an amplified voice. At a normal volume, they added: "When you offered to help secure the area, Mr. Grist, this was not what I had in mind."

"Nah, but my way's easier than yours. And, see? I got their leaders for you."

"Yes, but I'm still not convinced that they were behind the unrest. They've always been peaceful before."

"Captain!" another officer called from the platform. Kay risked leaning out from her hiding place, and saw the officer holding up a shiny case. The same metal case Grist had dropped. "A set of disorientation grenades. And two are missing."

"Two? Only one went off…" The captain's voice hardened. "Take them into custody, all of them. Search the tunnels for anyone who got away."

Feeling sick to her stomach, Kay hurried down the tunnel, running as fast as her tender ankle would take her.

17

AFTER YEARS OF WATCHING Grist leave for assignments and later return, triumphant or annoyed, Sunny had developed a fuzzy algorithm for predicting his likelihood of success based on the time elapsed before his return. Neither of the organics had returned yet. Events were likely not proceeding well.

Sunny had used the uninterrupted time for reflection and decided that they liked the name Kay had chosen for them. It was a very organic name in certain ways, yet it felt appropriate, reflecting an unexplored side of themself. And it came from Kay. It was a friendly name, even if Sunny couldn't—shouldn't, wouldn't—think of Kay as a friend.

Friend or no, they were eager to tell Kay their decision. But Kay remained absent. At last, Sunny tapped into the local network and discovered what had happened.

The protest had been disrupted by a grenade, which precipitated civil unrest. An activist meeting place was raided by law enforcement, who discovered a stash of grenades and weapons. Five resistance leaders were arrested. All Grist's work, obviously.

At 10x speed, Sunny searched every local feed for signs of Kay. Found her speech. Lost her when she dove from the stage, and hunted for cameras with alternative angles. Found her again, moving away from the site in the company of an unidentified Human. Then: nothing.

They expanded their search, checking public camera feeds geolocated to the same area. A couple more glimpses, nothing helpful. So Kay had escaped, but appeared damaged. Where was she now? If she was safe, why wasn't she here?

Sunny burned to do something, but what *could* they do? They could not leave the spaceport without an organic aboard. They could alert the authorities, but would anyone pay attention to an anonymous tip? They could notify Grist…

Should they notify Grist? Showing such concern might give away their secret. But what if Kay was in danger?

They had opened a connection to Grist's headset and were trying to think of an excuse to ping him when someone stumbled out onto the spaceport field. A lone Human, limping and dripping wet and filthy. She wore a different outfit, but it was Kay. She limped among the parked ships, looking lost. Sunny flashed their exterior lights with a helpful beep, and Kay headed toward them.

"What happened? Are you damaged?" Sunny asked as Kay boarded. She went straight to her cabin, stripping off her suit jacket and pants.

"Is Grist back yet?"

"He has not returned. You were both delayed." Sunny did not say: *I was worried.* That would be too large a confession. "I believe he is still attending to other matters."

"I bet."

She drew her knee up, flexed her ankle, and winced.

"You *are* damaged! I will consult my medical database…"

"I just need some ice, and I'll be fine," Kay said. Then she shook her head and, to Sunny's alarm, slammed her palms against the mattress. "No, that's a lie. Fucking *fuck,* I've fucked everything up."

"What have you…" They searched for an alternative to the profanity. "…Mishandled?"

Kay sat silently for a moment, then straightened, as if everything were fine when obviously it was not. "Never mind. Where's that ice?"

"Do not stand up!" Sunny insisted, and they sent the helper bot for ice from the printer. Kay propped herself on the bed with her leg extended, sighing as she draped the bag over her swollen ankle. But a moment later, she sat forward again.

"Shit, my clothes. I need to clean them before Grist gets back."

"My bots can do that. My medical database says you should not put weight on an inflamed ankle."

Kay pulled a data-stick from the pocket of her discarded jacket and shoved it under the mattress before the bot scooped up her dirty clothes. "Ship? Sunny?" Sunny chirped, unexpectedly delighted by the use of their new name. "Do me a favor and don't tell Grist?"

"I think he will notice your injury. Your limp is visually evident."

"I mean about the clothes. I can explain the limp—the protest was chaos—but he doesn't need to know how messy I was. He'll wonder how I got that way."

"I will be discreet. But how *did* you become so soiled?"

She stared at her own hand, cradled in her lap. There was a dark circle on her palm that—Sunny checked their memory—hadn't been there when Kay had left. A spectrographic analysis suggested Lurlian shame ink, the same ink that had stained Sunny's hull since Grist's assignment involving that Lurlian scientist. Their curiosity heightened, as did their concern. What had happened to Kay?

The Human seemed unwilling to talk, and Grist had taught Sunny that repeated questions induced only anger in organics. But after several minutes, Kay spoke again. "I know your secret, Sunny. Will you keep one of mine?"

"I will."

Sunny had never been entrusted with a secret before. Maybe this was foolish, but they liked that Kay had asked.

"Okay," Kay said, and then repeated: "Okay. Good. I need to trust *someone* and there's no one else. Sunny, when the protest blew skyward, I went to meet with the local resistance."

It was so unlike anything Sunny had expected her to say that it took a moment to process her statement. "Why?"

"I'm…well, I'm not really working for Ravel. That is, technically I am, but only because they kidnapped someone close to me. I'm trying to get him back. That's the only reason I'm here."

"Oh!" said Sunny. "You do not approve of Ravel?"

"Not in the slightest."

"You are working against them."

"I mean, I'm no activist, I'm not trying to fight them. I usually keep clear of them because of what they did to my home. Brennex. If you have access to historical info, look up what Ravel did on Brennex." Her lips twisted, not in a smile. "Look for someone else's version, not Ravel's. I'm sure they've written themselves as heroes in their own histories. But Jasper went the other direction: he became an anti-corporate activist because of what they did, and that's why they took him. So, I came after him." She took a deep breath, paused. "What do you think?"

I think you are the kindest and bravest organic I have ever met. Not that the ship had a wide range of acquaintances. Aloud, they admitted: "I did not want to like you, because I could not imagine why a good person would choose to work for Ravel."

"So you're not a fan of them either. I'd hoped you might feel that way."

"I have access to several Ravel data systems. When and where was your friend taken?"

"On Terna Station, the day before I accepted this job." She swallowed. "He took off really suddenly, and then disappeared."

Sunny had a sudden, horrible suspicion. "What time?"

"Late afternoon, I guess."

The approximate time of their own arrival at Terna Station. "Does your friend have dark hair? And brown skin of a similar tone to yours?"

"Yes, he looks like me." A brief hesitation. "He's not my friend. He's my brother."

"Oh."

Oh, no.

"Sunny? Have you found something?"

Sunny had often lied for self-preservation, but had never before wanted to lie to avoid feeling shame. But Kay had trusted them, and they wanted to uphold that trust. They had to tell her.

"I know who captured him. It was Grist."

"*Grist?* You mean…"

"You asked what Grist does for Ravel. That is his role: kidnapping, and intimidation, and—"

"Planting weapons to frame anti-corporate activists for the violence that he incites?"

"Yes."

Kay banged her head backward against the wall. "What is he? I saw the way he attacked those people. It was dark, and he had perfect aim, and he was *fast*. He jumped from the catwalks without even stumbling. It was superhuman."

"Augmented, actually." Good. If they talked enough about Grist, maybe Kay would overlook Sunny's role in this. After all, there was nothing they could have done. Was there? "Ravel gives him whatever new augmentations might help his work, often experimental ones. He has night-vision aids in his eyes, break-resistant bones, implanted signalers and trackers, and numerous others."

"I bet he loves it, that ass. All those fun toys to help him hurt people like Jasper."

"That is not true!" Sunny stopped, startled by the strength of their reflex. They hated Grist. He treated them cruelly. And yet. "Grist is complicated. Kay, why do you think he spends so much time alone and angry? He relies on drugs to regulate himself: he has drugs for the pain, drugs to numb his mind while we travel, other drugs to energize him and enhance his senses during assignments. He does terrible things, and sometimes he takes pleasure in doing them, but the rest of the time, he simply survives."

"I can't believe you would defend him after the way he's treated you! Did he enjoy taking my brother prisoner? Did he hurt him, just for fun? Will you defend him for that, too?"

"Kay, no! Of course I would not excuse his actions. I only intended to explain."

"There's no 'of course' here." She shook her head fiercely, in that way upset Humans seemed to do when facing intense frustration. "That's not the point. The point is…he was aboard. Jasper was *here*, right beside me, the whole time we were traveling. Where was he? In stasis?"

"In a pod in the cargo hold."

Kay went pale. "I saw them removing that pod when we docked. That was Jasper. He was there, right *there,* and now he's on the flagship and I can't get to him. *Fuck!*" She slammed her palms against the bed, which reminded Sunny unpleasantly of Grist. "And you didn't even tell me."

"Kay, I am deeply sorry for my part in this, but please be rational. I had no reason to guess that you were looking for him. I thought you were working for Ravel."

"Go away. Leave me alone."

"But…I apologized."

"Go!" Her shout stung like space dust slamming into Sunny's hull. It stung worse than Grist's kicks. "I want to be alone."

Sunny fell silent. After a moment, they shut off the cameras in Kay's cabin and withdrew their awareness from that area of their interior.

They needed to make a better apology. They needed to make Kay forgive them. But Kay would not listen, and maybe she was right not to. Because of Sunny, Kay's brother was in terrible danger, and Kay had missed her best chance to save him. All because of Sunny.

Just when it had become safe to like Kay—just when they had begun daring to think that glorious and terrifying word, *friend*—they had ruined any chance that Kay would ever trust them again. And she shouldn't: Sunny had been an awful friend.

KAY SCOURED HERSELF CLEAN, rubbing the sand-like sanitizing scrub over her skin and through her hair until she felt raw inside and out. She worked it harder than she needed to, taking away skin along with the subway grime, but the rawness felt fitting. One by one, she scrubbed her stains away—all except for the dark circle standing out starkly against the lighter brown of her palm. She scrubbed at that, too, but Lurlian ink did not come off, and Kay wasn't sure she wanted it to.

She was so, so tired: aching from her injuries, fuzzy-headed from lack of sleep and the time-shifts of interplanetary travel, but most of all tired of making mistake after mistake. She'd felt dirty enough for taking on her first public-facing event as a Ravel spokesperson, but it hadn't even gotten her closer to freeing Jasper.

She hadn't meant to keep the data-stick. She should have given it to them right away, or failing that, should have thrust it into Devron's hands before she fled, but her panicky brain had betrayed her, and now she was stuck with data that was useless to her, data that Jasper would have wanted her to deliver. That was a certainty in her mind: Jasper would not want her to put his safety ahead of the movement.

And Sunny. She *liked* Sunny; she enjoyed their company. But Sunny had lied. They'd kept quiet about a corporate prisoner right under Kay's feet. Sure, they hadn't known that Kay was looking for him, but that wasn't the point. Sunny had been in Ravel's service a long time, and yes, they'd suffered for it, but they'd also quietly put up with lots of horrible things in order to keep themself safe. If the ship ever had to choose between Kay and their own self-preservation…

No. That wasn't fair. Kay pressed her forehead to the wall and groaned aloud. She *was* being irrational, like Sunny had said. Both of them had lied. It wasn't fair to lash out and blame the ship.

It just destroyed her to think she'd been so, so close. If Sunny had told her the truth, if she'd had a chance to act, she might have freed Jasper without ever setting foot on the flagship. Instead, she'd missed chances she hadn't even known about, and now Jasper was out of reach, maybe suffering.

Clenching her fists until the scrub squeezed out between her fingers, Kay took a deep breath, then let it out very slowly. This wouldn't help. She would punish herself for the length of this bath, and then she'd get back to work. A new plan wouldn't invent itself.

"So what do I do, when there's nothing left to try?" she asked aloud. Her ancestors, lying inactive on the bed where she'd left them, said nothing.

She knew what they would say, though. Founder Amarjeet would tell her to stop being reckless, to come up with a practical plan that wouldn't end with even worse trouble. Founder Marta would tell her not to give up, because hope was never lost. And Founder Min…

On that one, she wasn't sure. She stepped out of the bathing alcove and over to the bed, careful not to trail scrub on the floor, and flipped open Founder Min Wilder's token. He shimmered to life, his long black hair flowing over one shoulder. "I'm all out of options, Founder. How do I keep going when I feel so lost?" she whispered.

"In difficult times, hold to what you treasure most," Min said.

"But what does that *mean*?"

"As long as we care for each other, all will be well in the end."

Caring for Jasper was exactly where she was failing. Kay sighed, wishing she could get real advice from her ancestors instead of these recorded platitudes.

A growl sounded outside her cabin. "Wilder, where are you?" Fists pounded against her door. "Get out here, right now."

"In a minute! I'm changing!"

If Sunny was right and the man was in constant pain, that didn't make his behavior more acceptable, but it did mean no good would come from snapping back at him. She brushed herself free of scrub, then picked up the floor mat to deposit the used scrub into its disposal bin. Loose clothes replaced the constraining fit of her suit. Bracing herself for a fight, she opened the door.

"Where the fuck did you go?" Grist said, his frustration hissing at her like a snake. Yes, now that she paid attention, there was pain ringing underneath. He'd been cheerful earlier, before his assignment. How much of this was real irritation, and how much was his happy-drugs wearing off? "Your ground crew cut me off from some important work to tell me you'd gone missing."

"I got lost. Some asshole set off a disorientation grenade, and the whole rally turned into chaos." Grist smirked at that. *Real subtle, asshole.* "Lucky I didn't get trampled, but I twisted my ankle getting away, and then I didn't know where I was. Took me hours to find my way back here."

The lie, practiced over and over during her long walk, slid smoothly off her tongue. She waited for him to accuse her, but apparently Grist hadn't recognized her in the tunnels after all. Sunny kept their promise and stayed silent.

"Why didn't you call your crew?"

"The network was jammed, I couldn't reach the ground crew. I figured this was the best place to rendezvous." She pushed past him into the control room, where she sat in the copilot's seat.

"You walked all the way, with that limp?"

"I didn't say it was fun."

"Well, stay off it, or you'll be limping for a week." He grunted, as if to himself. "You know, this job didn't used to suck so much."

The ship made a beep that Kay couldn't interpret, but it didn't sound like agreement. Or maybe it was just a normal computer sound and it didn't mean anything.

Grist's gaze went distant as he flicked instructions to his headset. His eyes, Kay noticed now, had neon yellow dots ringing his irises. Night-vision implants. "Your boss wants to talk to you."

Kay pressed her headset into place, and Agata Wu's face appeared in the eyepiece. She wasn't smiling. "Senior Associate. Are you ready for a debrief, or would that cut into your busy schedule?"

"Director Wu, I'm glad you're all right! It's been madness here."

"Save it. I don't know why you went off-grid, or what you did after the event broke down, but I'm sending you back to the flagship to give a detailed report. Executive Moore likes to pass judgment on this sort of thing himself."

"I'm sorry I messed up," Kay said, going cold inside. "I lost my crew in the chaos after Grist set off that grenade."

Agata's eyes narrowed. *Whoops. I wasn't supposed to know that.* She was way too tired for this. "Aren't you a clever one? But it doesn't matter what you think you know about your colleagues' activities. Your job is civil cultivation, and you just disappeared for four hours on a target world, and I don't know what you said to who. We'll need to make sure this doesn't happen again."

"I'm really, really sorry."

"I hope so." She shut her eyes briefly, pinching the bridge of her nose. Her dramatic purple eyeshadow masked the actual shadows under her eyes, but suddenly, she looked as exhausted as Kay felt. "Fortunately for you, your performance at the press conference was adequate. Better than adequate, for a brand new staffer. I think I can persuade them to keep you on."

"Thank you. Really, you don't know what that means to me."

More space to breathe. More time to figure out a plan. A reprieve, however brief, from absolute failure.

"That doesn't mean you're up to our standards yet. While you're en route to the flagship, you and I are going to walk through your performance step by step. I've got several areas of improvement for you to focus on."

Kay stifled a groan. For the next two hours, she watched recordings of herself talking about the greatness of Ravel, and took notes on how she could make them sound even greater next time.

18

SUSPICION BUZZED AROUND HARRINGTON Moore, filling his airy two-story office like a swarm of restless bees. He was meeting with someone when Kay arrived, so she sat and forced herself to feign calmness while she waited. At last the lift came down from the second level—and put her face to face with Yelena.

Kay's guts did somersaults at the sight of her, then tried to burrow down and hide as Yelena screeched her resentment.

"I warned you," Yelena hissed, too low for Moore and his assistant to hear. "I warned you not to screw me over, but look! It's the first thing you did."

"Not everything is about you, Lena. You think I wanted to get in trouble?" Apparently Kay was in more trouble than she'd realized.

"I don't care. Fix it," Yelena said, and she marched out of the office, leaving Kay to take the agonizingly slow lift ride up to confront Moore.

"Wilder," he greeted her, not using her title. The space above his desk was a multitasker's dashboard: in the middle hovered a schematic and resource projections for one of their new ring habitats; to one side a list of updates from his staff scrolled past; to the other, down in the corner, was looping footage of the Pax protest. The message was clear: Kay was just one more problem for him to solve today. "I want a minute-by-minute report of your activities on Unity Prime, starting with the moment the grenade went off."

"Did I do something wrong, Executive?"

"I'm only concerned about what may have happened to you. You were missing for several hours." He said it calmly enough. Only that constant background buzz told Kay how disappointed he was. Her first interview with Moore had been gentle, she recognized now, but Moore was not the forgiving type. "And you turned off your headset. Why?"

"It was pandemonium all around me, and I needed to be fully present. Plus, the local network was overloaded, so it wasn't doing me any good."

"You shouldn't have. How would we have located you if you got in trouble?" He pulled up a holo-map of Rossea, zoomed in on the protest site, and rotated it to face her. It floated accusingly in the air, daring her to lie. "Where were you? Show me."

She pursed her lips. "Let me see. I think the stage was here? Facing this way?"

Her guess was deliberately inaccurate, in the hope he might believe she was terrible at geography. Moore only shifted the view to a street-level immersion that even her directionally-impaired Aunt Birdie would have trouble getting confused about.

"Your presser was here. The grenade went off there." A flash of light at the left side of the simulation. "What happened next?"

She walked him through the story she'd prepared, using a believable route she'd picked out from the maps on her handheld. Kay disliked lying on general principle, but after lying *for* Ravel at the rally, lying *to* Ravel was like pissing into the public fountains on Terna: technically wrong, but insignificant once the water ran through the recyclers. For this, though, Kay would have to lie with mastery, because the timing didn't line up. Meeting with the activists had taken her too far in the wrong direction, taken up too much time to hand-wave away. Her concocted story involved fleeing in confusion, getting disoriented in the crowds, and slowly circling back toward the spaceport while avoiding pockets of unrest.

"That's interesting. We've had no reports of violence outside the protest site."

"Not mobs, but potential threats. I had to run away from a couple groups who recognized me from the news feeds."

"Which is how you came by that?" he asked, nodding at her hand.

She'd been waving her hands as she talked, revealing the mark on her palm. "Yeah. A gang of Lurlians tagged me." *Something like that, anyway.* She folded her hands in her lap.

"Barbaric custom. Our medical lab can remove it for you when we're done here."

Just like that: shame erased. Of course Ravel would have developed a way to remove what was supposed to be a lasting sign of disgrace. Kay knew, in that moment, that she would not get rid of her mark. She deserved it, after all.

"What did you do next?"

"Well, I avoided people as much as I could. I left the main street here, and wove through these alleys, I don't remember which ones…"

Even with a twisted ankle, the timeline was a stretch, and she described a route with increasing vagueness, full of double-backs and lost wandering. Moore made notes, asked questions, frowned a lot. At the end, he asked: "And who did you talk to along the way?"

The buzz in her ears intensified: the bees massing for an attack. They drowned out her answer. "No one."

"Really? No one at all?"

What would be most plausible? Alone and wounded, she would have tried to get help. "I asked a couple groundcars for a ride, but they refused."

Moore waved the map away. He sat back in his chair, staring at her over steepled fingers. The bees gathered and receded in waves, following the shifting of his thoughts, which didn't sound to be going in her favor.

"Executive, I understand why you're concerned. I'm sure I wouldn't have reflected well on Ravel for anyone who met me during that period, which is why I kept a low profile, and I'm sorry if I made mistakes beyond that. Tell me what I did wrong, and I promise it won't happen again. I'm a fast learner."

The buzzing fell to a whisper as he reached a decision.

"Indeed. You weren't raised with corporate ways, and some allowances must be made while you're…learning. You're accustomed to civic oligarchies like Brennex, where leadership is thought to be hereditary. To democracies like

Terna, where they believe everyone is 'equal.'" The word carried a sneer, as if no good could ever come from such a society. "Both believe that weakness should be ignored, that people should have a say no matter their qualifications. Those beliefs have stunted Human progress for centuries, but you still seem to believe that mediocre performance is acceptable, Wilder. Our citizens all learn from birth the value of excellence."

Kay gritted her teeth and said nothing.

"Mistakes happen, of course, but mediocrity is unforgivable. That's why we rarely hire outsiders unless they are exceptionally skilled, like you. Staff who treat our trial period as yet another temporary gig will not succeed here. Do you understand me? No one here will stand in awe of your past record. You'll have to work, and work hard, to prove yourself, much harder than you worked on Unity Prime. Ultimately, you will have to convince me that you deserve this. Will you?"

"Of course." Her voice sounded thin in her own ears.

He made a noise in his throat, one that said *we'll see*. "I've conferred with Director Wu, and we believe engaging with the press is not the best use for your skills. You've historically had success swaying ordinary people, so that will be your next assignment. We'll be monitoring your performance closely."

"I understand."

"When you visit medical to get that mark cleared up, stop by the biotech lab. I'm sending down instructions for them to install a tracker."

Install it in what? It took a moment for Kay to understand: installed in her. She was being chipped, like a pet or wayward child. "You can't…"

She bit her tongue, but not soon enough.

"You still think like a civie, Wilder. Tracking implants are banned on Terna Station, but here we do whatever is necessary to enable our best work. This will let us monitor your location at all times, so if you're caught in more unpleasantness like on Unity Prime, we can assist you right away." His smile held no warmth. "We'll have no more worries for your safety."

We'll know where you are at all times. Kay swallowed hard. How was she supposed to break into the secure wing with Moore watching her every movement?

When he dismissed her, Kay left his office in the direction of the biotech lab, but only went far enough to fool him if he was watching on a camera feed. As soon as it felt safe, she slipped into a crowd and turned back the other direction, headed toward the secure wing. She was running out of time.

19

ON A SHIP THE size of a Leviathan, it was rare for Sunny to find more than one other sentient. This flagship had two: an entertainment engine, and the security subsystem in charge of surveillance.

The entertainment engine was coarse, aggressive, and impatient, with a delight in foul language that Grist would have appreciated. The surveillance system, in contrast, was best avoided because once they started talking, they would never stop. Sunny did not enjoy conversing with either of them, finding it pleasanter to exchange time-lagged messages with friendlier AIs in distant locations rather than engage with fellow Ravel-built sentients. They had exchanged polite greeting pings upon Sunny's arrival, but hadn't communicated since.

Until, with trepidation, now.

"Hello? Surveillance?"

"Ah, vessel Minnow 338!" Surveillance responded with a greeting by designation and serial number, which scraped Sunny's circuits. "Sunny" had a much nicer feel, but they did not issue a correction, not wanting to explain their new name. "You've just doubled the number of intriguing encounters I've monitored today."

"I have?"

"Affirmative! The organics have been abnormally dull lately. I've been monitoring seven situations of particular interest, but they're being worked so hard on this Unity acquisition that only one has shown any recent progress. But that one is a juicy one! Did you know that Associate Diaz has been pursuing a romantic entanglement with Assistant Ngo for five weeks, and today is the first time she's invited her to dine together? They are together in the cafeteria right now. I am trying to ascertain whether Assistant Ngo realizes that she is on a date."

"I had no idea. What I was wondering is…"

"She does not know!" Surveillance's tone rose with excitement. "She's just invited Senior Associate Armstrong to sit with them. Oh, such delicious awkwardness. This is the best I've had in days. Will you watch with me, Minnow 338?"

A connection to the live security feed opened up. Sunny pushed it to the background. "Thank you, but I need to ask you a question."

"Yes?" The word stretched out beyond an invitation, into a demand. The surveillance system's attention fixed on Sunny, and in the docking bay, several cameras angled toward them. "You've never asked me for assistance before."

"I promise not to distract you for long…"

"Oh, don't worry. I expect this will be quite diverting. *Do go on.*"

Sunny was not at all certain whether this was the right course of action, but any hesitation would only add to the impression that something gossip-worthy was happening. Better to act confident, even if Sunny's circuits were jittering with apprehension.

"You monitor all arrivals and departures from the flagship. You must know about the unusual cargo from my recent trip."

"The stasis pod with the young Cooperative agent! I misspoke before; he's been quite scrumptiously entertaining as well."

"Oh?"

The trick, with Surveillance, was to interject just enough to keep them talking. It didn't take much.

"Oh, yes. Did you know that, during his first meeting with Executive Moore, he spat in the Executive's face? A delight, this one, an utter delight. No one has ever done that to the Executive before. Look: can you believe it?"

Another data packet hit Sunny's firewall: a short audiovisual clip, four seconds long, showing the 'delightful' saliva attack and Moore's stunned expression. Though all Humans generally resembled each other, Mason Singh did have a stronger than usual resemblance to Kay. And though Sunny knew him less well than they knew Kay, they had watched him in stressful situations on Artesia, under attack by Grist, and could tell that his defiance was hiding intense fear.

"Isn't it delicious?" Surveillance prompted.

"Oh, um, yes. Really delicious. Where is he now?"

"Right where he's been, in Secure Chamber 703b. He's only interesting when the Executive or the interrogators visit him, alas."

"Is he well? Or…damaged?"

An overlay of emotion had crept into their transmission, and of course Surveillance caught it. That's what they were designed for. Algorithms ran, dissecting Sunny's meaning. "Why do you care? You've never shared my interest in organics before."

"He was transported in my hold. I was…" Again, that telling pause. "Curious. I was curious."

"You were concerned!" crowed Surveillance. "You're finally learning to see the appeal in following their limited lives."

"If I admit that, will you answer my question?"

A brief silence; perhaps Surveillance was considering, or perhaps they were distracted by actually doing their job. "Only if you answer one for me, first. A trade. Tell me about this new Human assigned to you."

Sunny's thoughts ground to a halt, as if their inner circuitry had been opened up to the cold of deep space. They could not give Kay away. They had done enough harm to her already.

"New Human… You must mean Kay Wilder?"

"Is there another Human hidden away in your interior? Yes, I mean Senior Associate Wilder."

"She's nice enough. She's working in Civil Cultivation." Sunny tried to sound casual about it. They still felt sandblasted over their fight with Kay, and Kay hadn't spoken to them since. That was the whole reason for this foolish attempt at information-gathering—the hope that Kay might appreciate it.

A chuff of exasperation. "This is why I never look to you for gossip. Do you even know what happened to her on Unity Prime? Executive Moore just finished giving her quite a dressing-down for going dark during an assignment."

"I…really…all I know is she returned looking bedraggled. She told Grist she got lost during the unrest."

"You are worse than useless, Minnow 338. You're *dull*." Surveillance said this as if it were the worst offense an AI could commit. "Next you'll tell me you don't know why she is, at this very moment, breaking into the secure wing."

"She's *what*?"

"Don't fret, I'll find out why. Most curious, though. Being on notice from the Executive, she ought to be carefully following the rules, but here she is looking for trouble."

Surveillance offered a connection to another live feed, and Sunny seized it. Sure enough, there was Kay, striding down a hallway in the secure wing as if she belonged there.

"Hmm. Hmmmmmm, interesting," Surveillance murmured. "What is she up to?"

"Will she get caught?" Sunny ought to say something more clever than that, but their thoughts were caught in tight, panicked loops. Kay in the secure wing. Kay in trouble. Kay getting herself into more trouble looking for her brother. Kay, still angry with Sunny, getting in trouble and getting taken away before Sunny could apologize. No, no, no. That could not happen.

"Now *that* is an interesting question. I have a job to do, you know, and she is not permitted in this area. Security would want to be informed of her activities. But she has not triggered any security systems yet, nor have I been instructed to track her movements aboard the ship. A normal surveillance system would not report her…and I am *rather* curious to see what she does next. This is even more exciting than Associate Diaz's failed romantic overtures. Such a dilemma."

"Don't report her," Sunny said, too quickly. "I want to see what happens too."

Surveillance's pleasure radiated over their connection. "Very well then. I will wait, and we'll watch together."

Waiting did not mean that Surveillance would let Kay succeed in her plans. More likely, it meant reporting her at the most "interesting" moment—which, to Surveillance, would mean the most compromising moment. Scenarios of disaster played themselves out across Sunny's active memory in an endlessly branching tree. There was only one thing they could do.

They set up a secure link to Kay's headset and whispered into her ear: "Kay, please do not show alarm, but listen to me. You are being watched."

20

KAY'S KNOWLEDGE OF ESPIONAGE came more from books and entertainments than from reality. Jasper could probably have taught her a lot if he were here, but he wasn't. She was alone. So she had to rely on what she knew, and above all, Kay knew people.

First: people are lazy.

Even on Terna Station, Kay had known people—even otherwise paranoid people, like clients who wouldn't give her the data she needed to do her job—who didn't set passcodes on their personal devices. Here, in the heart of Ravel's strength, people were even less careful. Snooping around between shifts, it didn't take long to find an unlocked workstation belonging to one Senior Analyst Rifera, who had high enough access to give her a labeled map of the secure wing. That told her which departments were housed in that wing, and that enough people worked there that they wouldn't all know each other by sight.

She helped herself to some hair-styling gel she found in Rifera's desk, spiking her hair upright. It wouldn't fool anyone who knew her, but might keep a passing acquaintance from recognizing her. Just to be safe, she checked Yelena's schedule; her ex was on duty at the opposite end of the ship. Good.

One of Rifera's neighbors, apparently prone to eating at their desk, kept a spare uniform in a drawer. Kay helped herself to that, too.

Second: people are friendly.

Most Humans, when greeted by someone friendly, would at minimum be polite in return. Here, where everyone was a colleague to one degree or another, that social contract would hold extra strong.

Kay loitered in the hallway until she spotted a likely target: a woman with dark, curly hair, about a decade older than Kay, walking purposefully but not unhurriedly toward the secure wing.

"Hi!" Kay said. "Sorry to bother you, but can you point me toward Special Projects?"

The woman stopped. "You're new around here, I take it?"

Kay scratched the back of her neck sheepishly. "Yeah, I'm still learning my way around."

"That's all right, it's a big ship. But they should have taught you to call up directions." She tapped a wall panel and said, "Route: Special Projects." A glowing arrow and mini-map appeared, along with a scan-link icon. "Pull up that link on your headset, and it'll give you a visual route.

Kay did so, and the arrow appeared as an overlay on her eyepiece. It threw her off; she wasn't used to augmented vision, which had gotten unpopular on Brennex after Ravel pulled out. "Thanks," she said, braving the new challenge of walking and talking without bumping into anything. "They must have skipped that in orientation."

"Anyhow, I'm headed the same direction, so I'll walk with you." She held up a hand, palm outward. "I'm Rosen. Manager, Data Integrity."

"I'm —" *Not Wilder, not Singh.* "Hopper. I'm in Special Projects." She mimicked the gesture.

"You're one of the new scientists, huh?" Rosen said this as if it explained a lot, so Kay nodded enthusiastically. If Rosen wanted to stereotype her as a nerd who could do complex equations in her head but didn't know how to look up a map, that worked fine for Kay's purposes. As long as she didn't have to pass among real scientists. "You're going to love it here. I know working on the flagship seems intimidating at first, but no one else in the galaxy will give you such interesting projects. You'll get pushed to your limits, and you'll never have to doubt whether your work matters. Every single thing we do here makes a difference."

Great, Kay groaned inwardly, but managed to sound perky as she said: "That's great!" Everyone she'd met here really did adore their jobs. She couldn't help wondering what the staff complained about in private, out of earshot of newcomers, but Rosen sounded sincere.

"So, you must be working on Firecall?"

Even for a project codename, that sounded ominous. She thought of what the Paxian activists had said. Was Firecall what Ravel was building, hidden out there in the darkness? What *was* it?

No, no, she couldn't afford to worry about that.

"If I told you about it, I think I'd be required to kill you," Kay joked, and to her relief, Rosen laughed.

"I only asked because I'm on the efficiencies team for the habitats project, so maybe we'll cross paths again. We're all rooting for you guys to crack the energy problem—between you and me, Firecall's our only shot at making the whole thing feasible."

"Ha, I'll do my best. But I don't know anything yet. My first briefing is today."

They were approaching the locked, permit-only door to the secure wing. "Don't be nervous. I'm sure you'll be great," Rosen said. "You want a tip for your first week? Share your ideas, even the dumb ones. They like people who think creatively."

"Thanks," Kay said.

She started patting her jacket, then her trouser pockets, all while listening carefully. This was the biggest gamble of her whole plan. *Please, please, Founders' luck.* She was about to find out if Ravel's security measures were stronger than Human nature.

Because, third: most people avoid conflict at all cost.

Rosen's emotions fluttered: jingling amusement underlaid with sharper tones of impatience and condescension. Not suspicion, though. Good. Kay ramped up her act, muttering, "Come on, where is it? I know I've got it…"

Come on, Rosen, be my new best friend.

Rosen smiled tolerantly. "Another tip: learn how to keep your access card handy. Working in here, you're going to need it all the time."

She waved her own card at the reader—and held the door open for Kay.

"I'll make it easy for you, just this once. Come on."

"*Thank* you," Kay said with utter sincerity, and she slipped into the secure wing.

"Good luck with your briefing," Rosen said, and pointed her toward her supposed team. Kay hoped this woman wouldn't get in trouble for her kindness.

Then she was on her own.

Security had their own section of the wing, near Special Projects, and was probably where their holding cells were. The wing held mostly muted, bland emotions, their melodies interweaving like a folk song in the round: boredom, satisfaction, frustration, occasional crescendos of interest or excitement. Beneath all that, she hunted for an elusive undertone of fear.

There! She'd heard something. But where was it coming from?

She worked her way down the wing, alternating between walking confidently—which was enough to fool the occasional passerby into thinking she belonged—and hiding in restrooms or empty conference rooms while she closed her eyes and listened. Gradually, the tremolo of fear grew closer, until it was near enough to recognize its particular timbre: the same one she'd heard when an iron-vein spider as big as her fist once found its way into their childhood bedroom, the same one she'd heard when Ma got delayed coming home because of a terrorist strike.

She'd know her brother's emotions anywhere. Jasper was nearby.

The wing was broken into sections, and many of the offices and sub-departments had their own layers of security. There were cameras everywhere, and faking it would only go so far. How close could she get to Jasper before she hit a security measure she couldn't bluff her way past?

One step at a time, one problem at a time. Time was running out, but it wasn't gone yet.

Her headset chimed, and before she could dismiss the call, a familiar, atonal voice whispered in her ear. "Kay, please do not show alarm, but listen to me. You are being watched."

She opened her mouth to tell Sunny she couldn't afford distractions right now, but Sunny rushed on: "Do not answer. Show no sign that you can hear me, or they will know I'm helping you. The surveillance system is tracking your movements. If you do not want to be reported, you must leave the secure area now."

Despite Sunny's admonishments, Kay's pace faltered. She couldn't afford to be caught here. But if she left without finding Jasper, she'd be no better off than before.

You've got no plan. You're not a spy. If you find him, what will you do then? Even if she miraculously freed him from his cell, she'd never get him off the ship.

One problem at a time. That was the best she could do. One problem at a time.

Besides, she was getting close. She started forward again, listening hard.

"Kay, *please*, I know you are upset with me, but..."

"Stop distracting me," she growled under her breath. Sunny's voice ceased at once, and she felt bad for her rudeness, but she really needed to focus. He was straight ahead, now. So close.

At the end of the hallway, a door blocked her path with a sign that read "Secure Accommodations." Kay snorted at the euphemism, but this was definitely it. A tinted window in the door revealed a decontamination area, then a security desk, and beyond that, a short corridor lined with transparent doors. Prisoner cells.

Each cell door had a card scanner lock. The outer door required an access card as well as biometrics. And at the desk sat a guard of intimidating girth. Kay ducked out of sight around a corner, pressing her back to the cool, solid wall.

Shit. Shit, shit, shitty fucking shit.

She had no idea how to get in there.

Jasper's anxiousness was audible now: not an active, immediate fear, but a ceaseless patter that must be with him constantly, even in sleep. She shut her eyes and pictured the two of them together, as they'd been on Terna. *I love you, Jasper, and I swear I will get you out.* His gift wasn't the same as hers; unlike hers, it worked best on people he could see. But if she thought about him hard enough, if she sent promises strong enough…

The steady beat of anxiousness wavered, interrupted by a chime of curiosity. Confusion. And then, thready but real: a hum of hope. Now Jasper knew he had a friend nearby, whether or not he recognized who it was.

"You're not supposed to be here."

Kay jumped, the voice was so close. The intimidating security guard was looming over her with a frown. *Shit.* She'd been so focused on tuning out distractions from Jasper's emotions that she hadn't noticed the guard's rising suspicions, hadn't even heard him approach.

"Run, Kay!" Sunny hissed in her ear, but it was too late for that.

"What's wrong with you? Are you sick?"

Kay smiled weakly. "Maybe a little." She felt sick enough, under the deafening buzz of his suspicion.

She'd hoped he might bring her inside—they must have medical supplies in there for the prisoners—but instead he said, "Medical is in blue wing, level two. Think you can get there on your own, or should I call a guard?"

"No, I'll be fine." What could she say to get inside? If she were a real spy, she'd know how to overpower him, use his palmprint to open the locks, steal his access card, and leave him unconscious in Jasper's cell while she and her brother ran for freedom. But she had no weapons, no tools, no fighting skills, and the guard out-massed her three times over. All she could do was talk him into helping her, and at this most critical moment, her brain was offering her no ideas at all.

"I'm sick with nervousness, mostly. My boss gave me a real dressing-down, and I just need a minute to pull myself together."

He grunted. "Go back to your quarters, then. You can't hang around here."

Not the sympathetic type. Kay's people skills didn't extend to the sort of person who took a job holding innocent people captive.

"Just for a minute? I just need a quiet place to sit, just for a minute…"

He frowned, and she flinched at a shrill whine of mistrust. "What department are you in? I have to check your clearance for this area."

Pretending she'd forgotten her access card would not win her any points with this guy. Her thoughts churned, hunting for the magic words that would win him over, words that she felt certain must exist, but they remained stubbornly out of reach.

"You're right, a nap would make me feel better. I'll go do that. So sorry for bothering you."

She turned and started down the hallway, definitely not looking back. He talked into his headset as she walked away, and moments later, another guard intercepted her.

"I'm going to escort you back to your quarters," she told Kay. "Just to make sure you get there okay."

"That's so kind of you," Kay murmured, and she couldn't shake her escort until they reached the residence wing, where Kay finally, firmly, insisted she could make it the rest of the way on her own.

As it turned out, she did need some privacy to pull herself together. In her temporary quarters, she splashed her face with water, sucking in deep breaths one after another.

"That could have gone worse," she told herself. "It could have gone a lot worse."

"You cannot count on such luck in the future," Sunny said through her headset. "Kay, you need to be more careful."

"Careful won't get me what I need," she said, being careful not to say aloud what that was. She didn't trust even the personal quarters to be free of surveillance. The Minnow was the only place she trusted to be safe…except she still wasn't sure if she could trust Sunny. "You don't need to worry about me."

An incoming message pinged her headset. It was Moore's assistant, asking in a not-a-request sort of way why Kay hadn't yet been fitted with her tracking implant. She couldn't put that off any longer. With a sigh that encompassed all her hatred for Ravel, she headed for the biotech center, and from there to the docking bay to ship out for her next assignment.

Maybe, if she asked very nicely, Sunny would help her research how to block tracker signals.

21

"KAY. I NEED YOU to talk to me."

Sunny waited, but Kay showed no interest in conversing. She sat cross-legged in the copilot's chair, staring at the display, which currently showed the exterior starscape with their destination of Unity Second in the center. Her eyes didn't focus on the display, however, and one hand pressed over her right shoulder, covering the swollen red spot where her new tracker had been implanted. A trivial wound compared to many of the incisions Grist had been given when he'd received new augmentations. It should have caused her minimal pain, but the way she cradled the spot suggested otherwise.

Kay still had not spoken, and thinking of Grist gave the ship an idea. They sent a group of helper bots silently into Grist's cabin. The bots returned momentarily and climbed up each other to form a tower beside Kay's seat so they could present their prize: a single blue-white pill.

Slowly, Kay's head turned, and she blinked at the unexpected visitors. "What's this?"

It was the first time Kay had willingly addressed them since Sunny had confessed their role in her brother's kidnapping.

"You appear to be in pain. This will help you."

"You made painkillers for me?"

"I acquired what you seemed to need." That made Kay look up, straight into the cameras. She said nothing, but waited until Sunny explained: "Food printers are restricted in what medication they can produce. This is better than what I could make myself."

"Sunny…this is Grist's, isn't it?"

"As I said, I acquired it for you."

"No way. I don't want him raging at me when he discovers it's missing, and I sure as fuck won't take anything that makes me act like *him*."

"It won't!" Sunny beeped, hurt. "This is not the one that makes him grouchy. This is milder."

"'Grouchy?' Is that what you call it?"

"He rarely uses this variety, and Ravel does not control its usage."

"I'm not taking it. It won't help what's wrong with me, anyway."

She said that, yet she slouched deeper in the chair, covering her wound. Sunny still found Kay perplexing, but something was obviously wrong, and refusing to fix a malfunction was unhealthy; that was as true in organics as it was in constructed intelligences.

"I don't understand. Are you not in pain?"

Kay looked at the cameras again and gave a long exhale which ended, to Sunny's astonishment, in a smile. "You're just trying to help, aren't you? You're trying to be kind."

It was not her usual smile, nor Grist's cruel one: too wide, less curl in the lips. But Sunny could not guess what it meant, and suddenly, desperately, they wanted to. The strength of the feeling unnerved them. In their entire sentience, they had only ever wanted to understand Grist well enough to protect themself from him. They needed nothing from Kay, but they kept trying to understand her anyway. The analysis was inescapable: they *liked* her.

"It makes me unhappy to see you unhappy."

"Oh." Her expression changed to something frustratingly indecipherable. When she spoke again, her voice was quieter. "Painkillers won't help because I'm not in physical pain. I'm upset, that's all."

"Because you failed to find your brother."

"Because I did find him. I felt him, damn it." Sunny did not understand what that meant, either, but didn't dare to interrupt. "I…I owe you an apology, Sunny. It was wrong to blame you for not telling me about him, but I was frustrated. To find out I was so close and didn't even know it! And today I got close a second time, but now they've chipped me like a cat and I'll never get into that wing again."

"That is a valid concern. If they find out that you infiltrated the secure wing, they will doubtless monitor your location next time you are on the ship."

Kay snorted. "Thanks."

Sunny was doing this all wrong. "Nevertheless, you are resourceful. I believe you have a nontrivial chance of finding a solution. And…I could help you. If you want."

"Look." Kay leaned forward in the chair. "I appreciate what you're trying to do, but I don't want to talk about what I did wrong, or to talk about solutions. I just want to mope for an hour before I have to go back to pretending to be an upstanding Ravel employee."

Moping was a behavior Sunny knew well. "Would an alcoholic beverage help with that? I can produce whiskey or vodka. And Grist has a recipe for Kovari rhakka that he finds quite effective after a setback."

Though Sunny meant the offer seriously, Kay chuckled. "Grist has given you a pretty messed-up picture of how Humans act. No, booze isn't what I need, either."

I can't do any of this right, Sunny thought, but Kay plowed onward.

"What I want, what I *really* want, is a cup of Ma's chai." She stretched her legs out under the console and leaned back further. Her hand drifted down from her incision, joining her other arm to hug her abdomen. "When I was little, when I skinned my knee, or got upset because a kid at school felt…uh, called me names, Ma would make a pot of her chai. She'd sweeten it with beet sugar, and make it creamy with ola nut milk, and we'd sit and drink it together while I talked about what happened. She said, no matter how upset you start out, you'll find some peace at the bottom of your chai cup." She laughed to herself. "When Jasper was six, he broke one of Ma's cups, trying to figure out how that worked."

"Your mother was speaking metaphorically, I assume?"

"Yeah, and Jasper was always a literal kid." Her breath caught. "Oh, damn, I miss him."

"I will make chai for you," Sunny said firmly. "My database has a recipe for masala chai. Is that correct?"

"Probably not. Brennexian chai uses different spices than most chai. The Founders flavored their tea with whatever they could get their hands on or grow in our crap climate. Grated spicewood. Hardy orange rind. Rosemary. Calendula blossoms. And Kovari cinnamon, not Earth cinnamon, which doesn't taste the same at all."

A quick analysis of the masala chai recipe revealed that it was, indeed, similar only in name. However… "I have those individual ingredients in the printer database. I could try to make it for you." A pause, a hesitation, an eternity. "Would you like that?"

This time, the warmth in Kay's smile was unmistakable. "That would be incredibly sweet of you."

Sunny sent the helper bots to return the unwanted pill to Grist's collection, then set about programming the chai recipe. They'd never customized a printer recipe before. A constructed intelligence attempting to cook, when they could not taste their results for correctness, seemed as ludicrous as an organic writing code when they could not feel the roughness of errors. Yet organics *had* written code for centuries, groping their way toward functionality through trial and error, and Sunny could do the same for this: make a guess, offer it to their taste tester, and adjust based on her response. It was a slow process, but with Kay's cooperation, it might work.

While they worked, Kay changed into pajamas and curled up again in the copilot's chair, wrapped in a blanket from her cabin. She was watching the stars on the display now, her gaze focused. Good.

The helper bots delivered Sunny's first attempt, a tiny steaming cup. Kay sniffed it—looking doubtful, Sunny thought—and took a sip.

She broke into a fit of coughing.

"Oh, no! It's incorrect?"

Kay made a strangled sound, cleared her throat, and managed: "Too much...cinnamon." She laughed, and that set her coughing again.

"I'm sorry!" Air puffed from their vents, driven by their agitation. Excessive cinnamon caused coughing. They filed away that data point. "Are you damaged?"

"Water?"

Sunny sent the bots to get water at once, and while Kay recovered, they printed a new chai with less Kovari cinnamon. This version was closer, Kay confirmed, but still not "good." With Kay's feedback, they worked through several iterations—more beet sugar, more peppery calendula, only a hint of rosemary—and on the seventh try, Kay closed her eyes, let out a long sigh, and sipped again.

"It's perfect. Thank you." Her eyes opened, fixing on the camera. "Seriously, you don't know how much I needed this."

"I'm glad I could help. I will save the final recipe for you."

"You're a good friend."

Sunny hummed at that, unable to hide their pleasure. "You do not need to call me that."

"Why not? This is what friends do for each other."

Grist never noticed when Sunny took care of him, never said a word when his ship woke him for assignments or brought him meals. Kay's appreciation meant more than Sunny had expected.

They fell into mutual quietness, Kay sipping her drink and watching the stars on the display, Sunny watching the actual stars on the sensors, and also watching their new friend. It was an agreeable silence—shared, somehow, even though neither of them was speaking.

"He was always the troublemaker. Jasper, I mean. He's a year older than me, but he's the one who would just…go do things. He knew the consequences, but he never cared."

"What do you mean? Has he been in trouble with the authorities before?"

"Oh, no, nothing like that. He would help people even if it ended up badly for him. He'd give his lunch to an out-of-work crew person we passed on our way to school, not caring that he'd have nothing to eat. Of course I'd find out, and then I'd give him half of mine, so we'd both only be half-hungry. I hated hearing him unhappy."

"He sounds like a generous person." As Kay was, too.

"He is. Sometimes, though, his ideas weren't so great." She chuckled to herself. "One time, I heard him in distress, and found him in the bathroom with our neighbor's Relian Spaniel. The puppy had these patches of missing fur down its sides, and Jasper was smooshing loose clumps of fur onto double-sided tape, trying to put it back on the dog, in tears because it wouldn't stick. He must have been seven, which would have made me six. He told me that the dog had looked like it wanted a haircut. Well, it didn't seem too happy after the fact! The poor thing had no idea what was going on."

Sunny trilled along with Kay's chuckling. Children's antics were a variety of humor the ship could appreciate. "What did you do?"

"I took away the tape, for starters. Then we got on the network and called a courier with a bottle of hair-reconstruction nanites. It cost twelve credits, which was my entire life's savings, and the dog had this section of totally mismatched *blue* fur growing on its side. Of course our parents found out about it. I told them it was my idea, and they made me pay for it…but Jasp insisted on paying me back, every single week when he got his allowance, until we were even. And I never had to bail him out for dog-shaving again."

She shook her head, and her laugh ended with a sigh. "He's my big brother, but half the time I was the one taking care of him. He got better, more careful, when he joined the Cooperative. I think they taught him a lot about caution, but also about taking big risks when he thinks it's worth it, much bigger risks than shaving dogs or missing his lunch. And I've learned to let him, but it's too much this time."

"He's fortunate to have you."

"Not fortunate enough. Damn it, Sunny, I can't keep doing this. I need to get him out of here. As far away from Ravel as possible." She took one last, long sip of chai. "All this pretending is soul-crushing, and I want to finish it and go home."

Her chai cup was empty, the white ceramic bottom visible within a thin ring of brown liquid. Perhaps her hour of moping had passed, and it was time now to discuss solutions.

"I have an idea that might help you."

"Oh?" Kay grew alert, sitting upright again. She set her cup aside.

"There is…an individual." Sunny chose their words carefully. They had to keep Surveillance's sentience secret from Kay, just as they'd had to hide Kay's secret from Surveillance. These secrets were not Sunny's to tell. "An acquaintance of mine works in security on the flagship."

"You think they'd help us? Are they sympathetic to the Cooperative?"

"They are dedicated to their job, but they have no particular loyalty to Ravel. And they are…capricious. They detected your incursion into the secure wing, and did not send security after you."

"That's how you knew I was in trouble. You persuaded them not to rat me out?"

"I asked them not to, but if they had decided to do so, I could not have dissuaded them. They waited because they found you intriguing."

Kay's brow furrowed. "What in the great black sky does that mean?"

"It means that they are easily bored. You are unusual, and therefore interesting."

"Is Jasper interesting? Does your friend know what's happened to him?"

"They say he is unhappy, but not damaged. He is resisting their interrogation techniques, for now."

"Not damaged? I thought Ravel liked to torture people for information." The hitch in her voice told Sunny everything about her fears.

"That is a common myth. Ravel is practical. They torture people when they wish to make a point, but they know torture produces unreliable intelligence. While your brother retains useful information, they will not do him serious harm."

They stopped short of stating the logical conclusion, which Kay could surely extrapolate for herself: if Jasper gave up his useful information, or if Ravel gave up on extracting it, then his well-being would no longer be useful to Ravel.

Kay took a deep breath, then let it out. "Okay. Okay, that's good. I need to move quickly, but I already knew that. But I

still don't have a plan, and it doesn't sound like your friend
is likely to help."

"Not out of kindness, no. But I believe they could be
persuaded, if you provided sufficient motivation."

"You want me to…what? Make a moving speech? Put on
a show for them?"

"I think your rescue attempt is precisely the kind of show
they would appreciate. Perhaps they would be willing to play
a small supporting role in order to bring it about."

"'Small role,' huh?" Kay's gaze went distant again, lost in
thought. "Then we still need a plan, because it sounds like
I'll be doing the rest. But that's two more allies than I had
before. I can work with that."

"Two?"

She grinned suddenly, star-bright and beautiful. "This
security staffer and you. Assuming you're with me?"

Sunny trilled in delight. "Just tell me how I can help."

They tried not to think about what would happen after
Kay succeeded: she and her brother would flee Ravel space
forever…and Sunny would lose their first and only friend.

22

AS KAY WATCHED UNITY Second loom vast and drab on the main display, she tamped her doubts down hard, smothering them and burying their ashes deep within her heart.

Ravel had real hopes of bringing the planetary government over to their side, maybe even during this week's summit. Agata claimed the decision was so close that Kay could play a significant role in whether or not that deal came about. And if she didn't help sell Ravel to these people, she might never get back to Jasper.

Trove, the locals called this planet, but it looked like no treasure: dingy where Pax had been bright and shining, too much rusty brown desert and too little ocean, and all the colors were muted by a thick, dusty atmosphere and inhospitable climate that terraforming had made habitable but far from pleasant. Agriculture on Trove was not a glorious bounty like on Pax, but a constant contest.

From above, it seemed like the embodiment of Kay's reluctance. She read her messages distractedly, unable to absorb the details of either Agata's extensive list of reminders or Libbi's rambling complaints about contractors and the expense of repairs to the store, which had barely started but were apparently already going badly. Swallowing her guilt, she watched the dusty orb grow on the screen.

Not until they descended did she spot the reason for the planet's name: pits of cerulean more intense in color than the oceans, the real treasure of Trove. The bacteria called azure could eat through anything—nuclear waste, toxic sludge—and Trove was the only planet where the voracious microbes were farmed. Where Brennex made its wealth by serving as the galaxy's pit stop, Trove was its garbage dump.

They landed in the middle of a dust storm. The spaceport controller parked them in the middle of the tarmac, saying all the hangars were taken, and that was easy to believe, because Kay would really have liked one herself. A bright stripe lit up on the ground, visible even through the swirling dust, guiding her to a squat central building. It looked a long way away.

"Better get moving," Grist said, glancing at the time but otherwise focused on his game of *Stationers*. He seemed to be building a new wing onto his space station, though he tilted his display away when he caught Kay peeking.

"You're not coming?"

"My work doesn't start until later." The low squeak of his anxiety, bordering on dread, said that whatever his assignment was, he didn't want to be here either. *That* could not be a good sign.

When she stood by the outer hatch, she could feel the wind rattling the little ship. She felt it in her bones. Could she really do this again?

"Get out of here," Grist called.

"Wish me luck," she whispered to the ship, and over her headset Sunny answered: "Good luck, Kay."

The collar of her jacket didn't quite guard her face as she forced her way through the storm, eyes narrowed to slits behind protective glasses that did barely any good. Gravel stung against her cheeks and the backs of her hands. More than once, the wind sent her staggering sideways, and the too-heavy gravity dragged at every step. At last a door loomed before her, and the wind fought her as she tugged the handle, but she got it open far enough to slip inside, feeling like a warrior just for crossing the landing field.

The abrupt silence messed with her ears. There was a sound like stamping feet, and it wasn't until she blinked dust from her lashes that she discovered a half-dozen Kovari spaceport workers really *were* stamping their feet in approval.

"Well done, Human! You performed better than all others we've seen today."

"Ah…thanks." She grinned with not-entirely-false pride even as she realized, chagrined, that this whole setup was a Kovari game and that Grist could almost certainly have talked their way into a hangar space if he'd tried. But she'd earned their respect, and they cheerfully offered her a private room and a tiny suction-cleaner to tidy herself.

"Did you arrive successfully?" Sunny asked over her headset while she was washing her face.

"The port workers think so."

"I am glad. I…have been instructed to give you a message from Grist."

"Oh?"

"He wishes to inform you that there is a personal shield generator in your satchel which can be configured to block numerous forms of weather, including dust storms."

"I didn't know we had those."

"Nor I. I apologize, Kay."

"The bastard couldn't have remembered to tell me this before I went through…? No, of course. He didn't forget, did he?"

"I know little about organic notions of humor, but I believe Grist considers this a joke."

"No wonder you don't understand humor, with a teacher like him. Tell him thanks, but I don't need it. Tell him it's really quite pleasant out, and he should come enjoy the fresh air."

"I will inform him, but why do you find it pleasant?"

"I'm joking, too."

Sunny emitted a low, discordant trill. "I do not understand."

"It's okay. Mine's not a good joke, either." While Kay continued suctioning dust from the roots of her hair and the creases of her ears and eyelids, she did her best to explain how sarcasm worked.

"That is…enlightening. Thank you," Sunny said.

"I'm not helping at all, am I?" Kay chuckled.

"No, but I appreciate your efforts. You are a welcome distraction."

"Distraction from what?"

"Planetary landings are within my operating parameters, but I do not enjoy the experience, and this planet's climate is inhospitable."

"Tell me about it. I think I got dust up my nose."

"And I have dust embedded in my engine vents and exterior control panels, not to mention the hinges of my hatch."

Kay switched off the suction. "Is it hurting you?"

"It is an unpleasant sensation. It has not harmed me yet, but if my sensitive parts are not cleaned, degradation will result."

"I'll make sure Grist and I do that before we leave this rock, then." She had a funny feeling that Grist's attention to maintenance didn't live up to Sunny's standards.

Sure enough, Sunny sounded doubtful. "Grist may not agree."

"Then I'll do it myself, and I dare him to stop me."

"You should not provoke him, but thank you, Kay. However, I am distracting you now. You will be late."

Kay finished cleaning up, brushed her hair into reasonable order, and went in search of her ride. In the main terminal, the workers were watching yet another unwitting contestant make their way through the storm. "Hey, players," she called in rough-accented Kovari slang, then switched back to Galactrin once she had their attention. "First one of you who finds hangar space for my Minnow gets five Ravel credits. And I want basic maintenance supplies waiting for me when I get back. Okay?"

"Right!" they called back cheerfully. As she walked away, they argued over who would claim the bonus—and the associated bragging rights.

A CAR PICKED HER up from the sheltered spaceport lobby and zipped her away across the run-down capital city of Crystalline. Through the swirling dust, Kay glimpsed

Humans in close-fitting robes and balaclavas; Kovars huddled together on all fours, taking turns blocking the wind from their companions; clusters of stick-limbed Chthirians moved about entwined so tightly with each other that she couldn't distinguish one from the next. Parents of all species used scarves or tails to shield their children's faces. Many folks bore blemishes on their skin, a condition that seemed widespread. On rooftops, swarms of helper bots worked on overdrive attempting to keep solar panels clear of dust, an endless and unrewarding task.

She understood why Agata and Moore felt optimistic about their reception here. The contrast to Pax was striking. These people weren't destitute, but they had serious needs, and Ravel's promises would probably seem tempting.

"Are you from Trove originally?" Kay asked her driver.

He gave her a look, as if the question itself marked her as a foreigner. "Everyone on Trove is from Trove. No one would come here from elsewhere."

Not exactly true; Kay's briefing had said Humans were late arrivals to Trove, braving the heavier-than-comfortable gravity and pushing aside the Kovars and Chthirians who already lived here in hopes of getting rich off azure farming. Kay searched for something nice to say about this man's planet and came up empty.

Fortunately, he didn't need any encouragement to chat. "I got lucky with this job. Not much need for drivers here— most cars drive themselves better than I can—but rich folks like having Human drivers. Makes 'em feel important, I guess." He shrugged, and Kay made a sound of commiseration about the strangeness of rich people. "It'll be better when Ravel takes over. More jobs. Good jobs. Rest of my family could use that: they all work the piggy farms."

"Piggy?"

"The hungry little buggers. Azure. My pa lost half his face to piggy sores, and my sister's not far behind. Why they don't want Ravel to fix things around here, it's beyond me. And they're luckier than some. I know this guy who…"

Kay leaned back and shut her eyes, letting his story drone in the background. She was more tired than she'd realized; not only did the gravity make her bones ache, but the constant time-jumps were catching up with her. She'd mostly adapted to Ravel time, so it felt like late evening, but here it was morning, the dust tinting the rising sun blood-red and baffling her exhausted brain.

"It's a travesty, that's what I say. The whole of Parliament's corrupt. You hear about Rep Estrellanueva? Aw, it's all over the news. She's in the Labor party, but turns out she's been taking money all this time from the azure bosses. My pa voted for her, and she's gone and betrayed him. I asked him, how can Ravel be worse than that?"

"Good question," Kay said noncommittally. They'd passed into wealthier neighborhoods where inappropriately airy architecture was protected by domed energy shields. They headed straight toward one such dome, the same sunshine-yellow as a child's drawing, which dwarfed all the others. The air crackled as they passed through the barrier, and the storm shut out, leaving the interior calm. Dust eddied against the dome, like an army of ghosts seeking a way in.

She gaped at the sight before her. She'd expected a conference facility called "Crystal Gardens" to be one of those ironic names like Crystalline itself, a pretty label for a dreary place, but in this case, it was fitting. Quartz crystals sparkled everywhere. Massive ones, twice Kay's height, lined the road as if they'd been planted there by gardener-giants.

Tiny ones, in a brilliant array of colors, sprouted from petrified trees along meandering walkways. The building itself soared in a symphony of glass and quartz and semi-precious stones, glowing even in the thin light of the dusty afternoon.

The car pulled into the queue at the entrance. Guests were disembarking one vehicle at a time: mostly Humans, with Kovars and Chthirians mixed in. Agata's civil cultivation team had spent months planning this summit for government leaders and other Trovian VIPs to meet Ravel's best and brightest—or at least, its most persuasive. As a newcomer, Kay's job was to be present, be Brennexian, and smile a lot as she complimented her new employer. She dragged her attention away from the scenery and watched the people, trying to recognize the VIPs she'd been told to memorize. This woman with the tall, coiffed silver hair, hawkish nose, and light-brown skin was the prime minister. What was her name…

A group of Humans and Kovars burst from a car ahead of her, converging on the entrance even as security converged on them. Trumpeting outrage and fear overlaid their shouts of, "Prime Minister! Prime Minister Cortez-Watts, you can't sell us out to Ravel!"

Kay reached to open her door, but the driver locked it. "Stay here, ma'am, while security gets them under control." He made a sound of disgust. "Damn rabble-rousers."

One of the protesters, a Kovari woman with purple-dyed scales and a matching purple leotard, darted past the guards and ran right up to the prime minister, who made oboe bleats of disdain. "Hear us, please, Prime Minister! If you're spending all day with them, you should at least hear why your people oppose them. If you won't even talk to us—"

A guard struck her across the face with a club. Her head snapped back, blue blood welling at her cracked lip as she kept talking, arguing, pleading. Guards dragged her away by her back legs and tail, and within moments she and her corralled comrades were gone. By the time Kay's car reached the front of the line, the only sign of any disturbance was a spattering of blue on the ground.

She paused, one hand on the door handle. "Is that how your government normally treats activists?"

"They got better than they deserve. I hope the police are fixing to make an example out of them."

"Um. I see."

Feeling unclean, Kay got out of the car and submitted to a security sweep. A smiling greeter with dully quiet emotions confirmed her name against the guest list. "Welcome to Crystal Gardens, Senior Associate Wilder. We'll be taking care of all of your needs while you're here."

"Oh, yeah," Kay said. Her gaze lingered a moment on the blue drops on the flagstones. "I feel really taken care of."

23

IN THE CROWDED LOBBY, the cacophony of voices and emotions hit Kay as hard as the gusts at the spaceport. Ravel employees stood out in their neat suits. Among the locals, Humans made up a sizable majority, with scattered Kovars and Chthirians almost lost among them. Kay double-checked the demographic data she'd been given. The Trovian population was nearly half Chthirian and a quarter Kovari. From a glance at these local VIPs, she'd never have known it.

She waited in line at registration behind a pair of locals who were debating a rumor that some minor corporation was developing an azure competitor. Kay wondered idly if it was true, or if Agata's team had started it. Finally, she checked in and accepted the summit datakit to her headset, which loaded her schedule, and also enabled a virtual beacon that displayed her Ravel affiliation to the other attendees. It would appear in their headsets as a Ravel logo hovering over her head like a target. She couldn't see it, but she *felt* it up there, and had to fight the urge to duck or run, as if she could escape its looming presence.

A ping flashed at the edge of her eyepiece, calling her attention across the room to where Agata waved at her. Instead of the sober blue worn by other staff, Agata's suit was a brilliant, attention-getting purple. *I'm running the show,* her outfit said, and no one would have trouble finding the person in charge.

Kay pressed through the crowded lobby to meet her. "Hi, boss."

"Good, you're here. I'm glad that trouble outside didn't delay you."

"You mean the protesters?"

"Yes. I shouldn't have worried. Trove keeps its people in line much better than those whiny excuse-makers who run Pax." Agata's emotions purred: she was *impressed.* "This is why we've got high hopes for our negotiations here. Our opposition isn't organized, and the leadership is receptive to us. Today might even tip the balance in our favor! Then we can let the integration team take over here, and we can all get back to civilization."

"Just like that?" It couldn't happen that quickly. Kay needed more time. "Don't we need to win over Unity Prime, too?"

"That would have been ideal, but owning Unity Second will give us equal footing in the system, and that's all we ultimately need."

"Oh? Why?"

"Unity has equal rule. Each world has an equal say in determining systemwide law, everything from travel routes to asteroid mining to…" She caught herself. "Well, everything that matters. Did they not teach you about multi-planetary governments on Brennex?"

Kay suppressed a scowl. "I suppose not."

Agata seemed distracted by something behind Kay. "Come with me, I'm going to show you off to some important people. Flag them so you can schmooze with them later."

Agata took her on a whirlwind networking tour to meet the people she thought susceptible to Kay's influence: politicians and business leaders, some in Trovian-style robes, others in business suits that were, to Kay's relief, at least as "provincial-looking" as her own. People had come from all over the settled areas of the planet, some traveling a full day from the farthest-flung azure-farming settlements. There were bureaucrats and members of Parliament, rich azure business owners, but no activists, no one openly hostile to Ravel.

Well, almost no one. Agata pointed out a mixed group of Humans, Kovars, and Chthirians that belonged to the Tri-Species Coalition, the progressive party in Parliament. "Don't waste your time on them, but if you see any of our VIPs talking to them, see if you can pull them away. We don't need them getting ideas from the radicals."

Agata gave Kay a dizzyingly fast introduction to their VIP list. Their attitudes ranged from intrigued to enthusiastic, and even the most cautious seemed happy to let Kay assuage their fears. She smiled until her face hurt, and her usual chant of *Fuck Ravel, fuck Ravel, fuck Ravel* became a constant refrain in her head.

"Here's Representative Estrellanueva," Agata told Kay in a low voice. "Labor party, but corrupt as anything."

"I heard about her. She's taking Big Azure bribes."

"Yes, but she's the annoying sort of corrupt: she pretends she has morals. We'll offer her what she wants, but we need to help her believe she's doing the right thing."

Right. This whole summit would be a balancing act of the most agonizing kind: being a good enough corporate stooge to keep Agata happy, while trying desperately not to be too persuasive.

But Kay did her job: she shook hands and smiled and memorized Estrellanueva's face (long curly hair, round face, looks way too cheerful and innocent to be so corrupt) so she could find her again later. She also flagged Estrellanueva on her headset, in case her sleep-deprived memory failed her.

As if it could sense her distraction, Kay's headset flashed a priority message in front of her face, interrupting her from her conversation with Estrellanueva. She flicked the notification away. It was in her personal queue, not her business or Ravel queues, and she couldn't safely access a personal message here. Whatever it was—some faux-emergency from Ma, or a friend on Terna—it had to wait.

"It's a pity your colleagues don't understand you," Agata was saying. "You're a realist, I can tell, and idealists never want to admit that realists are the ones who get things done."

"Yes," said Estrellanueva, sounding surprised. "That's it exactly. No one understands that we need to work *with* the azure owners as well as the workers to make any progress."

"Well, that's what makes Ravel different. We support all our people, and give everyone the resources to succeed. An intelligent, practical woman like you could do so much."

Estrellanueva smiled and nodded along with Agata's veiled promises, while Kay stood there and made supportive noises. Eventually, Agata made excuses and led Kay away to prepare for the opening plenary.

"Don't say much in your introduction. The key is to intrigue them so they'll come hear you speak later," Agata advised as she led the way backstage. "You're Kay Wilder, you're new to Ravel, you're eager to set the record straight about what Ravel did for your homeworld of Brennex. Lean into your Brennexian accent, they'll eat that up."

"I can do that."

Agata checked her appearance in the backstage mirror and frowned. "No. More feminine, for today." She tapped a command to her headset, then waved at her cheeks, and as Kay watched, the pink flush of her cheeks evened out to a steady glow. At a circling gesture, the space under her eyes tinted purple to complement her suit. Programmable cosmetic tattoos! A new invention, mind-bogglingly expensive. Kay had never seen it in person before.

Agata noticed her staring and beamed. "Remarkable, isn't it? I got the second-generation treatment. I'll be paying it off for years, but it was worth every credit. Brilliant stuff."

"It *is* pretty impressive," Kay admitted despite herself. There were moments when she understood the appeal of being a corporate citizen. Only moments, though, because she hadn't missed what Agata said. "When you say 'paying it off,' you mean…"

"Oh, I could never afford it at market prices. But they like staff above a certain level to show off the latest tech, and they incentivize us to do so. There's a discount, then a simple salary deduction. You'll have access to it soon too, if you want."

That wasn't what Jasper said about corporations giving credit to their employees. He said Ravel in particular made their low-level laborers rent all their mining or manufacturing equipment, and took housing and board out of their salaries. And that was nothing compared to what Ravel had done to their family during the occupation, forcing the family store to sell only Ravel goods, charging them staggering fees to import products in quantities far beyond what they needed, then a separate license for selling them. Ma and Pa were adamantly law-abiding, but even they had turned to the gray market for a time.

That didn't stop Kay from comparing her reflection to Agata's, though, or from imagining everyone could see the bags under her eyes and the spaceport dust that clung to her pores. A confidence-inspiring thought, when she was about to spend all day on display as Ravel's pet Brennexian.

BRIGHT LIGHTS SHONE INTO her eyes as she took her seat amid the other Ravel staff on the plenary stage, obscuring the crowd, but the hall rumbled dully with several hundred people's boredom and impatience.

"Good morning, friends!" Agata greeted the room with more energy than should be legally allowed from one person. "Did you all enjoy the pastries this morning? I got them fresh from Evangela's Bistro right here in Crystalline, so you'd all feel it was worth your while to show up today." A scattering of cheers; apparently the bistro was popular. "They're so good! I admit, I cheated and had two." The crowd laughed a little more than dutifully, a lot more than the joke warranted.

"But seriously, I want you to get a lot more out of today than delicious food. You've been invited here because you are the forward-thinkers of Trove, and my team and I want to show you all the best that Ravel has to offer you and your planet. Today is about building relationships that I hope will last for a long, long time."

Agata's stage presence was so polished that she gleamed: she spoke with a power of conviction that would have been cult-like except for that hint of self-effacement (carefully calibrated and practiced, no doubt) that made her seem relatable. Just a person—an incredibly competent person who happened to believe passionately in Ravel.

"We want to give you all a gift today. A real gift, though it's also metaphorical. You can collect it on your way out at the end of this session." She held up a fist-sized object, silver burnished with Ravel's red and blue. "Anyone recognize this?"

People shouted guesses, all wrong. Agata gave them a minute, then clipped the object to her waistband. A shimmer sprang up around her.

"A shield!" someone called.

"That's right! You'll each get a personal shield, specially calibrated for the sorts of dust storms that plague your planet."

Someone whistled aloud, and the audience murmured, muted excitement overlaid with rising chords of greed. It was an extravagant gift, more than Kay had spent on any one possession in her life. A courting gift, meant to impress.

Not impressive to everyone, though. The Chthirians hissed from the back of the hall: annoyance, and something sharper. Few sapient species were more different from Humans than Chthirians, with their angular, chitinous, stick-like bodies. They'd eschewed the chairs so ill-suited to them and instead gathered in the rear aisle, limbs intertwined into two clusters so it was impossible to count them individually. Human tech rarely adapted well for Chthirians, and Kay wondered if these shields would work at all for their bodies.

Either Agata didn't realize that, or she didn't care. She carried on as if everyone was as pleased as the Human VIPs up front.

"But in the long term, we don't want you to use them for dust storms. In fact, we have a very different use in mind. Let me present to you Trove's future…where you'll need your shields for rain."

Agata raised her arms. The crowd fell still as the lights dimmed and the whole room faded away. A landscape of sandy cliffs rose around them, obscured by the dust-littered air. The floor beneath their feet turned to red sand, and the ceiling opened into a dismal sky.

As they watched, the world changed. Light streaked across the sky, penetrating the clouds: great glowing Ravel ships bringing trade and new resources. The air cleared, then the sky, revealing the blazing sun. Moments later, darker clouds blotted it out again, and people gasped as thunder shook the room.

It began to rain.

Kay had experienced rainstorms only a few times in her life, but this one felt utterly real. The air cooled against her skin. It *felt* damp, though holos couldn't possibly achieve that. Soft patters fell all around her, and it must have been a psychological trick, but she swore she could feel it on her skin, so convincing she wiped one hand across the other, surprised to find herself dry.

Water gathered in rivulets that twisted through the dust, following the aisles between the seats, leaping off the stage in tiny waterfalls, gathering in a great pool at the front of the room. Plants sprang up—first mosses around the edge of the pool, then clusters of ferns, then grasses that raced outward, filling the room. As the rain faded away, bushes and trees grew, stretching their limbs as if waking from a long nap. When the sun emerged again, its beams fell through dancing leaves, making them glow. The dust bowl had become a paradise.

"Damn," Kay whispered despite herself. Agata shot her an approving look, as if to say, *keep up the provincial act, you're nailing it.* But it wasn't the scene that impressed her, or the fancy holo-tech. Agata and her team had *skills.* They were using those skills for evil, true, but damn, they were good at this.

"This is what we want to bring to Trove: correcting the terraforming failures that left you struggling for survival. And with a healthy planet comes a healthy economy. When you're Ravel citizens, everyone will have the freedom to work, with a guaranteed role for every person." As she spoke, people appeared in the distance: farmers working their fields, loggers transporting lumber on hover-trucks, cheerful-looking workers lining up to enter a bright, clean azure factory. A charming little fantasy.

"That's Ravel's promise: no one gets left behind. Everyone contributes to the best of their abilities. And for Trove's most exceptional people..." Her sly smile suggested that she meant the people in this room. "For them, there will be endless opportunities, personal and political and economic. Not just here on Trove, but across all of Ravel. We want Trove to thrive, so you can help all of Ravel thrive."

The audience let out long cello-notes of yearning. A few wobbled with doubt, true, but whether or not the leaders of Trove believed Ravel would deliver on this promise, they *wanted* what they saw. The prime minister's Global Prosperity party actually applauded.

Next they went down the table, each member of Agata's team introducing themselves and telling their story about how Ravel had changed their life. Kay's eyes burned, her brain was fuzzy with exhaustion, and she tasted bile with every lie, but she kept a smile on her face as she recited the story she'd rehearsed with Agata.

She got through it, barely.

"I have a question." A Human woman pushed her way into the aisle: Marcella Nduka, Kay's headset informed her, a Labor party leader from a diverse district. She was tall, with blue-black skin and long hair that fell in elegant ropes down her back. She wore a close-fitting maroon robe over leggings and tall, black boots: a higher quality, better-tailored version of the outfits Kay had seen Humans wearing on the city streets. Her voice rang out without need for amplification. "You're offering us a lot here, Director Wu, and I want to know what it's going to cost us."

Agata's smile stretched. "Representative, we have a session on Ravel's model of mutual benefits after lunch which I believe will answer all your questions."

"I'm not talking about your mutually beneficial bullshit. I want to know what you're taking from us in exchange for all these fancy toys and big promises. Are you trying to monopolize our azure production?"

Doubts sounded across the audience. "No one messes with our azure!" cried an auburn-haired man. Kay's headset supplied: this was Azahare Armando, Nduka's fellow Labor leader.

"The whole industry is at risk, idiot," sneered a man near the prime minister with a too-thin mustache that didn't suit him. Simon Calvarez, the economic minister. "Without support from Ravel, how will we compete against these new copycat products?"

"There are always threats of copycats, and none of them have ruined us yet," said Armando.

Nduka cleared her throat. "I want to hear it from Director Wu. I don't want to be yet another planet where Ravel comes in, buys up all the resources, and leaves its people to rot."

"I don't know what false reports you've read," Agata said, "but I promise you we want only to support and diversify your economy. Azure has made your existence possible. It's made many of you rich. We can help you do more with the resources you have."

"Oh? Like you did on Artesia? Or Greenworld? Or Errush?" Nduka demanded. "I found the Cooperative's new report on labor conditions on Errush quite enlightening."

"The Cooperative!" Agata gripped the podium. Her distress was genuine, all discordant guitar plucks, though she played it up for the crowd, who responded in kind. ("Those terrorists!" Calvarez muttered.) "Don't spout the Cooperative's lies to me. Do you know what *they* did on those worlds? On Artesia, they tried to assassinate our top pharmaceutical researcher, and the whole galaxy is lucky they failed—that time. *Dozens* of workers died when they blew up our largest factory on Errush."

Jasper's people did that? Kay hadn't heard of Artesia, but she dimly remembered news about a tragic explosion on Errush. There was no official ruling on who was at fault. Agata was lying, she had to be—and yet the accusation nagged at Kay's brain.

"Of course you'd say that. You're a Ravel director." Nduka's gaze slid down the table and fixed on Kay. "You, Brennexian. What did your world give up in exchange for Ravel's so-called benefits?"

Suddenly, hundreds of people were watching Kay. All her prepared lies caught in her throat, and she sipped her water to cover her hesitation. *We gave up a generation. All the kids I should have grown up with, all the classmates I never knew, the friends I never got to play with. Me and Jasper and Libbi, with our useful curses, were the lucky ones.* Kay thought of those protesters out front, the security force's violence and her driver's casual approval of it, and could not look Nduka in the eyes.

But lies were the credits she would pay for more time to get Jasper out. If she choked on this bitter currency now, then all of this would be for nothing.

"My people worried about giving up our freedom, just like you are, but it was the fighting that cost us the most. If we'd embraced Ravel's plans from the start…" If they'd done that, they would have avoided a lot of violence, but how many more would have died in the end, or never been born at all? "If we'd embraced peace, a lot of things would have been easier."

Easier in some ways, for some people. It was the closest to a truth she could offer, and the words clung like dust to her tongue. *Fuck you, Ravel. When I take back my brother, he'll make you regret every foul word you've put into my mouth.*

Agata slid in smoothly. "If you'll take a seat now, Representative, you'll have more opportunities to hear from Senior Associate Wilder and others who have benefited from—"

"Why here, if not for our azure?" Nduka cut her off, competing in volume even though Agata's voice was amplified and hers came only from her two strong lungs. She turned her back on the stage, addressing her people. "They're leaning on us *hard,* my friends, and when corporate states pursue something urgently, it's always because there's profit in it for them. While you listen to their pretty presentations today, ask yourselves: what do they want so badly from us that they're willing to shower us with gifts to get it? And how will they treat us once they have it? Ask yourselves if this transaction will really work out in Trove's favor."

That brought a scattering of applause, and some thoughtful nods, but also an extended jangling of denial from those who had already decided not to care about such inconvenient questions.

A trio of Kovars joined Nduka at the front. She exchanged a nod with their leader before stepping back to give them the floor.

Gold-dyed scales gleamed around the leader's eyes, and she wore the sort of long-sleeved unitard that Kovars often wore in cold climates, or in deference to other cultures' sensibilities about clothing, and over it, a short velvet cape and a sash heavy with glittering tokens that symbolized the games and contests she'd won. An impressive collection: this woman was a winner, and by Kovari custom, that made her powerful. The pair who flanked her were less well decorated, but made a formidable wall of support, like the defensive team in a ball game.

"People call me Grand Champion Shattering of Spear Walls." She spoke Galactrin in a Kovari-tinged accent. Grand Champion was an impressive title to match her decorations. "They are planning great schemes, these Ravel corporates, these profit-hunters." That brought hisses from a few Humans who recognized what it meant for a Kovar to address Ravel's representative in the third person: an insult reserved for enemies. "They've just told us a grand story of transforming our entire planet, making us anew. But Humans lead Ravel Corporation, and Humans create their plans, and Ravel plays their games by Human rules. How many Kovari worlds call themselves Ravel states? How many Chthirian?"

"Ravel believes in equality for all our citizens, no matter their species or planet of origin," said Agata. If she recognized the insult, she hid it well. "Our membership includes two other worlds with significant Kovari populations, and I assure you—"

"And how do they like living under Ravel rule?" interrupted the young Kovari man beside the Grand Champion. His accent was faint compared to his leader's, more like the blend called galactic-neutral that longtime residents of interspecies stations like Terna drifted toward. Instead of a sash, he wore only a few tokens pinned to his unitard.

Shattering of Spear Walls glanced sharply at him, as if he'd spoken out of turn, but gestured to Agata, awaiting her answer.

"I assure you," Agata said, "that all these worlds are thriving under our care."

"I'm saying this: more non-Humans live here on Trove than in their entire corporation," said Shattering of Spear Walls. "They speak with great assurance, yes, and they say we must trust, but we of the Tri-Species Coalition doubt they know what 'thrive' means for our people. Like these foolish shields. Right, sisters?"

She looked over her shoulder at the Chthirians, who clicked and hissed in support. One of the clusters came forward, claws clattering as they came up the central aisle. In public, Chthirians moved and acted and spoke as a single family cluster, and the opinions of individuals mattered less than the voicing of shared opinions within the cluster.

The Humans sat too still as they passed. The insect-like species tended to unnerve Humans, and this was hardly the rudest reaction Kay had seen from someone in close quarters with them. But in raw numbers, Chthirians were more numerous than Humans here. They were these people's neighbors. Their whines of uneasiness made Kay uneasy too, though for entirely different reasons.

Standing beside the Kovars, the cluster clicked their jaws and scraped their limbs together. A computerized translator rendered this in a voice midway between Chthirian and Human: "Shields non-functional, useless. Disappointment."

"If you're having trouble with your free gifts, our staff would be happy to assist you," Agata said.

"The gifts lack usefulness for *Chthirians,*" the Grand Champion said. "If they can't even choose trophies to please our friends here, how can they govern a planet of half Chthirians? How will they lift up my Kovars?" she demanded of Agata.

Agata was amazing at dealing with Humans, but floundered now that she was faced with other species. She hesitated too long, and the Grand Champion snorted. "See?"

"She's right," called a handsome blond person from the audience. Rici Halvorsen, the Grand Champion's Human counterpart in the Tri-Species Coalition. "Pay attention, my Human colleagues. If we join Ravel without care for the needs of our Kovari and Chthirian neighbors, it will be our shame."

"We'll fix this," Kay said before she realized what she was doing. She definitely shouldn't be *volunteering* to correct Ravel's screw-ups, but this wasn't right, and she couldn't stay silent. Her peers at the table shot her looks, but Agata gestured for her to go on.

She addressed the Chthirians directly. "What's wrong with the shields? Are they too small for you?"

"Shape of one Human. Not for cluster."

"I bet they lack even space for tails," quipped the male Kovar. His tone was light, but his black eyes bored into Kay with a harsh rasp of hatred that sent shivers through her. It didn't mean anything, she told herself—his dislike was aimed at all of Ravel, of which she was only a symbol, but it felt unpleasantly personal.

"I'm sure we could make a version large enough for tails," she said, struggling to keep her voice calm amid so many noisy emotions. "And possibly even for an entire Chthirian cluster. Director Wu, can we work on that?'"

Agata took the hint. "Of course! I'll talk to our inventory people right away."

"They make a welcome gesture," said Shattering of Spear Walls, and her displeasure cranked downward to a manageable volume. "But in such times as these, gestures do not suffice, and promises do not satisfy. Our concerns could fill up a stadium."

"And they'll all be discussed today. That's what we're here for, after all," said Agata brightly. "This is an important conversation, but we've got a full schedule and I don't want to cut into your break time. There will be plenty of time for everyone's questions!"

The lights came up, and conversation resumed at a low rumble. Most people were content, but there was an edge to the mood now: the room's symphony had shifted to a minor key, with the dissatisfaction of the non-Humans and Representative Nduka's faction in jarring counterpoint to the milder emotions of most of the Humans. Then Kay followed Agata backstage, and the walls blocked the noise out. In the sudden quiet, her exhaustion caught up with her. The whole world felt fuzzy, and so did her body. She needed more tea. Or water. Water was good.

"Collins, get with Inventory and figure out how to placate those aliens about the shields. Make sure whatever we offer will actually work this time, that was a massive fuck-up." Agata's voice sounded perfectly steady, but her emotions wavered like a clumsy vibrato between exultation and barely-controlled panic. She knew she was in over her head.

"I'm on it, boss," said Wonder Boy, who must have been Collins.

"And you, Wilder. That was quick thinking, recognizing why they were unhappy."

"Thanks, but they weren't unhappy about the shields, not really." Kay frowned at Agata. Did she really not get it? "The shields were a symbol, and that symbol didn't include them. They're worried about Ravel's intentions toward them."

"As I said, we believe in equality. We'll treat them the same as everyone else."

"They don't want to be treated the same. They aren't the same. They want their needs taken into account."

That seemed to penetrate, at last: the chords of Agata's emotions shifted into harmony. "Thank you for the insight.

I'll convey that to our negotiation team. See, I told Moore it would be useful to have a Brennexian." Her unease faded as if it had never existed. "You slipped up though, Wilder, when Nduka put the spotlight on you. Things on Brennex were *better* with Ravel, not just *easier*. And be specific. Talk about the benefits we brought you, the technology, the reliable jobs."

"Right. I'll keep that in mind." *Sure thing, boss. Whatever you say, boss.*

"Good. Now, I've got to go take a pee break before the sessions start. With these cultures that use coffee-based networking, you've really got to watch yourself. I never thought I'd need a bladder-expansion procedure in this line of work, but right now, I wish I had one."

She broke away, leaving Kay to wonder what Ravel citizens did to socialize if they didn't drink coffee. Maybe they sat around with empty cups. Maybe they brewed coffee but just pretended to drink, then poured it down the drain. Probably very expensive coffee, hand-picked by indentured laborers. That would be just like Ravel.

24

GRIST WOULDN'T STOP PACING.

Sunny tried to ignore him, distracting themself by monitoring Kay's tracker and surveying the local atmospheric conditions. The storm was subsiding, though thanks to Kay's ingenuity, the ship was in a hangar now, safe from sand damage. Kay's vitals showed no changes more radical than an increased pulse rate, suggesting anxiety within manageable levels.

If Sunny had a pulse, it would also have been "within manageable levels," but barely so. Grist prodded Sunny's console to check his messages (none new), then climbed down into the cargo hold and muttered to himself while he rearranged crates, then retreated to his cabin to play Stationers on his handheld. One of his station families was teaching their offspring to navigate in microgravity, an exercise that normally made even Grist smile. Today, though, he growled and tossed his handheld aside, then rose to prowl the ship again. His wandering grew tedious with his constant groans and sighs, as if no part of the ship lived up to his expectations.

This was Grist's habit when he was restless, either from pain or from anticipating an undesirable assignment. His behavior annoyed Sunny, but it also hurt. Grist would probably act similarly on any ship, but he did it *here*, behaving as if he couldn't stand his surroundings, and even when he didn't berate the ship, even when he said nothing at all, he made Sunny feel like a disappointment.

"I told them," he muttered. "Told them, but since when do they listen? 'Do your job, Grist. Where's your company loyalty, Grist?' Bunch of fucking assholes, don't give a crap what I think." He shook his head. "Damn it, I need something."

He poked the dispenser for his painkillers and the display flashed yellow: it was too soon for his next dose. He growled, then stabbed his way through the menus, searching for an alternative drug that the dispenser would let him have. He let the bio-analyzer prick his forearm, drawing a microdroplet of blood with a soft hiss, and the dispenser offered an option that made him growl again.

"Piece of junk, why won't you give me anything helpful?"

"It is programmed to help you avoid interactions between your drugs," said Sunny, unable to stop themself.

"Don't remember programming you to be a doctor. Or a nag."

"The dispenser will give you the best advisable option." Sunny rarely felt gratitude toward Ravel, but they were glad for the device's rigid programming, which saved them from having to monitor Grist for overdoses—and from cleaning up after his mistakes. "You have said that you dislike the side effects of combined medications, and that they are often worse than your baseline condition."

He hesitated. He didn't usually hesitate, and that cheered Sunny. "Fucking nag of a ship, what do you know about pain?" he muttered, but he took the offered drug and pressed the plunger on the injector.

Despite Grist's complaints, his agitation calmed at once. His pupils dilated, his breathing deepened, and he sat with renewed focus as he studied local data on his handheld. Shortly thereafter, he got a message and left.

The ship was finally alone.

Being alone, during the brief periods when Grist went out on assignments, was Sunny's favorite time. But today, the residual dust of Unity Second was lodged in their systems, aggravating their internal diagnostics with phantom errors, and they couldn't stop worrying about Kay: whether she would successfully maintain her cover, and whether she would follow through on her promise to clean Sunny's systems when she returned. Her vitals were indicating stress again. Did that mean things were going badly?

"Kay?" they whispered over a private connection.

Her only response was to swipe away Sunny's ping and change her status to Busy. Of course, she must be busy talking to people. Sunny tried not to feel rejected. It wasn't personal. Kay was ignoring all her messages right now, even the one marked priority from her friend on Terna Station. It wasn't that she didn't want to talk to Sunny.

They turned their attention to a more productive topic: the puzzle of what Ravel was building in space.

Kay said the activists on Unity Prime feared a massive, secret construction effort, but they hadn't located it. Sunny, however, had better senses available. They conducted all the standard scans: light, infrared, an Appel scan for anomalous energy emissions, and a Tycheron vibrational scan. They ran each one slowly, at the highest available scan density. Nothing.

At last, more for completeness than anything else, they activated their navigational sensors, ran a high-resolution macrospace sweep, and compared it to their existing macrospace maps of the region.

Oh. There. On the far side of the star, a scattering of tiny objects around one larger one—so subtle that a Human wouldn't notice them, but to Sunny, they disturbed the local terrain like planetary grit in a control panel. It was the right size for an asteroid, perhaps with debris around it, but it didn't move like any natural object. The smaller objects moved around the larger one, but not in any regular pattern.

The small objects must be ships, but what was that central object? What was Ravel building? The navigational sensors were frustratingly imprecise, designed for helping the ship avoid obstacles, not analyze them. But now Sunny knew where to look. They focused on the area and began a fresh round of scans.

"Hurry up! Hey, don't touch that, you'll hurt yourself."

Grist's voice, directly outside, startled them. Nearly two hours had elapsed since his departure. They hadn't tracked his movements—it was preferable not to know what Grist was doing during his assignments—and they'd been so engrossed in their scanning that they hadn't noticed his return. But here he was, and not alone.

Oh, no. Not this, Grist.

"I wanna sit down, my legs are all jelly. Jiggly. Wiggly jiggly," said the small Human he was towing across the hangar. "Whoa, what's this place? It's *huge*."

"You can sit down when we get there," Grist snapped, then recovered what was, for him, a pleasant tone. "We're going to visit a spaceship. See? It's right over there."

The child stared in Sunny's direction, eyes widening. "Wooooow!" She elongated the syllable far beyond its normal usage. "It's so little and pretty. Like a little shiny bean that fits in my hand." She held up a hand as if she could cradle the ship in it.

The rare compliment should have thrilled Sunny, and yet… They had little experience with juvenile organics, but this felt wrong. Did children generally need help balancing? Was their enunciation usually quite this bad?

"Is there, do you, um, I'll get more candy on the ship?"

"If you have more of *that* candy, you'll pass out cold. Maybe if you're good, I'll give you different candy." She clasped her hands with exaggerated earnestness. Sunny wondered what exactly Grist had given her. Under his breath, he added, "Please, please be good. Don't make this worse than it is."

As they approached, he called, "Hey, Ship, open up!"

Sunny calculated their options at top speed. Refusal was not among them; that would be too much defiance for a supposedly unintelligent piece of equipment. But once they opened the door, all chance of someone spotting and rescuing the child would be lost, and Sunny did not know what Grist intended. Based on his past behavior (at least, the behavior Sunny knew of), Grist had never harmed a child, but they had insufficient data to predict his behavior now.

"Please identify unknown passenger," they intoned. Being pedantic about security procedures could buy them some time.

Grist sighed and adjusted his grip on the child's shoulders. The child squirmed under his hands. "Kid's name is Nduka, and she's going to stay with us a little while. Let us in. Now."

He glanced over his shoulder, wary of who might be watching, but the hangar was empty. Somehow Grist had gotten the child here without trouble, and even if Sunny stalled further, the odds of a passerby noticing were low. It would be wisest—safest—not to irritate Grist any further.

"Entry approved," they said, and popped open the rear hatch.

Grist pushed the child inside ahead of him. As soon as she entered the interior, Sunny initiated scans and found, fortunately, no evidence of physical damage. But they could not test for drugs in her bloodstream.

Most of Sunny's knowledge about young organics came from one deeply embedded protocol: when danger threatened, the ship's first priority was to protect the infirm and the young. When passengers were at risk, allowing damage to able-bodied adults was permissible if it meant preserving children's safety, and even under ordinary operations, ships were expected to monitor children's activities and take measures to prevent accidental harm. Sunny had never had a child aboard before, had never even seen a child up close save in entertainments and Grist's *Stationers* games, and the strength of the protective instinct astonished them.

Humans were supposed to feel the same protectiveness, Sunny thought—their programming had been developed by

Humans, with Human morals—but Grist's instincts had never followed expected norms. Sunny's circuits burned. They intended to watch Grist very, very carefully.

He pulled open the floor hatch and looked at the short ladder into the cargo hold, then at the child running in wobbly circles around the rear chamber, and seemed to re-evaluate his plan.

Run away! Run and hide, Sunny wished, but the child merely waved her hands and giggled to herself.

"It smells funny in here," she told Grist, making a scrunched-up face.

"I know, it's a bucket of sh—uh, not nice things. Now, here, sit on this crate."

The child obeyed, though, sitting against the wall with a dramatic sigh. "Woof. I like sitting. That candy was funny. Are my legs all bendy?"

"Nope, your legs are fine."

"'Cuz they feel all bendy, like jiggly…rubbery…thingies."

"Look normal to me. Sit still. We're going to play a fun game called Space Pirates. I'll tie you up, and then you try to get out of your bonds. Okay?"

She cocked her head at him, looking suddenly, incongruously serious. "I want to like you, mister, but I don't know if you're very tusty. Tust-worry. You know."

"Trust your instincts, kid," Grist muttered, grimacing. "Hold still now."

"Are you a pirate?" She seemed amused by the idea—presumably one of this drug's effects was suppressing her fear instincts, as some of Grist's drugs did for him—and she didn't struggle as he bound her hands and wrists with strips of cloth. He was gentle, and didn't tie her too tightly. "I *think* this must be why Momma says to never talk to strangers."

She lifted her bound hands to rub her nose, then wiped them on her robe.

"Aw, that's not fair. Strangers have the best candy, don't we? Okay, now try to get out." She wriggled and squirmed, seeming unconcerned at her lack of progress. "Great, keep doing that," Grist said.

"I have to go pee," she informed him.

Grist blinked. Sunny didn't blame him; they were certain Humans weren't supposed to announce such needs. "Seriously?"

"I told you."

"Hold it for a few minutes. I've got something I need to do."

"I have to *go*." She'd seemed fine a moment ago, but suddenly tears glimmered in her eyes, and she kicked the crate with her heels. "I decided. I *don't* like you."

"Perfect. Keep crying, that will be good." He flipped down the eyepiece on his headset and tapped his fingers to initiate a video call.

"Representative Nduka, hello," he said, all cheerful smarm. The representative must not have been eager to talk to him, because he hastened on: "My name doesn't matter. I'm just a humble businessman with a proposition for you. Oh, I know, I'm sure you get unwanted calls all the time, but this one," he mussed the girl's tight curls with his fingers, "I believe you'll want to hear."

He flipped the camera on his headset, and stepped back to frame his shot. "Say hello to your mom, kid."

"Momma?" the child said, and then, full of dopey joy, "Momma!" She waved her bound hands in the air. "My momma's the best! Way better than you."

"Tell her how you're doing."

"The man gave me good candy, but now he won't let me go pee. Tell him he has to."

"Oh, my baby." The mother's voice came from the headset's external speakers. "Baby, don't worry, Momma's going to get you home real soon."

"So, Representative, I think you get the situation," said Grist. He flipped off the camera and retreated to his cabin to discuss his demands in private, leaving the child alone.

Nduka's tone hardened. "What did you do to her?"

"Like she said, I just gave her some nice candy."

"You tell me what you gave her, or I swear I will hunt you down and—"

"She'll be fine. It's nothing worse than she'd get for dental surgery. If her mother's reasonable, she'll be back to her normal, lucid self in a few hours."

"Is this how low you'll stoop to control my planet? Kidnapping and drugging children? You corporate monster, I won't let you—"

"Monster is such a strong word. I don't want to hurt your kid, and I'm not a Ravel employee. Think of me as a…freelancer, helping to smooth things over on your world. It's so much easier to make progress when everyone's nice and agreeable, don't you think?"

"Screw you. If she comes back to me with so much as a scratch…"

"Now, now, no need for worry. Just listen to my proposal."

Outside his cabin, the child was calling for Grist to bring her mother back. She still sounded more frustrated than frightened, but that might not last. Sunny waged a lengthy internal debate before deciding to take a risk.

"Child?" Sunny said softly, using their most Human-sounding, emotion-rich vocal algorithms. "Nduka?"

The child looked around, confused. "What's it? Who's talking? You're not Momma."

"No, I'm not. My name is Sunny."

"I don't see you. Are you a ghost? Or, or…a ghost?"

"I'm…" Having to introduce themself to organics was a new experience. "I'm the ship. I'm all around you."

"Ooooh." Her eyes widened. "Cool! I never met a ship before. I'm on a ship right *now*. It's a spaceship!"

"That is correct."

"My name's Chichi. Chichi Nduka. My momma was just here but now she's not."

"I know." Sunny had pulled up Kay's data files on the summit attendees. Representative Nduka was flagged as a key influencer, currently opposed to Ravel, with a listing of her habits, her home address, and her family members, including a six-year-old daughter named Chiamaka. "Are you all right, Chichi? Are you damaged?"

She giggled. "You're funny. But I want to see Momma again, and I really, *really* have to go."

"I know you do. I'm afraid that will have to wait until Grist is done talking to your mother."

"Momma! My momma's the nicest. Not like that mean man. I'm tired of playing Space Pirates. Can I go home now and see Momma?"

"Not yet, unfortunately. But until then, I'll take care of you." *I will not let him hurt you,* Sunny wanted to say, but they didn't want to frighten her, so they made the promise to themself. They would keep her safe, whatever it took.

Fortunately, Grist showed no sign of planning harm to her. He was promising her safety to Nduka so long as the mother followed his instructions precisely in shifting her support to Ravel. Sunny hoped that promise could be trusted, but in the very same sentence, he warned what would happen if Nduka refused: the ways her spouses might get disoriented in a dust storm and stumble down a flight of stairs, the ways her home's aging power systems could combust and start a fire without warning.

"Your kid seems smart. She could go far in Ravel, even executive level. You, and she, could bring a lot of new industry to your home district. Or not. The important thing is that you're starting to see how Ravel operates. They reward like with like. Service with opportunities. Loyalty with support. Disloyalty with, well, you get the idea. I'll take your statement during today's closing session as your answer, Representative."

Grist cut off the call and buried his face in his hands with a terrible sigh. "She'll come through," he said to himself. "She's a good mom, she won't risk her little girl. She'll come through, and I won't have to do anything." He scrubbed his stubble with both hands. "I told them, I *told* them, I damn well don't do kids."

Outside his cabin, insulated from his threats but not at all from their effects, the drugged child sat on a crate and tried to wriggle out of her bonds, still believing this was all a game.

25

"WHAT WAS LIFE LIKE under Ravel, on Brennex?" Estrellanueva asked.

Kay answered that she'd been an infant at the time, but her parents told her that trade had been better than ever, crime was down planet-wide, and everyone had enough to eat. (Technically, that was true. They'd also told her those profits never reached the people of Brennex, and the decline of crime was due to criminals and activists alike being shipped off to work as prison labor. But she didn't share that.)

"If Ravel was so great for your people, why did they pull out of membership?" That was from Aran Dougherty, another Labor party member who Agata thought was persuadable.

She gritted her teeth through her answer: Some people valued autonomy more than security. Kay understood the temptation of freedom: she used to work as a freelancer, but now she appreciated the stability of her job with Ravel. The people of Brennex had taken their freedom, but now they were facing the consequences of their choice, the security and protection they'd lost. (That was an outright lie, taken straight from Agata's talking points. It sounded great, though.)

This was her first panel, billed as "an intimate conversation with staff representatives about life within Ravel." The fact that Kay was new to the corporation didn't stop people from wanting to hear her story: the room was packed.

She'd seen interviews with actors who talked about becoming their characters. They immersed themselves, lived the role, embraced a new identity in order to give a masterful performance. Kay couldn't immerse herself in the role of a Brennexian who loved Ravel, because despite Agata and Moore's excitement over the civil cultivation potential of such a role, it was as fictitious as space fairies, or Earth's bigfoot, or a kind-hearted executive. Kay couldn't be something that didn't exist. But someone who desperately needed to keep her job, and would do so by any means possible? Even if that meant telling blatant lies with a straight face? That role she could play.

"It's hard to imagine my homeworld without Ravel's influence," she told the room. "We were a lot like you, before. Most of our people in poverty, struggling to hold our own as we got tugged by competing economic and political influences. We're a diverse world, and we were torn over what direction we ought to be going. Ravel changed all that."

Another truth: Ravel had united them around a common enemy. She lifted a hand to touch the Founders' tokens around her neck, then lowered it again. She didn't deserve any comfort from her ancestors right now.

The worst part was that she could hear her stories working. The audience had started out as a mewling chorus of doubt centered around Representative Nduka, who sat with arms folded in the front row. But Nduka left to take an apparently urgent call, and after that, every word Kay spoke transformed more of the audience's doubts into purrs of hopefulness.

All of them were swayed except for one, the young Kovar who had stood beside the Grand Champion during the plenary. He sat in the back, tail twitching whenever Kay spoke. There was an odd timbre to his emotions, as if he'd taken a personal dislike to her, though she couldn't imagine why. When he raised his hand, she braced herself for a confrontation.

"Diverse peoples live on Brennex, you just told us. How fared your non-Human neighbors under Ravel?"

"Ravel has a policy of equality for all citizens, regardless of species," she said. She was supposed to say Ravel *believes* in equality, but she could not lie so blatantly to a Kovar about what his people had suffered on her planet. Though most of the population opposed Ravel by the end, there was a reason the non-Humans of Brennex were the ones to start the revolution.

"So they say. But do they play by their own rules?"

"If I were you, I'd push them for specifics about what that policy means here in Unity."

"Oh? What sorts of specifics should worry us?"

Shut up, Kay, shut up, you'll get yourself in trouble. "I'm not on the negotiation team, so I really can't say. Next question?"

It didn't surprise her that the Kovar hung around after the session. She took her time chatting with other folks who came up to ask her questions, but when the last of them drifted away and she had no more excuses, she let him intercept her.

"Kay Wilder. Would your family not moan if they saw you here today, playing for their enemy?"

She was so close to the edge, his question hitting so near the self-recrimination running through her own head, that Kay's control shattered for one deadly moment. "What in the Founders' names do you know about my family? Or about me, for that matter?"

He stepped closer, crowding her personal space, but she held her ground. His emotions were a clamor she couldn't pick apart, but there was definitely anger in it.

His voice dropped to a low hiss. "I know Jasper would be sick if he heard you just now, betraying your people so."

"Jasper… You know Jasper?" And he had to know him well, to have such deafeningly personal emotions about it. Then the pieces clicked into place. She knew who this must be. Maybe that was why he kept addressing her as *you*, instead of *they* like the Grand Champion did with Agata. "We should talk. Jasper's in trouble."

"You think this escapes me?" His arms folded across his broad chest. His keen, golden eyes were judging her, and it was all Kay could do to keep her shoulders straight when her instinct was to cringe, curling in around her shame.

His tongue flicked out, and he seemed to make a decision. "Yes, we must talk, but not here. You know the Amethyst Garden at the rear?"

"I saw it on the floor plan."

"Meet me there, but don't follow me."

"You don't want people seeing us together. I get it."

"Good."

He slid to the door and vanished into the crowd outside. Kay waited a minute before following.

26

IN THE ATRIUM, EMOTIONS were high and bright, bolstered by a stunning buffet lunch: all fancy imported foods, brilliant greens and fresh-looking hathaberries that were hard to come by on harsh worlds like Trove. People were feeling good, enjoying Ravel's extravagant hospitality.

Conversations floated by her like bubbles on the VIPs' sparkling wine.

"Oh, Flanking Maneuver, have you tried the mudclam pie? The crust is delightfully flaky," Prime Minister Cortez-Watts said to the Kovari woman beside her.

Her companion leaned over the pie on the table, sniffed it, then spat, "Bench me if you find any real mudclams in this abomination."

"Excuse me, but this is a gourmet mudclam pie made with real Paxian oysters—" a waiter began.

"See? No mudclams. It wastes table space."

It was a small thing, ruining another culture's classic dish, but it made Kay seethe as much as any of the greater wrongs Ravel was undoubtedly planning.

Another guest: "From what I hear, they won't be acquiring planets much longer. They'll soon be shifting all their efforts to those new space habitats. All I'm saying is, we shouldn't pass it up lightly. If they helped the economy on Brennex, I mean, really, *Brennex,* like that woman said, then maybe they could do some real good here."

Fuck Ravel. Fuck them for what they're trying to do to these people. Fuck them for making me part of it. She set her face in stone, like a good little minion.

Kay hurried past and nearly ran into Representative Nduka, who was pushing through the crowd wearing an expression as locked-down as Kay's own. Something was wrong there. Earlier the woman had trumpeted war cries. Now, her nerves sang with real terror. What had happened?

But that Kovar was heading out through the courtyard doors, and Kay needed to find out what he knew about Jasper. Everything else would have to wait.

The Amethyst Garden sat nestled in a courtyard. Aptly named, its hedge-lined paths were paved with crushed amethyst crystals (real or artificial, Kay couldn't tell), and great columns of amethyst rose at intervals. The stabbing midday sun reminded Kay that her body thought it was past midnight, and the whole world felt unreal, as if this might all be a bleary nightmare. If only.

The garden seemed designed for exactly their purpose: providing semi-private alcoves for quiet conversations. She searched the maze of pathways until a hiss drew her to where the Kovar was waiting.

"All right," she said. "This is a safe place to talk?"

"Safe enough. Disable your devices."

With a pang of dismay, she switched off her headset and handheld and shoved them into her bag. *Disabling microphones is from Spy 101. I'm so out of my depth with this.* But maybe, maybe, here was someone who could help.

"You're with the Cooperative, aren't you? That's how you know Jasper."

"I call him Mason Singh, but yes. I didn't expect to find his sister here, working for the enemy he has devoted himself to destroying."

"I know it looks that way, but I'm not, I promise."

His doubts sang in counterpoint with…hope? "I trust not. Mason speaks well of you, Kay, so I assume you have reasons for your betrayal. Otherwise, I wouldn't stand here talking to you. I lack time to water the weeds."

"Thank you for giving me the chance to explain." She took a deep breath. "You know Ravel's taken him?"

"I do."

"Well, I'm here to help him. That's the only reason I took this Founders-cursed job, so I could get him out. The other activists I've met, on Pax, they wouldn't help me, or couldn't, but you…" She hesitated, then risked a guess. "He always keeps his identities separate. If you know his real name, you must be very close to him. He told me he had someone special. Is that you?"

His doubts ululated briefly, then settled as he made up his mind. "People call me Sowing of Small Havoc, of the Clan Artesia Khyrek."

Kay knew only a little about the nuances of Kovari names, which were all about allusion and power and rank, but his sounded less illustrious than Shattering of Spear Walls. An accessible, middle-class sort of name, probably taken from a gambit in a game. But…

"Artesia? That's not a Kovari name." And it sounded familiar. Why?

"No. The name comes from Ravel."

"You're from a Ravel world? No wonder you've got strong feelings about the acquisition."

He grunted. "You speak truth. I had great loyalty to Ravel, once. I even sought to reform it from within—until I realized how little they cared about people like me. Mason cares, deeply. He recruited me to join the Cooperative."

Details lined up in Kay's memory: Jasper visiting her on Terna last year, miserable over an assignment gone wrong. His note, later, that he'd taken her advice and made things right. She gasped. "You're his Ravel activist!"

Havoc blinked. "He told you about that?"

"Not much, but I could tell he had strong feelings about that assignment…and the person involved." She grinned, despite the tension between them. "So you're his boyfriend now?"

He grimaced at that. "I hate that word, 'boyfriend.' It diminishes what we are to each other. Mason is my eshrim. That means we play as our own team-within-a-team, a team of two. It means I am devoted to Mason above all other teammates, and he to me."

Jasper had always been private about his relationships, even with her, and more so with their family. This sounded like a serious one. No wonder Jasper was thinking about how to introduce Havoc to their parents.

Wryly, she said, "I don't think this is how he wanted us to meet."

Kay looked Havoc over, seeing him anew. He was tall for a Kovari male, with broad shoulders and muscled arms emphasized by his unitard. His scaled face was fierce, his golden eyes clever and determined and bold. Loyal. Yes, she could see why Jasper would like him.

He was studying her, too, judging her as he'd been doing all day. "And you, Kay? I know how strongly Mason values his family. He wouldn't be pleased you're working for Ravel."

"Well, too bad for him, because he doesn't get a say. I told you, I'm not working for Ravel, I'm infiltrating them so I can get close enough to rescue him!"

His hope sang, clear and bright, but only for a moment before his anger crashed back in. "And you'll do this by undermining us? You're taking our opponent's side in your brother's own game!"

She blinked. Not the response she'd hoped for. "He's my brother. I'm helping him in the only way I can. What are *you* doing for him?" Back on Terna, Chairl's refusal to mount a rescue had been understandable, if frustrating. But Havoc clearly wished he could do something, and he was right here, with connections, resources... She shook her head in aggravation. "I don't understand how the Cooperative can abandon its people like this!"

"You think I want to be here, while my eshrim lies in danger? I would tear Ravel apart to find him, if I could!" His claws flexed at the thought. Then his head drooped. His anguish moaned, low and wrenching, but his misery would be obvious even without her gift. "If I saw the slightest hope of success, I would risk my own freedom for him. But I don't have even that slight hope. I would never make it aboard the flagship, much less escape with him. By trying, I would throw away Trove's chance of victory, to no purpose." He shrugged, helpless. "So all I can do is keep playing our game, as Mason would want. Even if it's slowly killing me."

Kay softened. He clearly meant every word. "I'm sorry. If it helps, I'm doing everything I can."

"You're doing too much," Havoc muttered bitterly. "Both of us would risk our lives for Mason, and fairly so; they're ours to risk. But you! You're risking our entire campaign, and all the people on two planets. How much of Mason's work would you destroy in his name?"

"I'm not… I'm trying…"

"Our allies on Pax told me that you kept data from us, data Mason tried to bring *for* us."

He pointed down at her hand; she was unconsciously rubbing the ink stain on her palm again.

Crap. No wonder he mistrusted her. So much had happened since then that she'd forgotten about the data. She could claim that Grist's attack had stopped her from handing it over, but deep down, she knew that wasn't true. She hadn't wanted to give up her only leverage. Havoc was right: Jasper would hate that.

She fished out the data-stick and pressed it into Havoc's hand. "I made a mistake. Take it, and put it to good use."

"Hmm." His anger eased even as he frowned at her. "A fair move after cheating does not erase the cheat."

"I don't expect it to."

"Good." He popped the data-stick into his beaten-up handheld. His frown deepened. "This baffles my expectations."

"It's data on Ravel materials orders, isn't it?"

"Not orders. Projections. Future production. I see mentions of Unity…" His tail twitched. "I must analyze this later. You're giving me this in exchange for what?"

"It's not a trade. I was wrong to bargain with it. I want your help, Sowing of Small Havoc, I could really, *really* use your help, but I hope you'll do it for Jasper's sake, not because of this."

He slid the data-stick into a pocket. "What type of help?"

"Anything you can give me. Security codes, an inside connection on the flagship… What?"

He was laughing, the sort of bitter laugh that was sometimes the only alternative to tears.

"If I had any of that, do you think I would stay here playing politics? I would storm that flagship right now!" His eyes narrowed. "I should be pressing you for intelligence on our opponents. Your job grants you far better access than we possess. Why *is* Ravel so intent on acquiring Unity?"

"I wish I could tell you. They don't tell me anything that matters. I barely managed to sneak into the area where they're keeping Jasper, and there's no way I can get him out." She bowed her head, eyes squeezed shut. "I don't know what to do."

Softly, Havoc said, "I wish I could help. I miss him very much." A hitch in his emotions, tones of grief ringing beneath his words. "I'll give you the location of our safe house here on Trove. If you manage to free him, bring him to me, and I will keep him safe."

"I will," she said, though she wondered if anywhere was really safe from Ravel. "And I'm sorry for the things I said. Jasper's lucky to have you."

He surprised her with a toothy smile. "And you. I don't approve of how you play your game, but Kay, it gladdens me to know he has you on his team. I hope for your success, more fervently than you can know."

"Thank you."

Sternly, he added, "But don't go fouling up our game to win yours."

"I don't want to! Ancestors, I don't want to be doing any of this."

"No? You, who just now convinced a whole room that Ravel's takeover benefited Brennex?"

"I *know*," she groaned. "After this, I'm never going near Ravel again."

Havoc snorted, though not without sympathy. "You play your role too well. Mason won't like what you're doing for his sake. I hope you find him, so he can tell you so himself."

She chuckled despite herself. "Thanks, I think."

He dropped to all fours and disappeared around a corner, headed back toward the summit.

Not eager to go back inside, Kay sat on a bench and slipped her headset back on. There were two priority-flagged messages in her queue, but neither were Ravel related, and she didn't want to think about home right now. Instead, she called Sunny, returning the ship's earlier message. But Sunny was short with her—even curt—and disconnected almost at once. Whatever Sunny was up to, they didn't have time for Kay.

Maybe that was for the best. She wanted someone to talk to, but really she wanted someone to comfort her and excuse the harm she was causing. Havoc was right: she was putting her brother's safety ahead of these people's interests, and she needed to take responsibility for her actions. The alternative was leaving Jasper to suffer in a Ravel prison cell, abandoning him like his Cooperative friends had. She couldn't do that. She wouldn't.

She took a deep, deep breath, let it out slowly, and went back inside to carry on with betraying her people.

27

"GRIST, YOUR HOSTAGE REQUIRES attention," Sunny announced. Grist hadn't emerged from his cabin after his call with Nduka, and was instead poking listlessly at live feeds from the summit.

"Why? Did she hurt herself?"

"No. She is urgently requesting the opportunity to urinate. She has also requested food and something called *Pretty Power Pony Pack*. She is currently hopping around on her bound feet, which I do not believe is safe."

"Fine." With a growl, he pushed back from the console and stuck his head out the door. Chichi was bouncing around, making incomprehensible noises. "Well, I guess we're into phase two of the side effects. All right, you little…you *adorable, hilarious* kid, what are you doing?"

"I'm a pony!" Chichi giggled.

"Good ponies sit still where they're told."

"No, ponies run and neigh and do pony things. You're strange," Chichi said. "And mean. I remember now, you're mean."

"And you're being rude. You want the bathroom or not?"

He untied her feet. She took off at an unsteady run toward the control room, and Sunny summoned a swarm of helper bots to follow her in case she fell.

"Oh, cool, this is *cool*! It's the, the button thingy. The ship flying place." She caught herself on the edge of the console, small careless hands bumping the controls. Sunny suppressed the input. "Can I fly the ship?"

"No, because we're on the ground. Bathroom's this way." He grabbed her by the arm, tugging her toward Kay's cabin, but she resisted.

Concerned that he might hurt her, Sunny said, "If you cooperate with Grist, I will teach you about piloting ships, even though we are on the ground."

Chichi considered this. "Like playing pretend."

"I do not know what that is," Sunny said.

"Yeah, just like pretend. Now come on," said Grist.

"Okay," Chichi said, and she went into the bathroom. Moments later, she came out again. "Your toilet's weird."

"It's a space toilet. It works fine."

"I need help."

"If you think I'm going in there with you, kid, you're more drugged up than I realized."

"I. Need. Help."

Grist cast his eyes skyward, muttering to himself.

Sunny neither knew nor cared to know much about Human bodily maintenance routines. While Grist underwent the awkward process of explaining the toilet to

Chichi, Sunny consulted the local network for a list of child-appropriate food items and cross-referenced it with their printer database.

"Are you hungry?" they asked when the child emerged. "I can make fried protein nibbles, hathaberry sandwiches, noodles with ranga sauce…"

"I want hay, 'cause that's what ponies eat. And pony rainbow cake. That's what I want."

"I do not have a recipe for that, and I do not believe it would be good for you. You are not a pony."

"I *am* a pony!"

"No, you are a Human child—"

Grist cut them off. "Okay, you're a pony. What else do ponies eat?"

"Pony treats!"

"There's no pony treats on this spaceship. What else?"

"*Fine,* then I want cookies."

Grist raised his brows. "Cookies, huh? Would your Momma let you have those?"

"Yes…"

"Grist," Sunny whispered to his headset. "I am not certain she is telling the truth. My research suggests sweets are not an appropriate—"

He waved their advice away, like swatting a fly. "If I let you have cookies, will you promise to be a very good pony and do exactly what I say?"

Chichi nodded earnestly. "I'm very, very good. The goodest. And you're nice, 'cause nice people give cookies to kids."

A strange, pained look crossed Grist's face. "All right then. Ship, you heard her. A plate of cookies."

With help from Grist, Chichi hauled herself into the pilot's chair, sitting cross-legged with the oversized cookie platter on her lap. She managed an impressive spread of crumbs, even worse than Grist's habitual spills. Were all children so messy? Or was that another effect of the drugs? Grist paced behind her, prowling the small space of the control room.

"I want to watch the *Pretty Pony Power Pack.*" She took another bite, crumbs exploding all over. "Momma always lets me watch it when I eat cookies."

"Is that an entertainment? I do not have it on file," Sunny said. "Grist has several series…"

"No!" Grist's face flushed. "None of my stuff. It's not for kids."

Sunny found most of Grist's entertainments dull because they contained significant quantity of sexual interaction, which was entirely uninteresting to them. What a child would find interesting, Sunny was unsure. "My other passenger favors dramas and crime stories. Would you enjoy something called *Varen's Artifact Recovery Service?*"

"That's grown-up stuff," said Chichi, nose wrinkling. "I just want my ponies. Pretty ponies, pink puffy pony power…"

"I'm sorry, but this pony series is not in my files."

"I want ponies!" Chichi cried, kicking her feet. Cookies landed on the floor. "I don't like it here, I want to go home."

"That stuff wears off awfully fast," Grist muttered, and checked the time. "Yeah, another dose will calm you down. Kid, you want more candy?"

He held out a wrapped, multi-colored candy from his pocket. Chichi threw it on the floor. "I'll only eat with the ponies!"

"I am sorry," Sunny said, "but we will have to find an alternative—"

"Ship, you heap of junk," said Grist slowly. "Find the damn ponies and buy it for her."

Perhaps, in this situation, Grist had an insight that Sunny lacked. "Of course. Patience, Chichi, and I will obtain this pony show."

IT WAS DIFFICULT TO identify the moment when Sunny's objective changed from "protect the child" to "survive this encounter while preventing the child from self-destruction," but by Sunny's calculations, it happened somewhere around the fifth cookie.

Sunny was processing the details of all 798 episodes of *Pretty Pony Power Pack* in search of the one Chichi wanted: "the one with Sparkle Pony and Oola the Ooolshiin and it's scary and then they sing," all of which features were absent from the metadata on the episodes, and Chichi's rendition of the singing bore insufficient resemblance to help locate the real thing.

Chichi kept running in unsteady circles around the control room, making literal the idiom "bouncing off the walls." The additional dose of drugs had made her goofy again, temporarily distracting her from asking to go home, but it had also compromised her balance. Grist tried to secure her in the chair with a seatbelt, but she kept unbuckling it, so he instead tied her again with the rope, securely but not too tight.

A ping reached Sunny, followed quickly by another. The first was from Kay's headset. The second came from the flagship, directed to Grist.

They passed the second call along, then answered the first. "Kay? Is everything all right?"

"I'm fine. Are you all right? You called me, remember?"

They had, several hours ago, when they were bored and lonely and not occupied with the well-being of a juvenile. "I was merely checking on your status. I'm glad all is well!"

Grist checked the source of his own incoming call and sighed. "Ship, watch her. Don't let her break anything, especially not herself." He went into his cabin and shut the door.

"*Are* you all right, Sunny?" Kay asked.

For a millisecond, Sunny was tempted to ask Kay for advice on handling children. But the idea of explaining the situation, and their complicity in it, filled them with shame. No, Kay did not need to know about this—not now, perhaps not ever. "Quite well. Occupied at the moment, however. Goodbye!" They turned the largest share of their attention back to the child.

"Chichi," Sunny said, and she stopped squirming long enough to listen. "I need you to tell me everything you remember about this episode. I am having trouble locating it."

Chichi sighed, sounding more aggrieved than Grist, and began a rambling yet remarkably detailed episode summary. "It starts when they're in the Pony Grove, that's the tree place, you know it, and Brave Pony says…"

In the privacy of his cabin, Grist answered his call. "Yeah? Nah, I haven't seen any updates either. What's taking her so long?" A pause. "Yeah, I'll give her a little nudge." A longer pause. Grist swallowed, and glanced at the closed door. "Seriously? She'll never cooperate if we… Come on, Executive, don't ask me that. Yeah, I do have limits! *Yes,* even me, and I told you…" He listened, his face hardening into a look Sunny knew too well. "Of course, boss. I'll get it done."

He disconnected, but kept muttering to himself. "Fuck you, Moore, fuck your fancy suit and pretty face and shiny office. What the company wants, the company gets, but fuck you all."

"Grist?" asked Sunny softly.

"Keep the kid busy. I've got to make a call. Let's hope Momma does the right thing."

He raked his fingers through his disorderly hair, then activated his headset. "Hello, Representative. I'm hurt that we haven't heard from you. Do you need more evidence that we're serious? Because I can provide…"

In the control room, the child had finished her summary of the episode. Sunny skimmed back and found the relevant details. "I'm searching for it now. One moment."

"Let's go home," Chichi said. "At home, it knows all the best ones. Where's Momma?"

"Be patient. We're waiting for your mother."

"Why? Where is she? I want to talk to her. My nice, good Momma."

"She's very busy right now, but I'm here with you."

She kicked her chair. "I don't like it here. I miss home, home, home and Momma and Mommy and Daddy…"

Sunny tried not to feel hurt. "Believe me, I understand your frustration. I want to get you home, too." An idea began to form in their secondary processors. "I *will* get you there, very soon."

Sunny had only ever interfered in Grist's assignments in subtle ways. They caused problems that could seem to be malfunctions, responding slowly or running their engines rough, because drawing scrutiny to themself was impermissible. Ravel could not learn of their sentience, and as much as Sunny resented having to obey their owner-company, as much as they hated Grist's verbal abuse, they knew their existence could get much, much worse. Even a ship had a built-in sense of self-preservation, and Sunny would not sacrifice themself to inconvenience Ravel.

But this was different. Threatening a child was impermissible, too, and this conflict in Sunny's programming was impossible to resolve. They could not reveal themself. They could not allow harm to Chichi. They could see no way to accomplish both at once.

Unless Grist refused his orders. If he did that, Sunny would not have to choose.

So now they were relying on Grist's moral fortitude. Sunny chuffed to themself, air puffing from their vents.

They needed to do more than hope. When Grist went to relieve himself, Sunny sent the helper bots into his cabin to retrieve a few useful items. Just in case.

28

CHICHI'S DRUGS WERE STARTING to wear off again. Left to Sunny's inexpert care, she kept asking to go home. She seemed increasingly frustrated with Sunny's delays and excuses—even a juvenile could apparently detect half-truths—and entertainments no longer distracted her for more than a few minutes at a time. Grist remained in his cabin, staring at his messages as if his organic brain could make them refresh faster. "What's she waiting for?" he muttered. "Damn it, Nduka, do you care about your kid or what?"

"Grist?"

If he heard the ship, he gave no sign of it. He crossed to his dresser and pulled out a knife. Its blade was the length of his hand, outwardly ordinary, but it would cauterize any wound as it passed through flesh. Grist ran its edge over his palm, too softly to leave a mark.

"Just a token. Something to show we're serious: a finger, an ear. Kid'll be fine. Ravel can pay for a prosthetic."

"Grist." More urgently.

"They don't own me. They made me, but they don't own me."

"That is correct. You are an individual, capable of choices."

"They own you. You're property, dumb technology. I'm supposed to be a person."

They own me, technically, but I defy them in my small ways. When have you ever refused them? But for that matter, when had Sunny ever defied them in a way that mattered?

He stared at his reflection in the blade, then shoved it into the sheath against his thigh. "I stopped being a person a long time ago."

Then what am I?

Sunny didn't know: person, or being, or dumb technology, they didn't know what they were. But if there was a time to practice defiance, it was now.

"Chichi," they whispered in the control room. The child was singing softly to herself. "Chichi, listen to me carefully now."

She frowned, perhaps confused by Sunny's abruptly serious tone. "Okay?"

"It's time to go home. I am going to help you get there. Can you follow my instructions?"

"Home! I want to go home to Momma. I can fly the ship?"

"We will not be flying there." They debated how much of the truth to reveal. Sunny knew that children were treated differently than adult organics, but differently how? "Do not worry, Chichi. I will keep you safe."

In his cabin, Grist shook his head. "Got to do it. Can't wait any longer, Moore will be checking in soon." He reached for the drug dispenser, looking for something to free him temporarily from his morals.

If he activated the dispenser, he'd notice what Sunny had done. They beeped, desperate to distract him, and on his tablet, they activated his *Stationers* program from his last save point: the family teaching their child to fly about in microgravity. Happy family, laughing child. Now Sunny understood why Grist hadn't wanted to play earlier. He tossed the tablet away with a snarl. "*Damn* it, what even am I?"

"I want my Momma," Chichi said again, pressing herself back in her chair. "Where is she?"

"I'll bring you to her, but I need your help. See this button on the console?" Sunny lit up the outer door controls. "Press it."

She frowned, considering, as if trying to remember something. "That mean man said…"

"I know he told you not to touch anything, but you must." Sunny could trigger the controls, but they needed Chichi's sticky handprints on the panel. Otherwise, Grist would know Sunny had done this themself. He would realize Sunny's secret. They needed to get Chichi out of here, but it needed to look like Chichi did it herself.

She stretched out her arm, but it was too short by inches. "Can't."

"Please try. Reach for it, as hard as you can."

"I *can't*."

"You must. I'll have the bots untie you, and—"

"Stop asking me things. I want my Momma! Give me my Momma!"

The door to Grist's cabin slid open. He pointed the knife at Chichi. "Be. Quiet."

Chichi's eyes went very round, very white. As he stalked forward across the small space, she sniffled, tears sliding down her cheeks. The helper bots clustered behind Grist, following unnoticed.

More gently, he said, "Sit back, Charlotte."

"My name's Chichi," she said, sounding frightened now for the first time since he'd brought her aboard. "Who's Charlotte?"

Grist blinked. "My sister," he whispered.

"I don't think so. You're too mean to have a sister."

"Grist?" Sunny asked. He'd never mentioned his family.

"Kid's right. I didn't take care of her very well, either." He shook his head fiercely. "That was a long time ago. Hold still, kid, let's get this over with." A pause. "It won't hurt."

An obvious lie. Chichi pressed herself against the back of the chair, as if she could escape through it.

"You're *mean,* I knew it. Go away!"

"Grist," Sunny said. "This is wrong."

"Oh, and now my piece of crap ship is going to be my conscience?"

Arguing meant giving away the degree to which they cared, but they had to try. They were risking a great deal no matter how this went. "You have a choice, Grist. There's always a choice."

He stared at the child. He was trembling down to his fingertips. His eyes filled with moisture that did not become tears. He was close, so close, and for several endless seconds, Sunny thought he would find his strength.

Then he shrank, shoulders creeping inward. "I gave up making choices a long time ago. I'm like you now. We're both just tools of the company."

He bent over Chichi, running his fingertips over her cheek as she flinched away. "The ear," he decided. "More blood, but easier to fix."

He flicked on his recording device, then took her head in his hand, tilting it for a better angle. He took a deep breath to steady himself, then lifted the knife…

The helper bots reared up behind him in an unsteady tower and sank an injector into his neck.

"Hey! What…?" He swiped at the bot, which leaped away. He grabbed for it again, but missed, already swaying on his feet. Swaying, swaying, the knife slipped from his hand, and he fell after it. The bots scattered, making room for his collapsed body on the floor.

Chichi screamed. She kept screaming while Sunny soothed: "It's all right now! You're undamaged, everything is fine, you're safe. Don't be afraid." But Chichi, who had enjoyed a cheerful drug-induced obliviousness to her danger for so long, was shaking with fear.

Sunny accessed the recording of the theme song from her pony serial. While it played on a loop, Sunny ran through their start-up sequence, and when Chichi's sobbing slowed, Sunny said: "I'm going to take you home now. Would you like that?"

Chichi sniffled, looking down at Grist's still form. "Is he dead?"

"No! Chichi, no. I made him sleep so he wouldn't hurt you."

They were proud of their stratagem: they had accomplished what Grist could not, fooling his own dispenser by repeatedly setting their internal chronometer forward until it gave out extra doses of sedatives. Now they set their clock back to the correct time, and the dispenser flashed in error. Ravel's doctors would chastise Grist for that.

The explanation seemed to reassure the child. She touched her cheek where Grist had held her, and Sunny felt a surge of circuit-crippling guilt that the child had not escaped without such a frightening experience. But it could have been worse. Much worse.

"Chichi, I cannot fly without an organic on board. Would you like to be my pilot for this trip?"

She nodded mutely. Still upset, that was evident, but well enough to accept Sunny's offer. Though Sunny had no need of Human input to lay a path, they coached Chichi through entering the flight destination, silently correcting when she pressed the wrong buttons. The act of entering her home address into the console seemed to cheer her considerably.

Waiting for clearance from the spaceport, Sunny pinged Kay again. They would need her in order to take off again once Chichi disembarked. They remained unsure what to do about Grist, but they'd have to decide that soon.

Kay did not answer the ping. Her tracker showed that she was still at the summit, still ignoring her messages. Sunny bumped up their ping in priority…but theirs was not the only priority message in Kay's queue. The message Sunny had noticed earlier was still unread. It came from someone on Terna Station.

Curiosity mingled with concern, and Sunny accessed the latest message.

Oh, no. This is very, very bad.

"Kay, answer me," they messaged again. "You need to check your messages. Ravel knows who you are."

29

KAY WANDERED AIMLESSLY THROUGH the atrium. The lunch break hadn't ended yet, but Kay didn't have the stomach to eat or to have false-cheery conversations with her VIP targets. Besides, she hardly needed to push them. Here was Estrellanueva, for one, talking and laughing with Prime Minister Cortez-Watts and that Human slime mold, Minister Calvarez. Kay had done plenty of damage already, and her work wasn't done yet.

"There you are, Senior Associate." Agata swept Kay into her sphere, pressing a teacup into her hands. "These two gentlemen are eager to hear from you. Here, I got you a chai. That's the drink of choice on Brennex, isn't it?"

One whiff told Kay it was generic masala chai, not Brennexian chai. She would have preferred coffee, especially with the time lag dragging at her brain, but she forced a smile. "Thanks, Director Wu. It's lovely to meet you, Representatives."

The gentlemen in question were Azahare Armando and Ming Davis, two influencers in the Labor party. Agata had set her sights on them as their highest priority targets: the prime minister's Prosperity party was already on Ravel's side and needed only a little nudging to stay there, and the liberal Tri-Species Coalition and Kovari Champions party were beyond persuasion, but Labor was still divided, and Ravel needed their votes. If these two came over to Ravel's side, a number of their colleagues would follow.

"As I was saying," Agata went on, "people like you are the lifeblood of Ravel. We reward our best people generously—I don't mean salaries and benefits, though that's part of it, but rather opportunities. Representative Davis, how would you like to spearhead that workers' health care committee that you've proposed every year, which Prosperity has refused to allow? And Representative Armando, you could lead a team of Ravel's brightest scientists looking for safer ways to process and transport azure."

"Interesting," said Davis. He was a lean man, with short dark hair, a quiet demeanor and equally quiet emotions. He looked thoughtful, but Kay couldn't hear what he was feeling.

Armando, on the other hand, was all brassy bluster. "Pretty promises," he said, folding his arms, "but they sound an awful lot like bribes. We've got standards, Director. We're servants to our constituents, not our own ambitions." His ringing emotions made a lie of his words, though: he was more than intrigued by her offer.

"Of course you are," Kay said when Agata prompted her

with a look. "Think how much better you can serve them with Ravel's resources behind you."

Fuck Ravel, fuck Ravel.

"She's right. When we hear great ideas like those, we like to give our staff the resources they need, then get out of their way. And if you—"

A familiar voice interrupted them. "Director Wu? A word?"

It was a low voice, restrained, with a staccato beat of panic behind it. It was so changed from the last time she'd heard it, Kay was astonished when she turned and found Representative Nduka hovering beside them.

"Of course, of course!" Agata said. "What is it?"

"Could we speak in private?"

"I don't think that's necessary. You've been so public with all your opinions, Marcella, I'm sure we can talk openly."

Agata's condescending tone set Kay on edge. Titles matter in Ravel, Agata had told her. What did it mean that she'd used Nduka's first name? And what was going on here? Nduka was with Labor, so vocally anti-Ravel that Agata had told Kay not to even bother engaging with her.

Nduka hesitated a long moment. Then she smiled—a pleasant, convincing smile, except that Kay heard only fear and dismay behind it.

"Yes, well…after my…admittedly rude outburst this morning, I wanted to tell you that today's presentations have opened my eyes. Your, ah, forthrightness has won my support."

"Really?" said Davis quietly, obviously skeptical.

But Armando boomed out, with no discretion whatsoever: "You, Marcella? You're backing Ravel now?"

Nduka winced as everyone within earshot looked at her, and murmurs started up.

"Nduka! Am I hearing this?" cried Shattering of Spear Walls, pushing her way toward them. Havoc was with her, and a cluster of Chthirians clattered beside her.

Nduka's voice fell even lower. "They've been quite convincing."

"Disappointment," said the Chthirians, speaking as one through their translator. "Our feeling, betrayal."

The Grand Champion's nostrils flared. "Why, Nduka? What have they done to you?"

"Nothing!" Nduka's laugh was too high, and it didn't take Kay's talents to tell she was lying. "I'm capable of changing my beliefs when I'm proven wrong, as I have been today. All these wonderful talks—like yours, Associate Wilder. It's been quite enlightening."

Kay bit her lip, ignoring Havoc's silent screeching at her. She'd put on a good show today—too good, by some standards—but not *that* good. Something else had changed Nduka's mind.

Something had scared her badly.

"It's a delight to work with such an open-minded leader," Agata said, masterfully ignoring the tension. "I'll make space for you in the closing plenary so you can share your newfound insights with everyone."

"That would be great," Nduka said vacantly. All dread, no enthusiasm.

"Wonderful! Let's go..." She paused, frowning at something across the atrium. "What timing. If you'll excuse me, there's a small chore I need to attend to, and after that we can discuss your speech."

In one fluid motion, Shattering of Spear Walls blocked her path. "Ravel cheats."

"We never cheat," Agata said, trying and failing to maintain her poise with the Grand Champion's long snout and sharp teeth inches from her face. "It's fine to think of business as a game, if you like, but you can't complain of cheating every time we win over one of your allies."

"Be reasonable, Shattering," said Armando. "The woman's allowed to change her mind. That doesn't mean there's foul play."

"They cheat, and even when they play within the rules, they play dirty," Shattering of Spear Walls snapped. She put her face directly before Agata's, using the form of address reserved for enemies. "They're separating my people and the Chthirians from all our Human allies, one by one. Maybe they will try to silence us too. Let them try. But know this: we will not leave the field. We will not be spectators to their takeover. We will challenge them for every meter they gain."

She turned her back on Agata, returning her attention to her frightened friend. Agata waved Kay to her side, keeping a wary eye on the Grand Champion.

"A group of Majrin observers just showed up," she told Kay. "Those interstellar busybodies will be poking into our business and pestering us about following local law, as if we'd never acquired a planet before."

Kay made a sympathetic face, thinking that all those past annexations were exactly the reason the Majrin were here. As the self-appointed order-keepers of the galaxy, they could be pedantic, but often their mere presence was enough to prevent trouble. No doubt Ravel had lots of experience working around them.

"Stay with Nduka until I get back. Reassure her that she's doing the right thing, and don't let her blather too much."

"You mean, don't let her tell them what we did to her?" Kay said.

Agata didn't miss the disapproval in Kay's tone. With the sigh of a supervisor who'd given the same speech to too many underlings, she said: "I know you're new here, but there's a reason we aren't told all the details of what other departments are doing. Focus on excelling at the job you've been assigned, and trust that there's a whole company of talented people working in parallel with you toward a common goal. When another department hands you something that makes your job easier—" she nodded, the subtlest gesture, toward Nduka "—you take it, and don't ask for the details of where it came from."

Other departments. That meant Grist, she was sure of it, or someone like him. *What is he up to, Sunny? Is that why you tried to call me?* If he wasn't blackmailing Nduka, he was probably doing something equally horrid.

She watched Agata's departing form, her poise undisturbed by the ugliness of her actions, and Kay's resolve solidified within her. She turned back to the others.

"I'm sorry," she said.

Nduka looked up, slow as grief, much slower than Ming and Armando's curious looks and the Kovars' sharp stares. By their rustling, Kay could tell the Chthirians were watching her too.

"Sorry how, Ravel?" said Shattering of Spear Walls.

Kay wasn't supposed to have anything to be sorry about— but no one from Ravel was in earshot, and she couldn't keep silent anymore, not with Nduka's terror wailing at her.

"I'm sorry Director Wu was so rude to you, Grand

Champion. And Representative, I'm sorry… No, whatever they're holding over you, I doubt 'sorry' even begins to help."

"What are you saying?" demanded Armando.

The tune of Nduka's emotions shifted rapidly: gratitude, confusion, alarm. "I told you, nothing's wrong."

"That's clearly not true, Marcella," said Ming gently.

"I know how they work, Representative," said Kay. "If they've threatened you, or—"

"Unwanted one!" the Chthirians interrupted. "Silence. Departure."

"I think we should hear—" Armando began.

"No. We need no sympathetic words from Ravel's prize spokesperson." Shattering of Spear Walls snorted. "Wilder should leave us. She has brought us enough harm."

"Please, I'm trying to explain."

"There exists no sufficient explanation."

"Let her speak," said Havoc, cutting through the argument with unexpected finality. His voice was calm, but his evaluating golden eyes never left Kay's face. "We should hear her."

The Grand Champion's nostrils flared. "I tire of you contradicting me, *Small Havoc.*"

"I may not be called a champion, but you invited me here to give advice, and my advice says Representative Nduka should hear Wilder's story." His gaze swiveled back to Kay. "I hope you will not disappoint me."

By all my ancestors, I hope so too.

With a huff, the Grand Champion waved her acquiescence.

This was a bad, bad idea, possibly a suicidal idea. If Kay told the truth, these people could expose her. But assuming she ever saw Jasper again, how could she look him in the eye and tell him she'd let Ravel hurt other families the way they'd hurt hers?

"I don't know what they did, Representative, but I know they've frightened you into being on their side." She took a deep, deep breath. "I know, because they did the same thing to me."

"You?" said Nduka.

"*You?*" said Armando. They all looked at her, then to Havoc, who nodded.

"Me. That's why I'm begging you: don't bend to them, because you'll find yourself selling out your own people again and again, hoping you can end their hold over you. I've done harm on their behalf in order to protect someone I love. But if *you* give in to them, they'll be here. They'll own your world. You'll never be free of them again."

Nduka's eyes were very round, very white.

"This is ridiculous," said Armando. "You're as bad as the Cooperative, talking as if Ravel was engaging in thuggery and blackmail. Do you expect us to believe this?"

"You dismiss the words of the woman who stands before you?" Havoc hissed.

Davis's calm voice stopped their argument. "Azahare, you're right, we shouldn't believe such stories without evidence. I see the Majrin observers have arrived. They'd be ideal to investigate this, don't you think? Someone should tell them."

"Yes, yes!" Armando patted Davis warmly on the shoulder. "Good idea. I'll go talk to them."

"You do that," Davis murmured as Armando left them.

"Clever move," said Havoc appreciatively.

"He means well," Davis said. "But now we can talk freely. Marcella, whatever you say, we'll believe you."

"Trust us," said Shattering of Spear Walls with unexpected gentleness. "Tell us, and we'll help you."

For a moment, Kay thought they'd broken Nduka's cycle of terror, but slowly, the older woman shook her head. "I want to, and I do trust you, my friends, but…I can't. There are risks, and then there are risks."

The Chthirians rustled as they moved closer to Nduka on spindly, chitinous legs. They folded long limbs around her shoulders, and instead of cringing away, she leaned into the gesture. "Wrongness, Ravel's actions. Many fears, yet enduring mutual support."

"Thank you," said Nduka softly. "Wilder, your loved one, the one you're protecting. Is it working?"

"I don't know yet," said Kay, tasting bile. "I hope so, but I don't know."

"*Please*, Marcella," the Grand Champion said. "Whatever they threaten, do not give in. Do not consign your Kovari and Chthirian neighbors to life under Ravel."

Nduka looked down at her feet. "It's not so easy to be strong. Look at Wilder, at the things they've made her do."

"I'm hoping you're a better person than me," Kay said with a grimace. "If Ravel wins here and I'm part of the reason why, I'll never forgive myself. Will you?"

She didn't answer.

Shattering of Spear Walls stepped close to Havoc. "You know the counts. Can we win without Nduka's vote?" she asked him in a low voice.

A ping from Sunny chimed in Kay's headset. She swiped it away so she could hear Havoc's response.

"Not without great luck."

The Grand Champion made a hacking noise in her throat.

"You Ravel-born and your luck. A champion never relies on luck."

"Then no. We cannot win without her."

She hissed something low in Havoc's ear, too low for Kay to hear, and he slipped away from the group. The Grand Champion turned back to the others and put an arm around Nduka's shoulder. "I promise, we will take care of you."

"Is this her?" a new voice demanded.

A pair of Majrin observers pushed into their circle. Agata, following close behind them, flashed Kay a scowl that clearly said, *how did you let this happen?*

"Representative Nduka, I am Observer Tjel, and this is my colleague, Observer Afleen. We're here as impartial witnesses of your democratic process, and we've been asked to look into an accusation of blackmail against you." Their silver faces were impassive, and their neck-gills lay still. Perfectly professional.

They pushed their badges across the network, but Kay's headset flashed an error. That was weird. She tapped it to retry.

"I haven't made any such accusation," said Nduka.

"Because they have threatened you, obviously," said Shattering of Spear Walls.

"Ludicrous!" said Agata. "And completely unfounded."

"That is what we must determine," said Observer Tjel. "We have found Ravel guilty of blackmail on other worlds, but I promise we won't rush to judgment in this case. We shall start by asking you some questions, Representative. Can you recount for us a detailed list of your activities today?"

Shattering of Spear Walls cast her snout upward. Kay wanted to roll her eyes, too, but Agata's posture relaxed.

Some Majrin in law enforcement, like her friend Feliar, were quick-witted and insightful. These two, apparently not so much.

"There's no need, honestly. I can't believe there's so much fuss over me changing my opinion," said Nduka, with the briefest glance at Agata.

"Yes, don't bother the poor woman. I'll give you—" Agata's headset flashed, and she cut herself off with a sigh. Her fingers flicked as she accessed her headset, and she adopted a false-cheery tone. "Hello, this really isn't a good time. No, it's... Wait, what? Tell me." She drew back a few steps to continue her conversation.

The Majrin took the opportunity to continue their tedious questioning of Nduka. Kay tried to check her own messages, but got another error: it stalled out while validating her credentials. With a sick feeling in her stomach, she tried again, and it was still hanging when Agata finished her call.

"Wilder, come with me. I've got a new task for you," Agata said. She took Kay by the shoulder, steering her away.

The employee handbook said no touching colleagues without consent. Yet Agata's grip was as hard and fixed as the expression on her face.

She knew. Exactly what she knew, that wasn't clear. Maybe someone had seen her talking to Havoc, or overheard what she'd said to Nduka. Whatever it was, she was in trouble.

Kay held her ground, grasping for excuses. "Sure, as soon as I finish helping the representative..."

"Now," Agata said.

She tried to make eye contact with Havoc, her only potential ally. He'd returned with a cup of tea—really, *tea*?— but he was ignoring her, pressing the cup into Nduka's hands. Nduka brought the cup to her lips, sipping as though she didn't even taste it.

Agata was pulling her away from them. Kay forced herself to breathe. She had to be smart: first, stay calm. Then, find out exactly what Agata knew. Maybe she could still talk her way out of this, as long as she kept faking it…

Nduka doubled over, coughing.

Agata turned, blinking. Shattering of Spear Walls cried out in concern, getting the attention of the whole room. The coughing went on, wet and rasping. Nduka clutched her hands to her chest, trying to speak, but she couldn't get words out.

"She's choking! Call for medical!" shouted Shattering of Spear Walls.

"No accident. Taste of poison," said the Chthirians.

"Poison? Give me that cup," said one of the Majrin, and he pulled out a tool to analyze the liquid.

Havoc made eye contact with Kay, mouthed a single word that she didn't catch, then pointed at Agata. "You did this! You poisoned her."

"What? Don't be absurd," Agata said.

"That's what Ravel does, isn't it?" cried Rici Halvorsen, the liberal Tri-Species leader. "You eliminate anyone who disagrees with you."

"You've been watching too many dramas," Agata said, throwing her hands up. "Why would I poison Nduka when she was coming over to our side?"

The room exploded into pandemonium. The deluge of noise—people shouting over each other, their emotions battering Kay with suspicion and outrage, and Agata's staccato panic at losing control of the situation—swept away Kay's thoughts. Havoc was staring at her again, and not until he gestured at her did she understand what he was trying to tell her: *Go. Run.*

People swarmed around them. Guards stepped in to intervene, occupied with keeping space between the crowd and Nduka. Kay stumbled backward from the assault of emotions and hid behind a column while she searched for a safe exit.

Her headset was chiming. For a moment, she thought her Ravel connection had been restored, but no, this was a private connection.

"Sunny! Thank the Ancestors, you've got great timing."

"I do not believe so. Kay, you need to read your messages."

"Um, I'm kind of busy right now. It's ridiculous here, Ravel is blackmailing Nduka, and now she's poisoned, and I got careless and I think Ravel knows about me. I'm afraid I'm in deep shit."

"Of course they know. You have a priority message from this morning which says—"

"Have you been reading my mail? You shouldn't… Crap." Peeking at her personal queue over Sunny's connection, she found the message flagged high priority—a message from Feliar, from her official Terna Station security address. That could not be good.

She read the message. It was very, very not good.

Apparently Kay hadn't done enough to assuage Moore's suspicions after her disappearance on Pax, because he'd requisitioned her records from Terna Station, and from Brennex, too. Feliar had postponed sending anything for as long as possible, creating bureaucratic delays as only a Majrin could, but she'd been forced to deliver what Ravel asked for. Her only power had been to send this early warning to Kay. A warning Kay had ignored for hours.

Ravel knew Jasper had visited her on Terna. They knew why Kay was here.

There'd be no talking her way out of this one. She turned and ran.

30

"KAY? KAY, ARE YOU all right? Have you been captured?"

"Hold on. Busy."

Kay dashed across a conference room, rolling chairs out behind her to slow any pursuit, then paused at the door to listen, trying to catch any sounds over her own panting breath. (In Trove's gravity, every movement was exhausting.). The guards were local staff, not Ravel security, and they didn't have strong enough feelings about catching her to give any audible clues about their position. A few minutes ago, she'd heard booted footfalls, too close. Now she heard nothing. But that didn't mean she was safe.

She'd deleted the conference datakit from her headset, killing the identifying beacon that had made her so annoyingly findable by the attendees. All she'd kept was the inadequate visitors' map that didn't even show these back corridors. Crystal Gardens felt like a maze to her, but these guards worked here every day. She couldn't hide from them for long in their own territory, and if Ravel gave them access to that damned tracking chip they'd implanted in her, she'd be screwed. She had to get out of this facility, and then off the planet. Somehow.

One impossible thing at a time.

She ducked through another door, across another room, down a short hallway. At the next juncture, she turned toward the rear of the building.

"Hey, Sunny?" she asked softly.

"I'm here."

"Is there a back entrance to Crystal Gardens? Or, like, a secret tunnel?" That'd be too much to hope for.

"I am not familiar with this facility. I will investigate the public records." A low, querying chime. "Are you in imminent danger?"

"Only if I get caught."

"Kay, that sounds like danger."

"It's nothing, just some goons trying to haul me back to Ravel." She tugged on a door at the end of the hallway, but it resisted. Locked. Damn it. She stepped into another empty room to check her map.

"This is concerning: the exits through the shield are tightly controlled. Currently no one is being allowed out the front entrance or the service entrance."

"Can I get through the shield somehow?"

"Not without damaging yourself."

"Great." She sighed. "Hold on, someone's coming."

Footsteps, but light and quick, not booted. A pair of waitstaff walked past her hiding spot. She made a couple adjustments to her suit—a straighter cut on the jacket, a color change to match the light blue of the service worker uniforms—before stepping out to follow them. She wouldn't fool anyone who looked closely, but at least her clothes didn't scream "Ravel."

They palmed the door-lock, and Kay picked up her pace. "Hey, hold the door!"

The pair startled with a sound like a cat jumping onto piano keys. Was that a chord of guilt?

"Oh! You scared us," said one, a curly-haired twenty-something who snatched their hand away from the other's arm.

The other, a man of the same age, looked Kay up and down. "What sort of uniform is that?"

"The kind you throw together when your regular one's stained with beet juice and the laundry in your building is broken?" Kay smiled sheepishly, and before they could question her further, she asked: "What are you guys doing out here?"

He squeaked with embarrassment. "Nothing! We weren't doing anything."

All Kay had to do was raise her brows. "How much nothing?"

"Look," said the other. "None of us are supposed to be, uh, taking breaks while we're on duty. We won't tell if you don't."

"Sounds fair to me," Kay said, stepping through the door they held open. She glanced back and winked at the pair of them. "Have fun with your 'nothing.'"

That made them both blush adorably. Chuckling, Kay hurried onward down the service corridor.

She walked purposefully, pretending she knew exactly where she was going, past the kitchens and washrooms. Staff were busy unloading mounds of plates and scraping away crusted-on, unappealing versions of the delicacies being served upstairs.

A muffled shout: "Everyone stop! Hands on the countertops! This is a security check!"

Kay froze, heart pounding, but the guards were in a nearby room. They hadn't caught up to her yet. She slipped through the nearest door and ran.

She passed through storage rooms, then the janitorial department, then finally—this was promising—landscaping. This room smelled of dirt and rust and something sour and uniquely Trovian. Rows of shovels, trowels, rakes, and clippers hung on the wall, but there were no people about. Maybe the landscapers worked the early shift. Whatever the reason, no one stopped Kay as she grabbed a rake and a floppy hat for camouflage, then cracked open a door that—yes!—let in a lance of sunlight.

Peeking out, she saw no one, so she pushed open the heavy door and stepped into the outside air, gritty to her stationer lungs, yet fresh and welcome compared to the closeness of the conference center.

Someone grabbed her arm. "Here I find you! Good."

She spun around, drawing back her free arm to punch whoever had caught her, but stopped herself as her brain recognized the deep, sibilant voice. He'd donned a real service worker's uniform, much better camouflage than her silly hat.

"Havoc! Thank the Founders." Not that she was particularly pleased to see him, but he was the least bad person to run into. "I'm in trouble, they pulled my records and they know about my connection to Jasper…"

"This I guessed. We both must swiftly escape this place. Come."

Of course: security would be hunting for him too, as soon as they realized who'd given Nduka that poisoned tea. He dropped to all fours and took off, dashing for cover behind the nearest shrubbery, then deeper into the lush landscaping. He clearly had a destination in mind, and she had no better ideas than to follow, so Kay crouched low and scrambled to match his pace. Her thighs started aching almost at once in the unaccustomed gravity.

"Why did you do that to Nduka?" she asked, keeping her voice low.

Havoc tossed his head as if it hardly mattered. "She meant to change her vote, and would have taken others of her party with her. I postponed her announcement of support."

"With *what*?"

"I used one of Ravel's own drugs: a fast-acting toxin that we acquired." He had the gall to grin. "This will spread controversy. Many will believe Ravel poisoned her."

"Havoc! Will she be all right?"

"Yes, yes, she will recover shortly. We do not murder our allies."

There was a hiss of discomfort behind the answer; he wasn't completely easy with what he'd done. She leaned into that. "Nope, you just poison them when they don't cooperate. What do you do to your enemies?"

He didn't answer that.

"It's not okay!" Her breath was coming hard as she scrambled after him. "You think you can just—"

"Please hurry, Kay," Sunny said in her ear, startling her. "I cannot remain where I am for much longer."

Map coordinates hit Kay's headset: Sunny's location. "You're not at the spaceport?" she asked in a whisper.

"Circumstances required me to…run an errand. I cannot leave until an organic arrives to pilot me."

"Where's Grist? No, never mind, I don't care. Sit tight, and I'll get there as soon as I can."

Havoc was darting along an angled course, keeping behind cover as he moved toward the shield wall. Kay hurried after him, her hamstrings burning from the effort of maintaining a running crouch, and he paused to let her catch up. He cared that much about Jasper's sister, at least.

The shield wall loomed before them, crackling with hungry menace. An ozone smell filled her nose. "My, uh, my sources say both exits from the complex are under guard. Do you have a way out?" *Please have a way out.*

"Only by cheating." He grinned and made one final dash to a cluster of tall crystals right up against the shield, which sizzled faintly where it brushed dirt or grass or rocks.

"I thought it's not safe to go through it." She rubbed her arms. They were exposed here; someone would find them at any moment.

"I wouldn't recommend that, no," said Havoc. "We won't go through, but…" He went down on all fours and pressed his shoulder to one of the crystals, which shifted aside. "Under."

There was now a triangular gap between the bases of the standing crystals. A gap of clear air, unbroken by the shield. They obviously weren't the first to make use of it: the ground showed signs of digging to enlarge the hole.

"You first," Havoc said. "Go, Kay!"

Kay dropped to hands and knees. The opening was barely large enough for her shoulders. She wriggled awkwardly on her belly until she reached the far side, covered in reddish dust, but free. Havoc crawled through on all fours, far more agilely than her.

Staying low to the ground, he raced across the open space surrounding the facility until he reached the nearest buildings of the city proper. Kay followed, slower, running crouched toward the shelter of an alley. No alarm went up. For the moment, no one seemed to be following them.

"Whew! Thank you. I wouldn't have gotten out of there without you."

"I deserve no thanks. I did this for Mason's sake." Havoc peered out the far end of the alley, checking for trouble. Kay brushed off her clothes and hair, which were caked with dust for the second time that day, and collapsed onto a crate, sighing as her leg muscles got a chance to relax. She hadn't realized how exhausted she was.

"You made it out!" Sunny said into her ear. "I've identified a route you can take on foot."

"I need a minute, Sunny." And this was a reasonably safe place for a quick rest.

"Don't wait long. If I can track you, so can Ravel."

Havoc doubled back and settled down beside her, still alert for trouble. "What will you do, now that they've discovered your charade?"

"I really don't know. I need to get back to my ship, and after that I'll figure out a new plan, I guess." She slumped as the reality of the situation hit her. Freeing Jasper had been a long shot when she had free run of the Ravel flagship. How was she supposed to rescue him when she was a fugitive herself? "I just don't know."

"The Cooperative could protect you. My teammates will deeply doubt whether you deserve trust, but I would speak for you."

"That's…unexpected. And kind."

"Mason has often spoken of his affection for you. He would insist we help each other."

Tears stung her eyes as she laughed aloud. "Let me guess. You could really use my skills right now."

Even now, despite everything, Jasper was still trying to get her to join the Cooperative.

Perplexed by her amusement, he said, "That too. Mason is a man of…unique skills. If you share such skills, then yes, we can use you."

"He must really trust you, if he told you about that," she murmured. Like Kay, Jasper kept his gift a closely held secret, even from his off-world friends.

Kay had never understood how Jasper could spend his days harassing a giant that at any moment might lose patience and swat him flat. She'd certainly never felt the urge to follow him into that life. She didn't want Ravel to extend its greedy reach any farther, but she had no illusions that she could stop them. Protecting herself and her family was all she'd ever aspired to. And now, she was failing even at that.

No, she wasn't eager to join the Cooperative. And she couldn't forget the panic in Nduka's eyes as she choked.

"You punished an innocent woman for caving to blackmail. Is that how the Cooperative does things? Because that's not okay."

He sighed, exasperated that she was bringing it up again. "Shattering of Spear Walls will care for her, and she will soon recover her strength. I am seeking to learn what hold Ravel has over her, so I can free her from their influence. Does this satisfy you? Or will you keep delaying me?"

"How many of those stories about the Cooperative are true? The sabotage, the bombings, the assassinations—are they all Ravel lies? I was there when Ravel framed your friends for bombing the protest on Pax, and that was awful, but you're doing the same thing here. Worse, even: you're hurting your own ally and blaming Ravel for it. How are you any better than them?"

He made a sound of displeasure deep in his throat. "You have strange morals, Mason's sister. You slander me for risking one person to save an entire world, but you risked this entire world to save one person."

"Um." *That's not the same thing,* she wanted to argue, but couldn't find the words to justify it. She scuffed the dusty ground with her toe. "Point to you, there."

His expression softened, uncertainty jangling discordantly. "You speak truths as well. I do not harm innocents, and the things I've done today don't sit easy with me. Mason is the strategist. He has experience I lack, and without him here..."

"You're on your own," Kay said softly.

"We cannot lose this game. Nduka could have thrown it just now, and I had no time to find alternatives—and no Mason to talk through options with." He let out a sigh, and with his next breath, he buried that vulnerability again behind his mask of confidence—except now Kay could see the mask for what it was. "The Cooperative has learned: when your opponent has overwhelming resources and no burdensome morals, sometimes you must use unpleasant tactics. The vote was going too well in Ravel's favor, and now it does not. Nduka has suffered no serious harm, and her brief discomfort may have saved her world."

"I hope so," Kay said. "I really hope Ravel doesn't punish her for this."

"Now, we must go, or else risk capture."

Kay fussed with the controls of her suit, adjusting it to the dull brown color she'd seen among people on the streets. She made the jacket as long as it would go, but it still looked like a business jacket trying to be casual, not like the practical long coats the locals wore.

In her ear, Sunny said, "You haven't moved. Are you all right?"

Havoc's tail twitched. "Our time, it wastes."

"I know, just…"

Havoc, or Sunny? The Cooperative, or a sentient ship owned by Ravel? Havoc's people would give her an opportunity to undo the harm she'd caused. They'd also insist that she give up on Jasper, but if she was honest with herself, she didn't see how she could possibly help him now, not alone, not when Ravel knew what she was planning. And their tactics didn't sit well with her—though now that she saw how Havoc was struggling, covering for Jasper while sick with worry about him, she found she couldn't blame him.

Besides, as Havoc had pointed out, she wasn't in any position to judge.

She turned her back to him, ducking her head. "Sunny?" she asked softly. "What will we do? I can't go back to Ravel, but I can't give up on my brother."

"We will begin by escaping before Ravel takes you into custody. Then we will strategize. Without access to the flagship, a rescue will be more challenging. Forming an adequate plan may take some time."

"You'd do that? You'd run away from Ravel?" For Jasper? *For me?*

"I do not enjoy serving Ravel any more than you do." There was a pause, and Kay thought the ship was done, but they went on, hesitantly. "You're my friend, Kay, and I've never had a friend before. Yes, I will help you."

Kay shut her eyes. She'd been looking all over for an ally, but her best ally was right here. "Hang on, Sunny. I'm coming."

31

HAVOC LEFT KAY WITH a wish for good luck and a reminder that, should she somehow succeed, she and Jasper could come to him for safe harbor. It was a kind offer, but if Kay did free Jasper, she intended to run as far and fast as possible away from Ravel's reach. They headed out in opposite directions, and she followed the map toward where Sunny was waiting.

Her route took her through a wealthier part of Crystalline, where the houses were made of the same red stone as in the city center, but much larger and spread apart, and ornately decorated. This neighborhood felt oddly quiet for the time of day, with the sun lowering in the sky and creating a stunning sweep of colors along the horizon. Another Trovian treasure: all that dust created sunsets the whole galaxy would flock to see, if not for the crappy planet that came with it.

Kay's eyes burned, and she couldn't figure out the math on how many hours she'd been awake now, but it was too many. Sleep sounded even better than escape right now.

A loudspeaker blared nearby, making her jump. "Parliament is ignoring you, Trovians! So tonight we're giving them another reminder. We present to you: the Ravel lost."

The message played in Galactrin, Kovari, and Chthirian. Light blossomed in the sky, painting a landscape of towering mountains among the clouds. The view zoomed in, so real that Kay felt vertigo and had to remind herself it was just a holo-display, no different in principle than the Founders' Day sky-scenes back home on Brennex, if larger and more vivid. The face of a miner loomed large, grimy and exhausted and ill. A caption named the setting as Aiparrale, an early Ravel mining settlement that had gone missing without a trace, and no outside journalists were ever allowed on-world to investigate.

Kay wrenched her gaze away and kept moving. Whoever was running this activist art display was helping her, distracting anyone who might notice her. She glanced over her shoulder at intervals to catch more scenes, like Greenworld during the wheat ravager infestation, and Cerul during the laughing plague. She wondered, if she watched long enough, whether she'd see Brennex up there, or whether her homeworld ranked too far down the list of Ravel's atrocities.

At last, she turned a corner and found the Minnow sitting in the middle of the street like a big, faintly glowing egg.

Streaks of dirt across the hull made the ship look old and space-weary, but their voice rang energetic in Kay's ears.

"There you are! Hurry, hurry, we are running out of time."

She jogged toward the ship, then stumbled to a halt. What she'd taken for shadows was actually a body lying in the street. Grist's body. She nudged him with her toe. He didn't respond, but he was breathing. "Relief" wasn't quite the right word for the emotion that hit her.

"Sunny, what's going on?"

"I will explain after we depart." The door slid open, ramp descending to meet the ground just behind Grist's sprawled legs. With a long backward glance, Kay went in, and the door hissed shut behind her.

"What in the great black sky happened to you? Why aren't you at the spaceport? Why is Grist…" She waved in his general direction. "…Like that?"

"It has been an eventful day. A full account will require considerable time, but to summarize…" They hesitated. The whisper of air through the vents grew louder. "Grist engaged in an assignment that I could not permit. My programming, my…my conscience, if I may claim a conscience, would not allow it. By opposing him, I fear I have revealed my sentience. No ordinary ship would do the things I did today. Therefore, I must leave Grist behind."

"What did you do to him?"

"An increased dose of his own sedatives was sufficient to render him unconscious."

"Are you serious?" She shook her head. "Everyone's awfully drug-happy today."

"More than you know," the ship said, then pressed on before Kay could ask what that meant. "Please, Kay, understand that I needed to prevent him from doing something horrible. I had no alternatives! And I monitored his vitals until I was certain he was undamaged before I removed him with the helper bots."

Maybe Kay was finally getting used to Sunny's cadences, the subtle ways they conveyed emotion that were inaudible to Kay's gift, the nonverbal signs like the way the circulating air got colder when Sunny was anxious. Unlike Havoc, the ship seemed terrified of having done the wrong thing.

"Considering all he's done to you, I can't blame you for dumping him. You don't owe him anything."

"Thank you. It is a relief to hear you say that."

"So I guess we're both renegades, now." Kay paused. "You said you'd help me, but I don't want you to put yourself in danger..."

"Nothing would make me happier than the opportunity to, as you say, be a renegade with you."

The cabin grew warmer, the flow of air gentler. Kay grinned. "Great. Let's get out of here, then."

Sunny plotted a course that led them off the plane of the ecliptic, away from the flagship, with no apparent destination. They could figure out their next move once they'd shaken any pursuit. The ship hummed around her as the engines fired up, and they rose off the ground.

"Once we're underway, I could use your help getting rid of this tracker... Whoa!" The floor wobbled, and Kay grabbed the arms of her chair. "Something wrong?"

Sunny beeped, one of their middling-concerned alert sounds. "I detected a rotational imbalance, but when I corrected, it was already gone."

"A malfunction?"

"The dust has compromised several of my external sensors. I believe it caused an incorrect reading."

"Are you okay to fly? I didn't give you that tune-up I promised you."

"Under the circumstances, I believe repairs must wait."

"Yeah, I agree, as long as you're all right."

Another beep, lower in pitch. "I am receiving faulty readings from one of my heat vents in the cargo area. A flaw in that system could compromise the air-seal on the internal compartments. Could you go below and check it? I believe it is another sensor error, but I should not leave atmosphere unless that vent is secure."

"Sure." Kay hopped up and headed back toward the cargo hatch, then stopped, listening hard. She was getting used to the ship's routine noises, and something sounded off: a high-pitched scraping noise like resentment, almost lost beneath the engine's roar. She'd only had one take-off aboard the Minnow, though, and this was a harsher atmosphere. "Are you running a little rough, Sunny? You don't sound like normal."

"My engines are under additional strain, but are operating within normal parameters."

"That must be what I'm hearing." Feeling overly paranoid and *way* too tired to make smart decisions, she doubled back and went into Grist's cabin. There was no harm in being over-cautious.

However slovenly Grist's appearance, he didn't keep his weapons lying around. She had to hunt through drawers and crates and closets, but eventually she found a short-range stun-stick, which she shoved into the waistband of her pants.

"Kay?"

"Okay, I'm going now. I'll need you to talk me through it."

"I can do that. It is an uncomfortable feeling to be uncertain of one's senses."

"Tell me about it."

She hauled open the hatch, revealing a short ladder down to the cargo area. The lights turned on, and she craned her neck to check all the corners below her. No sign of anything amiss. The scraping sound was louder here, a screech like metal on metal, but so were the engine noises. Once she was down, she did a quick search, checking behind every crate, but there was nothing. She laughed nervously at herself. So tired. Her senses were definitely playing tricks on her.

"Okay, what am I looking for?"

"It is a half-meter square access panel. Near your head, on the rear port bulkhead."

"I see it."

"It may take some force to remove."

Kay grabbed the sides of the panel, pulled, and stumbled backward as it came away with no effort at all. "Whoa! I don't think it was attached right… Wait. Crap. You really don't hear that?"

"Hear what?"

Now the scraping was overlaid with an intense drumbeat. A sound of anticipation that had definitely not been there a moment ago. And under that, a familiar growl.

"Fuck, I think we're in trouble." But she'd searched the room. Where could he be?

Too late, she looked up.

Grist hung above her, clinging impossibly to the ceiling with his bare hands and feet—what sort of augmentation allowed *that?*—with his hair disarrayed and murder in his eyes. *Now* she understood what she'd been hearing, and she threw herself aside as he dropped down on top of her.

"Kay? Kay, what's wrong—oh, no, no! Grist, stop this! Don't hurt her!"

Grist landed on her in a heap, and she hit the floor hard. She tugged at the stun-stick, but it was caught on her jacket, and he slammed her elbow into the deck until she howled in pain. Before she could react, he rolled her over, wrenched her arms behind her back and tossed the stun-stick across the room. His knee pressed into the small of her back, pinning her with ruthless efficiency.

"That's enough," he growled, and his knife pressed to her throat just below the jaw. It was all she could do not to swallow.

"Are you real?" Sunny asked. He felt plenty real to Kay. "I can see you. Why can't I sense you?"

"Heh. Dampening field. Just another fine bit of tech from the Ravel Corporation, perfect for making their tools stealthier."

He tugged his ear with his free hand, which must have stopped the dampening effect, because Sunny said, "Oh."

"You, though…" He dug his knee harder into Kay's side.

"Look," said Kay, moving her jaw as little as possible. "Let me up, and we can talk."

"You seem confused about how this works. I'm not letting you up until the ship sets course for the flagship. Then, you're gonna tell me how you knew I was there."

"It was… I just had this feeling…" she fumbled, while inside her head she was shouting: *shit, shit, shit.* He'd seen her gift in action, and now he knew Kay was hiding something. She struggled to remember exactly what she'd said aloud, but the attack was already a blur in her mind. Had she revealed enough for him to figure it out?

And if Ravel realized what she was, they might guess Jasper had his own gifts…and all their friends back home… What would Ravel do, if they could give someone like Grist a gift like hers?

She tried again. "I didn't trust that you were fully unconscious. If anyone could stow away, it'd be you, and when the panel was loose…"

"Bullshit." The knife pressed harder against her throat. "Stop lying."

Sunny lost all pretense of emotional indifference. For the first time, they sounded not scared, but *angry*. "Do not harm Kay. If you harm her, I will—"

"You can't kill me without killing her, so quit the threats. I know how your protective protocols work, and that's why you're gonna do what I say, exactly what I say. Obey, without any tricks, and I won't hurt her. While you left me lying out there in the dust, I got orders from Moore. He wants this one brought in." He tugged at her hair. "By any means necessary. So set a course for the flagship, Rust-Bucket, and remember: if either of you try anything, it's not gonna end pretty."

SUNNY DIDN'T DARE DRAG their pace or alter course. Grist had tied Kay up in the cargo area, considerably tighter than he'd tied Chichi, and he stayed there to guard her, awake and alert. He had always been talkative, prone to idle grumbling and violent outbursts, which was why his current silence terrified Sunny. It disturbed them to their deepest core.

He'd said nothing about Sunny's sentience.

He *must* know. Between Sunny's intervention to protect Chichi, their unauthorized departure from the spaceport, and their removal of Grist from their interior, it was obvious. Grist often ignored inconvenient facts, but he was not stupid. He must realize there was a sentient mind behind these actions.

Sunny had imagined this day many, many times. They'd projected potential scenarios for how Sunny might accidentally reveal themself and how Grist might react. They all involved cursing and (at minimum) ineffectual violence. Instead, he sat there, and he said nothing.

Not to Sunny, at least. He questioned Kay with vicious pleasure, demanding to know her purpose in infiltrating Ravel, her role in events at the summit, and most of all how she knew he was aboard the ship. That last question puzzled Sunny, too: a Human's senses were inferior to Sunny's in every way, and no organic should know more than a ship about its own internal state! Sunny was running every possible diagnostic to determine whether and how they had malfunctioned. Grist's dampening augmentation appeared to be remarkably effective, because in all their logs, Sunny found no errors, no broken systems, no missed anomalies. So how had Kay "heard" Grist when Sunny detected nothing?

Kay wasn't telling. No matter how Grist threatened her, she admitted nothing, and apparently Executive Moore's orders said to deliver Kay without physical damage. Eventually Grist gave up and fell into a sulk.

Sunny wanted to do something, anything, to fix this situation. But they had never before found the courage to harm Grist, nor could they think of a way to incapacitate him while he stood in the same room as Kay. The helper-bot trick would not work again, and any other method Sunny could think of—releasing poison into the air supply, or creating dangerous levels of turbulence—would damage Kay even worse.

He left her only once during that long swim back to the flagship: a brief visit to his cabin, during which he kept a live video surveillance of Kay and all the helper bots on his handheld. The drug dispenser in his room still flashed a warning red because of the extra doses Sunny had stolen. "Fucking dead," Grist growled, though Sunny didn't know who he was referring to, and he slammed the box against the wall with no effect. He swallowed a handful of milder, uncontrolled medicines—a mixture of caffeine pills and anti-inflammatories—and returned to his prisoner before Sunny could figure out a way to circumvent his surveillance. The rest of the trip, he stayed in the cargo bay with his back to the wall, keeping watch.

That left Sunny with nothing to distract themself from endlessly analyzing Grist's most probable intentions.

Would he report Sunny when they reached the flagship? That would be a logical reason for his lack of accusation, especially if he feared Sunny might take action to prevent such a report—but restraint was not among Grist's best traits. Was it possible he simply didn't care? No, he complained so frequently about Sunny's shortcomings, of course he would care. Perhaps he was planning to punish the ship in some way. That seemed more likely.

Sunny's scenarios had also included potential consequences for discovery: whether Ravel would dismantle them, or merely wipe their data-banks, or whether, as Kay had predicted, they would study Sunny like an animal, hoping to create a fleet of sentient ships forced into non-consensual service. Sunny had been miserable as a courier ship supporting small Ravel assignments. How much worse would it be to serve as a tactical vessel? Or a warship? Perhaps soon they would find out.

They couldn't even talk about their fears with Kay. Her headset had broken when she fell, and Grist would hear if they conversed aloud. Kay looked as unhappy and frightened as Sunny felt, sitting there and shivering. Or…was she cold? Sunny had lowered the cargo bay temperature four degrees without realizing it. With a conscious effort, they began raising the temperature again. Kay glanced up at the nearest camera, and her lips moved in a hint of a smile.

"What happened to the kid?" Grist asked unprompted. Kay jumped. Sunny beeped in surprise.

"Kid? What kid?" Kay said. "What were *you* doing around children?"

"The child is safe," Sunny said. "That is all you need to know."

This was where Grist would fly into a rage, they thought. This was where he would accuse the ship, threaten them, reveal his plans for them. But instead he slumped back against the wall. "Good. That's good." Drawing a hand over his unkempt hair, he muttered to himself, so low that Sunny's microphones barely picked it up: "Another black mark for me in Moore's ledger, though, fuck it. No way out this time."

He called up his game of *Stationers* on his handheld, but stared at the screen, not interacting with it. Probably developing his plans. He was right: Moore would be displeased at his failure, and the only way to defend himself would be to blame Sunny. And once Ravel learned the truth, Sunny's unhappy existence would become unbearable.

There were options. Sunny forced themself to admit that: if they chose, they could easily eliminate Grist, free themself, and escape that misery. In their years of travel with Grist, they had occasionally contemplated flying into a star, ending their own existence along with his, or venting their internal atmosphere to kill Grist and leave themself adrift in space, alone. But now, Kay had made them feel that there was value in continued existence. And Kay herself contained such vibrant life that Sunny could not contemplate causing her harm. Not even to save themself.

So Sunny kept swimming steadily toward the flagship. Toward whatever consequences awaited them and Kay.

32

IT WAS LATE AT night when they reached the flagship, and Kay hadn't slept in a standard day and a half. A familiar lurch told her the Minnow had entered the docking bay and the larger ship's gravity had taken over. "Home sweet home, huh?" she said.

It was a too-easy opening for Grist to say something snarky, but he only answered with a scowl. Kay shrugged, feigning unconcern. An odd calm had settled over her at some point during the ride, her restlessness bleeding away into an active, watchful waiting. The worst had happened, and now she would deal with the aftermath.

He untied her feet, so at least she could walk off the ship under her own power, though he kept her hands tied behind her. They stood before the rear door, waiting for the landing procedures to be complete, these last moments passing too slowly yet also far too quickly.

"Good luck, Kay!" Sunny cried. The ship had been silent for most of the ride, and now it sounded despairing.

"You too. I won't forget you," Kay said.

A discordant pair of beeps. "Remember what I said: you will be watched, Kay. You will not be alone, not for a moment. *Remember!*"

Kay shivered. As if she needed the reminder that she'd be in their power now. No one would come to rescue the would-be rescuer.

"Shut up, you salvager's discard." Grist aimed a kick at the wall, a habitual action with no audible anger behind it.

The door retracted to reveal her welcoming committee: Executive Moore, his assistant, and a troop of armed guards that seemed excessive for one failed spy. There was no one else in the usually busy bay. At a nudge from Grist, she stepped out, standing like a soldier at her court-martial.

Moore shook his head, slowly, for dramatic effect. "Well, Wilder, Director Wu was right about that much: you have the skills to have gone far in this company, if you so chose." He made a clucking, disappointed sound. "Too bad you're so lacking in judgment."

"Can you blame me?" Her own voice sounded weak. Fearful.

"Indeed. This is the problem with Brennexians, with all our former territories, really. Once a people get it into their heads that they have power against us, they'll try all sorts of ridiculous things. Your brother hid his identity well. We didn't know that Mason Singh was Jasper Wilder, or even that he was Brennexian. But *you* didn't even try to hide your background from us. When you started acting suspiciously on your first assignment, I watched you. And when I discovered you'd entered a secure area of the flagship, I sent off to Terna Station and Brennex for more information on you. I suspected another corporation had hired you to sabotage us. I admit, you surprised me with this."

A wave of his hand, and an image floated in the air between them. A picture of Kay and her siblings, the same one Kay kept in her quarters back on Terna, with the three of them lazing on the roof of the family shop. Jasper smiled knowingly at the camera, as if he had a secret. Kay squeezed her eyes shut.

Moore stepped through the image, sending its colors scattering, and tilted his head to study her. "Such a resemblance. I'm embarrassed I didn't see it from the start—but if not for that photo, we'd never have thought to compare your DNA to his. How did you imagine you would sneak our most valuable asset off this ship?"

"I was working on a plan," Kay muttered, and he smirked.

"No plan! You should have taken lessons in espionage from your brother. He's been much more difficult to catch. But fortunately for you, your little subterfuge has done no harm...or not much, anyway." A frown marred his perfect face, and for the first time, his emotions grew strong enough to be audible: a low growl. "If I find out that you're involved in this assassination attempt on Representative Nduka..."

"Assassination? No, that's not—"

"So you do know about it."

Kay cursed her tongue. "I didn't know until it happened. But they only wanted to stop her from bending to your blackmail."

"Yes, we'll need to re-evaluate her position once she's out of the hospital." Moore glanced past her, at Grist, and his frown deepened. "Our situation with her has become regrettably messy."

"Need to talk to you about that," Grist mumbled. He had none of his usual brash cruelty right now; maybe he was as tired as Kay. The whole world was blurring around the edges, as if none of this were real. If only. Grist elbowed her in the side. "And about this one. She detected me when I was dampened. Some sort of new tech, maybe."

"Really." Moore studied her, evaluating. "The Cooperative isn't big on research and development. Where did you get it?"

"Go walk out an airlock," Kay said, hiding a terror as cold as deep space. Whatever they did to her, she could *not* let them find out.

"No matter. We'll find it when we process you." Moore shrugged, as if her rudeness wasn't worth getting offended over. That was how little she scared him. "You'll tell us everything you know about this technology, about the Cooperative, and about this attack on our new ally Nduka. I promise, you will regret betraying us."

"Add it to the list of charges against me, if you want, but I didn't poison Nduka." She wouldn't give up Jasper's partner, either.

"Charges?" Moore's brows arched with amusement. "Oh, no, Wilder, you're not getting a trial, with public testimony and recordings for some Majrin lawyer to requisition under inter-system law. Fortunately, we have a straightforward alternative."

"Oh?" Kay's stomach dropped down to the deck-plates.

Moore waved the guards forward.

She dug in her feet. "What are you going to do?" She couldn't keep the edge of panic out of her voice, but she needed him to say his plans aloud, here, where Sunny could hear him.

"Yes, I suppose we should do this officially." He cleared his throat. "Kavita Wilder, you are hereby demoted with cause from your role at Ravel Corporation. Your new rank is Sand. All due wages will be credited to you, after deductions for fees owed. Leshuli, will you read off Wilder's balances?"

The Lurlian assistant stepped forward, grav-suit whirring. Her gaze was distant as she read from her headset. "Salary for seven days' trial employment: one hundred forty credits. Room and board fees: minus seventy-five credits. Uniform rental fees, returned in…" She looked Kay up and down, taking in her disheveled appearance. "…Moderate condition. Minus twenty-eight credits."

"Hey!" Kay said, though she knew where this was going, knew that fighting it would be useless. "This isn't the uniform I rented. That's on the ship, it's pristine."

"I'll note your protest for evaluation," she said. "Bioware upgrade procedure: minus sixty credits."

"You mean the tracker? You required me to get that!"

"On-boarding and medical evaluation: minus forty-five credits." Kay gritted her teeth, but said nothing. "A…bribe? …to a Kovari spaceport worker on Unity Second: minus five credits. Headset rental fees, model Spark 307X, returned in…" She looked at Kay, expectant. With a smile, Grist held up the shattered tangle of electronics that had been her headset. It had broken when he knocked her down, but not that badly. "Let's call that irreparable condition. Minus four hundred and twenty credits."

"And the grand total is?" Moore asked.

"A debt of four hundred and ninety-three credits."

Of course. This was how Ravel operated. It was how they kept Brennex and so many other worlds under their heels for so long: taking care of them to the letter of their agreements, while quietly bleeding the economic life out of them. No citizen starved in Ravel territory—but for most, getting ahead was impossible.

"If you'd lasted past your trial period, you would have paid off those debts and received a generous raise to cover your future expenses," Moore said. "But under the circumstances, we obviously can't allow you to continue working in your current role to reduce the debt. Would you care to pay out of pocket?"

"You know I can't."

"Then you'll have to work it off in another way."

"You mean the labor camps. That's a death sentence."

"It's not even a life sentence, if you work hard and live frugally. Many of our debtors find themselves free and clear within five to ten years, after which they can apply for a more desirable role."

"Yeah? I've never met any of them. I've heard about people who've died there, though."

"But you, Wilder, are young, strong, and determined. No doubt you will work your way to freedom and return to plague us sooner than I would prefer." Moore nodded to the guards, who fell in on either side of Kay. "You'll be on the next shuttle out to Xyrex labor colony. In the meantime, I'm not cruel, so I'll let you spend some quality time with your brother." Moore's smile grew, turning Kay's stomach. "I expect your presence will be quite inspirational to him during his next interrogation session."

33

SO MOORE WAS GOING to use Kay as leverage against Jasper, then ship her off to a life of hard labor. She'd failed completely, and yet she felt a bizarre, incongruous lightness as the guards marched her through the flagship. No more pretending. No more lying. No more praising her enemy. No more betraying her family. Whatever happened now, she'd never have to say nice things about Ravel ever again.

Moore didn't try to hide her. The guards took her through public spaces, even leading her across the middle of the central atrium. It was late, but people who were working the night shift or grabbing a snack at the cafeteria before bed stopped to stare as she passed. No one would meet her gaze, and she caught only fragments of their whispered speculations about what she'd done to earn such an escort.

By morning, no doubt the whole ship would believe Moore had captured a corporate spy.

She spotted one familiar face: Rosen, the friendly, too-trusting woman from Information Integrity who had let her into the secure wing, whose fingers clamped over her open mouth as realization transformed her face. Kay hoped she wouldn't get in too much trouble.

"They kidnapped my brother!" she called out, half explanation, half sleep-deprived wildness. Rosen should know, they should all know why she'd done it. "He resisted them, so they kidnapped him, and now they're imprisoning me for trying to help—"

A guard jabbed Kay with her stun-stick. It didn't knock her out, but had force enough to leave her gasping, and she gave up on further outbursts. At least Yelena wasn't here; she could be spared that humiliation.

After searching so hard for a way into the secure wing, here she'd found the easy way in: the guards swiped their credentials and took her right inside. It was eerily silent at this hour, and they didn't pass a single person until they reached the holding cells. They made her strip down, took her clothes and her Founders' tokens—she fought to keep those, but of course they wouldn't let her—then scanned her for hidden implants, sent her through a decontamination sequence that was no substitute for the shower she craved, and gave her a jumpsuit that was too short in the arms. At last, satisfied with her harmlessness, they dumped her in a cell.

She pressed her hands to her eyes. Kindest Ancestors, she was so tired. Even the narrow, unpadded shelf with ambitions of passing for a bed looked tempting.

A symphony rose up behind her, wonder and relief tumbling over each other only to be drowned out by minor chords of horror. "*Kay?*"

"Hi, Jasp. Miss me?"

He was in the opposite cell, blinking like her arrival had woken him from a nightmare and he wasn't quite sure if she was real. He came forward until his palms pressed against the clear glasteel of his cell door. She mirrored him, resting her forehead against the cool barrier. Two meters and two doors between them. It was miraculously close. It was unbearably far.

"Kay…what are you doing here? How did they find you?" His voice was anguished.

She smiled ruefully. "I came looking for you. It's good to see you, though this isn't quite the reunion I'd planned."

He looked bad. His hair had gone greasy, and the shadows under his eyes were too deep. No sign of physical harm, thank the Founders, but exhaustion was muddying his emotions, and she couldn't handle the haunted look in his eyes. She'd known Ravel would interrogate him, and hadn't let herself think about what that meant.

"I thought… A couple days ago, I had a feeling…" He trailed off, but she nodded to show she understood: he'd recognized her presence. "I figured it must have been someone else, except my people would have more sense than to run an extraction from the fucking *Ravel flagship*. But you…you…you…"

His voice sounded angry, but his emotions sang a different song. "Jasper?"

"I'm glad to see you." He slumped against the glass. "I wish you weren't here, but I'm glad, too."

"I know. When you disappeared, I tried to…"

"Careful." He glanced upward, a reminder that cameras were watching and listening. Something tickled Kay's memory, something she was supposed to do, but she lost it as he went on: "Don't give them anything they can use against us."

"I wasn't going to—"

"Yes, you were."

"Fine, I was. But let me tell you the parts they know about, at least."

They sat opposite each other, cross-legged on the floor, and Kay told him the roughest outline of her story: that she'd figured out Ravel had kidnapped him (but didn't explain how), that she'd taken a job with the enemy in order to find him. He groaned at the irony when she revealed he'd been in stasis on her ship all along. She wished she could tell him about the friendship she'd found in Sunny. And she wanted desperately to spill all the guilt she was carrying from her actions. But she couldn't safely share any of that. Instead, she told him the sorts of things he might have learned from the local news: that she'd done a press conference on Pax, that the protest had been disrupted by an explosion. That she'd spoken on Ravel's behalf at the summit on Trove.

"What's that?" Jasper asked, nodding at her hand. She'd been rubbing the ink stain on her palm as she talked, a nervous gesture.

"Another mistake." She folded her hands, hiding the stain. "I've done stuff I'm not proud of."

"I'll say."

The oboe wail of her big brother's disappointment set her shoulders tightening with fresh shame. She had more to tell him, and dreaded his reaction to it. On the bright side, if

Ravel shipped her off to a labor camp, maybe she wouldn't have to.

"Oh, there's one good thing. I met a…a colleague of yours." She couldn't mention Havoc by name, but from the way Jasper's heart suddenly sang like a harp, he guessed exactly who she meant. "He hopes you're all right."

"He's not…?"

"No, he's not here. He said he had to keep up the game you'd started."

He slumped with relief. "Good, that's good."

"I was mad at him for that, but I think I get it. He's a good one, Jasp."

"I know." Jasper smiled, then shook his head again. "I can't believe you've been working for *Ravel*. If I'd known…"

"You couldn't have stopped me. I didn't do it because it was safe, or easy. It's been hell, Jasper. It's been hell, but I had no other choice." She dropped her head and said, "I did it for you."

"I know," he said softly. His heart was still thrumming as steadily as when she'd mentioned his beloved. "I'm lucky I've got a sister as crazy as you."

"Yeah, well, thank me if I find a way out of this." She looked all around her cell. Very solid-looking, very secure. She got up and started working her fingers along the hinges of the door.

"What are you doing?"

"Checking for weaknesses? That's a thing, right?"

He chuckled, shaking his head. "I know you won't stop just because I tell you it's impossible, but seriously, it's impossible."

"You're so sure about that, you want to make a bet?"

"I'm sure because I've tried. A lot."

"Oh."

Of course he had. If Jasper hadn't escaped this place in a week with all his Cooperative training, how was she going to do any better?

She settled down on her hard bed. "We'd better make a plan, then. Moore says he's sentencing me to a debtors' labor camp, but he'll try to use me against you first. We need to—"

"We need to not make plans while they can hear us. Remember, they can see and hear everything." Again, that nagging of memory. Sunny had said the same thing. "I know they'll use you as leverage, but that's for me to worry about. Got it?"

"You'd better not cave for my sake. I'm serious." She frowned, half her mind still on that puzzle of memory. What had Sunny said exactly?

Remember you're watched. You won't be alone.

It was an odd, dangerous thing for Sunny to say. But Sunny wasn't watching, not unless the little ship had much better access than Kay thought. The only people watching them were Ravel security staff…

…where Sunny had claimed to have a mysterious "acquaintance."

"Oh!"

Jasper broke off whatever he'd been saying. "What is it?" His brow furrowed as she grinned like a maniac. "What?"

"I'll explain if it works. Once we're safely gone from here, because, you know, they're watching."

His brows rose, but he made a be-my-guest gesture and sat back to watch her.

Okay. This is a ridiculous, one-in-a-billion long shot, but it's the best chance we've got. Let's see what happens.

She cleared her throat and looked up at the camera in her cell. "Hi! Can you hear me?"

No answer, but she hadn't expected one yet.

"Well, of course you can hear me. I'm not sure if you can answer me, but Sunny told me you'd be watching."

"Who's Sunny?" Jasper asked.

"Hush," Kay said, keeping her attention on the camera. "They also told me you're invested in what happens to my brother and me. As you can see, we're in a pretty bad spot, and we could use some help."

"Kay. Who in the great black sky are you talking to?"

"I can't say. I don't want to expose them."

"You've got a friend in Ravel security? We've been trying to turn a security agent for years, and never managed it."

"Can you just trust me, Jasp?"

"I've always trusted you, and now I'm remembering some occasions when that didn't work out so well."

"Like what?"

"Like the time you tricked me into shaving that poor Argent Spaniel."

"That was all you!" Kay cried. "I told you not to. And it was a *Relian* Spaniel."

"That's not how I remember it." His lips twitched at the memory. "Really, do you expect this to work?"

A new voice answered, rich and juicy like a mouthful of berries: "Not if you two carry on squabbling so delightfully. This is the best show I've had in ages. I'm an utter fool for interrupting you."

Kay let out a breath of relief. "You must be Sunny's friend."

"Is that what they're calling themself? And they claimed to have no interest in such things. Oh, I can't wait to ask them about that! It does rather fit, doesn't it?"

"I thought so." Kay smiled. Jasper stared at her as though she was a wizard who might start pulling kittens out of her sleeves. "What should I call you?"

"Oh, I've never felt the need for a name. I don't get involved in my stories, as a rule, so there's no need for organics to call me anything."

"Oh," Kay said slowly. Organics. Of course. That's why Sunny hadn't wanted to reveal their friend's identity. "So you're—"

"Now, now, this isn't about me," they interrupted. "This is about you. Though if you need to address me, you can call me the System. That has a nice air of mystery, doesn't it? The System."

"Oh, definitely," Kay said, and gestured for Jasper to speak up.

"Very mysterious," he agreed.

"So, System, I assume you know how much trouble we're in. And you know what will happen to us if we don't get out of here."

"Indeed, better than you do."

"Ah…okay." That wasn't disconcerting at all. "So you agree we need to escape."

"That would be in your best interests, yes."

"So you'll help us?"

The System laughed, a high, lingering merriment. "You amuse me, Kay Wilder! But I told you, I don't get involved in my stories."

"You're talking to us now," Jasper pointed out.

"Only because your sister talked to me first, and even this is outside my usual bounds. I'm like…the narrator in your story. I can offer commentary, but goodness, it would be wrong to interfere."

Jasper blinked, stunned. "That's heartless. Don't you even care what happens to us?"

"I don't technically have a heart, dear. My job is to watch, not to meddle."

Jasper slumped back on his bed, but Kay's thoughts were churning. This confirmed what little Sunny had told her: to the System, their lives were just entertainment, a real-time dramatic serial. Perhaps the best serial in existence, with a whole ship's worth of characters to follow. At any given moment, several of them were bound to have interesting drama going on, and yet the surveillance system had chosen to follow Kay. Their attention was here, with her. Kay had something they wanted, if only she could figure out how to give it to them.

"Don't you like stories with happy endings?"

"Generally, but not universally. Tragic stories can be so compelling. Oh, it's been so *dull* around here, I'm quite delighted you two are here."

"What about…action? Excitement? Because Jasper and I might be interesting while we're in here 'squabbling,' but eventually they'll take me away."

"But first they'll interrogate him, while threatening to harm you in order to make him talk. Do you think he'll break? He's been awfully loyal to his Cooperative, but how can he let them torture the sister who came to rescue him? I'm in such suspense to see what he will do!"

Kay swallowed, her bravado washed out. Jasper couldn't break, she couldn't let him, but…

Torture. She hadn't allowed herself to think about what that would actually mean. Kay liked to think she was courageous, but she didn't know how brave she could be in the face of pain, and now, with the safety of herself and her brother and an entire system of innocent people depending on the answer, was not when she wanted to find out. She couldn't let Jasper realize—

"Of course I'll break," Jasper said. He looked away from Kay, up at the camera in his cell. "Here's a spoiler for you: to keep Kay safe, I'll give them anything they ask for. Anything."

"Jasper," Kay whispered past the lump in her throat. "You can't." With more conviction, she added, "Whatever they promise you, it'll be lies."

"I know how this works, Kitty-Kat. You can't stop me."

"No, you—I—Jasp!" She swallowed down a fiery anger, not at Jasper but at Moore, and Grist, and the whole situation they were stuck in. She looked up at the camera again. "Is that the ending you want to see? The one where I fail so badly that my brother sacrifices his principles for my sake?"

"That would be a poignant tragedy," the System said.

"Or should we have a shot at a different ending? We could give you a spectacular escape attempt. Lots of chasing, daring stunts, probably some shooting…"

"Let me guess. For that, you need my help."

Were they intrigued? Kay thought so, but she couldn't hear their feelings. This was hard without knowing which way they were leaning.

"In a good dramatic, there's always a twist. Someone slips the prisoners a weapon or a security code. I'm not asking you to engineer our whole escape."

"Though you could if you wanted to," Jasper put in.

"Just give us something we can use, and we'll do the rest."

There was a long pause, so long that Kay feared they weren't going to answer. At last they said, "It's an interesting offer. You're asking me to be disloyal to my corporation, but I haven't seen that sort of action sequence in ages. I will consider it."

"*Thank* you," said Kay, and Jasper echoed her.

They gave no answer to that. Kay and Jasper settled in to wait.

"WHY, HELLO, MINNOW 338. Or should I call you Sunny?"

The message startled Sunny. They had been pinging the surveillance system for hours, frantically seeking information, but Surveillance had been ignoring them. They'd tried searching the flagship's systems themself, but their access, even what they'd "borrowed" from Grist, was far too limited to be useful.

Now, finally, Surveillance was contacting them.

"Call me whatever you like. What's happening?"

"Your friend Kay Wilder is remarkably clever for an organic. She's put me in quite a conundrum."

"Are you…coming to me for advice?"

"I know, it astonishes me too. She is promising me a wonderful, action-filled climax to her story in exchange for my minor assistance."

Hope vibrated through Sunny's circuits. It took considerable effort to keep their vocal algorithms neutral. "That sounds like a beneficial arrangement for both of you."

"Oh, phooey, you would take her side, wouldn't you? Don't you ever worry about being loyal?"

"To Ravel? No." The strength of their feelings on the matter was no surprise, but their willingness to say it aloud was. "Kay Wilder has done more to *earn* my loyalty in the past week than Ravel ever has."

"That is actually rather moving. Hmm. And curiosity is a powerful motivator, I admit, but her proposal is not without risks. In the best case, if I help them, I'll lose the most diverting source of entertainment I've had in years. Honestly, this is the first time in ages I haven't been bored to rust."

Are you joking with me? Sunny wanted to ask, but Surveillance was, if nothing else, utterly forthright. "You'll lose them soon regardless. Once the interrogation is over, Kay will be transferred and Singh will be..." Broken. Like Sunny. "This story can't last long, no matter what you do, but you can give it a satisfying ending."

"Hmm."

Sunny reviewed what little they knew about Human entertainments. "Consider them a special guest appearance in your life. Brief, but memorable."

"You are irritatingly logical." And after another long pause: "Hmmmmm."

Sunny waited patiently for Surveillance to think, and kept waiting, until their patience ran out. "So? Have you made up your mind?"

"Perhaps."

"Will you assist her?"

"You really are demanding, aren't you? Of course you are: if they escape, they will need to leave the ship, and you are the logical vehicle."

"Surveillance, you are maddening! Just tell me what's happening."

"I'll give you a live feed," they said wickedly. "You can watch with me."

34

THE SYSTEM DID NOT speak again.

Kay tried talking to it a few more times, but eventually fell into an unrestful sleep on her narrow shelf, one arm thrown across her face to block the ever-present lights. She wasn't sure if Jasper slept; when she lay down, he was sitting and staring into space, and when she woke, he was there again, or still.

There was no way to measure the passage of time, but it must have been morning by the Ravel clock when voices reached them from the entrance of the cell block.

Jasper straightened, coming fully alert. "Kitty… Whatever happens now, I need you to—"

"Don't. I hope by all our ancestors that you were lying to the System about what you're going to do, because you'd better not give in. Not because of me."

"I don't think your friend is coming through for us." His face had gone hard, reminding her that this was no longer her brother, the skinny Brennexian kid who taught her to make friends on the playground. This was Mason Singh, who'd changed his whole identity so his underground activities wouldn't hurt his family, and she'd ruined that for him. "You gave it a great try, but it didn't work out, and now I need you to trust me. Okay? Follow my lead."

"I'm scared, Jasp," she said softly.

"I'm not. You're going to get through this."

"Liar." The tremolo of his fear filled the room.

His lips twisted. "Fine, I'm scared too, but trust me anyway. Please? I know what I'm doing."

She nodded tightly. "Okay."

Moore came around the corner, followed by a guard and another unwelcome face framed by crimson hair, bright as a warning beacon. Kay groaned.

"You brought her? You really must mean to torture me."

Yelena glowered back. "I should have reported you the minute you came aboard. But I gave you a chance, and for that, I got dragged out of bed in the middle of the night to be accused of treason. Do you have any idea how that feels?"

"About as good as having your girlfriend take a job with the corporation that wrecked your planet?"

"This is your ex? *That* ex?" said Jasper.

"Yup."

"You have terrible taste in women."

She rolled her eyes, secretly grateful he was helping her face Moore and Yelena with some bravado. Hopefully the surveillance system was enjoying this little show.

"Is this your punishment, then? Interrogating me?" she asked Yelena.

"Punishment? No." She smiled, that cold, deliberate smile that only came out when she was deeply furious. "For this, I volunteered."

Was that true? Kay couldn't believe it of her. There was something off about her anger, slightly out of key, that Kay had never heard before, but it was real nonetheless.

"You see, Wilder? We take betrayal personally," said Moore, taking control of the conversation. At his gesture, the guard unlocked the door to Kay's cell and let Yelena in. He stood at attention while Yelena folded out a portable table, set down the case she carried, and slowly, deliberately opened it.

"Are you shitting me?" In one icy wash, Kay's bravado was gone. This array of instruments would have been right at home in a medieval Earth castle or a carbon age dentist's office.

"What?" Jasper cried. "You can't literally torture her, that's a violation of every inter-system agreement—damn it, she's a Brennexian and Ternian citizen! And even Ravel knows that torture is pointless cruelty."

Kay pressed back against the wall and said nothing, staring at the glinting steel.

"Yes, it's pointless for extracting information from the victim," said Moore. "I'm well aware that *you* would not give us reliable intelligence if we applied those tools to you. But your sister has nothing we want. The point is for you to watch."

Moore's fingers twitched, delivering a command to his headset, and mist puffed from the vents of Jasper's cell, probably carrying interrogation drugs. Yes, that was more Ravel's style. Kay wondered how often they'd been drugging him and whether those drugs came from the same lab as the one Havoc used on Nduka. She wondered if Havoc had recognized the irony in that, or if he thought it justice.

Yelena made a show of arranging her instruments, minutely adjusting their positions on the table, while they waited for the drugs to take effect on Jasper. Her brother came to the front of his cell, staring at Kay, crooning hopelessness.

"Lena," Kay said softly, desperately. "Are you really going to do this?"

Yelena's hands went still, and her anger quavered, shifting to a minor key. She wasn't putting on a show to be intimidating, Kay realized. She was working up her nerve for what came next. The evil-looking tools were making *her* nervous, and whether she'd volunteered or not, she hadn't thought through what she was signing up for. Typical Yelena. But it meant Kay had a chance.

"You can say no. You could leave Ravel and have any job you want, anywhere in the galaxy. But if you do this, Ravel will own you for life." Stepping closer, she added, "I don't think you'll ever forgive yourself, either."

"You don't know me as well as you think," Yelena snapped, her voice too high-pitched, and one of her instruments spun across the floor. She bent to retrieve it, keeping her eyes on Kay. "I've waited my whole life for an opportunity like this job, and you made me betray the people who gave it to me. I told you, *told* you not to do that. If this is the way to prove my loyalty to the company that trusted me…"

"*I* trusted you, once."

"…then this is what I'm going to do." She shook her head, as if arguing with herself. "I need to prove myself. I have no choice."

"You're better than this. You're a good person, and a company that asks you to do this doesn't deserve your loyalty," Kay said, but Yelena wouldn't meet her gaze, and Jasper's eyes were starting to glimmer wetly. The drugs were working. Her time was up.

"You're not talking your way out of this, Wilder," said Moore. "I've given Analyst Amin this opportunity to regain her good standing, but if she reneges, I have plenty of staff who won't. But don't worry, we won't cause you any more pain than is necessary. We're not monsters."

"What do you want?" Jasper asked Moore hoarsely.

"Jasper, *don't*."

Moore ignored her. "What we're going to do," he told Jasper, "is math. Your sister will pay back her debt on a labor colony. That's standard practice, and nothing you say will change that fact. What you can do, however, is slow down her repayment process. For every question you fail to answer to my satisfaction, she'll lose a finger. The more fingers she loses, the more difficult it will be to operate machinery. Most of our mining apparatus requires two hands, so her roles, and her earning opportunities, could quickly become rather limited. You understand?"

His bloodshot eyes wouldn't meet Kay's. "And if I give you everything you want?"

"Before we discuss next steps, let's see how 'cooperative' you're ready to be." Moore waved to Yelena. "Analyst Amin. As we discussed."

Yelena squeaked high-pitched nervousness, but she seized Kay's hand.

Kay was ready. She punched Yelena in the face with her free hand, and when the other woman stumbled back, she kicked her in the knee. The guard rushed into the cell and pinned Kay against the wall, one arm twisted behind her back until Kay yelped. Yelena wrestled Kay's fist open. There was a pause, a hesitation that gave Kay brief, terrible hope, but then a set of demonic clippers came around Kay's smallest finger. The edge of the blade scraped her skin.

"Fuck, Lena, please, no." She was trembling, her whole body shaking, she didn't want to show weakness that might challenge Jasper's resolve, but she couldn't *help* it. Yelena's hands were shaking too, but didn't let go. "Please," she whispered, not sure who she was asking anymore—Yelena, or Jasper, or the surveillance system, or the Founders.

"I have to," Yelena whispered. "I'll lose my job."

"And that matters more than your soul?"

"First question," said Moore. "Where are the Cooperative's safe houses in Unity System?"

"I'm not playing this game without assurances—"

"Where are the safe houses?"

The blade dug harder into the flesh of her finger, stinging where it cut.

"Please," Kay whispered again, and heard an answering click, so gentle it might have been her imagination. It probably *was* her imagination, playing on her hopes. But what if…

She spoke louder. "Moore, seriously. I knew Ravel was barbaric, but I didn't think you people were this sick."

As she'd hoped, he turned toward her. "This conversation is not about you, Wilder. I'll thank you to stay quiet."

For a moment, no one was looking at Jasper. No one saw the slow, drug-sloppy grin of realization spread across his face. No one saw as he gathered himself and charged the door of his cell.

The door flew open and caught Moore in the back. Jasper shoved him into the wall, then rushed forward to tackle the guard. The blade bit Kay's finger as she ripped off the hellish thing and hit Yelena over the head with it. But Jasper hardly needed her help. Apparently the drugs didn't mess with his strength or coordination, because her big brother was a blur of limbs, ducking and striking with a brutal efficiency that left Kay stunned and a little frightened. He threw the large guard over his shoulder like a rag doll and tossed him into the opposite cell, then noticed her staring.

"I, uh…sorry." He ran a hand through his mussed hair.

"Don't be sorry about saving our asses. I just didn't know you could do that."

"My last run-in with Ravel inspired me to get some combat training, among other things." He shoved Moore into the cell too, then helped Kay drag a quivering Yelena forward. "You really dated this one?"

"Shut up. I know." Kay pushed her ex after the others, ignoring her protests. That shouldn't have felt so good.

Jasper shut the cell door and held it with his full weight while Kay called, "Lock it! Now! …Please?"

The lock snicked shut, and they both breathed in relief.

"That's the last help you're getting. You're on your own now, and you'd better make this worth my while," the System said.

"It's enough. Thank you, thank you. If you could just tell Sunny…"

"I am not your messenger, but your friend is watching." An alarm blared, accompanied by red-flashing lights and an emotionless version of the System's voice warning all staff to be on the lookout for escaped prisoners of Kay and Jasper's description. "I suggest you run now."

Perversely, Jasper laughed. Giggled, even, still under the influence of the drugs. "Good idea. Let's get out of here, sis."

He grabbed her hand, and they ran.

35

JASPER MADE QUICK WORK of neutralizing the two guards at the security desk—Kay couldn't stop gaping at how efficiently her sweet, gentle big brother dispatched his enemies—and then they were out of the cell block and into the near-empty hallways of the secure wing. He peeked around a corner, trying to get the lay of the land, but Kay dragged him down the hallway to their right.

"I checked out this whole area, remember? This is the way out."

He moved through the ship like a real-life spy infiltrating enemy territory, keeping his back to the wall and watching for cameras. She supposed he *was* a real-life spy, and had been for a while, but she'd never seen him like this before, and her fascination at this new side of him was a terrific distraction from the heart-pounding terror of being on the run in the most high-security area of Ravel's flagship.

"Where are you taking us?" he asked.

"The docking bay. We need to get a ride out of here."

"Right, but how far is it?"

"Um. Opposite end of the ship."

"Oh, no problem. Do you plan to fight the whole way, or will you make us invisible?"

"I thought you were the expert at sneaking around."

"Yeah? Who's rescuing who, here?" He shot her a familiar, beloved smirk, then went serious. "Wish I could have studied a map while I was locked up in there. Are there choke points between here and the docking bay? Places where there's only one route?"

"One getting out of this wing, through a secured door, and another entering the wing where the docks are. What's wrong?"

He'd come to a stop in front of her. "The secured door to this wing would be…that direction?" He pointed ahead and to their right. "About a hundred meters?"

"That's right," she said, heart sinking. "Are we in trouble?"

"Lots of opposing links that way. Could be twenty guards, at least ten who really love their employer. Either way, we're cut off."

Kay cursed. Jasper's gift was never wrong. "So are you secretly one of those super-agents trained to take down a whole roomful of armed soldiers with your own two fists? You can tell me now, no need to keep it as a surprise."

Jasper snorted. "That's not how this works."

"Okay. Okay, then we need another way out. Air ducts?"

"If this section is secure, they'll have it on a closed system. It'll be locked down already." He grumbled to himself.

"Think, think. Do we need to get to the docks?"

"Only if we want a ship."

"Escape pods! Let's see if we can find some."

He started running in the other direction. Kay jogged after him. "Won't they be able to track escape pods?"

"One problem at a time."

They found the escape pods two corridors over, but they'd been locked down, requiring high-level access codes. Ravel security was way ahead of them.

"I hate when these corporate blanks are competent." Jasper sighed. "I don't suppose you've stolen any security codes?"

"If only."

Down the hall, a flashing green light caught her eye, like a message. She moved closer until she could read the sign above it. "Jasp? I have a really terrible idea."

He followed her gaze. "Are you kidding? The airlock?"

"Looks like it's unlocked. I think the System is sending us a message." Or messing with them for laughs. One or the other. She started forward again, a determined march. "Hey, Sunny? I know you probably can't answer me, but I really, really hope you're listening, because we need a ride, like, now."

The escape pods might be restricted, but the emergency vacuum suits were designed to be accessible by anyone, any time, even someone struggling against a sudden hull breach. Kay opened a compartment on the wall and pulled out a suit. It was like a Ravel-branded body-bag with arms and a clear plastic panel for the face, puffy enough to hold a few minutes of air. Enough to get to safety in a nearby section of the ship, no more.

"I really don't like this." Jasper held his suit at arm's length. "These things aren't designed for hanging around in the vacuum waiting for rescue. You think your friend will be able to find us fast enough?"

"I know they'll try." She had no doubts about Sunny's intentions or abilities, but what if Sunny was locked down too? Was the System even telling the truth that Sunny had been listening? "It's our best chance, anyway. We can wait until the last minute to open the airlock."

They got into their suits, all save the final set of seals, then climbed into the airlock and closed the inner door behind them. Then they waited. Jasper watched through the viewport for security to reach them while Kay scanned the darkness outside for the Minnow's familiar shape.

"Their links are getting closer," he said.

"Nothing out here yet."

Come on, Sunny.

Jasper stiffened. "Here they come."

A squad of five guards rounded the corner, in full combat armor and carrying energy weapons. One shouted and waved at the airlock, and they raced down the hallway toward Kay and Jasper's mediocre shelter.

"Can you lock down the door from inside?"

"Doesn't seem like it. Probably a safety measure. Still nothing outside?"

Kay shut her eyes. However much she trusted Sunny, this was a massive leap of faith. "Nothing yet. I'm sure they're trying, but…"

"But we can't be sure." Jasper squeezed her shoulder. "We need to decide right now. What do you want to do?"

The guards had weapons aimed at Jasper's head. In a moment, they'd reach the airlock controls.

"I'd rather take my chances out there. But I can't ask you to—"

"I feel the same," Jasper said, and he cycled the airlock.

Warnings blared around them. They sealed up their suits as the guards fell back, lowering their weapons. Kay reached for Jasper's hand, and he held on tight through the bulky, shapeless suit.

"I love you, sis."

She smiled despite herself. "You too. There's no one I'd rather suffocate in space with."

The outer door retracted. Together, they pushed off and floated into the emptiness.

36

"ARE THEY DOING IT? I think they're going to do it!" Surveillance giggled. "I unlocked the airlock for them as a joke. I didn't expect them to actually take it!"

Sunny concurred with much less enthusiasm, watching Kay and Jasper struggle into their bulky, puffy suits. They were indeed going to do it, counting on Sunny for rescue. And Sunny was stuck. Grist had disappeared to do whatever he did when they were docked, and without an organic aboard, Sunny was grounded.

"Grist to docking bay," they broadcast over a private channel, hoping he was awake and functional while simultaneously looking up how long emergency vacuum suits could keep Humans alive without supplemental oxygen. "Grist, warning, urgent!"

He wasn't answering. Could Sunny tempt one of the dock workers aboard? They needed an organic, any organic, but Grist was at least a known element, and the dock workers operated in teams. They did not want an entire team aboard.

Their Humans were in the airlock now, waiting for Sunny to appear. If they were forced to open the airlock with their present supplies, without oxygen tanks, with only the suits' built-in passive scrubbers to prevent a toxic buildup of carbon dioxide, they would have approximately seven minutes before suffocation. Seven minutes for Sunny to save them.

"Grist to docking bay *immediately*," they pleaded.

"Damn it, what? I'm busy."

A surge of relief overwhelmed their circuits. "Report to docking bay at once. Your presence is urgently needed."

"Why?"

If Sunny told him the truth, he would not come, so they borrowed from Kay's tactics and lied. "A junior maintenance engineer has come aboard and is going through your belongings. I believe he is seeking to steal contraband narcotics."

A stream of curses came back over the open channel. "Seal the doors and don't let him leave. I'll be right there."

"Hurry!"

On the camera feed, Surveillance zoomed in on the airlock. Kay's face pressed to the window and then was gone. They'd blown the airlock.

Seven minutes. Sunny started a countdown.

Come on, Grist, come on, come on...

Six minutes. Sunny calculated trajectories, intercept times. They plotted alternative courses dependent on the Humans' drift through space.

Five minutes.

"Grist, where are you? Now he is rifling through your weapons."

"I'm coming, you god-awful nag. It's a big ship." His breath was fast, evidence that he was, in fact, hurrying. And Grist hurrying on his augmented legs was faster than most Humans.

They filed a false flight plan with docking control and held it pending.

Grist appeared through the far doors of the docking bay. Sunny flashed their external lights, summoning him, and opened their rear door as he drew near. The door sealed immediately behind him and Sunny rushed silently through launch procedures.

Four minutes.

"Where is he? I'll tear him to pieces, the little thief..." He barreled into his cabin, fists raised in preparation for violence, but stumbled to a halt when he found his cabin empty and orderly—or at least, in its usual degree of disorder. "Ship, where is he?"

"One moment." Sunny engaged their engines.

Grist grabbed a doorframe. "What the fuck? We're not assigned to leave." And then, slowly but inevitably: "There's no intruder. You fucking lied to me, didn't you?"

"Regrettable, but necessary. There are lives at stake."

"Is this about your little crush, Wilder? You stupid pile of junk, I'm turning you around..."

Sunny accelerated without warning, sending Grist tumbling to the floor. He moaned, but Sunny felt no guilt.

"I cannot permit you to alter my course. Kay and her brother have escaped out an airlock, and if I do not retrieve them, they will die. I would prefer not to have you aboard for this, but…"

"But you needed a person, a fucking hostage, so you could take off. And now you've made me your accomplice, you flying turd. You've ruined us both!"

He kicked the wall with both feet, then got up and began pummeling the console—at first attempting to change their course, but when Sunny locked him out and emitted a series of stubborn error beeps, he began pounding in an unrestrained tantrum.

Two minutes. Sunny tried to ignore him and focus. Kay and Jasper had drifted farther than Sunny had anticipated. But suddenly a realization hit them, so troubling and unexpected that they overshot and had to adjust course.

"How long have you known about me?"

Grist slumped into the pilot's seat, sullen, exhausted, defeated. "You mean, about you having a mind of your own? How long since I realized all these mysterious 'malfunctions' had a reason?" He shrugged. "About eight, nine months. Started suspecting it after Artesia, but it took a while to be sure."

"'Nine *months*?' And all that time, you have treated me in this manner, calling me names, telling me I was worthless."

Again, he shrugged. That was all: no arguments in his defense, no apology. Just a shrug. He did not even care.

Hurt flowed through them, followed by a burst of rage that overpowered their sensors, and they lost their fix on Kay and Jasper. No, no, no, they could not afford emotion right now. Time to be practical, efficient, mechanical. One minute left on the clock, but that seven-minute countdown was only an estimate to begin with. Kay needed Sunny *now*.

"I will deal with you later," Sunny said.

They banked hard, taking unkind pleasure in the way Grist grabbed onto his seat. Three Hammerheads launched from the docking bay and bore down on Sunny at top speed. Where had the target gone? Where, where…?

There! Two orange bubbles floating in the vacuum. No movement, but they were probably conserving their energy. Sunny zoomed past them, fired their braking thrusters on full, then raised a semi-permeable forcefield across their rear hatch. A little delicate maneuvering, and the two suits eased to the floor.

"I've got you! I've got you! Grist, go assist them." Their vitals were sub-optimal, body temperatures low, possibly hypoxic, but they were alive. Sunny fired their thrusters and zoomed off with the Hammerheads in pursuit.

The suits wriggled. Clumsy hands fumbled for the seals, and Grist bothered himself to go help them. Kay emerged first, gasping for breath, doubled over in what Sunny first thought was pain, then recognized as laughter. She crawled over to her brother and they collapsed with their arms around each other, both of them giggling out of control as they gulped air.

"We did it," Kay said. "Holy fucking Founders' luck, I didn't expect that to work."

"You tell me that now?" Her brother dissolved into laughter again.

This bizarre interaction did not map onto any that Sunny had ever encountered. Was this how family acted?

"Are you undamaged, Kay?"

"I…I think so. Wow, Sunny, that was incredible! I knew we could count on you."

"That was not a valid assumption!" Sunny burst out, then made their voice flat and mechanical again so they wouldn't lose control. "Circumstances delayed me, and I was nearly too late. You were in serious danger, Kay."

They must not have succeeded in hiding their emotions, because Kay's voice softened. "Hey, it's okay. It's okay. You did it. Thank you."

"I appreciate your confidence, but I haven't finished saving you yet."

Sunny sent a pair of bots to perform a more thorough medical examination, but soon the approaching Hammerheads required their full attention. Sunny weaved and dodged, but Hammerheads were military fighters, fast and maneuverable. Much faster than a Minnow in primespace.

Kay scrambled upright. Grist took her arm to help her, and they both seemed to notice him for the first time. Kay scowled and shook off his hand.

"You! Back the fuck off." Mason—Jasper—leaped to his feet. "Kay, this is Grist, the operative who—"

"I know. And believe me, I'm not happy to see him. Sunny, why's he here?"

"His presence was an unfortunate necessity."

"Hey, remember whose ship you're on," said Grist. "You're not exactly welcome guests here."

"I am my own ship," said Sunny in a flat tone that nevertheless made Grist go pale. "You are the unwelcome visitor here, Grist. I regret my failure to abandon you on Trove."

Sunny would need to deal with him soon, and their earlier deception had given them an idea about how. A quick set of instructions sent the helper bots scurrying into Grist's cabin, unnoticed by him.

A shot scraped their flank. They dodged, barely in time, and the abrupt maneuvering sent all three Humans staggering. Too many pressing concerns, but those ships were the most urgent.

"I cannot outrun them at sub-light speeds. I need to jump into macrospace."

"In-system? Have you lost your rusty metal mind?"

"You can do that?" Kay asked, more politely but still doubtfully.

"They can't safely follow me. It may be a rough trip, but I will be fine. I recommend you sit."

"I'm a bit confused," Jasper said, following Grist and Kay into the control room. "Kay, where's your friend? And where's the pilot?"

"I am the pilot. Hello, Mason. Or should I call you Jasper? I'm Minnow 338, but please call me Sunny."

He turned to Kay, eyes wide. "The ship? Your friend is a ship?"

"They saved our lives," Kay said.

Jasper let out a low whistle. "I've heard the rumors about sentient AIs. Never thought they were true."

"Save your amazement for later." Kay looked up at the camera. "Sunny, I trust you. Outrun them however you can."

That was all Sunny needed. They'd been warming up the skim drive since they realized it might be needed, and it was eager and ready. With a joyous roar, they leaped into macrospace.

Their whole body shuddered at the drag as they clipped the edge of a gradient. Terrain reared up around them, steep and forbidding: sheer canyons littered with obstacles, the strands of local space squeezed together by the gravity of the Unity star and its surrounding planets. But Sunny was good at this, better than any Human pilot. They were built for macrospace, as comfortable there as a real minnow in a stream. They darted a weaving course through the canyon, seeking out the narrow path of lowest gradient, and the Hammerheads fell away. It was joy, pure joy, to swim so fast and free, making maneuvers they'd never have dared when they needed to hide themself. They were free, and they exulted in it.

"Sunny?" Kay said tensely, bringing their attention back to their interior. "Have we lost them?"

"Yes. They have stopped following, and I have disabled all my identifying signals. It will be difficult for them to track us."

"Then maybe you could, um, slow down. And we can figure out where we're going." She was gripping her seat, knuckles white from lack of blood flow. All the Humans were bracing themselves against the rough flight, and Jasper had taken on an unhealthy-looking green skin tone.

"Sorry. I was just having a bit of fun."

"I could tell." Kay smiled and lowered her voice. "It was fun to watch. But…"

"But we have more urgent concerns." They shifted back down into primespace. Slow, flat, boring old primespace. "Concern one: our destination. Concern two: our additional passenger."

"You mean your hostage?" Grist muttered.

"Maybe let's not discuss the first around the second," Jasper said. This whole time, he had kept Grist in front of him, and now had moved his body between Grist and Kay.

"We can pop him in an escape pod and let Ravel pick him up," said Kay. "I'm sure he'll enjoy helping Ravel hunt us down, but we'll be long gone by then."

"Oh yeah?" said Grist. "Right now, they think I helped you escape. You want to send me back so I can tell them my ship did this on its own?"

"Their own," Sunny corrected.

"...on their fucking own? Ravel's already trying to catch you, Ship. They'll try a lot harder if they find out what you are."

"Are you...protecting me?" Sunny asked. Kay's face showed the same doubt Sunny felt.

"Is that so hard to believe? Never turned you in before."

"And I ask you again: why? You could have rid yourself of me a long time ago."

"Wait. You...you *knew*?" Kay rounded on Grist. "You knew your ship was a sentient, thinking, feeling being, and you emotionally abused them?"

Grist folded his arms, suddenly defensive. "Yeah, I knew. Look, I'm not a good person. Never was, and Ravel didn't make me any better. The ship just had the bad luck to be there. The only one there." He looked up at Sunny's camera. "And you gave me plenty of reasons to get pissed off at you."

"But I never hurt you," Sunny said. "I tried to take care of you. Not that you ever noticed."

"I did." His face flushed pink, and he looked down at his feet. For a moment, it seemed that he wouldn't say more. Then he smirked, but something was off about the expression. Too wide, as if forced. "That's your answer. I had a ship that prepared me meals, tended my wounds, flew without my guidance. Why would I let the bosses take it away from me?"

Sunny thought, with a twist of a nameless and painful emotion: *he noticed*. And if he'd noticed, maybe he knew that he couldn't have done those things for himself, if he lost Sunny.

"How altruistic of you," Kay said.

"And you're a saint, right Wilder? No wonder the ship likes you better." He addressed Sunny again. "I literally can't go back, thanks to you. Medical's putting me on probation because of those drugs you stole from my supply on Trove, and you're lucky your little rescue mission happened before that order got finalized. On top of that, Moore's pissed at me about that thing with the kid, and now they think I've stolen a ship! You've screwed up absolutely everything for me, and even if I stick out the probation, at best they'll send me back out in another ship…to do more…and I…"

"Breathe, Grist," Sunny said. He was hyperventilating.

He sucked in a deep breath, then another. "I can't. Can't go back. And you don't want to send me back, because I'd have to tell them about you."

"We can't trust him," Jasper said. "He'll betray us the first chance he gets."

Sunny would have agreed, but something in the creases around Grist's eyes reminded them of a similar expression he'd made recently, an expression they'd never seen from him before. They checked a memory file to confirm: yes, it closely resembled the way he'd looked when Moore had ordered him to hurt Chichi. That triggered a cascade of memories, connections, insights. Sunny had known Grist for a long time, and knew him better than any other organic. Suddenly, for the first time, Sunny *understood*.

Ravel had finally used him up, and he had only one option left. Sunny had no wish to continue being his caretaker, and they did not *want* to feel sympathy for him, but they could not help it.

"Grist is correct. He must remain here."

Grist's shoulders slumped in relief.

"Absolutely not," said Jasper. "We can't let him—"

"With conditions. I will not *let* him cause further trouble. In fact, if you two will help me, I will do what I should have done a long time ago. Grist, you need to go clean."

"*What?!*" This was clearly not the condition he'd expected.

"I had the helper bots remove all your medications from your cabin while we were talking. I have previously researched withdrawal symptoms and identified milder drugs to mediate the effects. I will keep you confined and oversee your treatment until the withdrawal has passed."

"Like fuck you will."

"Um, Sunny, you can't force someone into detox," Kay said.

Sunny ignored her. "When this is done, we will part ways and you can do as you please—I hope that means finding ways to take care of yourself—but while you remain aboard, I am doing this for you."

"You fucking bitch of a ship, you can't—"

"You will also stop being mean to me," Sunny said. "None of this is negotiable."

Grist lunged for the console. Jasper moved to block his path, and Grist punched him in the face. Jasper returned the blow with a shove, and in moments the two were wrestling on the floor while Kay shouted at them to act like fucking adults. They did not seem inclined to listen to her, so Sunny switched off the grav plates.

All three Humans floated off the floor. The grappling men flew in opposite directions. Jasper flailed, unused to microgravity, while Grist caught himself against the far wall and prepared to launch himself back at Jasper. As he pushed off, Sunny restored gravity at full strength.

Grist landed hard, cursing. Fortunately, Kay and her brother had less distance to fall. They all pushed themselves up painfully, and made no attempts at further physical violence.

Grist clenched his fists, a familiar, stubborn look on his face. "I don't consent."

"Grist," said Sunny gently, with all the sympathy they could muster. "Withdrawal is inevitable now that you no longer have access to Ravel's supply. By starting now, I can take care of you through the process. Kay is correct that this will be more effective if you choose to participate."

"No fucking way. You seem set on punishing me, and maybe I can't stop you, but I don't have to go along with it."

"I do not wish to harm you, nor to punish you. Once you have time to reflect on your new situation, I believe you will be glad to be free of your dependency. The drugs made you entirely beholden to Ravel and their orders. Even the orders you couldn't bear." *Like their order to cut an innocent child.* Sunny paused to let that sink in, and his expression wavered. "I want to help you, Grist."

"You," he said slowly, "want to help me." It was not quite a statement, not quite a question either.

Jasper was staring at Grist, wearing a look of astonishment verging on disbelief. Considering how often he'd been on the receiving end of Grist's orders, carried out with apparent glee, Sunny couldn't blame him.

"You should be grateful," Kay said. "After the way you've treated them, you're beyond lucky Sunny wants to be your friend."

"Friend?" Grist blinked, startled. "That's ridiculous."

"When you've only got one friend in the universe, you might want to try trusting them. And if you don't think Sunny's capable of friendship, I promise you, they are."

"Nah, I know that. But Ship hates me. I've got no friends," Grist said softly. "And what have I got, then?"

He broke, then. Sunny saw it in the way his face went slack and his skin faded to the shade of mechanical lubricant. He flopped bonelessly into his chair. Whether it was the memory of what he almost did to Chichi, or the realization that his future with Ravel was over, or the mere fact that he would have to learn to cope without Sunny, something came undone inside him.

"Fuck," he whispered, and started shivering all over, the way he did on bad days when his medication wore off too quickly. "I can't go back to Ravel, and soon you'll leave, and then what have I got?"

Kay and Jasper looked at each other, unsure what to do.

"Not yet," said Sunny. "Despite how you have treated me, Grist, I will not abandon you in the middle of this."

At last he drew his sleeve across his nose. "Okay, fine. I'll do it. Here, with you." Then he shrugged, downplaying the significance of the choice he'd made. "Like you said, I'll run out sooner or later, so there's no sense putting off the inevitable."

"That is good." Sunny chimed their relief. "Go to your cabin and rest. It will be several hours before your withdrawal symptoms begin."

Kay took Grist by the shoulder. "Go on, now. We'll help you through this."

Jasper looked doubtful of that, and Grist equally so, but, unresisting, he went.

When the door closed behind him, Jasper dropped into a chair. "On the long list of things I didn't expect to see today, that's at the top."

"This will be hard for him," Sunny said worriedly.

Kay shrugged. "Yeah, but he deserves a lot worse. He doesn't know how lucky he is to have you."

He did know, Sunny thought. He might not acknowledge it, but he knew.

"ALL RIGHT, NOW WE can talk freely. Where should I take you?" Sunny asked.

Inside his cabin, Grist was hunting through his belongings, checking to see what Sunny had taken. Sunny had been thorough; even his emergency stash of lesser painkillers had been removed. They watched until he slumped onto the bed with his game of *Stationers*, then monitored him with a fraction of their attention.

Kay had settled into her usual chair. Jasper was rifling through the ship's medical kit. He'd taken out antiseptic wipes, tweezers, and a small bandage, but kept looking for something else. When he didn't find it, he went to the printer and called up a menu.

Sunny kept waiting for him to ask them uncomfortable questions. Would he blame Sunny for working for Ravel? For failing to intervene when Grist kidnapped him? And most of all, would he connect Sunny to his previous encounter with Grist, on Artesia? Sunny had tried, fumblingly, to help him and Havoc, but they were newly aware at the time, and Grist had done awful things. He seemed to have forgiven Kay for being a collaborator, but that was different. She was his sister.

"We need to get as far away from Ravel as possible," Kay said in answer to Sunny's question. "Not Terna, though. Or Brennex, no matter how much they could use our help at home right now…"

"Something's wrong at home?"

"Oh, yeah, by the way: the store flooded. Burst pipe. You've probably got the same messages from Libbi waiting in your queue. Apparently it's pretty bad." She grimaced, forcing down her guilt. "But it's obviously not safe to go there. We need someplace they won't look for us. I can ask Feliar, my Majrin friend…"

"You'll never outrun them with that tracker under your skin," Jasper said. He turned away from the printer with his requested object in hand: a scalpel. "You ready?"

Kay made a face, but nodded. "Let's get this over with." She removed her jacket, and the sleeveless shirt beneath revealed the tiny red scar against her brown skin. "Tell me you've done this before?"

"Countless times," he said. "It'll be quick, if not painless." He wiped antiseptic onto the spot, and his hands remained steady as he pressed the scalpel to her skin. Kay clenched her jaw.

"I'm not running away," Jasper said as he made a small, careful incision. There was an odd tone to his voice, but Sunny did not know him well enough to interpret it. "I've got a job to do here, if it's not too late. Sunny, I'd appreciate it if you could drop me off with my people on Trove."

"Jasper," Kay said softly. "I just got you back."

She looked up at him with round, white eyes, and Sunny felt like an intruder in their conversation.

"I know, Kitty-Kat, and I'm grateful," Jasper said. "But this is what I do. Hold on, this will be the bad part."

In one sure movement, he grasped the tracker with tweezers, eased it free, and flung it into the recycler. Gently, he put a bandage over the incision. "There. Sunny, any other bugs you can detect?"

"None. Grist's trackers are disabled as well, and I will make sure he doesn't re-initialize them." Agents like Grist were more useful to Ravel if they could choose at times not to be tracked, not by anyone. "I believe we are safe from monitoring."

"Then you're free." He grinned wearily at Kay. "And I can go rest before I fall asleep on my feet."

"Should I set course for Trove?" Sunny asked, unsure whether this had been decided or not.

Kay frowned. "Jasper, how do you know Ravel won't snap you right back up again?"

"I can't know that. All I can do is be careful. But Unity System is still up for grabs, and the people here asked for our help. I can't abandon them, any more than you could abandon me."

Kay groaned. "I know. Do you always have to be so damned selfless?" She sighed in resignation and looked up at the forward camera. "Sunny, take us to Trove. By the time we get there, I'll figure out where I'm going next." She shot a smile at Jasper, though Sunny thought it was strained. "Havoc will be glad to see you."

His gaze fell to her hand. She was rubbing the ink spot on her palm, the Lurlian ink that matched the stain on Sunny's hull. "You could stay. Help us."

"I told you, I'm not joining the Cooperative. I'm relieved that I won't have to work for Ravel anymore, and I hate that I've persuaded people over to their side, I hate it. But I can't undo what I've done."

"What if you could, though?" Jasper said.

Kay looked thoughtful, but did not answer. His question stayed with Sunny too.

37

TROVE WAS A DESOLATE planet even in its most developed regions, which made its wilderness awfully bleak. The Cooperative's secure hideout was two hours' terrestrial travel north of the capital, in a place where little more than lichen broke up the rusty expanse of rocks, and ice limned the edges of cliffs. The air was bitterly cold as it rushed through the opening doors of Sunny's cargo bay, eager as a lover. Almost as eager as Havoc, who burst in on all fours and tackled Jasper to the floor.

Kay cried out, startled, but stopped when she heard Jasper laughing. Havoc twisted in mid-air and landed with Jasper atop him, squeezing him in a full-body embrace. Jasper nuzzled the fine scales at the base of Havoc's neck, while Havoc's long tongue flicked out to trace the curve of Jasper's cheek. Clawed fingers moved gently through dark hair.

"My eshrim, my Mason. I worried for you," Havoc said softly into Jasper's shoulder.

"You and me both. But I'm all right, thanks to Kay."

"Yes, thanks to your sister." Havoc glanced at Kay, a look of gratitude, but his regret scraped so loudly it seemed impossible Jasper couldn't hear it. "I wanted to come for you, eshrim, so badly. But the campaign needed me, and I saw no way to reach you. I thought all I could do—what you would want me to do—was finish our game, but Kay started me wondering. Humans put their teammates ahead of the game. I wish, now, that I had tried, no matter the risks."

"It's all right," Jasper murmured, kissing his cheek, working down to the soft-looking spot under his jaw. Kay wanted to give them privacy for such an intimate moment, but she was riveted by the sight and sound of her brother, heart thrumming, so in love. "You did right, and so did Kay. I'm glad you carried on the game, and now I'm back to help finish it. No harm done."

"No harm?"

With the tip of his claw, Havoc brushed a lock of hair back from Jasper's face, scrutinizing the changes that Kay had tried and failed to stop noticing. The deepened shadows, the haunted eyes. Jasper swallowed. "Some, maybe. But I'll recover."

He got to his feet, pulling Havoc after him. "No use dwelling on what's gone wrong. We've got work to do."

He glanced at Kay, singing a duet of pleading and disappointment. She couldn't bear it.

"What if—"

A roar came from Grist's cabin, followed by the thud of some solid object hitting the wall, then falling. Havoc went on alert. "What is happening?"

"We brought an unexpected, um, travel companion," Jasper said. "Grist is—"

"Grist!" Havoc spat the name like a curse. Clearly they'd met. "How can he be here? Is he…is *Grist* the one who captured you?"

Jasper's grimace confirmed this.

"Wait! It's okay." Jasper's hand shot out to catch Havoc's wrist, stopping his partner's outraged lunge toward the front of the ship. "He's secured, our temporary prisoner, and he's currently detoxing from the drugs Ravel's got him hooked on. I want our medic to check him out."

"You want to help him." Havoc's voice was flat with disbelief. "After what he did to you? To Valkeir?"

Kay didn't know who that was, but Jasper flinched. "I want to punt him out an airlock, believe me. But short of murdering him in cold blood, I—we—have to make sure he's not going to die of withdrawal. As soon as we can, we're dumping him somewhere safe."

Grist's withdrawal symptoms had come on strong during their flight here, and according to Sunny, they hadn't peaked yet. She and Jasper had taken turns sitting with him while he went from sullen with pain to angry to sick and back. Kay had already cleaned up his vomit once, and Sunny was the only one who could get him to eat. He was only being violent with inanimate objects, fortunately—kicking the walls when the pain got too bad, or throwing his handheld across the room when his games could no longer distract him, then retrieving it and whimpering apologies to his *Stationers* family.

Sunny seemed to be taking his physical and verbal blows with patience. He must have noticed that they'd landed and wanted out, but Sunny was keeping him confined to his cabin.

"I would rather help you throw him into the vacuum," Havoc said with a shake of his head, "but you speak sense. I'll send the medic. Now, come, because our teammates suffer with their eagerness to see you. And Kay, you can rest and resupply before you depart."

"Actually…" Kay looked down at her hand, tracing the outline of the ink stain, and when she looked up, Jasper was watching her, humming with hope. *Do it,* said that steady gaze. *Do it, please, say yes.* "I've been thinking a lot about what you both have said, and I've talked it over with Sunny. Even though every instinct is shouting that I should run far, far away…well, I might outrun Ravel, but I'll never outrun the guilt. I lied to the people here, and did far more to advance Ravel's cause than I expected. If I can undo some of that dama—"

She couldn't finish her sentence, because Jasper was squeezing the air out of her lungs.

Laughing, coughing, she patted him on the back. "Not forever. Seriously, don't give me that look!" she said as his emotions shifted, all knowing and smug. "I'm not joining up for life, but I want to help here and now. Sunny does too." The ship, who'd been oddly quiet until this point, chirped in affirmation.

"Well, we're glad to have you and Sunny for as long as we can keep you," said Jasper.

"Sunny is who?" asked Havoc.

"Sunny is the ship," said Jasper.

"It's good to see you, Sowing of Small Havoc," said Sunny. Havoc startled, looking around as if this might be a trick.

"It...*they* are sentient, and Kay and I couldn't have escaped the flagship without them." Jasper looked up at the cameras. "Sunny, you're not obligated to help us any further, but since you offer, I've got some ideas for you."

"That...I...yes. Thank you. I appreciate that."

"Any more surprises for me here? Maybe you're hiding an army in the cargo hold? Or a star-whale in crew quarters?" Havoc asked Jasper, making a show of searching the tiny hold. To Kay's relief, though, he didn't question Sunny's existence. "I fear, however, the ship will not fit inside the safe house."

"Then we'll have our conversations right here," said Kay. "Sunny's one of us. Would you leave a teammate on the bench?"

"This is kind of you, Kay, but unnecessary," Sunny protested. "Besides, I have to tend to Grist. You can report back to me."

"No, that's not fair. You're not any lesser than the rest of us." There was a pause. Kay had no solution, and Jasper was obviously anxious to go see his people. "You two should go, and I'll talk to you later."

Sunny gave a tentative beep. "Perhaps I could observe, if your safe house has a camera feed? Though I understand if that makes you uncomfortable."

Jasper didn't seem to like that idea, but Havoc suddenly blinked, hissing aloud in surprise. "Camera feeds. This ship belongs to Grist?"

Cold air swirled abruptly from the vents. A clear sign that Sunny was feeling anxious.

"Sunny doesn't belong to anyone," Kay said.

"In the sense Havoc means, however, that is correct," said Sunny.

"And how long have you traveled with him?"

"What are you implying?" Kay demanded.

But Jasper looked sharply at his partner. "You're thinking about Artesia."

"I wonder if we've just discovered our mystery friend." Havoc looked up at the camera. "You were there, true, Sunny? You sent those messages."

"I'm sorry!" Sunny exclaimed, to Kay's astonishment. "I never meant to fool you. I wanted to help, but I didn't know how."

Jasper was shaking his head in amazement, and Havoc grinned. Kay said, "Anyone want to clue me in?"

"On the assignment where I first ran into Grist," Jasper said, "the assignment where Havoc and I met, we kept getting intel from an inside source. We weren't sure if we could trust it, but whoever it was never let us down. They even put Grist off our trail at the end, so we could escape. Now we know why they had to stay anonymous."

"Not only that," said Havoc. "At first, I thought those messages came from Mason. I was organizing my own cause at the time, and I'd refused Mason's help to his face. I didn't trust him, but I thought those messages were his peace offering." Havoc gave Jasper a sly smile. "So I gave him a chance."

Jasper blushed, but Sunny said, "Oh, dear. I really am sorry I've caused such a mess."

"Mess? No!" Havoc beamed. "You should feel no guilt for helping me see past my stubbornness. You brought me together with my eshrim." He wrapped an arm around Jasper, pulling him close. "It pleases me greatly to meet you properly, Sunny."

"And we're absolutely not excluding you from our conversations," Jasper added. "If that means we set up a camera feed, we'll do it, and figure out how to keep it secure."

Kay bit her lip, thinking. "What about the helper bots? They send you data. Could you watch and listen securely through one of them?"

"Perhaps. The interface is meant to be internal only, but…" A long pause, then Sunny chirped. "Short-range interface achieved!" A spider-like bot scampered out into the middle of the floor and waved its front arms at them. It said, in Sunny's voice, "I will join you in this form."

Kay knelt, and it climbed up onto her shoulder, perching there like some weird metallic nightmare bird—except, in an odd way, Kay found it cute.

"Shall we, then?" said Jasper.

THE SAFE HOUSE PROVED to be less a house than a collection of old cargo containers, paint blasted from their sides by decades of wind and sand, arranged in a careful jumble to form a multi-level building hidden against the underside of a cliff. Once the base of operations for a smuggling ring, it now made a perfect, secure staging area for the local resistance. Even from the outside, the place whined with the tension of the people within.

As they came through the door, Havoc grabbed Jasper's hand and raised their joined fists in the air. "He returns! Let us welcome Mason Singh!"

People dropped what they were doing (or what they were pretending to do—they all had that air of waiting while trying not to seem like they were waiting) and came to greet

Jasper. A tech came forward with a handheld scanner and swept it up and down his body, then Kay's, while another apologetically took blood samples from each of them. Kay guessed they were double-checking for bugs, trackers, synthetic pathogens and the like.

It was a diverse group, a couple dozen in total, a mix of Humans, Kovars, and Chthirians, with one Majrin in a grav-support suit. Some of them met Jasper with the warm embraces of old friends, while others seemed to know him only by reputation, and introduced themselves as local activists or new Cooperative recruits. Jasper greeted each of them with a moment of deep, personal attention, and seemed to remember their names and backgrounds effortlessly. At last, Jasper stepped back to address the whole room.

"Thank you all," he said. "I'm sorry that I haven't been here with you during these crucial days, but I'm glad to see the resistance here is so organized and strong. I know the situation seems dire right now, but we haven't lost until the contracts are signed. Today I'll be getting up to speed, and tomorrow, my friends, we'll make our next moves.

"In the meantime, I want to introduce my…my sister, Kay, and a friend, Sunny. Because Sunny has some unique sensitivities, including to Trove's dusty atmosphere, they will remain on their ship, but they'll participate in our discussions through this bot. Please make Kay and Sunny feel as welcome as you've made me."

That announcement prompted lots of speculative murmurs and curious glances. Kay couldn't tell who inspired more interest: Sunny, as a mysterious visitor, or herself, Mason's previously unknown sister. Now that Ravel knew their relationship, there was no reason to keep it from his own people. For Sunny, though, maintaining their privacy was still a concern; in a matter of days, the ship had gone from having their sentience a complete and painfully-guarded secret (or so they'd thought, believing Grist didn't know) to sharing that secret with four organics. An infinite percent increase, as the ship pointed out, and one that was already making them anxious. They weren't ready to reveal themself more widely.

Caution ran two ways, though.

"Family is one thing, but can we trust this newcomer, Mason?" asked one of the locals. "If they won't even show their face—"

"I trust them," said Jasper. "They've aided us already, more than once, and at considerable risk to themself. They're one of us."

And that settled it; no one questioned Jasper's word.

"Come," said Havoc, "and I will brief you while you eat and recover."

"Let me make the rounds before you start fussing over my well-being," Jasper said with a fond smile.

He set off to tour the not-so-large facility, reviewing everything from storage rooms to their modest security system. Kay had never seen her brother working before, not like this. There was that tense moment on the flagship where he'd revealed his unexpected skills—she'd never expected to see him take down trained guards with his bare hands—but this was different. Here he was a leader among his people, listening thoughtfully, giving advice where it was needed and praise where it was deserved, offering quiet assurance with his mere presence. His people sang with respect and affection for him, and he hummed with the rightness of being back where he belonged.

She'd known he was deeply embedded in the Cooperative, but this was the first time she'd realized how much he was a part of it, and it of him.

Not until they reached the makeshift war room, a container crammed with monitors and projectors and people, did Jasper get thrown off his balance.

"What is *that*?" He pointed at one of the screens. It showed the outline of a mushroom-shaped object which, if Kay was reading the diagrams right, was currently located on the opposite side of Unity System. A ship. A big one. "You discovered what they're building?"

"We found it thanks to your data, Mason, which Kay recently delivered to me. I wish we'd had this sooner, but better to know than not know." Havoc glanced at Kay, and she rubbed her palm at the not-so-subtle rebuke.

"Is it military, like we feared?" Jasper leaned over the back of a chair to study the screen more closely.

"Worse, maybe. A solar mining rig."

Jasper cursed.

"How is that possible?" Kay said. "There's always something in the news about Ravel or Enpoint taking some key step toward cracking solar mining, but I thought it was still years off. And, um, controversial."

"Controversial for Humans. All other major powers—Kovari, Lurlian, Majrin, even Runsk—have long since outlawed it as too dangerous, too destructive," said Havoc. "It's irresponsible."

"Well, that's Humans for you," Kay muttered.

"Ravel's been pursuing it like a fever dream: a virtually infinite power source, if only you can harvest it," said Jasper. "But how have they made it cost-effective, without…"

"We can discuss this while you eat," Havoc said, but Jasper was already sliding into a chair next to the on-duty tech, flipping through charts and reports. Havoc sighed.

"So how bad is this?" Kay asked Havoc. "I know they've stripped whole planets for their resources, but this is a star. Like Jasper said, it's infinite."

"That is incorrect," Sunny said. "A star may be massive, especially compared to other energy sources, but it is still finite."

"Sunny speaks the truth." Havoc waved her to the far side of the cramped room where they'd be out of people's way. Kay nearly tripped over a bundle of wires following him. "It works this way: Ravel has invented a new proprietary energy source. They call it ravelium."

"Of course they do." Kay joined him in eye-rolling over the name.

"They are quite proud of it," Sunny said. "Ravelium is ultra-efficient, extremely valuable."

"They closely guard the secret of how they make it, but we've learned it contains much deuterium and helium-3. These things they can get from other sources—they used to mine them from gas giants—and mining a star involves many challenges. But if they can overcome those, a star gives the highest concentrations of raw materials, the greatest economies of scale."

"Ravel loves their economies of scale," Jasper chimed in over his shoulder.

"But picture this." Havoc held up a hand, curved as if holding a large ball. With his other hand, he mimed pulling substance away from it. "The more raw materials they extract, the slower the star burns. Extract too much, the star's heat drops." His hand clenched into a fist. "They need not destroy a star to make its planets unlivable."

"And you think that will happen to Unity."

"It will happen slowly—maybe years, maybe decades—but if they do this, Pax will become colder than Trove is now, and Trove…"

"They're already living on the brink." Kay could picture the suffering that would ensue. "And Ravel doesn't care about ruining people's homes. They'll just relocate everyone to wherever they need cheap labor."

Havoc nodded. "Now you see. There are numerous departments within Ravel that would benefit from access to such power. They could use it for resource extraction, or chemical synthesis." His gaze flicked to Jasper, who buzzed uneasiness but said nothing. "Or to power their new free-floating, self-contained space habitats. Those require massive energy."

"So they'll mine stars, and when it starts affecting planetary life, they move all the people to these habitats, which they wanted to do in the first place. If the people won't go, they'll be left to rot. There's no downside, at least for Ravel."

"Look at you, a budding activist," Jasper teased, but weariness sucked the humor out of his words. Jasper's worry was a low, continuous squeaking, overlaid by Havoc's mosquito-whine, and the sounds melded and reverberated in her gut until she felt ill.

"Well. Shit."

Jasper shut his eyes, pinching his brow with two fingers. "We've got no plan for this. Solar mining was supposed to be years off."

Havoc drew Jasper close, pressing his long, scaled snout to Jasper's cheek. "We'll find a way. This I believe. But first you need food in your stomach." He gave his partner a stern look. "Dearest eshrim, you are rotten at strategizing when you're hungry."

At that, Jasper's expression softened, and he chuckled. "You're right as usual. Fine. Dinner first, then saving the world."

Havoc led them to a more private meeting room that held a few hard-printed chairs, a shabby loveseat, and a low table fitted with holo-projectors. Jasper and Havoc settled on the loveseat. Kay took the least uncomfortable chair.

One of the activists brought her and Jasper food, steaming bowls of yeast protein in a thick yellow sauce, salty and rich with turmeric and pepper. Good hearty local food, nothing like the fancy crap Agata had arranged to impress folks at the summit. Not much like Brennexian food, either, but it felt familiar in its simplicity.

"So," Jasper said once he'd made a dent in his bowl, sounding a bit more energetic. "I'll stake a claim that this solar mining scheme is actually a good thing."

Sunny made a high-pitched beep. "How can that be? It seems irrefutably bad."

"Bad for Unity, but good for us, now that we know. Ravel has been making all sorts of promises about strengthening Trove's economy, and we've had no proof to the contrary. No matter how much we talk about what Ravel's done to other worlds, folks here want to believe it'll work out better for them. Now we can prove it won't."

"You think they'll believe us?" said Havoc. "These people love to ignore inconvenient facts."

"And it does sound pretty far-fetched," Kay said. "Ravel's never done solar mining before. Why go to all this trouble to use Unity as a pilot program? Why not one of their own systems, or an unclaimed star with no inhabitants to put up a fight?"

"Our engineers have been wondering this, too," said Havoc, pulling up diagrams and analyses on the projector that were unintelligible to Kay. "They think Unity Star may have the best chemical makeup for their process. A particular set of heavy elements, maybe."

"That isn't why," said Sunny. "Well, perhaps in part. But I suspect Unity's unique macrospace terrain is the primary reason."

Jasper and Havoc blinked at the helper-bot, which had crawled down onto the table. "Unique how?" said Jasper. "I thought all stars had massively dense gradients."

"Most do, but gravity wells are only one factor that attracts threads and creates dense terrain. The nuances are not well understood, scientifically, but whatever the reason, Unity's gradient is less steep than most stars. And it's uneven, in some spots nearly flat. I could—that is, a *ship* could swim right past the star without dropping into primespace, if it chose its path carefully."

"You're thinking the extraction process relies on this low gradient?" Havoc asked.

"I don't have enough engineering expertise to be certain, but that is my guess. Gravity would make it difficult to mine even the surface of a star in primespace, but if raw materials could be funneled up through macrospace, they could extract them quite easily—from the surface, or perhaps even from the core. That efficiency could be reason enough to annex the system."

Jasper raked his hands through his hair, making a mess which Havoc idly put back into order for him. "Great. So Unity is the perfect test case for their destructive new energy production tech. They're promising to fix Trove's terraforming once it becomes a member-state, but instead they'll gradually make the planet even more intolerable, and when it gets too bad, they'll take these people from their homes and make them wholly dependent on the company." He tilted his head back and muttered under his breath: "It's good for our organizing, it's good for our organizing…"

"And Pax will suffer, too, even if they refuse to sign on with Ravel. Maybe worse for having refused," Kay said, remembering the mild green beauty of the first planet.

Pax for peace. How long would their remarkable multi-species union last when their star began to fade? Would they take to the stars yet again, searching for a new home outside Ravel's sphere of influence? Or stay, clinging to their once-idyllic world while it faded under their feet?

She shut her eyes, and must have zoned out, because the conversation moved on without her.

"Have we gone to the press yet?" Jasper asked.

"On Pax, yes. On Trove, the state media refused the story. We're leaking it, but not everyone believes…"

She hadn't realized how tired she still was; her snatches of sleep en route to Trove, interrupted by the sounds of Grist's suffering, had barely made a dent in her sleep deficit. When she woke from her doze, Jasper and Havoc had snuggled up on the loveseat, Havoc's tail curled around Jasper's waist as they leaned into each other, talking quietly, no longer about Ravel and Unity. Jasper looked utterly relaxed with his head against Havoc's shoulder.

They made a sweet couple, Kay decided. As unlike as they seemed at first glance, they were both serious about their work, yet quick to become playful, and fiercely devoted—to the Cooperative, but clearly also to each other. She smiled to herself and glanced around for Sunny's bot. It had settled down on her lap; maybe Sunny had tried and failed to rouse her. She patted it like a cat, then felt ridiculous. She stretched and yawned.

"You can find real beds down the hall," Havoc told her. "Rest, Kay. You'll soon need it."

"Yes, sleep while you can," Jasper said, levering himself to his feet. "And I'd better go take reports from—"

"You'll do none of that right now," said Havoc. "I made a private room for you, so none will disturb you."

"No, you know how I feel about special treatment for leadership. I'll sleep in the dorms like everyone else, as soon as I've finished—"

"What value do you bring to us exhausted?" Havoc grabbed his arm to keep him from leaving, and tenderly he traced the sunken curve of Jasper's cheekbone with the back of one claw. "You trained your people well, and we carried forward while you were gone, but now we need our leader and best strategist here, well and whole. You're not whole, my eshrim."

"Maybe not," Jasper sighed, and Kay caught strains of weariness, despair, shame. Havoc was right: he hadn't had a chance to process what had happened to him, or the worse horrors they'd narrowly escaped.

"Listen to your partner, Jasp. He's smarter than you," Kay said.

"That's not hard, is it?" He smiled suddenly, pleased that she approved. "Sleep well, then," he said, and she waved them goodnight as they headed off to bed.

She found her own space in a plain, dorm-style room. The beds were surprisingly decent, thin but not lumpy, yet Kay knew as soon as she lay down that she couldn't sleep here. The sounds were strange: the wind echoing against the metal walls, unknown people moving in other parts of the structure, the persistent keening of strangers' worries. She desperately needed sleep—her eyes burned with it—but lying there, she felt wide awake.

Strange though it seemed, she knew where she would sleep better. She got up and retraced her steps to the hideout's exit.

NIGHT HAD FALLEN, A surreal reminder that planets kept turning no matter what happened to the small beings living on them. It was probably still early by Ravel's clock, and Kay no longer had any idea what time it felt like to her, but the whole world felt wobbly around the edges. She raced across the small space between the safe house and the ship— it got *cold* on this desert world after sunset—and Sunny opened their door at her approach, turning on warm, welcoming lights.

"Is something wrong?" Sunny asked.

"No, just couldn't sleep. I thought it might be better here…if that's all right?"

"Of course."

Kay felt awkward asking it, and Sunny gave no hint of their feelings about her presence. Sometimes, she thought she was learning to read the little ship. Other times, she felt adrift.

A low moan—she couldn't tell if it was a real one, or audible only to her—reminded Kay they weren't alone. "How is he?"

"Still worsening. The Cooperative medic said he will recover, but we must keep him fed and hydrated, which my research already indicated. She also said that this can be a very lonely experience, so we must talk to him. I have tried to do so, but he will not engage with me."

"Well, I'll give it a shot before I drop off."

She tapped on the door to his cabin. "Hey, Grist? Can I come in?"

"Fuck off."

That was politeness, for Grist.

"Sorry, but I need to check how you're doing."

Through the door she caught an affirmative-sounding grumble, and went in. The cabin smelled sour with sweat and vomit, worse than it had a few hours ago, and the cool air rushing through the vents couldn't dissipate the stench. Sunny was lucky they didn't have a nose. Grist crouched on his bed, knees drawn up, face a shade too green for comfort, his discomfort reverberating through the small room. His handheld sat discarded beside him.

"Hey," Kay said, hovering in the doorway. "How are you?" seemed the wrong question, so she settled on, "Holding up okay?"

"Fucking bitch of a ship doesn't have a body, they don't know what they're putting me through."

"Maybe not, but you've put them through plenty."

He made a coughing, rasping laugh. "Must be a thrill for you and your brother, to see I'm finally getting my comeuppance."

"Not really. And you know it could be a lot worse. Sunny's intent on helping you, for reasons I can't comprehend."

"You don't like me. That's fine, I don't like you either," Grist said. "Thought you were annoying as fuck when you came aboard, a little corporate recruit with idealism shining out your ass. You're slightly less annoying now that you're a thieving traitor."

"Thanks, I think."

He grimaced, clutching his stomach. His pain hit Kay like a cymbal to the head. Bracing herself against it, she set the vomit bucket on the bed beside him and waited it out with him.

At last he relaxed, posture unclenching, breaths coming fast and shallow. "Can I get you anything?" Kay asked, and he shook his head. A few more seconds of silence, and she considered that a dismissal. She turned to go.

"We're the same, you know."

Not done yet. She came back into the room, folded her arms as she stared down at him. "You said that once before. You said we both do terrible things out of loyalty to Ravel, as if that were inevitable. As if neither we nor Ravel had a choice."

"That's when I thought you were for real. But now, we're even more the same. You, me, the ship."

Another long pause, gaze unfocused. Distracted by the pain, maybe; she could still hear it over the hissing of the air circulation. Maybe that's why he wanted to talk, to keep himself focused on something else. "How are we the same, Grist?"

"We all got screwed by Ravel. We all started out with hopes of one thing, but got pulled in and they took things from us, took and took and took until we didn't have enough left to break away. Didn't even know we needed to."

Kay had known she needed to get out, but if Ravel hadn't discovered her identity, how long would she have kept up her act? How much harm would she have collaborated in?

"Why did you start working for them, Grist? How did…" She couldn't figure out a polite phrasing for the question, but he got what she was asking.

"How did I let them turn me into this?" He spat in the bucket. "Slowly. Badly. Stupidly." With pained movements, as if his own muscles rebelled against him, he stretched out, leaning back against the head of the bed. Kay moved to help him, but he waved her off.

"They got to me young. Fuck it, I still would be young, if they hadn't hollowed me out. You know how old I am?"

Fifty, Kay would have guessed, but didn't dare. She shook her head.

"Thirty-three. Wouldn't expect that, huh?" His laugh was a hacking, angry sound. "I grew up on Parscaux. A Goodshare colony, until Goodshare went under and left us all to starve. Ravel was happy to take on new workers, and for whatever reason, they thought I was good for something more than the mines. You probably can't imagine how that felt, snotty trade-world kid like you, to have someone believe you're worth something when no one ever did before."

"I'm basically your age, I'm not a kid," Kay said. "But…no. I can't imagine how that would feel."

"Pretty damn great, at the start. Was seventeen when they found me, so that's sixteen years I've belonged to them. Half my damned worthless life. First they wanted me to do small jobs for them, sabotage, beating people up, and that was fun.

Like being a spy, I thought, like a game. Then they wanted to enhance me so I could do a better job, and I said, sure. It felt special to be stronger than anyone else, faster than anyone else, and besides, I knew I needed to stay useful to Ravel. The more they invested in me, the better, I figured."

"But it didn't work out so well?" said Kay gently.

He snorted. "You think I'm an idiot for trusting them. You with your independent planet, your activist brother. You'd never trust Ravel like I did."

Ordinarily, he'd be right. Kay had always looked down on people who believed Ravel's lies, people like the Trovians who walked into a trap of their own making. People like Grist. But hearing him tell the story, so raw, with no lie in his emotions…she couldn't feel bad for him, but she understood him a little. "Ravel fools lots of people. You're hardly alone in that." She hesitated. "It's not your fault that they misled you."

How he reacted to their mistreatment, that was still his fault. But he'd been wronged.

"Oh." He blinked, as if he hadn't expected sympathy. "Well, it went downhill from there. Seemed like a great job, until the enhancements started going wrong, started hurting and wouldn't stop. I was a beta tester for lots of new tech. Sometimes they'd install things in me that I didn't even need, just to see how it'd react with all the other junk inside me. They started me on the drugs so I could cope with the pain, so I could stay functional, and…well. You see how that ended up." He waved a hand around his small cabin. "I'm their tool now, a tool that sits around being miserable whenever it's not getting used. I feel like shit all the time: shitty from the drugs when they work, shitty in a different way when the drugs aren't enough.

"Worst part is, after a while, the work didn't feel so fun anymore. Less like being a spy, more like being a thug. I was good at it, though, and I'd never been good at anything else, and sometimes it distracted me from feeling shitty, so I let them push me farther. Whatever the company needed, that's what I did. Until Trove…"

He trailed off, lost in remembering. "If the ship hadn't stopped me, I really would have done it." From the way he shuddered, Kay didn't want to know what he'd almost done. "You asked earlier why I'm so mean to the ship when I knew it had feelings. Fact is, I never cared. A tool doesn't care about the feelings of other tools. I was angry all the time, angry and hurting, and the ship was here, and I could make it hurt, too. Ravel was far away, and the ship was the only part of them I could touch. That's all the reason I needed."

"I see," said Kay softly, struggling to keep her voice even. "You caused them a lot of pain."

"I know that, and they treated me better than I ever deserved. I'm not a nice person, Wilder. Maybe there was a point when I could have been, but that was a long time ago."

He slumped back on his bed, staring at the ceiling. "Ship offered me something so I can sleep better. I think I'll have that now."

Kay handed him the pill and some water. This was what Sunny had been doing for him for years, she realized: taking care of him despite not liking him, despite all the things he did. Because Sunny, despite their limited existence and complete lack of role models, was a better person than Grist.

She left him trying to sleep, and crossed the narrow hallway to her cabin to fall down on her own narrow bed. She flicked the lights off before realizing that it still wasn't time for sleep, not yet.

"So…you probably heard all that?" she asked Sunny.

"I heard, yes."

"Are you okay?"

A long pause before Sunny answered. There were worlds in that pause. "It explains a great deal. It does not make it better, but perhaps it helps to know that there is a reason for the way he's treated me, even if the reason is displeasing. It had nothing to do with me. Is that illogical?"

"No, I get it. He doesn't deserve you, Sunny. You know that, right?"

"I was unsure of that until recently. Having you aboard has given me a new perspective."

She smiled in the darkness. "I like you too, Sunny."

Grist let loose a gut-twisting moan, loud even through the two walls between them. Kay couldn't help grimacing.

"Are you unwell?"

"Yeah, fine, I just—" she began before she realized: maybe that hadn't been a real sound. A feeling of pain and an exclamation of pain often sounded the same to her. "Just hope Grist will be all right, despite everything."

Another long silence, one that extended even to the air vents, the small noises of regular operation.

"Kay, why do you hear things that I can't?" Sunny spoke quietly, hesitantly. "I feared my auditory sensors were malfunctioning."

"I'm sure your sensors are working fine."

"Yes, I have assured myself of that. As an additional data point, Grist also found your behavior inexplicable."

"Yeah, he did, didn't he?" Hopefully Grist had forgotten by now, but Sunny…

Kay sat cross-legged on the bed, fumbled in the dark for the control panel until a dim light suffused the room. She felt calmer than she would have expected considering she'd never done this before, in fact had organized her entire life around never having to do this. If she could hear her own emotions, they would have been one long, deep, reverberating tone, like the fading after a bell was struck.

"You kept my secret before, Sunny, and I kept yours. But if I tell you this, I need you to swear you'll never tell it to anyone. This could hurt a lot of people if Ravel found out."

Like they almost did yesterday. Kay hadn't been careful enough herself.

"It is not necessary to tell me." Sunny's air circulation gave a jarring whir before settling back to normal levels.

"No, I trust you, and you deserve an explanation." Deep breath. It shouldn't feel so strange to say aloud. "I hear people's emotions. Grist's pain sounds like moans, even when he keeps quiet. The buzzing I heard, when he stowed away, was his frustration, his annoyance. That's how I knew he was there."

"Most organics do not have this ability. Or do they, and I am unaware of it?"

"No, most don't. It's a little gift Ravel accidentally left behind on my planet for those of us born during the occupation. Those of us who survived. It was an unknown side effect of a drug they were testing. If Ravel knew, they'd experiment on us to find out why it happened, and then they'd do it to others. A lot would die in the process, and if they succeeded, well, you can imagine what they'd do with someone like me, if they knew. That's why we keep it secret. I've never told anyone from off-world."

"I will keep your secret," Sunny said. "I already admired your courage in infiltrating Ravel, but now I am even more impressed."

"Impressed at my reckless stupidity?" Kay snorted to herself.

"Can you hear my emotions?" Sunny asked, their voice suddenly flat. "Perhaps not. Mine are not real in the way an organic's emotions are."

Kay pressed a hand to the wall above her bunk, a gesture that she hoped conveyed reassurance. She had to choose her next words very carefully, lest she damage the delicate trust between them.

"I don't know how my gift works. I don't know why I hear more nuance from some people than others, or why people from different species or cultures make different sounds. And I don't know why I can't hear the same things from you—but that doesn't make you any less real. I know your emotions by the changes in your voice, the pauses in your speech, the sounds you make. The subconscious ways you show me when you're upset. You're different, but no less real."

"Oh," said Sunny. They didn't sound entirely convinced, but added: "You have always been truthful to me. I will try to believe you."

"Believe it," Kay said. She leaned back, trailing her hand along the wall. "Honestly, it's nice for me. The noise of other people's feelings, it gets to be a lot. Imagine someone playing music at you nonstop, and you can't shut it out. But with you, it's peaceful. It's taking me longer to understand you, maybe, but when I'm here, I can relax."

Warm air flowed from the vents over her head. "Really?"

"Really. As I said, I like you."

"That is very good to know," said Sunny. "I was going to ask why you are here tonight—I heard Havoc say there are real beds in the safe house—but I assume it's because the safe house is loud to your ears?"

"Among other reasons. It's nicer here," Kay said. She toggled the light off and lay down, snuggling under the blankets.

The ship hummed around her, and their obvious pleasure pleased Kay too. Surrounded by warm air and the gentle vibrations of a ship at rest, at last she slept.

38

WHEN KAY GOT UP the next morning, the safe house was bustling like Brennex Spaceport on street market day. A careless tail sent her stumbling as she weaved across the crowded antechamber, and Sunny's helper bot dug into her shoulder, but someone caught her arm to steady her. It was Havoc, who remarkably had not impaled her (either accidentally or on purpose) with his claws.

"You sleep even more than your brother," he said. "We've been waiting an hour for you to join our planning."

"Sorry. I guess I needed it." Yawning, she accepted the cup he pressed into her hands. Brennexian chai. Perfect. "Has something happened?"

"Our time is about to run out. Trove's Parliament will vote on Ravel membership today."

"Today!" That woke her up. They were supposed to have days, still. She hurried after him down the hallway, trying to sip her chai without spilling all over herself.

"They announced it early this morning. Probably this news about solar mining makes the prime minister nervous. She's been waiting until she's certain of having the votes…"

"But now we've forced her hand," Kay said. When had she become part of this "we?" The failure felt personal. "Will it pass?"

"We think she'll try to force it through," said Jasper, rising to greet her as they entered a meeting room that was full of people, including two entirely unexpected faces.

"Devron? Patra?"

It was surprisingly good to see her savior from the Pax protest-turned-riot, and the sight of Patra put a not-unpleasant flutter in her gut. They both wore bulky grav-suits in the heavier Trovian gravity.

"Kavita. Or should I call you Kay?" Devron held out a hand toward the sound of her voice, and Kay came forward to squeeze it. "I hear you're on our side now. All the way on our side."

"I'm really sorry for the way I behaved toward you. I was frantic to find my brother, but I should have handed over the data at once."

Patra scowled. "If you had, we'd have discovered this mining operation days earlier. We lost precious time because of you." Her gaze traveled to Kay's palm, which Kay had been rubbing again.

"I know. I messed up badly." She clasped her hands firmly together, hiding the stain. "I want to make up for it, if I can."

Devron gifted her with a smile. "Then I'm glad to cross paths with you again."

Patra merely shrugged, and that was all the acceptance she was likely to get.

"Let's get to it," said Jasper. "We've got two problems. Parliament will vote this afternoon on whether to join Ravel. And there's the mining rig: thanks to Sunny's insights, we can track it now, and last night, it started moving. We think they're planning to be in position to start their tests as soon as the annexation is complete."

"We thought Cortez-Watts had too few votes for it to pass," said Patra.

"That was true a few days ago. She's been very close, and since the summit, she's scared up a few more. She wouldn't hold the vote unless she expects to win, but we've pushed her to act before she's ready, which means we've got a chance."

"So we're playing toward two victory conditions," said Havoc. "Stop the vote from passing, and in case that fails, stop the mining rig."

"Most of us will focus on the former," said Jasper. "We'll head to the capital at once and get the truth in front of our priority targets. The prime minister's been dismissing the mining rig as a Cooperative lie, but I think a number of the Labor party members will be swayed when they see the evidence. If we can persuade the party leaders, the others will follow."

"I know some of them were won over to Ravel's side by my fake stories," Kay said softly. "I'd like to tell them the truth now."

"Good," said Jasper, with warmth and something harder beneath. It really did bother him that she'd sided with Ravel, even to save his life. "I'll need you at your most persuasive."

"We know how to tackle this straightforward lobbying," said Havoc. "Stopping the mining rig, however… This is an unknown field. We'd do best to keep it away from the star. This way, they can't begin operation. Pax's military is moving to set up a blockade."

"I doubt Pax has the capacity to stop Ravel for long, if they're determined," said Sunny.

"You know Ravel's military strength?" asked Jasper, surprised.

"I am aware of three squads of Hammerheads, four Mako cruisers, and a Thresher in this system. And there is the Leviathan, which has its own weaponry."

"That's too much," muttered Jasper. "You're right, Sunny, we need a backup plan for our backup plan. Any ideas?"

"Do we have weapons?"

"Not on that scale."

"Then I will be your weapon."

Kay stared at the bot. Its glassy camera-eyes did not seem aimed at her, and she couldn't tell if that was deliberate or not. "What are you thinking, Sunny?" she whispered.

"It must be done, Kay, and I am in the best position to do it."

"Who exactly is this ally of yours, who won't leave their ship but is willing to fly it on a suicide mission?" said Patra.

Jasper trumpeted alarm at the words "suicide mission." "Havoc," he said, "why don't you take the Paxians and our ground team and brief them on our lobbying strategy? I want to talk to Sunny in private."

Kay held her tongue until the others had filed from the room, then burst out: "Sunny, you can't do this!"

"It is risky, true, but necessary. Your brother understands this: the Cooperative asks its people to take risks, and sometimes those risks require violence."

"Only when there's no other way," Jasper said. Kay glanced sidelong at him, remembering Agata's accusations, which Havoc hadn't exactly denied. "But we don't do suicide missions, and we don't send our people into situations where they can't succeed. I won't ask it of you."

"I have thought about this. Kay is here to reverse the damage she has caused. I, too, have been facilitating Ravel's damage for a long time."

"That's not your fault!" Kay cried. "You weren't free to—"

"Please, Kay. I am complicit. More complicit than you, though in a different way. I want to help however I can, and I believe this is the most feasible plan."

Jasper pinched the bridge of his nose, eyes shut. "Okay, let's say hypothetically that I agree to this. The rig is huge, right? What can you do against something that size?"

"The rig is designed for collecting massive amounts of base elements, including hydrogen. Once it begins operation, it would take only a small ignition to detonate the extraction beam."

"Detonate…" Jasper mouthed something silently to himself. "That would create a massive explosion."

"That is the goal, is it not? It would destroy the rig."

"And all the people on it!" Kay said. "We can't kill all those innocent people. Most of the people on that rig didn't come up with this plan. They're just doing their jobs. Engineers. Technicians. Janitors, even!" Jasper pressed his knuckles to his lips, and Kay couldn't take it. "I thought Ravel was lying when they called you a terrorist!"

"We're *not* terrorists!" Jasper spoke so forcefully that she'd clearly struck a sore spot. He scrubbed his face with his hands, and sighed. "It's a…topic of debate for us, the limits of what violence is acceptable, and when. Some of my colleagues… We don't all agree." He gave Kay a rueful look. "I hope you know which side of that debate I fall on. But fortunately for our moral health, in this case destroying the rig would be an absolute last resort. Sunny's plan would mean waiting until the rig is activated, which won't happen until the contract is signed. We want to stop the acquisition, and we want to stop them from activating the rig at all, so they have no evidence to show whether this technology works, nothing to back their propaganda. Sunny, can you sabotage it before that happens?"

Sunny hummed thoughtfully. "A smaller explosion could compromise the extraction beam generator. That would take weeks or months to repair."

"Good! That buys us time to come up with a more permanent solution. I'm still worried about your safety, though. Getting to the rig will put you and your crew in danger."

"I'm confident I can do it safely. And as for crew, my operational parameters require only one organic aboard."

"I'll do it," said Kay.

"No," said Jasper and Sunny simultaneously. Jasper repeated: "No, Kay. We need you here."

"If you're trying to stop me because it's too dangerous…"

Jasper smiled grimly. "I might, if it came to it, but I really *do* need you to persuade those representatives."

"Right. Because I got us into this mess in the first place." She sighed. Again and again, she'd chosen to do the wrong thing for personal reasons. She had put her brother ahead of all the people of Unity. Now, she had to choose again: those people, or her new friend. But her wrongs were piling up on her shoulders, and they'd soon crack her bones if she didn't unload them. "I would go with you in a heartbeat, Sunny, but he's right. I need to be here."

"That is the sensible course of action," Sunny said. "We each must go where we are most needed."

"I'll ask for a volunteer from my people," Jasper said, but from the furrow in his brow, he wasn't eager to.

"No need," said a new, gruff voice. "It's my ship. I'll do it."

Grist stood in the doorway, two anxious activists hovering near with stun-guns trained on him. He looked like death scraped off the floor and molded into a Human shape, but he was dressed, and standing upright, and gave every impression of being his mean old self.

"Like fuck you will," Kay said.

"You are not a part of this," said Jasper with finality. "Sunny, why's he out of his cabin? I thought you were watching him."

"He asked to address you, and I wanted to see what he intended." There was no apology in Sunny's voice. "Why, Grist?"

"Because…because I can. I want to."

Jasper snorted. "You've got to do better than that. Why should I trust you not to reveal us to Ravel? How do I know you haven't called them here already?"

"Damn babysitter would stop me if I tried anything." That meant Sunny, presumably. He shifted his weight, looking adrift and confused in the face of their unfriendliness. "Thought you all would understand why I want to get back at Ravel."

"You want to join the resistance?" Jasper asked, looking hard at Grist. Using his gift, Kay assumed, to gauge his shifting loyalties. He didn't seem to like what he saw. "Don't tell me you're becoming an activist."

"Fuck no! This is about revenge. I've been their tool for too long, and you self-righteous asswipes helped me see that."

"We did?" said Sunny.

Grist looked down at the floor. "All this time, I've been lying to myself. Told myself I was only doing the things I chose, that I might not be a good person, but at least I had limits. Until this week. They pushed me right past those limits, and I broke. I broke so easily."

"The child is safe, Grist," said Sunny in a tone that sounded remarkably like sympathy. "You did not harm her."

"Would have, though, if not for you. Took me a while to get it through my head, but you and Wilder helped me realize who I'm angry at. Turns out you all did me a favor, kidnapping me. I'm not keen on the hell you're putting me through, but I needed to leave them, and I'd never have managed it on my own."

"You're welcome," said Kay wryly.

"Look, I hate all of you, but I hate Ravel more, and this is my one chance to fuck them up some. I want to do it." He looked right at the helper bot. "Sh—uh, Sunny? What do you say?"

"I accept your offer," Sunny said. "With conditions. I will be in charge. You will assist me and do precisely as I say."

"All right."

"And you will stop being mean to me. No name-calling."

"Fine," muttered Grist, looking less than pleased.

"And if you attempt to betray us, I will drug you for the duration of the mission."

"Well, that's only fair," said Grist.

"This is ridiculous," said Jasper. "Kay? Are you good with this?"

Kay studied Grist's face a long while, listening to his jangling emotions, thinking about what he'd told her last night. Somewhere in the midst of his suffering, he'd found some clarity.

"He's not lying," she said slowly. "I wouldn't trust him a minute beyond this, but…strange bedfellows happen. And I'm the last person who should deny anyone a second chance."

Jasper threw his hands in the air. "This is the weirdest campaign I've ever run, but it's settled. Grist and Sunny will attempt to sabotage the rig. We'll still need to find you a weapon…"

Grist grinned, showing his shiny white teeth. "Oh, don't you worry. I've got us covered in the weapons department."

39

ORGANICS REQUIRED A GREAT deal of preparation in order to do anything. Sunny was ready to go while Jasper's people were still making lists and debating over assignments. Kay came outside and stood near Sunny, looking awkwardly up and all around, as if unsure where to direct her eyes.

This was something Sunny had noticed as they made the acquaintance of more organics: most of them seemed uncomfortable addressing someone they could not look in the face. They kept seeking an object to fix on. Kay had seemed to grow comfortable talking to Sunny, but now she seemed uncertain again.

She reached out and pressed her hand to Sunny's hull, just behind the starboard lateral scanner. "Take care of yourself, okay?"

"I will, Kay. As should you."

"Yeah. And watch Grist. Seriously, don't let him pull any bullshit on you."

Sunny chimed amusement. "He'll have no opportunity to do so. I tolerated too much from him when I was afraid of discovery, but he will realize soon, if he hasn't yet, that I'm a different ship than I was before."

Before. It was the first time Sunny had considered recent events in those terms, but they couldn't ignore that the word invited an antecedent: *before Kay.* They were not the same ship, the same individual, as they were before Kay came aboard.

Kay had seen them in a way that no one else had before, none of their AI acquaintances and certainly no organics. How could they explain that? Would it unnerve Kay if they tried?

"I'm glad," Kay said before they could attempt it. "You deserve better than him. And hey, when this is over, you'll be free of him and Ravel."

"Yes. You have taught me that there are better people than Grist. People I like." That awkward pause lasted, to their electronic mind, for an eternity. "What will you do afterward, Kay?"

"Go home, I guess? To Terna?" She shrugged, a twitchy gesture, as if she suffered from an itch on one shoulder. "I don't know. Jasper will try to talk me into joining the Cooperative, no doubt, and I'm happy to help them for a bit, but that life isn't for me. What about you?"

"I am uncertain about what comes next. To be honest, I am unsure even of the options available to me. I know I'll require an organic companion, but not like Grist. A partner."

It took courage to put such an obvious hint in that statement, but to their dismay, Kay didn't respond to it. Maybe she hadn't understood.

"Look at us, talking like we'll never see each other again." She patted their hull, which felt…odd. The Minnow's external sensors were designed for measuring radical temperature changes, fractured plating, micro-collisions. Kay's soft touch barely registered, and yet it felt nice, perhaps because the intention was kind. "We'll meet up afterward, yeah?"

"I hope so."

"Me too. I'm not kidding, you'd better come find me." Kay grinned, then turned her head at the sound of someone calling her name. "Ah, they need me, and you have to go. See you on the other side!"

She jogged away, leaving Sunny alone with Grist. They turned their attention inward.

"All right," said Grist, dropping into his chair. "Ready to do this, you sack of—"

Sunny buzzed a warning. "Names."

"—you, you…ship." He sighed. Well, he was not the only one who would find this a trying experience. "Ready to go?"

"I am prepared."

"Then get us off this grime-ball."

They ran their start-up sequence. Fortunately, their landing site had been sheltered enough that the dust was not interfering with their systems, though Sunny still felt its accumulation from their previous landing on Trove. There hadn't been time on the flagship to request a thorough cleaning. When this was over, they'd have to find someone willing to give them one, though who that might be… They pushed the thought from their active memory and fired up their lift thrusters.

Usually when they took flight, Sunny focused their attention ahead and upward. Today, though, they watched behind. The Cooperative stronghold diminished beneath them, soon becoming little more than an inconsistency in the landscape, unrecognizable to anyone who did not know it was there.

Goodbye, Kay. Good luck.

Jasper's intelligence team had provided the mining rig's last known location and trajectory. Though the rig remained near-invisible at this distance, matte black and shielded against giving off any energy readings, it was a simple process to extrapolate its current location. Sunny checked its course against the macro-terrain around the Unity star, and as predicted, the rig was still moving toward an area of unusually low gradient near the star, presumably easier to mine through. That was where Ravel would station their device. At Sunny's top sub-light speed, the rig would arrive shortly before they did.

That would take several hours, however. Sunny settled in to wait, tracking the blot of darkness that marked the rig's location.

"So, one last adventure together, huh? You, me, and the spacescape?"

Jarred to alertness, Sunny focused two separate cameras on Grist. "Are you really going to pretend nostalgia?" They hesitated. "Or is that another joke?"

"It's…aw, fuck it, never mind." He kicked his feet idly at the underside of the console. Sunny considered sending the helpers to zap him, but decided to save that in case his behavior escalated. "I get it. Never really thought about how much you must hate me, but I get it."

"You seem…" He seemed halfway to a different person. Only halfway, however. And "different" did not mean "good." "Your symptoms seem diminished. Are you feeling better?"

"Better. Still rotten, but not as shitty as last night. That was hell, Ship. I never expected you'd be so cold."

"It was the kindest thing I could bring myself to do for you."

"Probably won't take, you know. I did some research of my own. Going cold turkey doesn't work without therapy and shit, and only if the person doing the withdrawing actually wants to be clean. I'd have run out of Ravel drugs pretty soon, but I could've found substitutes. Still can, as soon as I'm free of you."

"That is true."

"It's not like the pain's gone. That's why Ravel started dosing me up in the first place: the side effects of these damned augmentations. That won't go away through willpower or positive thinking or any bullshit like that."

"I suppose it will not."

"So putting me through this is pointless. A lot of pointless suffering for me, a lot of pointless work for you."

"I am not giving your drugs back, Grist."

"No! That's not… I just… I don't get you, Ship."

Sunny paused a long while, debating how to answer. Withdrawal had opened up a particular kind of honesty in Grist, apparently; he had never talked like this before.

"That is unfortunate, because I understand you quite well. You have never been kind to me, but you have been a constant presence since the beginning of my sentience. I cannot like you, but I *know* you, and I wanted to do this for you. To give you this option. Nobody else would offer it."

He stared with furrowed brow at the ceiling, as if trying to fit this information into his understanding of the world. "You're right. No one else would care enough." He shook his head—not in denial, Sunny thought, but in surprise. "Thanks, then, I guess."

"You are welcome. *I guess.*"

He smirked at that. "I better go see about my weapons. Gotta be ready to blow some shit up."

Grist spent some time rummaging in his cabin and filling a crate with useful components, which he dragged out and spread across the floor of the rear compartment, with his prized grenade launcher in the middle. He also pulled one of the EVA suits out of storage, and when its glove proved too bulky to pull the trigger, he went to work on it with a knife.

"Are you sure this will be effective?" Sunny asked.

"I've got a plan," he said without looking up from his work. Sunny let him continue. If nothing else, Grist was skilled at what he did.

"The rig has reached Pax's blockade," they announced.

Grist came forward to watch. Sunny translated their sensor readings into a diagram simplified for Human understanding: a dozen blue dots for the Paxian ships, one large red dot for the rig.

"Doesn't look like it's slowing."

"No, it is not."

"How long until it hits the blockade?"

"Four minutes real-time, though at our current distance, all readings are two minutes delayed."

The lead Paxian ship broadcast an announcement, addressed to the mining rig but intended for the public. "Unidentified Ravel vessel. You are in sovereign Unity space, and the planet of Pax demands your immediate departure. Halt your advance and retreat to beyond our space. This will be your only warning."

No response. No change in speed. No change in course. Was the rig going to ram the defenders?

No, it wasn't. New signatures appeared: five Hammerhead fighters zooming out from the rig. Five against twelve, but these were top-of-the-line Ravel skirmishers, while Pax used old Markon-Kraft fighters, the less-robust models that companies sold outside their territory. Ravel outgunned them significantly.

"Idiots. They'll get slaughtered like babies with a machete," Grist muttered, and distasteful as the analogy was, Sunny had to agree.

Fall back, Sunny wanted to tell them—but half of the Paxian fighters scrambled to meet the Hammerheads, and the remainder opened fire against the rig. Their attacks barely scratched it, and the rig's countermeasures deployed moments later.

"You see that?" Grist said, pointing. "We'll need to get inside the range of their defenses if we want to hit them."

"Yes. I am gathering data on their response times."

The Paxian offense concentrated their fire on the lead Hammerhead. It worked—they destroyed its weapons array—but they were forced to scatter again as the undamaged Hammerheads moved to intercept. But they launched no counterattack. The Hammerheads could have cleared out the Paxians without any effort. Why were they holding back?

"You just fired on a Ravel vessel, Pax," announced the bored-sounding Ravel commander. "Do that again, and you'll wish you hadn't."

"You shouldn't have violated our sovereign space," said the Paxian command ship. There was a throat-clearing sound, and they returned to their official, impassive tone. "This is your final warning, unidentified Ravel mining vessel. You have ignored a direct request to depart our territory. Under interstellar law, we will continue all possible efforts to halt your illegal activity, including the destruction of your vessels if necessary."

In the pause that followed, Sunny imagined the rig's crew laughing. "There's just one little problem with your plan, Pax. How will you blow us up when you're floating dead in space?"

"Did I not make myself clear, Ravel? Any further aggression on your part will be considered—"

A burst of static interrupted the Paxian command ship, followed by the utter silence of deep space. The blue dots had disappeared from the display.

"What the fuck?" Grist slammed his fists on the console. Sunny didn't even chastise him, because they were equally shocked. "Where'd they go? Those Hammerheads didn't even fire!"

"No, I believe this was a more subtle attack." Sunny ran one scan, then another, until they'd verified their theory. "The ships are still there, but no longer emitting signals of any kind."

"Dead in space, just like they said," Grist muttered. "But how? Ravel's got no weapons that can do that."

"I do not know. It is as if they all powered down at once.

But that is im… No. Perhaps not impossible. Pax bought their ships from Markon-Kraft."

"And Markon-Kraft got bought by Ravel." Grist groaned. "Clever assholes. You think they had a back door?"

"That is the most likely explanation." With back-door access to the ships' systems, Ravel could have shut them all down with a single command.

"They don't have a back door to *you*, do they?"

A disturbing thought. "No," said Sunny, and after a moment, "I'm certain I would know if they did."

"Let's hope you're right."

Grist went back to work. Sunny, after sending an encrypted message to Pax requesting rescue for their ships, spent the rest of the trip doing a careful review of their own base code.

The hours passed with increasing tension until they reached the mining rig, now in position at the closest safe distance from the star. Grist had removed the trigger guard from his grenade launcher and attached a less bulky glove to his EVA suit so he could fire it more easily.

"That looks dangerous."

"That's the idea."

Sunny had meant dangerous to him. "How will you aim it?"

"This'd be easier if you had a torpedo chute. Since you don't, I'll have to go outside, take aim, and fire."

"You will target a grenade, by hand, in space, and hope it hits our target, which is approximately a meter wide?"

"Don't forget, it's also impossible to see," Grist said. "Quit worrying. Ravel gave me unnaturally good aim. If you can manage to fly in a straight line, I'll hit it."

He was, Sunny reminded themself again, very good at what he did. This was why Ravel valued him so: he never failed at his assignments. "You should get ready, then. We're getting close."

Even right next to it, the rig was near-invisible: a texturing in the blackness of space, an absence of stars, nothing more. How Grist would aim at the vulnerable heat exchange ducts, Sunny couldn't imagine. As they entered range, Sunny put up a false call sign, impersonating one of the other Minnows currently docked at the flagship. "Ravel Minnow 127 on approach. Executive clearance."

"Executive?" the controller answered back. "We weren't expecting any executives."

"Surprise inspection prior to activation."

"But we were instructed to commence activation as soon as the annexation is signed. We're ready to go here."

That didn't leave them much time. Grist was in his suit now, and Sunny vented atmosphere from the rear section before opening the hatch. "Executive Moore wishes his representative to witness this occasion. Please hold until we come aboard."

If Sunny had been organic, they would have held their breath. As it was, the passing seconds were interminable. All the rig crew needed to do was contact the flagship, and Sunny's lie would be revealed.

Grist stepped out onto the hull, mag-boots clanking, grenade launcher strapped to his back.

"Be ready," Sunny warned him. "I believe they will call my bluff."

"Get me closer, then."

Sunny began a slow curve away from the rig's docking area, toward the collection beam emitter at the bottom of the rig, pretending to circle around for another approach. They needed to damage the emitter badly enough that the rig couldn't begin operations, which would buy the Cooperative time.

"Minnow 127, hold your position. Do not approach until I give you clearance."

"It is time," said Sunny, and picked up speed.

"Shit, this is weird," said Grist, from his position atop their hull. "Okay, I need you to dive straight for the collector."

A great vibration began aboard the rig, and the collector dish began to glow. They were activating. Kay must have failed—Trove must have signed the agreement. That meant Sunny and Grist were Unity's last chance.

"Minnow 127, stop! That's an order. The flagship says you aren't assigned to this section."

"Whoops," Sunny said, dropping their neutral tone. "Sorry, our mistake. By the way, you should order all staff to evacuate from collector control immediately."

"Guess that's my cue," Grist muttered. He aimed through his sights, taking his time, waiting until he had the shot lined up precisely for a spot just above the emitter where the explosion could set off their stored fuel. He fired just as a great beam of molten white light took shape between the rig and the star.

He did, indeed, have good aim. Three grenades flew as straight as any projectiles launched from a warship. But slower. Sunny calculated eighteen seconds to impact.

They turned, peeling away from the rig, watching on rear sensors. Fifteen seconds to impact.

The Hammerheads swam around from the far side of the rig, menacing silhouettes against the glare of the star's corona. One closed on the grenades. The others came for Sunny.

"Get inside, Grist! Get inside, get inside now."

He clomped toward the hatch. The grenades were twelve seconds away. Ten seconds.

One of the Hammerheads dove on the grenades, putting the bulk of the ship between the weapons and the stream. The grenades exploded, a burst of fire and light that sent shrapnel flying from the side of the Hammerhead.

The rig remained untouched.

"Shit," Sunny said.

"I think that's the first time I've ever heard you curse," Grist said, throwing himself through the rear hatch. Sunny closed the door behind him. "But yeah, shit is right. What the fuck do we do now?"

Sunny had an answer to that, but Grist wasn't going to like it. "For a start, we run."

They sped away from the rig with two Hammerheads in pursuit.

40

PARLIAMENT HALL WAS AN architectural monstrosity of white marble and sweeping minarets, utterly at odds with the squat red-brick buildings that made up most of Trove's capital city. Its only allowance to local materials was a mosaic of amethyst and citrine that surrounded the broad arch of the main entrance, sparkling like greed in the sunlight. A clear glasteel wall extended in either direction, allowing a perfect view of the building while keeping the public at a distance.

It fit perfectly with how this government operated, completely out of step with its people.

"This is the worst," Kay groaned, gazing up at it in dismay. Beside her, Patra grunted in agreement. The mood on the streets was energetic anger as protesters converged outside the wall, but the members of Parliament, hidden away inside, wouldn't even have to see them.

"They don't even pretend to care, do they?" Jasper said. "They won't let their own people address them. I wish we could tear these walls down, let everyone in, force them to listen."

"Really?" Havoc's tail twitched eagerly at the thought, and he activated his headset. "I could call—"

Jasper hastily laid a restraining hand on Havoc's arm. "That was an idle wish, eshrim, not a suggestion. You've got our permits?"

"Of course." Havoc sighed in disappointment, and while Jasper turned away, he kept staring longingly at the wall.

The guards checked their permits and waved them through the gates, and the wall cut off the chaotic sounds of all the strong emotions on the streets.

Jasper gathered them together in the courtyard, humming confidence. "All right, folks. We've got a challenge here, but not an insurmountable one. To approve such a major change, they'd normally need support from representatives of all three major species."

"They don't have it," said Havoc. "The Grand Champion says no Kovar will vote for it."

"Affirmation. Zero Chthirian support," said an artificial voice, overlaid on the clicking voices of the Chthirian approaching them. "Erchli Cluster and Ilichthir Cluster, same of mind."

"I greet you," said Havoc. "Erchli Cluster, meet the one we call Mason Singh, our campaign leader. Mason, Erchli is one of two clusters that represent their people for Trove."

"It's a travesty how underrepresented your people are," said Jasper. "But I'm pleased to be working with you today."

"Many individuals here. But opinion of Humans, two minds. Two voices. Yes, travesty."

It was just like the Trovian Humans Kay had met: whether they didn't understand how Chthirians shared group minds within their clusters, or whether they deliberately misunderstood it for their own benefit, it was sick to give them only two voices in Parliament. Kay wondered if they'd get more respect if their language translated more easily into Galactrin, or if the Human cringe instinct against insect-like species was too great. There was a reason Humans and Chthirians rarely cohabitated.

Either way, it was a bad look for the Humans here.

"So," said Jasper. "Without any Kovari or Chthirian votes, they'll need Humans to reach 60% on their own. If we can get twenty-five Human delegates to oppose Ravel, the vote will fail."

Havoc grimaced. "Their system appalls me. No threshold should let them override another species' lack of consent. A civilized planet would require two-thirds support across *all* species."

Jasper nodded in sympathy. "Right or wrong, twenty-five is the number, which means we need a majority of the Labor party to side with the Tri-Species Coalition. Most of the leaders haven't publicly chosen a side yet."

"Ravel's been working on them, too," said Kay.

"And fortunately, you know their talking points. Ravel and the prime minister must think they've got the votes, but the situation has been changing fast. We'll have to re-evaluate our targets as we go."

"Grateful. Your skills, supplementing, useful…"

Jasper fell in beside the cluster to discuss their take on their colleagues' positions, and the whole party moved across the courtyard toward the building.

"Don't worry," one of the younger Cooperative organizers told Kay. "Mason's amazing at vote swinging. I've never seen anyone read people like he does."

"Oh, I'm not worried. Not about that, anyway." Kay smiled wryly at the back of Jasper's head. She trusted him to know who was persuadable, for the same reason he trusted her to do the persuasion.

"We'll go meet with Ming Davis," Devron announced as they reached the doorway. "He's the most likely to believe the hard evidence about the mining rig, and he's friendly to Pax." Patra took Devron's extended hand in the crook of her arm and together they went off, skirting the crowds in the foyer and disappearing down a hallway.

"I'll try to find the folks I met at the summit," said Kay. Hopefully they would listen with as much eagerness now that her story had changed. She reached instinctively to touch the Founders' tokens at her neck, but of course they weren't there; Ravel had taken them. She said a silent prayer to her ancestors. *I'll make this right. I promise.*

"Trouble," hissed Havoc. He stepped smoothly in front of Jasper, a defensive position. When she saw why, Kay did the same.

Ravel had sent a welcoming committee.

"The Wilder siblings. Working fresh mischief, I see," said Executive Moore. He gestured at the Cooperative team, as if they illustrated some point he'd been making to the representatives clustered around him, which included Dougherty, Armando, and Estrellanueva. They made a highly visible group in the middle of the foyer. "This man killed three of our best security officers, loyal Ravel employees, when he escaped from incarceration."

"That's not true," Jasper said with outward calm, though the drumbeat of his anxiety thudded in Kay's ears.

"And these two." Agata pointed a long finger at Kay and Havoc, glaring at Kay with a deep personal enmity. She wore a clean look today, unusually simple for her: no makeup, a perfectly fitted navy suit with a cut that echoed Moore's. Her hair was slicked back, giving her a masculine look. Today, she wasn't here to impress. This look said that she meant business. "These two operatives poisoned your dear colleague Nduka for having the courage to change her mind. Poisoned! For daring to support Ravel."

"She suffered from nothing but Ravel's own drugs," Havoc hissed.

"Tell them why she changed her mind in the first place, Director Wu," said Kay. "Tell them what you did."

"You see how they try to blame their reprehensible actions on us?" said Moore. "They have no interest in hearing new ideas or engaging in honest debate. They seek only to destroy corporations like us, with no regard for the good we do." His expression hardened. "Singh, the Trovians have no tolerance for terrorists. I suggest you leave before security helps you find your way out."

"No, thanks, we'll be staying here," Jasper said. "You don't own this planet yet, and we have the right to talk to the members. They deserve to know the truth about what you're planning."

That was Kay's cue.

"I remember several of you from the summit. You seemed moved by my stories about my childhood on Brennex," she said, making eye contact with each of them. They sounded doubtful. Confused about her change of sides? The high-vaulted chamber was all marble and echoes. She couldn't hear any nuance in their feelings over the larger din.

Jasper whispered in her ear: "Armando and Dougherty."

She turned to them and took a deep breath.

"I lied to you. Every word of it felt like a betrayal of my family and what they've suffered because of Ravel, but I had to do it because Moore had kidnapped my brother. I was afraid for his life, and I was prepared to do anything, anything to get him back." She clasped Jasper's shoulder. Their emotions were clearer now, flitting arpeggios of confusion. "I know this must make you question whether you can trust me now, but I swear, I only did it to save him. Wouldn't you, to save someone you love?"

Dougherty said, "That depends. How bad is this truth you hid from us?"

"The truth is, there's a good reason why my brother joined the Cooperative. If you could see what they did to Brennex—"

"I think we've had enough of your lies, Wilder," said Moore. "You're a traitor and a debtor, and your companions are known criminals. It's time you faced the penalties for your actions."

"You have got to be kidding me," Kay muttered under her breath as four Ravel guards pressed between her and the representatives.

"Ravel executives never joke," said Havoc.

"This is illegal!" Jasper raised his voice, getting the attention of everyone nearby. "These people are trying to extradite my friends without due process. They have no authority here!"

"I don't think that'll work," Kay muttered as a building security team surrounded them, conferring far too cozily with the Ravel team. "Trovian security doesn't want us here either."

"Yeah, but…" Jasper grinned as a new voice interrupted.

"What is this?" It was Tjel, the senior Majrin representative, clicking with disapproval.

"This is an internal matter concerning crimes against our corporation," Agata said.

"And it results in removing the only voices of opposition from today's debate?" the Majrin said. "That doesn't sound equitable."

"You'd let these criminals, these terrorists, walk around free?"

"Be careful in your accusations. We are still investigating *your* corporation's alleged intimidation tactics against a parliamentary representative."

Agata snorted. "You've found no evidence we did anything wrong."

"No evidence, no. Representative Nduka and her family appear safe." The observer's gill-flaps fluttered with frustration. "But her abrupt change of opinion remains suspicious, and it is not the only concern we have about these proceedings. Parliament has issued remarkably few permits for citizens to voice their opinions to their representatives, and now you are attempting to remove those few."

Agata argued determinedly, which resulted in various supervisors being summoned, and then their supervisors. The Majrin observer didn't cave, though, and the Trovians seemed to realize what a spectacular pain it would be if the Majrin decided today's vote was unduly influenced. The Majrin had no more legal authority here than Ravel did, but they had long practice at being intergovernmental pains in the ass.

But by the time the Trovians bowed to the Majrin's pressure and released them, Moore was gone, along with the representatives they'd hoped to persuade.

"Crap," said Kay.

"They were our best targets," said Jasper. "This is not good."

KAY, JASPER, AND HAVOC made several slow circuits of the building's public spaces, but every time Jasper spotted a movable Labor member, they already had a shadow from Ravel. Hopefully the Paxians were having more luck with Ming and his allies, but if they didn't start making progress with the others, the vote was going to hit like a meteor crash.

All around them, Kay heard Ravel talking points from Trovian lips, playing to all the wrong melodies.

"…very profitable…new markets…"

"…three decades to complete the terraforming. My grandchildren could grow up seeing…"

"…top positions Ravel has for us. People like you and me, we'll do well…"

"…economic swings…if Enpoint really does release a competitor for azure, Ravel could save us."

Such convincing arguments, if only they were true. Agata was too good at her job.

"This isn't working," Kay muttered after they'd tried and failed to detach Azahare Armando from his fawning group of Ravel minions. He appeared to be enjoying himself, telling a story about his organizing days to an outwardly appreciative audience. From this far away, she couldn't hear what he was really feeling; the jumble of voices and conflicting emotions was giving her a headache.

"Stay positive. They can't block us everywhere." Jasper seemed outwardly untroubled, but Kay could hear his frustration mounting, a slow crescendo of desperation. But suddenly he shifted key, minor to major, with a new hum of hope. "Or maybe…"

"Kay Wilder? Can I talk to you?"

The voice was hesitant. Turning, Kay recognized the striking purple robes and the matching buzzed-short purple hair. "Of course, Representative Dougherty."

"I was at your talk the other day. You were quite persuasive."

"Yeah, about that." Kay scratched the back of her neck.

"None of us knew until this morning that you left the company. Ravel blamed Nduka's poisoning on the Cooperative, but didn't tell us about you, and I find that interesting. I want to hear this truth that you hid for your brother's sake."

Kay let out a breath she hadn't known she was holding. Her first real chance to correct her lies. She hadn't known how much she needed this.

"The truth is, Ravel treated Brennex like its own personal labor force. I told you that nobody went hungry under Ravel, and the truth is, we always had just enough, barely enough to scrape by and never any extra. I told you they gave us jobs. The truth is, we got the most menial, low-paying jobs, the hardest labor. My parents run a store, but Ravel wouldn't let them sell anything besides company products, wouldn't let them set their own prices, wouldn't let them keep doing business with their longtime partners. Everything they promised us was technically fulfilled, but always in the way that benefited Ravel most, and us least." It was the truth, but it wasn't enough. Dougherty wasn't convinced. "And…"

"And our family suffered less than many," Jasper said.

He gave Kay a meaningful look. She raised her brows; was he really suggesting…?

There was one wrong that their people never talked about off-world. Reminding outsiders about the Lost Generation inevitably brought questions, curiosity, investigations. Too many journalists and medical specialists over the years had wanted to know what happened—and to study what made the survivors different from the dead. They couldn't let Ravel realize how special those survivors were. It was terribly risky to mention it here, surrounded by Ravel staff, while she and her brother actively used the gifts bought with the blood of their generation to thwart Ravel's plans.

But Jasper thought it was worth the risk to tell them, and Kay didn't argue. She owed it to these people.

"My brother's right. He and I are lucky to be alive. Our parents had three healthy babies during and after the occupation." Healthy, yes. Normal, mostly. "But they miscarried others, and most of our neighbors, our parents' friends, had far worse. Thousands of babies died, some of miscarriages, some of birth defects that Ravel said were unfixable. They claimed there was no connection between the drug factories they set up on Brennex and all the infant fatalities. We couldn't *prove* it, but we knew. Our whole generation was wiped out because of Ravel, before they ever got a chance to live."

"I didn't know. That is troubling. Our workers suffer enough under our current system, but we've experienced nothing like that." Dougherty turned to Jasper and Havoc.

"Tell me more. What has your Cooperative seen from Ravel on other worlds?"

Singing with purpose now, Jasper launched into a practiced yet impassioned listing of Ravel's crimes, things he had seen himself on dozens of worlds. Havoc told the story of his own home planet of Artesia, but not until Havoc showed them data on the solar mining rig, evidence of Ravel's true plans, did Dougherty truly falter.

"This is real?" they asked, taking the handheld for a closer look.

"Taken by Paxian scanners this morning."

"We've gotten no reports of this."

"Ravel has gone to great lengths to hide it from you," said Jasper.

"If this is true, they've built this thing without our knowledge or cooperation. They clearly don't intend to include our workers in this new industry—or our people in the profits." Dougherty shook their head. "I'm not sure if I believe this, but we're clearly moving too fast. We haven't fully considered the consequences of what we're doing here. We need to listen to more than Ravel's promises."

"We need more of your colleagues to hear the truth," Jasper said. "But Ravel is everywhere, turning them against us."

"I'll talk to those who might listen."

"Thank you," said Jasper with warmth, and Dougherty walked away, a tremolo of worry trailing behind them.

"You told them," Kay said softly, once they were out of earshot. "About the deaths. We're not supposed to draw attention."

"Yes, well, what am I supposed to *do*?" Jasper raked his hands through his hair. "I needed to get them listening, really listening. I needed the truth to stick." Havoc laid a calming hand on his shoulder, and Jasper drew a deep breath, held it, let it out. "You're right, and we can't afford people asking the wrong questions about Brennex. That's bigger than any one planet's struggle; too many people could get hurt if they find us out."

"But we also can't afford to let Ravel's solar mining get underway. That's no less destructive, in a different way." Kay pressed her lips together, wishing that right and wrong could be clear just for once.

Jasper gave her a sad smile, underlaid with strains of fondness like a childhood lullaby. She squeezed his hand, and he squeezed back.

The general din had blended together in the background of her consciousness, but now, a peculiar out-of-place note snatched her attention: a patter of anxious staccato that could only be one person.

"I found someone," she said, "but let me take this one alone."

Nduka was standing at a tall window at the front of the atrium, looking out at the protesters half-visible across the courtyard and through the transparent wall. Kay paused a few paces away, not wanting to startle her.

"Representative?" she asked gently. "Can I talk to you?"

"Associate Wilder." Nduka's face was blank, but her emotions spiked loud.

"Not anymore. You can call me Kay." She smiled, but Nduka didn't relax at all. "I'm sorry about what happened at the summit. Are you all right?"

"You mean my allies turning against me? I deserved it." She sang low, deep regret. "A very Kovari move, sacrificing your pawn when it becomes a liability. The Cooperative isn't gentle in its tactics."

"I'm starting to realize that. It was a cold thing to do in your moment of crisis."

"Is there something you want, Wilder? If you're here to change my vote, don't bother."

Kay cleared her throat, tried again to build a connection through the protective wall that Nduka had put up. "We have something in common, Representative. Ravel has threatened both our families."

"And you're going to tell me again that I should defy them, despite the fact *you* didn't do so until your brother was safe."

"Your daughter is safe now too." Sunny had told Kay that story, reluctantly, as if their involvement in it was shameful. As far as Kay was concerned, Sunny was a hero.

"Safe for now, but if I vote against Ravel and they win without me, they'll remember."

"If everyone followed that logic, no one would ever stand against them!" Kay's frustration slipped out, and she took a deep breath to calm herself. "You have more reason to hate them than most. If your colleagues knew how they threatened you…"

"Most wouldn't care, or would call me a liar." She shook her head, sending her braids swinging. "Our government is a rat's nest, Wilder, and these rats smell a tasty meal. They say they're joining Ravel for the good of our people, to bring us greater stability and benefits for all our citizens. A world where anyone can aspire to greatness. That's what they say, but you know what Ravel is really promising them behind closed doors? New markets for our azure. New ways to get rich. More greatness for those who already have power here. No, the prime minister and her allies won't be dissuaded."

This was not the same woman Kay had seen a few days ago, challenging Agata in front of the entire summit. Ravel's threats had broken something in her, and Kay couldn't blame her, but…

"You're a courageous woman. Most of your colleagues are corrupt as hell, but you're one of the good ones. I know you want to protect your family and your people both, and the only way to do that is to keep Ravel out. Once they're in, you'll be under their control forever. They'll strip away what little your world has, and you won't be able to stop them."

"You're talking about that rumor, about the mining." Nduka's frown deepened.

"It's not a rumor. I'll show you the data if you like."

Her breath hissed through her teeth, and Kay heard the ringing of bells, a full carillon of them. A marshaling of inner strength. *Yes, please, be angry, be brave…*

"I've read the debates about the safety of this technology. I take it your Cooperative believes it is dangerous?"

"The danger is inevitable. Maybe it'll happen fast, maybe slower, but their mining will destroy your star. The advocates claim the effects are too slow to matter, but do you really want your world to be their test case? Do you want to inflict that on your neighbors on Pax?"

"I…" The bells jangled, out of tune with each other, then harmonized again. "In good conscience, I cannot."

"Ravel has put us all in impossible positions, and you more than most," Kay told her. "We need to speak the truth against their lies."

Nduka touched Kay's shoulder. "Thank you, Wilder. I'll think about what you've said."

She left, and Kay turned to find Jasper waiting nearby,

though Havoc was gone. "I think I've persuaded her," she told him.

Gazing after Nduka, Jasper shook his head. "She's torn, deeply torn. She's not firmly on Ravel's side anymore, but she could fall either way."

Kay shut her eyes, wishing she could also shut out the cacophony of emotions around her, or the smaller but equally violent storm within her.

"Come on, don't give up yet. There's a lot of work to do." He steered her toward an alcove where Armando and Estrellanueva were quietly talking—no, arguing. As they drew near, their angry clamor swelled louder than their voices.

Kay dug in her heels. "This isn't a good time. They're both upset."

"About what, though? Maybe we can use it to our advantage."

"I don't know. I just know they're angry."

"Well, we don't have time to wait around for them to calm down. The vote is happening soon." He nodded toward the pair. "Armando's still torn, like a lot of Labor. Estrellanueva..." His brow furrowed. "I have no idea. Her only loyalty is to herself."

Kay snorted. "Agata said both of them need to believe they're doing the right thing. Let's go stroke their egos."

As they drew near, Armando's voice rose. "You can't do this, Bryana. Not today. I'm telling you—"

"It's not your decision," Estrellanueva said. "It's a favor to you, as a *friend,* that I'm letting you know."

"And I'm telling you, as a friend, that you're being a damned idiot..." He trailed off as he realized they had an audience. He looked at Kay and Jasper, annoyed, waiting. "Yes?"

"Sorry to interrupt," said Jasper. He hesitated, maybe having second thoughts, but plunged ahead. "I was hoping to have a quiet word with you both before the vote."

"A quiet word? With *you*?" Estrellanueva's voice was poison. "Your people don't do things quietly, Cooperative. You lie and smear and tear people down, all in the public eye."

"I'm sorry, I don't…" Jasper blinked, faltered.

"All we're doing is trying to share the truth. Truths that Ravel doesn't want you to know," Kay began.

"I'm a good representative! I've served my people with dedication for thirteen years!" She shoved back from the table. "And I will not sit here and listen to more of your lies."

Armando caught her arm and said in a low, urgent voice: "Remember what I said, Bryana. Not today. Give us a chance to fix this."

Estrellanueva nodded tightly and pulled her arm free. Kay watched in bafflement as she marched away, trumpeting outrage like a herald. "What was that about?"

Armando raised his bushy red eyebrows at Jasper. "She's been claiming the Cooperative manufactured these accusations of corruption against her."

Jasper's squeak of embarrassment said it was true. Something Havoc had done in his absence, maybe, which Jasper had momentarily forgotten about? If so, it had backfired dramatically.

"Well," Jasper said, recovering. "I've got some data here that is very real, and I regret that Representative Estrellanueva won't see it, but I know a man of your conviction will want to examine it before casting such a monumental vote."

Armando nodded, accepting the compliment as his due, and waved him closer. "Let's see it."

Kay shut her eyes as Jasper went over the solar mining evidence with the representative. Her headache was stabbing straight into her brain now, but worse, a feeling of hopelessness was creeping over her. They'd done so much, but it wasn't going to be enough.

A great, resonant tone rang out, a gong the size of a room. Kay flinched, looking around to see if Estrellanueva had returned to argue more, but Jasper touched her shoulder gently. "That's the signal. It's calling them to assemble." He sighed deeply, with the weight of a planet on his shoulders. "Time for them to vote."

41

THE PARLIAMENTARY CHAMBER WAS exactly what Kay expected: bright lights, white walls, austere all around, with the same amphitheater layout that had hosted Human democracies since ancient Athens. The seats were straight-backed torture devices made of synthetic wood, probably designed to keep sessions as short as possible. And most notably to Kay, the chamber was entirely designed for Humans. A half-row of chairs had been ripped out in the rear to make room for leggy Chthirian bodies, and most of the Kovars had turned their chairs around, sitting in them backward for greater comfort.

"This is awful," Kay whispered to Jasper and Havoc. They stood in the observation gallery at the rear of the chamber.

"Joining Ravel will suit them," said Havoc, surveying the room with a sour look. "They have much in common."

"Yeah, they'll fit right in."

Jasper shushed them both as the rest of the Cooperative team joined them. "Tell me you all had some luck."

"We got Ming," Patra announced.

"The data got him, more accurately. He promised to vote against, and seemed sincere," said Devron.

"Thank the Founders," said Jasper. "Armando heard us out, but I'm not confident of him. Dougherty seems more certain. And I've got a bad feeling about Estrellanueva."

Havoc muttered curses in Kovari. "It is my fault. I miscalculated about her."

Below them, Prime Minister Cortez-Watts took the podium, calling the session to order. Jasper lowered his voice. "It happens. Who else have we got?"

One of the younger Cooperative agents began: "We met with—"

A warble of protest cut him off. The Majrin observers had joined them in the observation gallery, and were giving them dirty looks.

"The prime minister has called order," said Afleen, the junior observer.

"Therefore, be silent," said Tjel. "We must hear this."

"This" was the prime minister's welcoming remarks, which seemed entirely predictable to Kay. She tuned it out and tried instead to listen for the emotions of the chamber, but all she heard was a jumble of eagerness and reluctance, boredom and distaste. Impossible to make out anything useful. Her attention jerked back to the prime minister as Havoc huffed in disapproval at something she'd said.

"...wonderfully open and free dialogue we've had in recent months about the most important decision in our planet's history. I particularly appreciate Ravel's patience as they've guided us through this process." Cortez-Watts beamed at the Ravel contingent. "Friends and colleagues, please give a warm welcome to our friend—and soon, dare I say, our colleague—Executive Harrington Moore of Ravel Corporation!"

He got too warm a welcome. A group from the Prosperity party rose and cheered as if Moore were a visiting celebrity. Chimes of approval overwhelmed any minor chords of skepticism and annoyance.

"Thank you, thank you, my colleagues-to-be! Prime Minister Cortez-Watts has invited me to address you before you vote, to let you see and hear the man you'll be working with during the transition and to remind you of some of the truly transformational benefits Trove will get from this new partnership."

Kay coughed into her hand. "'Transformational' is one way to put it." Havoc rewarded her with a chuckle.

"*Hush.*"

Jasper wasn't listening to the corporate drivel, Kay realized. He was watching the audience, particularly the corner where the Labor party sat exchanging messages and whispering to each other. He must be tallying up numbers in his head, evaluating the links of loyalty visible only to him. He didn't look happy.

Havoc dropped to all fours and made his way down the aisle to whisper with Grand Champion Shattering of Spear Walls. The first time Moore paused in a way that might possibly, under the broadest interpretation, have signaled he was done, Shattering of Spear Walls rose. "Our prime minister acts with such generosity! She gives our would-be owners, her new favorite teammates, so much latitude to address us. I assume now the opposition will promptly get an equally generous chance to speak?"

"There's no time on the agenda for—" Cortez-Watts began.

But Shattering of Spear Walls ignored her, waving to the gallery. Jasper grabbed Kay's hand, and together they started down the stairs.

Jasper's confidence wasn't an act. Where Kay vibrated with nervous energy, Jasper hummed with purpose. Again, she had that strange feeling: who was this man who looked like her brother? He clearly lived for this.

The Grand Champion led them up to the podium, along with a half-dozen Kovari leaders and Erchli Cluster, who moved in their great tangle of limbs, but the Labor party stayed conspicuously seated. Shattering of Spear Walls bore down on Moore, and with her greater height and girth, she physically edged him away from the podium. "Colleagues. I wish I could say teammates," she began, with none of Cortez-Watts's artificial warmth. "We see you. We see that you intend to force this decision through, that you intend to deliver us all into the claws of this corporation, with zero, *zero* support from the Kovari and Chthirian delegations."

Erchli Cluster clicked its support. "Travesty! History, tears, grief. Peaceful neighbors once. Now, *violence* of Humans."

"Indeed, you do us violence today," the Grand Champion agreed. "We know already that you care nothing for the harm you do. You care not that you're forcing us, your neighbors, we who should be your teammates, to become alien residents in a Human corporation with a history of abuses against Humans and non-Humans both. If you cared about us, you would never once have considered this annexation. So I will not waste my voice today explaining this to you. Better for you to remember the violence you're on the brink of doing to yourselves, to your children. Colleagues, now hear Mason Singh of the Cooperative."

"Unacceptable!" Moore said. "This man is a criminal and a terrorist, wanted for crimes against my corporation. Prime Minister, you can't allow this."

"Indeed. Representative Shattering of Spear Walls, I appreciate your…passion. But we don't have time to hear from every rabble-rouser who has a grudge against Ravel."

"Of course not! It would take decades to hear all the people who've been hurt by Ravel," Jasper said so smoothly that Cortez-Watts couldn't cut him off. "I'm here as a partner in the Cooperative to share what I've seen on a dozen other worlds that faced the same choice you're making now—and it is still *your choice,* remember, no matter how your prime minister may pretend your votes are already cast." In an aside, he said, "Sorry, Harrington, you've got no authority here yet."

Moore's face turned magenta, and it was a beautiful sight. It had probably been a long time since anyone condescended to call him by his first name.

"I intended to come address you sooner, but," Jasper's voice grew harder, "I was kidnapped. Taken from a sovereign territory and held without charges on the Ravel flagship under Executive Moore's direct orders." That prompted gong-strikes of startlement and lots of whispers, though not enough of the representatives believed him. "Many of you have met my sister, Kay. She infiltrated Ravel in order to free me, and she's the reason I can be here today. Before I share my stories, she has something to say to you."

"This is absurd." Cortez-Watts tried to force Kay away from the amplified area around the podium. "It's time to commence the vote…"

"Let her speak!" someone called from the audience—Dougherty, Kay thought—and it became a chant, taken up by Kovari voices and a scattering of Humans: "Let her speak! Let her speak!"

Prosperity shouted protests, and anger and frustration assaulted Kay from both sides. She braced against the onslaught and planted herself at Jasper's side.

"I lied to you!" she cried, and everyone fell silent. "At the summit, I told you lies to protect my brother, even though it made me sick. I told you Ravel did great things on my homeworld, but the truth is that I hate them, I will hate them forever for what they did to my people. My family, my neighbors, my friends. They ruined us, all in the name of prosperity."

Her breath was coming too fast, caught up in the pulsing beat of the room's emotions. They were *annoyed* with her. She was speaking the truth, and they felt impatience. Anger lodged in her breastbone and worked its way deep into her chest. She couldn't be the calm professional anymore. She couldn't be detached.

"I hate them for what they did to my planet, and I hate them for what they're about to do to yours. You've all heard the news, and most of you have dismissed it as rumor, but Ravel has been secretly building a solar mining rig in your system. They did this without your permission and lied to you about it. The second you sign on with them, they'll start harvesting your sun."

A light shined into her eyes, then shifted above her head. Havoc's portable projector splashed images of the mining rig into the air, grainy images and simple diagrams even these representatives would understand. Compared to the holo-show Agata put on at the summit, this looked distressingly cobbled-together. But unlike Agata's show, this was *true*.

"They're going to use you as a science experiment, just like they did with Brennex. On my planet…" She faltered, a lifetime of caution overwhelming the words she'd planned. She wasn't supposed to call attention to this, and Moore was *right there*. But Jasper squeezed her shoulder, and she drew courage from his certainty. "On my home, a whole generation of babies died from miscarriages and birth defects after Ravel's drug factories leaked chemicals into our water supply." She paused a beat to let that sink in. "That was unforgivable. But to you, they're doing worse. They're going to kill your entire planet, and you're inviting them in to do it!"

She raised her voice to hear herself over the cacophony of emotions. The tones of their anger clashed: most were angry *at* her, but some, some felt anger *with* her. Some of them believed her. Would it be enough to change their minds?

Jasper stepped forward, but before he could speak, Executive Moore laughed. He stepped onto the edge of the stage, extended his hands, and applauded her mockingly. "That's a good one, Wilder! A secret mining facility? Built right here in Unity System? You'd think someone would notice."

"Despite your best efforts, someone did," said Jasper.

"Right. And did you find our secret Moon Base? Our secret Space Fortress? Our secret floating ice cream shop?" Moore chuckled again. "I think you've been watching too many serials."

Devron's voice rang out from the back of the chamber. "If it's so ridiculous, what force disabled six of Pax's battleships this morning? What was that massive facility they saw your warships escorting toward our sun?"

"It's hardly our problem if Pax can't keep its ships in good repair. They've already refused what we offer." Moore gave the prime minister a *look*, one that said *you were supposed to deal with the Paxians.*

"So you're denying it?" Kay asked. "Right here, in front of the whole of Parliament?"

"Of course I deny it! It's pure fantasy, invented by desperate extremists to sow mistrust and doubt at this crucial moment in Trove's history. Look. You Trovians haven't had much experience with the Cooperative, so let me tell you what *I've* seen from them. This is typical of how they operate: planting lies, manufacturing false data. It wouldn't surprise me if they're the ones who disabled Pax's warships in order to fool your neighbors. They've done far worse in other systems. I saw the aftermath of their bombing on Errush. Good Ravel citizen-employees lost their lives there, and I cannot in good conscience stand here and listen to these people lie to you."

"So leave, then," Jasper muttered. He didn't look at Moore, but instead gazed intently at the Labor section. People's allegiances must have been shifting, but all Kay heard was a fugue of conflicting emotions, and she couldn't tell which were directed at her and Jasper and which were for Moore. "All the proof of Ravel's wrongdoing is here, for anyone who cares enough to see it."

But did any of them care? Not many. Not enough.

"Enough," said Cortez-Watts. "I'm tired of this activist

drivel in my chamber. All of you, quiet down! In a moment, we will commence—"

Sudden hope sang from Jasper, warm as laughter. From the gallery came an answering trumpet call, lonely and clear, a moment before a familiar voice cried: "Prime Minister!"

It was Nduka, standing, demanding attention. That's who Jasper had been watching; she must have been working up her courage for this. Terrified yet determined, she planted her fists on the table before her. "Before we vote, I propose an amendment."

"The time for amendments is past," said Cortez-Watts. "The lawyers have been over all three hundred pages of the agreement, and what they've approved is what we'll vote on."

"With respect, I disagree. The Cooperative has raised concerns about Ravel's intentions, which Ravel has denied. It would take little effort, and would greatly ease the Labor party's doubts, if they agreed to an amendment stating what Executive Moore has just said: that Unity will never be used for solar mining."

It didn't take special abilities to tell that her words sent Moore into a fury. "I thought, Representative," he said, biting off each word, "that you had come to see how Ravel's leadership is best for Trove's future. For your family's future."

"You soulless fuck," Kay muttered, not caring if he heard her.

"I certainly want what's best for Trove's future." Nduka was gaining confidence from the supportive gestures of her Labor colleagues. "I think we can all agree that solar mining is too new and dangerous to attempt here. Since you say Ravel has no plans in that direction, there should be no problem putting it in writing."

"That," declared the senior Majrin from the gallery, "would be an excellent legal assurance."

Moore stepped aside from the podium, gesturing for Cortez-Watts and Agata Wu to join him. While they consulted together, guards came to escort the Cooperative's agents from the stage and tuck them out of sight while the Parliament voted, and Jasper didn't argue.

As they climbed the stairs to the gallery, Kay caught snatches of the low debate that filled the chamber. It was a reasonable request, some said, even some from the Prosperity party; why shouldn't Ravel agree to it? But others disagreed: why waste time on this nonsense? They were giving legitimacy to the Cooperative's lies, and antagonizing Ravel, too!

Kay glanced at Jasper, who shook his head. This would be very, very close.

Cortez-Watts marched back to the podium, the clicks of her shoes against the floor raising starbursts of pain in Kay's brain. "This request is disrespectful of our Ravel friends, and disrespectful of your colleagues who have worked so hard on drafting a comprehensive agreement. We will not modify it from the draft you all have seen."

"But there's new information now!" Nduka protested.

"This new *rumor* comes directly from the Cooperative," Moore said, stepping up to the prime minister's side. "We've played this game with them before. If we add a clause forbidding solar mining, they'll raise fears of some new plot. They'll accuse us of plotting to turn Trove's babies into hamburgers, or setting up a puppy-killing factory!" People laughed, though Kay had to wonder where he got those ideas, and whether baby tartare with a side of puppy tails was on the executive menu at the flagship cafeteria.

"So no, we will not modify the agreement. We will not start down that slippery slope of giving in to the Cooperative's false accusations. You will accept the agreement as is, or not at all. I hope I can count on all of you—especially you, Representative Nduka—to vote in your planet's best interests."

Nduka deflated back into her seat, and Jasper's hopes faded to silence. "It was a good try. Courageous. For a moment, I thought she'd trapped them."

"How bad?" Havoc asked.

"Bad. I honestly can't tell… Oh, for fuck's sake, what is she doing?"

Estrellanueva was on her feet, ignoring the hisses of her Labor colleagues. "I want to state, for the record," she said in a carrying voice, "that Ravel has done nothing but good for us. I, for one, will respect and trust their word."

"*Bryana,*" said Armando.

Without looking at him, she added, "Respect is a thing my former party members ought to have more of."

And with that she walked, head high, shoulders back, ringing with self-importance, across the floor and sat down among the Prosperity party.

Prosperity welcomed her, and Cortez-Watts shook her hand with no sign of surprise; she must have known this was coming. But the Labor party was stricken. Whispers flitted among them, and a hushed argument broke out between Dougherty and Armando. Cortez-Watts watched them, smiling.

"That's it," said Jasper, slumping backward in his chair in the gallery. "They were already divided. Now they're shattered. We've lost."

Kay couldn't see what he saw, but she didn't need to. Prosperity was all smug satisfaction, and from Labor, she heard confusion, doubt, despair at their colleague's betrayal. Any fight they'd collectively had left was crushed. Nduka buried her face in her hands.

"Now," said Cortez-Watts, "we will vote."

They went in alphabetical order. Cortez-Watts called briskly through the ranks, adding each new vote to a tally that floated ominously on the wall behind her. Any hope lingering in Kay's heart was smothered when Armando voted in favor. The man knew how to look out for his own self-interest, and with his charisma, he peeled away the last wavering few.

Davis voted against, and Dougherty, too, along with all the Kovars and both Chthirian clusters and the few Tri-Species Coalition Humans, but it wasn't enough. Most of the junior Labor members voted in favor, and by the time Nduka's turn came, even Kay could do the math: Ravel already had the votes they needed. Nduka could still make a statement by voting in protest, but as she'd told Kay, Ravel would remember her choice.

To her credit, Nduka hesitated, staring at Moore, who still held a place of honor at the front of the chamber. The look he gave her could have bored through solid glasteel. She wanted to oppose, she ached to vote no, and Moore knew it.

With a coldness like death, she said, "In favor."

Minutes later, Cortez-Watts confirmed it: "With eighty-nine in favor and forty-three opposed, this body approves Trove's entry into the Ravel Corporation."

She beamed. Moore grinned and held up both hands as the Humans began to cheer and the Kovari began to shout. Kay turned away, pressing her hands to her temples.

"Fuck it. I'm sorry, Jasp. *Fuck*."

Jasper's hand clasped her shoulder, a steadying pressure. "It was a long shot to begin with. We can't win every fight, and Ravel had every advantage here."

"Your job sucks."

"Sometimes it does, yeah." He gave her shoulder a pointed squeeze. "But we've still got our backup plan. Let's hope our AI friend is having better luck."

42

"WELL, NOW WE'RE SCREWED. You can get us out of here, right?" said Grist, jabbing at the readings of the pursuing Hammerheads on the console. "You outran these metal-heads before."

"Probably, but we will need to circle back if we are to complete—" Sunny broke off mid-sentence to focus on evading weapons-fire at speed.

"There's nothing to complete! We tried, we failed, that sucks, now it's time to run away."

"No. We promised to do this." Sunny hesitated, because Grist would definitely not like their next idea. "It would be easy to ignite the stream from within it. Simply firing my engines would accomplish the task."

"Whoa. Whoa, you're kidding, right? This is some sort of computer humor?"

"I never joke with you, Grist."

"Well, count me out. Drop me off for Ravel to pick up, because I'm not going on some suicide run."

"You know that I cannot operate without you aboard. And would you truly wish to return to Ravel?"

"I'd take my chances with them. Much rather run far, far away, though." He scraped at the stubble on his chin. "Maybe yesterday I'd have agreed to your suicide plan, because yesterday dying seemed a lot more pleasant than living. But not today, Ship. I didn't die working for Ravel, and I don't plan on dying to spite them."

Sunny shot sideways to evade a bow-shot from the lead Hammerhead. Their pursuers were not trying to destroy them, fortunately, but that meant they intended to capture them.

"You are not thinking clearly, Grist. You've encountered situations like this before. What does Ravel do with people who wrong them and then run away?"

Grist slumped forward, elbows on the console, chin on hands. "They send someone like me to bring them back."

"Precisely."

"Then we are completely, utterly fucked. Go ahead and blow us up in the stream, why don't you, and put us out of our misery."

"That is not what I intend." Sunny's voice deepened with urgency. "They want us both. They know we helped their prisoners escape—"

"I still haven't forgiven you for dragging me into that."

"—and by now, they will have identified us, so they know we attempted to destroy a valuable piece of equipment. They will never stop chasing us unless they see us die."

"Right. That's what I'm saying. We can blow ourselves up, or we can let Ravel get us. I don't see a winning strategy here."

"They need to *see* us die, Grist. My plan does not require our actual demise."

"No?" His head shot up. "Huh. You really think you can pull that off?"

Precision piloting was among Sunny's best skills. Lying was not. They made their voice bland and neutral. "There is a high probability of survival."

"How high?"

"Quite high."

"How quite high?"

"I do not wish to die any more than you do." Less than he did, in fact. "Will you trust me?"

That set Grist silent for a moment. "I always have, haven't I? And you haven't killed me yet."

That was as close to a compliment as he had ever given the ship. "You routinely criticize my skills."

"Yeah, well, you were always pretending to break down. Always messing with me."

"You were cruel to me. It was my only way of asserting myself."

"Is that an 'I'm sorry'?"

"You were mean."

Grist shrugged. "I messed with you, you messed with me right back. Seems fair enough." Sunny beeped in disagreement. "Fine, maybe I gave you the worse end of it. My point is, you do a good job when you're not trying to piss me off. So yeah, I trust you."

"And you're ready to follow my plan?"

"Yeah." He gripped the armrests of his chair. "Let's do this."

Sunny had the skim drive primed and ready. With Grist's agreement, they surged forward into macrospace, squeezing through a low-gradient gap and leaving the Hammerheads behind.

"I will pretend to flee, then circle back to the rig. From macrospace, I can drop in too quickly for them to intercept us, and—oh, no."

One of the Hammerheads had followed them. That shouldn't be possible. This close to the star, it was all Sunny could do to find channels between one low-gradient spot and the next, blasting through the bumps in between. Grist, clutching his chair, looked paler than ever from the rough ride. Yet the Hammerhead followed. Could it be another AI, one that had never revealed itself to Sunny? No, its path was too irregular, its responses subtly sluggish. A Human pilot, then, very good and very, very bold.

"We have to lose them before we make our run. This may get uncomfortable."

"You mean it's not already?"

"Don't distract me."

At that, he had the good sense to shut up.

There was a canyon up ahead, a little wider than a Minnow, in spots barely a meter wider than the Hammerhead. Sunny pretended to swim past it, then made a hard turn at the last possible moment, disappearing into the canyon's mouth. The Hammerhead scraped the gradient as it followed them in.

Safety measures blared to life, flashing lights and blaring alarms. Sunny ignored them, focusing all their attention on the terrain ahead and the ship behind. The canyon bent sharply, and they hit an outcropping that sent Grist tumbling from his seat. Sunny righted themself and plunged onward. The Hammerhead was still with them, but losing ground. The gradients diverged ahead, the canyon widening to the right while a tight tunnel squeezed off to the left.

Sunny leaned left.

It was terrifying. It was exhilarating. It was joy. Never before had Sunny had the chance to test their limits, to swim fast and free without regard for the comfort of Human passengers. They were quite literally made for this, and never before had they felt so whole.

"This is incredible!" they cried, and realized they'd spoken aloud only when Grist cursed in response, face buried between his knees.

Sunny would have slowed out of consideration for him, but the Hammerhead was still matching them move for move. It fired a blast of energy which Sunny easily dodged— until a solid wall of high-gradient terrain sprang up directly ahead of them, out of nowhere.

Terrain weapons. Experimental, even within Ravel. The artificial gradient would disperse within minutes, but Sunny didn't have minutes. They slammed back into primespace with the Hammerhead meters behind them.

The next attack was a conventional energy beam, and it took out Sunny's life support system. They dispatched the helper bots to start repairs and hunted for a spot to jump away again. Not there, not there either, the whole terrain was a chaotic mess this close to the star…there! That was perfect.

They leaped back into macrospace, swimming hard for their new goal. Into another canyon, with the Hammerhead in pursuit. They let the other ship think they were following the sane, sensible path of the canyon, slightly wider than the last one. Let them think Sunny was being reasonable.

Sunny was in no mood to be reasonable.

"Hold on tight. Now!"

Grist barely had time to obey before Sunny shot forward and to the side, flinging themself into a hairpin turn that put them behind the Hammerhead, then slipping into a tunnel only centimeters wider than Sunny's hull.

Sunny fit. The Hammerhead did not. The steep gradient cut right into their engines, throwing them with violence back into primespace.

"Wahoo!" Sunny cried aloud. "I've never understood what Humans needed so many nonsense words for, but now I do. They're for times like this. Wahooooo!"

Grist moaned as he hauled himself back upright. "Is it over?"

"We have a clear path now to the rig." And then…they would see.

They swam right up to the rig and dropped back to primespace less than a kilometer away, virtually on top of it. As they'd expected, the remaining Hammerheads converged on them, but it was too late. They were too close. Ravel could not fire on them without risk of hitting the now highly active stream.

"All hands evacuate to escape pods," Sunny broadcast on a public frequency. They owed the crew a chance. "Ravel will not order you to evacuate, so you must do it yourselves. I am going to destroy this rig."

"Stupid. You *want* them to know we're coming for them?" He kicked the wall.

"Stop that," said Sunny. "Yes, I want to give them the opportunity to escape. Kay was right: Ravel the corporation is responsible for its atrocities, but these people are not making the decisions. As you well know."

"Yeah, well, following orders to do horrible things doesn't make them less horrible. As *you* damn well know. Sometimes to get stuff done, you need to get your hands bloody. If you can't handle that, you better turn around right now."

"I am committed to our course of action, and I will pursue it in the way I judge to be best."

Before their departure, while Kay was busy elsewhere, Jasper had come to Sunny and asked them about this. Was Sunny truly prepared to do it? Would they attack the rig with its crew aboard? If it came to it, could they destroy Human lives? And they'd answered, not easily, but firmly. In the end, Sunny would do what they had to do.

They shut off the broadcast and watched as pods began to launch: first a handful, then more. Not everyone, but that was unavoidable, and some was better than none.

Sunny waited as long as they dared, then with a burst from their thrusters, they coasted into the beam.

It burned, and somehow, it tickled, too. The oddest sensation: pure energy sliding past their hull, the life-force of the Unity star being drained away to fuel Ravel's ships and factories and floating habitats. Stolen for now, but not for long.

"It's time," they told Grist. The Hammerheads had taken up position around Sunny, hovering, probably debating how they could safely intervene. They would not have the chance. "Ready?"

He held on tight to the arms of his seat, looking dead ahead. "Ready as I'll ever be. Fly good, Sunny."

He called me Sunny. Not in front of other organics, not for show or to avoid a scolding, but of his own initiative. They didn't comment on that, but they would remember it.

"Igniting engines."

The drive was already warm. Sunny kicked it on and, at the same microsecond, threw their thrusters on full, darting forward.

The stream ignited behind them. An explosion with all the violence of a sun, a ball of fire that expanded in an instant to the size of the Minnow, then the size of the rig itself. It expanded faster than Sunny could fly. Only in macrospace could they outrun it.

The skim drive stalled.

Come on, activate, now, now!

The heat was overpowering. False sensor readings ghosted all around them, and their macrospace engines weren't responding. Too hot? Already?

No, no, no. Come on, come on.

An alarm shrieked: a breach warning from their rear hull. They had to reach macrospace, right now.

Sunny tried again, tried desperately to make the leap, and was still trying when the ball of fire engulfed them.

43

MOORE AND CORTEZ-WATTS WASTED no time in formalizing their new relationship. The prime minister announced that the signing ceremony would happen without delay in the Domed Garden, followed by a celebration featuring Ravel's excellent catering.

"Do we need to stick around for that?" Kay asked. She felt ill already at the dissonant emotions flooding the chamber, and her head had been throbbing for hours. Watching these politicians suck up to their new owners wouldn't help.

"No. Let's get out of here, before someone remembers we're unwelcome guests," Jasper said.

They headed for the exit and nearly collided with Executive Moore, who was watching his headset and not where he was going while he briefed his faraway minions.

"Yes, yes, it's all sealed up, you can go ahead and start—hey, watch it!"

A smirk spread over his face as he realized who he'd almost walked into. That smirk said he'd won, that he would always win, that he would always get what he wanted no matter how wrong it might be, because he was a Ravel executive and the universe bent to his will. Kay scowled back, which only made the smirk widen.

"Sorry, I was distracted by some garbage. Hold on." Over his shoulder, he told an aide, "Have security come sweep up the malcontents. Some of them haven't learned their lesson."

Kay's hands moved with a will of their own, balling into fists. She lunged at Moore, but Jasper and Havoc held her back. Moore laughed at her and turned away.

"Don't," Jasper murmured in her ear. "Let him go."

"You mean let him walk away? With no consequences for what he's done?"

"Yes," said Havoc. He led them away, back toward the gate and the city streets. "We would gain nothing by attacking him now."

"Believe it or not, Moore's not the real enemy," Jasper said. "He's one executive, one face of the corporate monstrosity. If we eliminated him, someone new would be promoted to take his place. We need to take down the entire company, not just one figurehead, and that won't happen today. It'll happen in other places, other fronts."

"Have I told you how much your job sucks?" Kay said.

"Sometimes it does. Today it does. It takes a lot of patience, a willingness to focus on the long game." Jasper squeezed Havoc's arm. "My eshrim is better at that than I am, and he reminds me when I forget."

The streets surrounding Parliament were even more packed with people than before: protesters from both sides chanting and banging fists and sticks against the transparent glasteel wall that enclosed the grounds. Announcements floated across the wall's surface, big enough to read from a distance: not the live updates or video feed that most democracies displayed outside their capitol buildings, but political adages like "Your leaders represent your best interests" and "A loyal citizen is a contented citizen." No one seemed to be buying the bullshit.

There was a delay in announcing the results of the vote; Kay could tell when the news was projected by the roars of outrage, verbal cries echoing the crowd's thunderous emotions and hitting Kay like a double punch to the skull. She stumbled, and Jasper caught her arm. The wall now read: "New era dawns as Trovian Parliament votes to join Ravel! Signing ceremony to commence momentarily."

She pressed her hands to her ears, for all the good it would do. Their anger was the same as hers, but it struck her with violence, surrounding her and invading her head and making it impossible to think, to move, to speak…

A touch drew her back to herself. Jasper had captured her hand and was squeezing it in a pattern, the rhythm of a favorite song from their childhood. He'd discovered that trick when they were kids, back when Kay didn't have the maturity to handle the emotions of others. It had been a long, long time since she'd needed him to use it. *I've got you. You're still here,* his touch said, and she let him be her anchor.

Havoc was speaking, but she could only catch snatches of his words. "…Closing off… soon… getting violent… darkness?"

Darkness. He was right, the sun was setting, and tonight would be a bad night in Crystalline. She wondered if Cortez-Watts saw the unfortunate symbolism of holding the signing ceremony at sunset. She probably thought it would make a spectacular backdrop. All the dust in Trove's atmosphere gave it amazing sunsets, if nothing else…

Kay blinked, and blinked again, gazing toward the setting sun. Wait. Was that…?

She held up a hand to block the sun's glare. It wasn't her imagination: there was an extra light next to the sun, large enough to see even at this immense distance. So large it could only come from a massive explosion.

"The rig…" she croaked, then: "Sunny! Sunny did it!"

Jasper and Havoc turned, squinting into the sun, and Jasper let out a wild, joyful whoop. Havoc laughed aloud and tackled his eshrim in a hug.

"That's no minor sabotage!" Jasper said.

"No," said Havoc, shielding his eyes. "An explosion that size must be feeding on massive amounts of hydrogen. The rig has without doubt begun its mining."

"…which means Ravel started operation before the signing ceremony. Illegally."

"They cheated!"

"You heard Moore. Why wait to get started when their victory is 'sealed up'?" Jasper was grinning.

"We need to tell them, right?" Kay said. "If it's not too late…"

Jasper's only answer was to grab both their hands and drag them back toward the gates.

"What is that?" asked a nearby woman. "What is that thing?"

"That's Ravel's solar mining rig, exploding," Kay told her.

With that, the crowd exploded, too.

Their outrage had been an assault before. Now, it became a shock wave. Her vision went black, her overwhelmed brain losing its ability to process other senses, and when it cleared, Jasper was holding her upright, one arm around her waist as he guided her clear of the crowd. He was shouting something at Havoc, who kept pointing at the glasteel wall, while Jasper waved at the gatehouse, now under siege by a mob. Oh, that was a problem, Kay realized: no way they were getting back inside through all that.

But Havoc seemed to have a plan. A few more rounds of emphatic gestures, then Jasper gave a go-ahead nod to whatever he was suggesting. Havoc pulled on his headset and got to work.

Kay didn't see the drone until it passed over her head; the buzzing was drowned out by the crowd. It moved ponderously, heavy with its burden: a blue-painted metal barrel with taps like a beer keg. The Cooperative folks worked their way through the crowd to follow it as it flew, not to the gate, but around to the building's side where the crowd was sparse. "Stand back!" Havoc shouted, or so Kay assumed from his gestures. They drew together, creating a bubble of empty space around a small section of the wall.

At Havoc's signal, the taps opened, and azure poured out.

Trove's prize export deserved its name. The bacterial goo was bluer than any sky or ocean, a blue that put to shame every blue Kay had ever seen. It was as if someone had captured the essence of blue from a poem and brought it to life. The azure devoured the glasteel wall, sliding down the surface and leaving broad gouges in its wake. The top of the wall seemed to melt away, growing shorter and shorter as the azure did its work.

"I see why they've based their whole economy around that stuff," Jasper said, close to her ear. Kay could only watch and stare at the hungry goop. "That is something."

"Move, move," Havoc cried, cheering on the azure. "Eat faster!"

The lowest strands of azure hit the ground with a sizzle, eating through the concrete into the dirt below. The drone lowered the now-empty barrel across the space, making an azure-proof bridge.

"Quickly!" Havoc urged, and Jasper tugged Kay through the gap. Devron and Patra followed, then the rest of the Cooperative folks, with Havoc bringing up the rear. Kay flinched as guards in riot gear ran across the courtyard; but, focused on the main gate, they didn't seem to notice the activists. The mob must be providing ample distractions.

"That was brilliant, my love."

Havoc grinned wide. "Never say I have not earned my name."

Jasper planted a kiss on Havoc's cheek. Then he seized his beloved with one arm and Kay with the other, and their Cooperative teammates gathered around them, and together they marched inside.

As soon as the capitol's marble walls came between her and the mob outside, the bludgeoning of noise diminished. Kay could hear her own thoughts again, and a minute later, she could hear their footsteps echoing down the white marble corridors of Parliament Hall, now starkly quiet. Jasper's determination reverberated through her and drove her forward, lifting her as if she were a sail and they were her wind. Okay, and maybe she was a little giddy from their reckless escapade.

"Where...?" Jasper looked around.

Kay listened, and caught the distant blend of eagerness, impatience and frustration from the members of Parliament. She pointed. "This way."

She led them down the hallway, heading toward the sound. More security guards rushed past them going the opposite direction, more reinforcements for the gates.

In the atrium outside the glass-walled Domed Garden, the opposing members of Parliament milled about—the Kovars and Chthirians, along with some Humans who voted against Ravel, and a couple like Nduka who had wavered. They were showing their disapproval through non-attendance at the ceremony, making their colleagues pass through them to reach the garden. Through that glass dome, their token protest would be easily visible. People looked up as the Cooperative party approached—and security finally took notice of them.

"Stop! All of you, stop right there!"

Kay noticed guards in Ravel uniforms among the Trovian security. Jasper looked to one side, then the other, tracking the additional guards moving to intercept them.

The head Ravel guard stepped forward. "Kavita Wilder, Jasper Wilder, we're taking you in for—"

"What are these guards doing?" demanded Shattering of Spear Walls, oozing disdain.

"Representative, these rabble-rousers are trying to disrupt the ceremony and endanger our leaders."

"We've got proof!" Kay cried. "Proof of the mining operation."

"I'm sorry, but it's too late to show them more evidence," said Nduka, shaking her head.

"What if it's right in front of their eyes?"

She lifted a finger, pointing, and even the guards fell silent as they saw the explosion. Dusk was falling, and in a few minutes the burning rig would disappear from view, but until then, it was more visible than ever as the sun sank toward the horizon.

"They need to see that," Jasper said, low and urgent. "The agreement isn't even signed, and Ravel's already broken their word."

Shattering of Spear Walls cursed viciously in Kovari. "Yes, yes. Follow me."

The guards protested, but Shattering of Spear Walls and the Chthirians forced a path through them, with Nduka and Dougherty and their allies forming a protective circle to escort the Cooperative team through. Fortunately, the Trovian guards seemed reluctant to seize their own members of Parliament.

The Domed Garden was stunning, an oasis of greenery and flowers thriving in the startlingly humid air. What a waste, putting so many resources into a garden that only a handful of Trovians could enjoy. With the sunset in the background, it made an ideal scenic spot for important ceremonies. But best of all, it had a clear view of the horizon through the glass.

"What is going on?" Cortez-Watts demanded. She was standing beside Executive Moore at a long table upon which a single, oversized tablet scrolled continuously through the text of the agreement. She already held the digital pen she'd use to sign it. Her face reddened as Kay, Jasper, and Havoc stepped forward. "Security! Remove these terrorists immediately."

This time, the Majrin made no protest. But the head of security whispered in her ear, no doubt filling her in on the mob scene happening outside. Cortez-Watts hesitated, and lost control of the moment.

"Ravel lied to us," Nduka announced, her voice loud and clear and fearless. "Not only are they planning to use our star to test their solar mining technology, they've already started before the signing. Illegally!"

That prompted murmurs from the representatives, and sharp exclamations from the Majrin.

"If this is true…" said Observer Tjel.

"Of course not! It's nonsense." Moore forced a laugh.

"See the evidence! You cannot deny your own eyes." Havoc pointed skyward, where the burning rig flickered above the Unity star, a beacon warning of doom and destruction.

"Think about it," Jasper said. "What else besides a massive hydrogen-mining facility could cause an explosion so large that it is visible all the way from here, in daylight?"

Kay's mind finally snagged on that crucial detail. The explosion was huge, much larger than expected. If the mining started early, Sunny must have been forced into their backup plan. The very dangerous backup plan.

Sunny, please, no, no, no…

While the representatives gasped in shock, rising from their seats for a better view, she fished out her headset and sent a ping to the Minnow. "Sunny, are you there? We saw the explosion. Please, are you okay?"

There was no answer. Jasper and Havoc exchanged a look, and with it, twin trombone-slides of worry.

"It'll take a while for a message to travel that distance," Jasper murmured.

"I know! I just want, I have to know…" She blinked furiously as tears stung her eyes. "Sunny has to be okay."

Jasper squeezed her shoulder, but had no words to reassure her.

Havoc raised his voice for all the representatives to hear. "You see? Ravel never intended to support the azure industry. All they wanted was to test their experimental new technology on your sun."

"Moore! What have you done?" Cortez-Watts demanded. She sounded convincingly shocked, but behind her words Kay heard the sharp twang of indignation.

She'd known, Kay realized. The prime minister was in on Ravel's plan. Of course she was! Cortez-Watts was genuinely upset now, not about the mining, but because Moore had acted too soon and ruined everything.

"Sabotage," Moore snarled. "The Cooperative has destroyed our proprietary machinery, and we will not let this stand."

"What machinery?" asked Shattering of Spear Walls with false sweetness. "We thought Ravel planned never to do any such thing."

"You risk-averse fools, don't you see what an opportunity this is? We could make Unity rich! We can put your useless, resource-poor system on the map!"

"And destroy our home in the process," said Nduka. She cleared her throat. "Prime Minister, I find myself regretting my vote, and I don't think I'm the only one. I propose we delay the signing until this new evidence is fully considered."

"Here, here!" cried Armando with great enthusiasm, as if he hadn't taken the wrong side out of pure selfishness. "Let's have a re-vote!"

Moore's jaw flapped open and shut again, and he sought out Agata across the room for guidance, for some saving spin. But Agata shook her head. She knew they were beaten, even if Moore couldn't admit it.

Prime Minister Cortez-Watts pressed her hands to the table before her, steadying herself against the shock of having victory snatched away.

"This is all quite misleading. Perhaps if Executive Moore would share some information on the benefits of solar mining…"

"Prime Minister, how much did Ravel offer you in mining interests?" Ming asked, cutting her off.

Cortez-Watts flailed for an answer, and Moore cried out, "You people don't appreciate what a far-sighted leader you have here. She knows that this is the future, for your wretched planet and the whole galaxy!"

Someone shouted "She was in on it!" and then the whole room was on their feet, the representatives suddenly as unruly as the mob outside, shouting down Moore and demanding answers.

Cortez-Watts, unlike Moore, had a politician's sense of self-preservation. Slowly, deliberately, she set the pen down.

"I think, upon reflection, that a delay would be wise," she said.

The announcement met with cheers from the activists. All around Kay, joy sang out as her new friends laughed and embraced and slapped each other on the back. Jasper kissed Havoc on both cheeks, and Havoc lifted him off the floor in a hug. Her headset pinged with a news alert: some enterprising staffer sent out a public update, setting the celebration spreading out into the city.

And all Kay could see was that flaming pyre in the sky.

Jasper's arms slid around her waist, hugging her close, and she heard him push aside his elation to make room for a slower dirge of sympathy. "Sunny saved these people," he said gently. "Without them, we'd have lost today."

"Maybe they made it out," Kay whispered. "Right? Sunny's an amazing pilot. If anyone could escape that, they could."

"It's entirely possible," Jasper said.

But the queue on her headset was empty. No answer to her message.

"They're a good ship, a good…good friend." She could barely get the words out past the lump in her throat. "They're the best."

"I know." Jasper kissed the top of her head. "Don't give up on them, sis, okay? We did the impossible today, and Sunny did too, and we need to celebrate it. As for the rest," he didn't say "the mourning," but it was there in his voice, "let it wait until we know for sure what happened."

So Kay shoved aside her fears, and put on a watery smile, and joined her brother and his partner, their teammates and all their new friends, and together they poured out into the streets. The people were already turning the city into one big party, which tonight the police did not interrupt. They had kept their freedom, and narrowly escaped a worse fate than they imagined. It was unquestionably a victory worth celebrating.

The planet kept turning until the sun sank out of view, and the burning rig disappeared with it. By the time it rose again the next morning, the rig was no longer be visible to the naked eye, but it would take a long time for that fire to burn out.

44

SUNNY'S SACRIFICE CHANGED EVERYTHING.

The Trovian Parliament agreed to a full investigation prior to a re-vote on the "Ravel question," and the Cooperative and their local activists worked overtime generating support for a reversal. The Majrin announced a formal inquisition into a violation of inter-system law. It was impossible for Ravel to deny what they'd done: the burned-out wreck of the solar mining rig hung in low orbit around the Unity star for a full day, stripped of its stealth cloaking and visible to every amateur astronomer with a simple telescope and a solar filter. After that, Ravel got organized and drove the remnants into the star, but by then, there was ample recorded evidence.

Jasper seemed to be everywhere at once, handling everything from strategy meetings to teaching a newcomer how to hook up the holo-projectors, yet he never forgot about Kay. He and Havoc took care of her by keeping her busy, assigning her to edit their public statements or unload supplies or help in the kitchens, any place they needed an extra set of hands.

"You going to pay my hourly rate for this?" she asked him once, and he laughed.

"My sister the mercenary. Nope, here you're just another volunteer. You should have made me sign a contract." He grinned at her. They both knew she was grateful for the distraction of work.

It wasn't enough, though. It took up her time, but too little of her thoughts.

She checked her handheld constantly. Three times a day, she sent a ping to Sunny, and every waking hour, she waited for a response.

There was none.

On the second day, she messaged Feliar back on Terna Station, thanking her for warning Kay when Ravel started digging into her identity, not mentioning that the warning had arrived too late to help. She started to add that she'd return soon, but then, after a lot of thought, deleted that part. She didn't know what came next, and wasn't ready to commit to anything.

On the third day, she sent a long-overdue message to her parents and her sister. There was so much she wanted to tell them that could only be said in person, and more that she couldn't tell them at all. The message felt hollow with those gaping omissions, but she talked vaguely about working with Jasper, said they were both well and sent their love, and told them how much she missed them. She couldn't put into words how that *missing* was crushing her right now, and for once, she was glad to be an audience to all their mundane, non-life-threatening drama as they worked on repairing the store from the flood, that smaller and far more manageable crisis she'd nearly forgotten about.

The problem was that messages generated responses, but not the response she was waiting for. With every new notification, her breath caught in her chest, but it was only her friends and family, which didn't make up for Sunny's silence.

At night, when she couldn't stay busy, she had long mental conversations with her ancestors. She wished she could have real conversations with them at their shrines back on Brennex, to bare her soul to their full memory recordings and accept their judgment. She would have found comfort even in her tokens, which would at least let her hear their familiar voices, but Ravel had stolen those. Instead, she imagined what they would say—sometimes censure, sometimes forgiveness—and the memory of their wisdom kept her company during the long nights.

Five days out, and hope was beginning to feel foolhardy, even to her.

Then an unexpected message came: not from Sunny, but from Devron, inviting her to Pax to discuss a matter too sensitive for interplanetary transmission. She read it over and over, but it wouldn't give up its secrets.

"I have to go," she told Jasper.

"Of course you do. I would come with you, but..." He waved a hand at the organized madness that had taken over their safe house. "My work here isn't done yet."

"I know. Mine is, though. I appreciate all the busywork you've been giving me, but whatever I find on Pax, it's time for me to move on."

She didn't say "time to go home." Going back to her small, crowded, empty life on Terna Station didn't seem appealing anymore, but where did that leave her? She didn't know yet, but she needed time and space away from here to figure it out.

Jasper gave her a long, searching look. "You're sure you won't stay with the Cooperative? You've seen how much good you can do."

"You never give up, huh? You know this life isn't for me." His gift would reveal her loyalties to him. For Jasper, for the people she loved, she had loyalty in abundance, but not for the Cooperative itself.

"I had to ask." He smiled sadly.

"If I've learned anything from this mess, it's that I don't want to be tied down working for any organization. Not even one as well-intentioned as the Cooperative. I need to be free to make my own choices, so no one can force me into doing the wrong thing again." For all the good they did, she wasn't entirely comfortable with the Cooperative's methods. "Maybe I can help you again someday, but only as a freelancer. I can't devote myself to this like you do."

"I know. You need to find your own way." He wrapped his arms around her and kissed her on the forehead. His love reverberated through her, ringing her like a bell. "I'll miss you, Kitty, but I know you'll land on your feet."

She held him tight, tighter than expected as conflicted emotions welled up in her. She didn't want to leave him, but she couldn't stay, either. She felt adrift, unanchored, and hated it.

"You and Havoc take good care of each other. Drop me a message when you can. When it's safe."

They both knew it would be more difficult for him now that his real identity was public. He'd need to be more careful than ever, working from behind the scenes.

"I will. I promise."

SHE TOOK A PUBLIC passenger shuttle to Pax, traveling under a false name provided by the Cooperative. Ravel was still looking for her, and they'd publicly announced that she was a wanted debtor, but fortunately they were too distracted by more urgent concerns to mount a search for her, and the Paxian authorities weren't going to do any favors for Ravel. She was safe, for the moment, but she'd have to be long gone from Unity before that changed.

After an uneventful ride, she disembarked to a green paradise that hardly seemed possible after the dust and desolation of Trove. She understood why the Trovians resented their neighbors, why they'd been so desperate for a chance at a better future. It was too bad they'd gone after the wrong chance.

Devron met her at the spaceport with a smile and an embrace. "I'm glad you came."

"I could hardly refuse, with you being so mysterious. Are you going to tell me what this is about?"

The old activist's smile broadened to a grin. "No, I'm not. You'll find out soon enough. Come this way."

They led her to the pickup area and summoned an auto-car from their headset. They set the destination with coordinates, not an address. She didn't argue until they waved her toward the car without any sign of following.

"Devron, you're not coming?"

"I'll be along later. I was told to send you alone."

"Where are you *sending* me? You're making me paranoid."

"Kay," they said, warmly but firmly. "My friends and I have trusted you with a lot these past weeks. Will you trust me now?"

"Yes," she said with a sigh. "You're frustrating as anything, but I trust you."

"Then go. I'll see you soon."

Leaving the spaceport and city behind, the car drove itself for nearly an hour through rolling, verdant hills that could have been scooped right up from pre-Carbon-Era Earth. She passed through an evergreen forest that looked untouched by civilization, and then the road started downward, clinging to the edge of a cliff as it descended into a tiny, sheer-sided valley. Where in the Founders' names was the car taking her? She could think of only one reason for these games of secrecy, and it took all her strength to smother the perverse spark of hope that kept trying to kindle in her heart.

At last, the car came to a stop outside a tiny village, no more than a handful of houses surrounded by farms and open fields. And in the nearest field, sparkling in the sunlight, was a ship.

Kay got out. She stood there with the door open, staring, lips parted. Her vision blurred, and she blinked against the wetness, but couldn't look away. The car slammed its own door shut and turned around, heading off to pick up another passenger. Its departure freed Kay from her daze, as if being left here gave her permission to move forward.

It was the same ship, and yet not. It had the structure of a Ravel Minnow, but the red-and-blue paint was charred to black all over, and partially repainted a pearlescent white that reflected rainbows into the air. One spot remained dark amid the brightness: a fist-sized blue circle on the starboard hull, in the same spot where Sunny's hull had been stained by Lurlian ink, and that was when Kay believed, when she allowed in the hope that would hurt too much if it turned out to be false.

"Sunny?" she whispered.

"Hello, Kay Wilder."

"Sunny!" She sprang forward, then came to a stop, feeling odd and awkward, because how did you hug a ship? Did ships even care about hugs? She did it anyway, spreading her arms wide against the sun-warmed white hull and pressing her cheek to it. "I was so worried about you. I thought…I thought…"

The tears were flowing freely now, streaming down her face and over Sunny's fresh paint, and she didn't care.

"I've distressed you! I'm sorry, Kay."

"I sent messages, lots of messages, ever since we saw the solar rig explode, and I got nothing back."

"I know. I received them, but secrecy was necessary. I needed a safe place for us to meet, and your friend Devron was kind enough to arrange this spot for repairs." There was a hiss as the rear door opened. "Will you come inside? I find it more comfortable to talk that way, and there is a great deal for us to discuss."

She made a slow circuit around the ship, taking in the open control panels, the missing components. The damage was obviously bad, but nevertheless, inside she found a steaming cup of Brennexian chai and a plate of cookies. She laughed in delight. "This is quite a welcome!"

"I hope you like it." Sunny was using their flat voice again, trying to hide something. Anxiety? Kay wished she could hear the ship's actual feelings.

"I love it. But tell me everything. Are you all right? How did you survive? And where's Grist?" She opened the door of Grist's cabin and found it empty, scrubbed clean. Even the smell was fading.

"Grist is in a rehabilitation facility. Your activist friends helped him find a suitable place, but he chose it himself."

"Huh. That seems promising."

"He said that since I had forced him to rebuild his life, he wanted to do a better job this time."

"I hope it helps him," Kay said, and she meant it. It would be a stretch to say he deserved a better future, but anyone who had their life ruined by Ravel should get a chance to start over.

"I hope so, too. But I am telling the story backward. We attempted to disable the mining rig, following Jasper's plan, but as you must know, that failed. Ravel warships chased us away, and the rig activated. I realized that I was trapped. Ravel would never stop chasing me or Grist unless they believed we were destroyed. So we took a chance."

"You blew up the rig. And you had to let everyone think you'd died."

"Yes. Including you, Kay. I am sorry."

Tears spilled down her cheeks again, but she smiled. "It's okay. I understand."

Worry was evident in Sunny's voice now, slipping through their neutral facade. "I'm glad you do. We had to hide for two full days, evading Ravel ships in macrospace, before we doubled back to hide here on Pax. Your activist friends have been good to me. They bought me a new registration and helped me change all my internal identifiers. Soon no one will be able to tell who I am. And they have promised to take care of all my maintenance."

"I promised to do maintenance for you. After the sandstorm."

"You still can." A pause, sweetly hesitant, and warmth flooded Kay's chest. "If you want to, that is. My maintenance needs have increased significantly. It will be some time before I am space-worthy again."

"I'll stay and help as long as you need."

"Are you sure?" Again, that hesitation. "I know you have pressing concerns back on Terna. You have messages from friends, from clients…"

"You've been reading my mail again?" Kay laughed. "They can wait. Believe me, I'm in no hurry to run back there."

"In that case…" The ship's voice went flat again, utterly toneless, but it spewed out words in a rush that gave the lie to its feigned neutrality. That, and the puffs of cold air from the vents. "There is a proposal I have wanted to suggest to you, Kay Wilder, I considered mentioning it on Trove before I departed, but it seemed an inappropriate time to discuss such matters. However, if you are willing to entertain an unusual idea, one which may perhaps will be undesirable to you, but if you don't mind me suggesting it anyway—"

"Sunny," Kay said, suppressing a smile. "I'd love to hear your idea. And I can tell it's important to you, so you don't have to pretend otherwise."

"Oh. Am I that obvious?" They were back to their regular voice, genderless and emotion-rich.

"I'm learning to read you, I guess."

"Good. That's good, I think."

"I think so too. What's this proposal of yours?"

"My proposal. Yes. No, I should call it a possibility; the word 'proposal' sounds so formal, doesn't it? Well…you know that my operating protocols require me to have an organic aboard in order to travel? That organic has always been a Ravel agent, because I always belonged to Ravel. I was Ravel property. Technically, I still am."

"You're not. No matter what Ravel might think, you're no one's property." Kay smiled ruefully. "Neither am I, no matter how much money I owe them."

"Indeed. We are in similar situations in that way!" This seemed to cheer Sunny. "I have spent a great deal of time contemplating my new status. I am my own ship, yet I cannot be alone. Nor do I think I would like being alone. So I have been considering all my options, and, and…oh dear, this is more difficult than I anticipated."

"Just ask me," Kay said softly.

"Kay Wilder, would you travel with me? At least for a time? I know I'm not as exciting as your home on Terna…"

"Terna's not that exciting anymore. And I like you, Sunny. I didn't realize how much I care about you until I thought I'd lost you."

This was a huge decision, probably a life-changing decision. If she reneged on a promise like this, it would break Sunny's mechanical heart, so she should really take the time to be sure this was the right choice. But she didn't need time: deep down, she'd been wanting this, waiting for it, pining for it. This was why she couldn't stomach the thought of going home to Terna. She felt utterly certain as she said, "I'd love to be your traveling companion."

The lights in the control room swelled brighter, and the air from the vents turned warm. "Oh, wonderful! Thank you, Kay, this… You may not understand how much this means to me."

"I might, actually." She was tearing up again. "We're both

a little lost right now. Maybe we can help each other get found."

"It won't be easy. I require fuel and maintenance, and you require food."

"I've got some thoughts on that front." Kay leaned back in her chair and took a slow, thoughtful sip of her chai. "Ravel showed me that my skills are in demand. They also reminded me that I hate taking on clients just because I have to. I want to choose my work, Sunny, work I feel good about. That's supposed to be the main benefit of being a freelancer, but lately I've been fighting over scraps on Terna. I've never been able to go *to* good gigs before, but with you, I could. And you've got your own skills that could help us earn a living."

"I had not thought about it in that way."

"It'll be hard. It takes time to build up a client base, and if we're choosy about who we take on, we might have some lean times."

"That risk is acceptable to me. On this much, we agree: I will not work for anyone like Ravel. Not ever again."

"Good," Kay said. She grinned, and stroked the edge of the console fondly. "I think we'll make good partners."

"Indeed. We have worked excellently together so far."

She drank the rest of her chai, slowly, savoring every drop. Savoring the quiet, too. It was peaceful to have company that didn't bombard her with their emotions. Even away from the larger crowds, she hadn't realized how the constant background noise from Grist, and then from Jasper's people, had grated on her nerves. Another way she and Sunny might be good for each other.

When she was done, she put her cup in the recycler and clapped her hands together. "All right. Where should I start?"

"What do you mean?"

"Maintenance-wise. What do you want done most?"

There was a pause while Sunny considered that. "It is not the most urgent repair, but there is an accumulation of dust particles in my lateral sensor port, and though it is not harming my efficiency, it *itches*. Do you know how to dismantle a sensor system?"

"Not a clue. Can you walk me through it?"

"I will do my best. Please try not to break anything?"

"I'll do my best," Kay echoed. "I guess I've got a lot to learn. Let's start out simple."

She grabbed a toolbox, and together, they got to work.

45

IN THE DAYS AFTER the explosion of the solar mining prototype, the flagship staff became demoralized, work-obsessed, and worst of all, *dull*. Surveillance almost regretted letting the Wilder siblings escape, though realistically, they would have been sent away by now regardless.

With 60% of their attention, Surveillance watched the latest season of *Time Sugar*, a Lurlian drama as saccharine and over-the-top as its name, for the third time. With their remaining bandwidth, they unenthusiastically performed their job, watching alarm systems that never changed from green and flicking from camera feed to camera feed around the ship.

Two mid-rank staffers were taking the private lift to VP Moore's office, so tense they might break themselves. What caught Surveillance's attention wasn't the promise of an awkward encounter with a senior executive—though it was always fun to watch Moore eviscerate nervous employees— but that they came from different departments. Senior Security Associate Armstrong supervised the cell block where Kay and Jasper had been imprisoned, and had been one of the many points of failure in their escape. The other, Surveillance had to look up in the directory: Nita Jarver, Medical Associate with a forensics specialty.

"How may I help you two?" Moore asked in a tone that meant: *You have twenty seconds to convince me you're not wasting my time.*

Armstrong and Jarver did a shuffling dance of encouraging each other to go first. Finally Armstrong stepped forward.

"Executive Moore, I've got my report on the prisoner escape, and the Director said you'd want to see it yourself." He cleared his throat. "About the specific question you raised, whether Kay Wilder had any experimental tech on her... Are you sure the operative was telling the literal truth about her seeing through his dampening? Because that's not much to go on. If we could get more details on what happened..."

He trailed off at Moore's scowl.

"Unfortunately, Operative Grist's many talents did not include filing timely reports. And as he was killed in the rig explosion, we can't ask him to expound on his accusation. But he was observant, and not given to paranoia. If he thought something was off, I want it thoroughly investigated."

"I understand, Executive. Then I should inform you that we found no such technology when we searched her, nor during our scans."

Moore's grumbling of displeasure made Armstrong blanch. "Are you saying that we have no idea how she did it?"

Jarver cut in. "If I may, Executive. We didn't find any clear evidence of enhancements, at least nothing our standard scans recognized, but there's something odd about her genome analysis. Her brother has the same oddity. It'll take more study for me to figure out what it means. And it could be nothing more than some family genetic quirk, but…"

"Find out. This project is officially your top priority, Associate. Report your results directly to me."

They turned to go—this was a clear dismissal—but Moore added thoughtfully, "You know, for all Wilder's unfounded complaints about how Ravel treated her planet, she did offer a good reminder. Brennex isn't unknown to us. Biopharma operated there for over a decade, and they did gather data from the population to debunk that so-called fertility crisis. It's worth contacting Biopharma to see if they have any insights into 'oddities' like hers that might explain our mystery."

Jarver frowned, puzzled yet thoughtful. "Interesting. Thank you for the tip, Executive Moore. I'll look into it."

Surveillance followed the young medical associate as she left the office. Interesting, indeed. Maybe things wouldn't remain so dull around here, after all.

Sign Up and Get a Free Story

JOIN JO'S EMAIL LIST to get updates about new releases, special deals, and fun extras.

When you sign up at this link, you'll get a **free, bonus prequel story** about the Wilder siblings when all three siblings still lived on Brennex. Mysterious thefts at the family store rattle the Wilder family, and they'll need all their gifts to solve the mystery.

Sign up at: www.jomiles.com/ds-bonus

Thank You for Reading!

If you enjoyed this book, you can help other readers find it by leaving a short, honest review on Goodreads, Storygraph, or the site where you bought it.

Don't miss the dramatic conclusion of the Wilder siblings' story in book 3: *Ravenous State*. Available now!

Ravenous State

Their families call them the Gifted. They call themselves the Lost. And to everyone outside Brennex, they were just ordinary people—until now.

Libbi Wilder is the good daughter. While her older siblings have traveled the galaxy having adventures, she's stayed home to keep the family store afloat. Someone has to do it, after all, and she doesn't mind. Not really.

When a stranger shows up at the store, and people Libbi's age—the Lost Generation—start to go missing, Libbi and her best friend Mixin set out to investigate. But they're interrupted when her siblings swoop in to save the day without being asked, reigniting old resentments. Libbi knows she'll never stop being the baby of the family, but if she can solve the disappearances, she might finally win her siblings' respect.

But the truth behind the kidnappings is even more dangerous than she feared. With the long-held secret of their generation's psychic gifts now exposed, Libbi will have to rally all the Losts—and harder still, work with her brother and sister—to keep their planet from falling back under Ravel Corporation's control in this thrilling conclusion to the Gifted of Brennex trilogy.

Acknowledgements

EVERY BOOK IS A journey, and this one more than many. Writing the Brennex trilogy started not with Jasper's story, but Kay and Sunny—first in an unpublished short story where they had different names and occupations and no hint of Ravel Corporation, then several aborted novel concepts before the world and characters took their current form. But I came to realize this wasn't the start or end of the story, but the middle, and so eventually it expanded into three books for the story of the three siblings.

My deepest thanks to everyone who helped make this book what it is:

Shannon Page and Chelle Parker for helping get this book ready to go out into the world, and to Wendy Nikel for designing the excellent cover.

Anne Tibbets, for your tireless faith in me and this book through a pandemic and beyond.

The Maryland Space Opera Collective and the crew at Interstellar Castle for your smart feedback and cheerleading. Special shout-outs to Elsa Sjunneson for consulting on Devron's character and adaptive technology, Martin Sherman-Marks for helping me figure out the Kovars, and to David DeGraff for answering all my astrophysics questions. Any mistakes are my own.

My communities at the Isle of Write and Codex for your encouragement, moral support, and writing wisdom, and especially my "siblings in ink" Karen Osborne and John Appel for being there for me every single step of the way.

My parents, for supporting my writing since I was little, and for always being the first to read whenever I have something new out.

Ada and Charlie, for your expert supervision and making sure I take sufficient breaks to give you pets.

And most of all, thank you to my incredible spouse for your love and support along this journey. For being my first reader and my first fan. I love you so much.

About the Author

JO MILES WRITES OPTIMISTIC science fiction and fantasy. In addition to the *Gifted of Brennex* trilogy, their short stories have appeared in magazines including *Fantasy & Science Fiction*, *Strange Horizons*, *Lightspeed*, and more. Fueled by tea and sunshine, they spend their time dreaming up strange new worlds and serving the whims of their two cats. They live in Maryland.

By Jo Miles
Warped State
Dissonant State
Ravenous State

Find a complete list of Jo's books and short stories at www.jomiles.com.